Colorblind

RANDY GREEN

Chapter 1

HE STOOD OFF TO THE BACK OF THE PLAYGROUND. He always tried to stay invisible. If he didn't get noticed, then he didn't get picked on; at least that's the way he tried to get through Westside Elementary School. It was a tough place for an awkward kid. The other kids were running all over the place, swinging on monkey bars, playing jump rope, and some of the boys that he tried to avoid were playing tackle football. He got asked to play one time, but he soon realized he was in the game just to get pounded. They would give him the ball and tell him to run, but the other team was always ready, and they would dog-pile him.

That was what happened when you get tackled and every guy on the other team would pile on you – except in this case, his own team would join in too. It really wasn't a big deal to him. He found it quiet and peaceful at the bottom of the pile and was just a little fascinated with the fact that he could be in the middle of the playground on a perfectly sunny day and be encased in pitch-black darkness. At least at that moment he wasn't alone. He was ok with the dog-pile game for a while, they all seemed to get a good laugh out of it which made him feel like he was a part of the group, but then they started doing mean things to him when he was at the bottom of the human pile. Mean things that hurt and made him cry, then they would laugh even harder, so he stopped playing the dog-pile game. He stood off as far as he could without the teachers yelling at him that he was too far away.

He knew every kid in the school, he knew their parents and even knew if they were smart or dumb. He didn't care either way if they were smart or dumb, he just liked to know what he was dealing with. The smart ones were calculating and mean, and the dumb ones were just mean. The dumb ones were the most dangerous because they felt like he was dumber than them, which made them more powerful, or something. He never understood that. His big sister told him one day it was because of a man named Darwin and he subscribed to a theory that only smart people or strong people or something like that survived.

His big sister was his best friend. She was already in high school and she was the prettiest girl in all of Mississippi. She never cared whether he was fast or slow or smart or dumb, she always had time for him. He really liked it when she would take him to get a milk shake at Milholen's Drug Store in downtown Webb. When he was with her, nobody picked on him. It was actually quite the reverse! When he was with her, they all sucked up to him, especially the big boys that would be mean to him when she was not around but be super nice when she was. They would rub his head and say things like, "Hey, big man, how you doing? You're looking strong there, sport-o!", or maybe it was *champ*, but there were always a whole bunch of other dopey names. When his sister wasn't around he was *twerp, slime ball*, and one big kid had even called him a *mattress stain*. He wasn't sure what that last one meant but he knew it couldn't be nice. Yeah, in no way was he stupid; he knew when people were lying.

Today he stood off and watched her. She was jump-roping with a bunch of other girls; she was the best there was at *Double Dutch*. When she was on her best game, her feet moved so fast he could hardly see them. Today she had the cadence and was really on her game, the ropes were barely visible as she pounded at the ground in rapid fire with her feet. Her cadence today was one of his favorites, it always made him laugh, ***"I know something, but I won't tell, three little monkeys in a peanut shell, one can read, and one can dance, and one has a hole in the seat of his pants!"*** When she was done with the monkey cadence she would jump out of the swinging ropes and would be congratulated for making it all the way through the cadence without tripping on the rope. The girls would laugh and giggle. She always wore a bow in her hair that matched her dress. Today she was wearing a yellow skirt that looked like overalls to him because they had straps that came over her shoulders. She had a white shirt on and he could already see the sweat rings getting bigger under her arms, but he didn't care.

She was the most beautiful girl in all of Mississippi; well maybe behind his sister but that was different, his sister was a grown-up and this girl was his age. He could hardly breathe when she was around, but he liked it when she was around.

She didn't seem to mind that he was a misfit; she was the only kid in school who spoke to him. It wasn't always, sometimes he would say, "Hello" to her and she would ignore him, but most times she would say, "Hello". Any day she spoke to him seemed like a better day. He figured he would marry her someday, but it would have to wait at least until they were in middle school. He needed to work up some courage to talk to her and tell her that he thought she was pretty. That's what his sister told him to tell her when he told his sister about Jeannine Martin. She teased him a little, but he didn't mind. She always stopped the teasing to give him some good advice and never failed to tell him that he was special and one day he would realize how special he was, and on the day he realized it, nobody would pick on him anymore. It wasn't always exactly like that, but it was close.

She had a different version of it for whatever pain he was going through at the moment. She was the closest thing he had to a momma. Their momma had been shot at the Sumner Dance Hall that she and his daddy liked to go to on Saturday nights. Two fellas got into a fight in the parking lot as his momma and daddy were leaving and one fella pulled a gun and shot at the other fella but missed. Instead, he hit his momma right in the stomach. He remembered seeing her hooked up to some tubes in the hospital; she looked so pretty laying there but she wasn't awake. He tried to tell her that he loved her, but he wasn't sure if she could hear him. She lived for a few days, but his sister came out of the room crying one day and told him that his momma had gone on to heaven and that Jesus was taking care of her now. He wasn't for sure what he was supposed to do. Everyone was crying except his daddy.

His daddy just looked mean and mad. Since people always told him to try and be like his daddy, he decided it was best if he didn't cry. Although he tried to look mean but wasn't sure if he knew how, no matter what mean face he came up with, people just kept asking him if he needed to go to the bathroom. He really missed his momma.

Chapter 2

HIS DADDY OWNED A BIG OLE BAIT AND TACKLE STORE that everybody had to pass by on the way to Swan Lake. He loved to go there and hang out in the summers. Sometimes he would help customers dip the minnows out of the tank or he would run back to the storeroom where the refrigerator was and grab a small cup of big nice juicy worms. When he was helping his daddy at the store, nobody seemed to mind that he was a misfit. The grown-ups all talked to him like normal, if there was a normal. His daddy knew everybody in town. That's how he knew everybody; not only did his daddy own the only bait and tackle shop on the way to Swan Lake, he was the Tallahatchie County Sheriff.

Being the sheriff meant that he could carry a gun if he wanted to, but he rarely did. His daddy would wake him up early in the morning during the summers and they would head off to work, as his daddy called it. He didn't see how it could be work because it was so much fun being there in the bait store. The store sold more than bait though; they had all kinds of cool stuff. They sold jigs and lures and fishing poles. They had all kinds of food and they even had a flat grill off to the side that his daddy would fire up and make the best hamburgers in the Delta. That's what he called them. He didn't think they were the best, but they were close. He loved the hamburgers at Donnie's Hamburger Shack over in Clarksdale. He figured they were the best hamburgers ever made but he still liked his daddy's hamburgers. The customers would come in early and fill their coolers with ice and beer and all kinds of food and then on the way back they would stop and have a beer in the back of the store where daddy played poker sometimes. They would tell stories about the fish they caught or the big one that snapped the pole or sometimes that the fish were runnin' too deep because it was just too damn hot. They said that *damn* word a lot. Not him though, his momma would whack him a good one if he said anything close to bad like that. His daddy would cuss a blue streak when he got around some of the guys that played poker in the back. Seemed like the more beer he drank the louder he got and the dirtier the words got. Decker knew them all, after all, he was almost in sixth grade and even though he was a misfit, he'd seen a thing or two in his day.

Sometimes his daddy would let his sister run the bait shop and just the two of them would go fishing all day. They didn't have a boat like some of the customers did but he would take a couple lawn chairs, fix up some bologna sandwiches and they would sit by the bank in the shady spots and fish all day. Those were his favorite times, sitting right there on that bank eating a bologna sandwich and watching his bobber in the water. His daddy would tell him that he was the best bobber watcher he had ever seen, and truth be known he was. He could sit there and stare at that bobber all day. He imagined that little minnow with a hook stuck through it trying to swim off the hook, creating a fuss under that water which attracted the big ole catfish. The thrill of seeing that bobber start flickering in the water was almost more than he could handle. He would see it jiggle just a little and cause a little ripple and his whole body would tighten up. He just knew it was coming and he needed to be ready to set that hook. As soon as he saw the bobber go completely under the water he would yank back on his cane pole and set that hook. There was nothing better than wrestling with a catfish or feisty crappie. He just loved it. His daddy would laugh so hard when it happened, but Decker could tell he liked it just as much as he did.

They would head back when it started to get dark and his momma would turn the back porch light on so they could see to clean the fish. That was the part he liked least of all the fishing parts. He hated cleaning fish. The guts were slimy, and they stunk. The catfish was the worst. You had to peel their skin off and it was like pulling a wet pair of britches off; it was a slow process. His momma would make such a fuss over his catch. She would say things like, "That's the biggest catfish I ever saw!" or "Oh, I can't wait to get that big ole crappie into the frying pan!" He would gush with pride. His momma really knew how to make him feel normal. After his momma got shot in the belly and went to heaven his daddy didn't take him fishing anymore. He really missed that. So many things had changed after his momma went to heaven and he couldn't think of any of the changes that were good.

Chapter 3

THE SIGN ON THE SIDEWALK WAS ONE OF THOSE sandwich board signs that was hand painted. It read, "Re-elect Sheriff Elmer Davis, Strength and Integrity". Elmer stepped into the barbershop. It was election season, which meant campaigning, and he hated campaigning more than anything in the world, but he loved being sheriff. Since it was campaign season he was in full uniform, which meant that he was in all brown. He had a small belt holster for his .38 because he hated the standard-issue belt that had all the cuffs and nightstick and whole bunch of unnecessary crap on it. That giant belt always made him feel like his pants were going to fall down, plus he could never sit down in the damn thing. "Come on in Elmer, you up for a cut today?" Mac Hibdon was the local barber; he cut everybody's hair except the women, they had a beauty parlor over on the square that Decker thought smelled funny. It burned his eyes when he went in there with his momma. He only liked going in there because Ms. LuLu, the lady who owned the shop, would give him big ole gum balls for free right out of the machine that other people had to pay a nickel for.

There was another barbershop just south of the railroad tracks but the people that went to that barbershop weren't Mac's customers. Decker had been in there with his daddy a bunch of times and everything seemed the same to him in that barbershop as it was in Mac's except that the customers that were in that one were all a different color. It seemed to Decker that his daddy was just as happy in Dub Martin's barbershop as he was in Mac's. As far as he could tell, folks were the same in both of the barbershops. He always thought that Dub gave a better haircut and Dub played the guitar sometimes when the place wasn't so busy. Decker loved the guitar and could listen to Dub as long as his daddy would let him. Dub actually let him sit in the chair, hold the guitar and strum it. It was the best thing maybe besides fishing with his daddy that he had ever done. Dub would show him where to place his fingers on the strings to make the C note. Dub would tell him that if he got good at holding the C note and people liked it, he might make a C note. He would laugh this huge belly laugh when he said it. He had no idea what that meant but his daddy would laugh right along with everybody else.

Decker thought of he could learn how to play the guitar, he might like to be a barber someday because people were usually happy in the barbershop and didn't seem to mind that he was a misfit, but he figured his name was too long to be a barber seeing how the town had a Mac and Dub. He figured it must be a requirement that to be a barber you had to have a name with only three letters. Dub Martin would give his daddy a haircut and two days later Mac Hibdon would give his daddy another haircut. Decker loved going places with his daddy. Before his momma went to heaven, he went everywhere with his daddy.

It was in Dub's barbershop that he first saw Jeannine Martin. She was Dub's granddaughter. The minute he walked into that barbershop with his daddy and saw her sitting there in the second chair that nobody ever used… he was in love. He didn't know what to say to her, but he didn't have to say anything because she did all the talking. On this day, his daddy was waiting his turn talking to everyone in the shop; it seemed very noisy, noisier than normal that day. The chatter was so loud that nobody even noticed him talking to Jeannine. Talking to anyone, *especially* a stranger, was something that Decker just didn't do. He heard them talking about a man named *Bobby Kennedy* and some other fella they called *Sir Hand*. He must have been pretty important because they had to call him *Sir* before his name. It was very hard to talk to Jeannine over all the noise the grown-ups were making but he didn't mind. She was so pretty. Her hair was like nothing he'd ever seen before. It was curly and she had a bow in it. She smelled like a girl; to him that was sort of a cross between a nice smelling cake in the oven and that pretty soap his mom kept in a dish beside the tub. He never used the soap because she had told him that it was girl soap and he would turn into a girl if he used it. He wasn't about to be a girl because he liked fishing too much. Girls definitely did not go fishing. He would sit in the tub and stare at the soap, though. He would put his face right up against the dish, as close as he could without touching it, so he could really smell it, and he did it so long one night he was in the tub, he fell right asleep.

His momma came in and saw him snoozing with his wet face lying right over the dish of soap. She didn't spank him, but she sure gave him the what-for on falling asleep in the tub and how a person can drown doing something silly like that. His momma was so pretty. She was always dressed so nicely. He loved it when she and his daddy would go over to Sumner on Saturday night to dance; she would wear her string of pearls and looked like she was a movie star he had seen on TV. She had red hair just like the movie star and his momma loved to laugh. He thought the lady on TV was probably funnier than his momma because she was always doing stupid stuff and getting into trouble, but it was close. His momma could tell some really funny jokes sometimes, *Lucy*, that was her name. That was the lady his momma looked like. Everybody said he looked like his daddy except for the red hair. He had red hair like his momma. He didn't know any other people in his school or anywhere else for that matter that had red hair except for him and his momma.

The ladies in Ms. LuLu's shop would make all kinds of comments about how pretty she was and how they all wished they had red hair. It wasn't the same deal for him; his hair just got him picked on more. He didn't like it so much on himself, but he loved it on his momma. He really wished that man hadn't shot her in the belly. "Lois Davis was a beautiful woman, she didn't deserve to die like that", his daddy used to say. He started to say that pretty regularly, especially when he would drink a lot. He remembered talking to Jeannine in that barbershop that day he couldn't wait to get home and tell his momma about her.

Chapter 4

⁘

IT WAS A FRIDAY NIGHT IN MID-OCTOBER. THERE was just a little nip in the air and they were all getting ready to go to the Choctaw game. That was west Tallahatchie's mascot. The Choctaws. Decker didn't know what a Choctaw was, but he loved to go to the football games. He was sure he liked football because of the weather. It was fall, and the leaves were changing, and his momma would make this thermos full of hot chocolate and bring some blankets and they would sit in the stands with the rest of the town and cheer like crazy.

Tonight, they were going to play Clarksdale, which was always a good game. The Choctaws had a quarterback that Ole Miss was coming to see every game. His daddy would talk about him all the time. His name would come up at both barbershops and people would go on and on about how *Donnie had a cannon for an arm* or that *Donnie could outrun a rabbit* or *Donnie is going to be a professional football player one day*. Naturally, Decker had to jump on the Donnie Ray Richards bandwagon with everyone else. It just seemed like the natural thing to do.

Decker really liked football; except for the dog-pile games the boys would make him play at recess. He didn't like those at all. Tonight, Clarksdale was coming to town undefeated and they had their own star quarterback, and it was said that the Mississippi State Bulldogs were following him all over the state. He could smell the air and the grass and that big thermos of hot chocolate as they waited on his daddy to get home to load the car and head out. The phone rang, so momma went to the kitchen to get it. He wasn't allowed to answer the phone, but he had practiced many times in case the need arose. When nobody was around he would run to the phone, grab it off the cradle and say, "Davis residence, Decker speaking." He was always careful not to twist that cord attached to it. It was long and if it got tangled up it was a mess to get untangled and worse, they would know he had been playing with the phone. That would have been against the rules and he would probably get a whoopin'. Momma came back into the living room and said that daddy was going to be late and he would just take the sheriff's truck to the game and would meet us there. So, his sister and momma loaded the car with the stuff and drove to the game.

It wasn't uncommon for his daddy to get hung up, but it was uncommon to get hung up on a football night. Most everybody in town, white and black, would be at the game. Decker thought it was probably the most exciting thing around. He loved the band and the noise and the cheering and especially the popcorn. He could eat a whole box all by himself at the game. As soon as they got situated in the bleachers, his momma would give him a dollar and send him to the concession stand to get himself a box of popcorn. He always felt like a big-shot holding that money and making the exchange like a grown-up.

He didn't need any help, he knew what he was doing and most of the time, he knew the people working back behind the counter and they knew he knew what he was doing. Tonight was no different, his momma laid out the blankets on the bleachers and got all the bags situated underneath their feet. She reached for her purse and took out a crumpled-up dollar bill and handed it to Decker. She tried to give him the normal instructions of, "Don't go anywhere but the concession stand, don't talk to strangers, don't this, don't that...", blah blah, but he didn't give her any time to finish. He snatched the crumpled dollar from her hand and he was off as fast as a bullet. He weaved his way in and out of the crowd as they all walked too slow for his taste. He pretended he was Donnie Ray Richards and was dodging tacklers and put his best move on a lady with a stroller; sort of a spinning motion where he had to actually turn his back on the helpless tackler for just a minute. He executed it flawlessly and was standing in front of the concession stand.

He wished he had gotten there just a little faster because there was a whole family of fat people in front. He was sure that they were going to buy all to popcorn before he even got there. He tried looking around the fat man in front of him to see what they were all getting; he thought about cutting in line, but he knew if his daddy found out about his rude behavior he'd get a lickin' for sure. He edged as close as he could to the fat man, hoping that maybe the pressure of so many people in line behind him would cause him to panic and leave, but it didn't work. He could hear the band and they had started to play! He was missing it all because some fat folks were hoggin' up all the food. He tried to watch the field behind him and keep an eye on the line in front of him, but it was difficult.

As he was looking back at the field, he thought he sensed the line had moved up a few steps, so he stepped forward too. His face planted right into the backside of the fat man and worse the man farted! He thought he was going to be sick. The smell was awful, so he backed up a step and held his breath for as long as he could. Just about the time he thought he was going to pass out, he let out the air and took a breath. The stink was everywhere. He decided it was best if he just held his nose and breathed through his mouth. That seemed to work. He did that all the way up until it was his turn at the counter. Once he had the popcorn box in his hand and the fat guy was out of his way, he bolted back towards the bleachers. He was running as fast as he could and dodging people all the way when he tripped. He tried to break his fall with his left hand and hold on to the popcorn with his right hand but it all happened so fast that he ended up landing right on the point of his left shoulder and then right on his face.

The pain that he felt on his face was nothing compared to the pain he felt shoot through his shoulder. He thought for sure that his arm had somehow caught fire. Just as he was about to cry he heard them laughing. He looked up and there were four boys from his school that always wanted him to play football. They weren't the smart ones that were mean, they were the dumb ones that were mean and dangerous because they enjoyed being mean. He knew he couldn't cry now or they would intensify their little game and it would just get worse. He looked around and saw the lid to the popcorn box had popped open in the fall and some popcorn had spilled out onto the ground. "Hey, moron, you dropped your popcorn, here let me help you pick it up." The kid kicked the box like he was kicking a field goal and the rest of the popcorn in the box exploded out of the box and all over the ground. They all yelled and laughed; the kid that kicked the box yelled with his arms in the air, "Miller nails the game with a winning field goal and the crowd went wild!" He mimicked the referee raising his arms like they do in the real games.

The other boys started patting him on the back and yelling. "Leave him alone, you boys better hit the bricks, or I will give you something to yell about." Decker felt the pain throbbing in his shoulder, but he had to turn his head to see who that voice belonged to. The four kids from his school took off running like they had seen a ghost. He sure was relieved. They were sure to beat him good tonight. They just looked like they were in a meaner mood than ever. They had tripped him, and worse, he had lost all his popcorn.

He got his head turned around but before he could find the voice, he had a hand on his arm trying to help him up, but it hurt so badly when the hand touched him that he screamed. Everyone stopped and turned to see a black man standing over a crying white kid. Quickly, there was a crowd around them and Decker heard them ask them what he had done. Decker saw that it was Bobby Martin. Bobby was Dub's son and he was Jeannine's daddy. He was a local kid that was a great football player back in his day. He got a scholarship to play football for the Arkansas Razorbacks, but he got hurt in the big game against Texas one Saturday and never played again. He came back home with a bad knee, self-esteem issues, and a drinking problem.

Later, he got a job out at Parchman as a guard, but they say he got fired when he was a little too rough on some of the inmates. Folks said he broke a guy's arm or something like that. Decker didn't care about any of that for right now; he was just grateful that he had run those kids off before he got beaten up. "Man, I didn't do nothin', them other kids was kicking his popcorn and picking on him and get out of my face." The crowd was getting a little too close to Bobby and he didn't like the way they were looking at him.

Maybelle Richards stepped in front of all of them; she was a big woman who had a loud voice. She yelled for everybody to back up and *give this baby some air*, is the way she put it. Decker didn't care much for being called a baby, but his shoulder hurt so badly that he didn't argue about it. She had a big hat on and she took it off and started fanning him; he wasn't sure what that was for because he wasn't hot, he was in pain. She bent over and tried to help him up, but that hurt him so badly he yelled and this time he cried. Nobody noticed that Bobby slipped away, and Decker hadn't had a chance to thank him, so he made a mental note that if he ever ran into Bobby Martin again, he would definitely thank him. Maybe he could talk Bobby into beating all those kids up for him.

It seemed to Decker that everyone stepped a little easy around Bobby. His daddy said Bobby was a good kid that caught a bad break and developed a short fuse. Maybelle realized something was more wrong than just a skinned knee or bloody nose. "Baby, where does it hurt?" She had a deep booming voice and it was nearly impossible for her to speak softly. Decker pointed at his shoulder, so she touched it with two of her fingers. It was a soft touch, but it made Decker wince and recoil. Decker knew Maybelle was a nurse at Coahoma County Hospital. Actually, she was the nurse in charge of all nurses. His daddy told him that back in her day she was fast as greased lightning and said she was quite the looker too. She went to Grambling State College on a track scholarship. She was one of the first black ladies to get a scholarship in Webb and she made the most of it. Her son was the quarterback that everyone came to see tonight and here she was fussing over this misfit. He said she put all that weight on after she had Donnie Ray.

Decker felt bad that he was keeping her from watching her son play but the game hadn't started yet so all he needed to do was get up and get back to the bleachers and the commotion would be over. "Oh, Lord, you are Elmer's boy, good Lord, where is your daddy?" She looked around to see if she saw him but made eye contact with someone in the crowd. "This is Elmer Davis's boy, Decker. Go find his daddy and let him know I think this boy has a broken collar bone, chop chop now!" Decker scrambled to get to his feet, but it hurt to move, so he told her that his daddy wasn't here just yet and it was just him and his momma and his sister. Maybelle continued to fuss over him and he found he actually liked it.

She had something in her manner that made him feel better. Maybe it was just her size and voice. She wasn't ugly at all, she had a very pretty face, but she was pretty large. She had soft hands though and she had the nicest smile. Decker didn't mind her fussing over him. He just couldn't imagine her ever running fast. He was imagining this woman running a race in her present shape and it sort of made him laugh. Maybelle asked him what was so funny and before he could make up story his momma was right there rubbing his forehead and kissing his cheek and making an even bigger fuss over him than Maybelle had. Maybelle let his momma know that she thought he might have a broken collarbone. She was explaining how she could tell when the football paramedics showed up. Those were the guys that would just hang out by the ambulance in one of the end zones waiting to cart someone off that got hurt. Decker thought that maybe they should park their ambulance at Westside Elementary for those football games; he could have used them a few times.

Chapter 5

✦

HE NEVER GOT TO SEE THE GAME, BUT HE HEARD that Webb lost. Decker was glad he didn't see that in person. It would have been tough to take. The Choctaws were undefeated to that point and the prospect of a State Championship was all people could talk about. Decker was sitting in a temporary hospital bed. They told his momma that he didn't need to stay overnight but they needed to monitor him for a few hours to make sure he was ok. The hospital smelled funny to him. It didn't stink like feet or a fart or anything like that, to him it smelled too clean. His momma would use some stuff to clean the fish smell off the back porch after he and his daddy were done cleaning fish. That's kinda what it smelled like to him. His momma had gone down the hall to see if she could find some popcorn. He was pretty upset that he didn't get to eat his popcorn at the game. She told him that if she couldn't find any at the hospital she would make him a batch on the stove when he got home.

He didn't want to tell her, but he liked the concession store popcorn way better than any other popcorn in the world. There was something about eating it at the football game, but he also liked his momma's popcorn she would pop on the stove. It always made the house smell good. She still had the thermos of hot chocolate and she was bound and determined to make her little boy feel better. Since there wasn't much that could be done for a broken collarbone all he could do was sit up in bed with his arm wrapped in a sling. It really didn't hurt anymore now that he knew what was wrong and nobody was trying to grab him and stuff. He was thinking about the smell of the popcorn when his daddy walked in. He was still in his brown sheriff clothes. "Hey, buddy, heard you took a spill at the game." Decker told him the story about running and falling but he left out the part where the kids tripped him. He didn't like to tell his daddy that he got picked on. He knew that it made his daddy mad. He could never tell if he was mad because kids were picking on him or mad because he didn't take up for himself. Either way, it was a subject he had learned to avoid. It just made everything easier if he didn't tell.

His momma came back in the room without any popcorn in her hand. She kissed his daddy and gave him a hug. She inquired about the band aid over his right eye, a detail that Decker had not noticed until now. His momma fussed over his daddy just like she did with him earlier. She was so good at kicking up a fuss and making someone feel like they were the only people in the world and that her one function in life was to make them feel better. His daddy pretended not to want the attention, but

Decker could tell by the way he smiled, and his face would turn a little red, or maybe it was a little pink.

He told her that there was a little scuffle at the Jackpot. That was a pretty rough bar and dance hall where he often got called to go out and break up a fight. He said that the Martins and the Buckles were at it again and he had to toss a couple of them in jail and that Brett had popped him a good one in the scuffle. Brett was the second oldest boy of the Buckles and he was mean. He got into trouble all the time and his daddy was always throwing him in jail for something. Folks in town say he lit a cat on fire and let it run through the street screaming. Decker didn't see it, but he heard his daddy talk about it. His daddy happened to be having lunch at the diner when he heard the commotion.

He saw the cat run past the store all lit up and he knew Brett was up to no good. When he told the story, he always got a sad face when he got to the part about having to shoot the cat to keep it from suffering. There wasn't a law against cat abuse in Webb, so he couldn't lock him up, but he sure gave him the what-for. There were four Buckles boys and five Martin boys, and they didn't like each other for some reason. Decker knew the oldest Buckles boy who everybody said was like the daddy of them all since their own daddy was up in Parchman. Everybody also said that he was generally a good kid, but he had too much responsibility heaped upon him. Decker heard his daddy say that he was a good boy, just not a good daddy. The oldest was in Viet Nam. He also knew that the other Buckles boys got meaner after he left, and his daddy told him to steer clear of them. He had no idea what *In Viet Nam* meant; he didn't know where anything was outside of Tallahatchie County. He had been to Charleston, Sumner, Clarksdale, and Grenada.

He had been to Grenada to visit a second cousin or something like that. He didn't have much fun. There weren't any kids
his age and the grown-ups just sat around and drank coffee and
talked about stuff he didn't care about. He tried to go outside
and climb some trees, but it was almost too hot to do anything,
plus he climbed this Magnolia tree and came within a few inches
of accidently touching a stinkbug. His sister had told him that
they bite you and after they bite you nobody would come near
you because you would stink and no matter how many baths
you took or even if you used momma's pretty soap you'd still
stink. He was forever on the lookout for stinkbugs from that
day forward. This one was so close to him that he got scared and
nearly fell out of the tree, so he went back inside and stood in
front of the air conditioner that was in the front window. That
was always one of his favorite things to do in the summer: to go
outside and get good and hot and sweaty then come inside, lift
up the back of his shirt then stand in front of the air conditioner;
it felt so good, it almost tickled.

As his momma was still fussing over his daddy's hurt eye,
in walks Maybelle Richards, the same lady who had helped him
at the football game and the same lady who was the momma to
the star quarterback. His momma reacted as if she had just seen
a long-lost relative, she hugged Maybelle and they did this little
circle dance while they hugged. It looked kinda funny to Decker
to see two women dancing and hugging in a hospital room. His
momma must have told her *thank you* what seemed like a thousand times to Decker. When Maybelle was done hugging his
momma she went right after his daddy. She hugged his daddy
and did the same little circle dance. She said she wished Lois
hadn't beaten her to him because he sure was a good-looking

man. His daddy's face turned beet red and he told her that she was just too fast for him and every other guy in school and that nobody from their class could catch her. They all laughed but it was a funny laugh to Decker, not a real one.

He heard his daddy mention Donnie's name and asked if he was all right. Decker perked up at that. *What happened to Donnie*, he thought? "Oh, Elmer, he is just fine but that poor boy's football season is over for this year." She said that those "thugs" from Clarksdale broke her boy's collarbone. Decker couldn't believe his luck! He had the exact same injury as the star quarterback of the high school except his got broken by thugs from Webb, not Clarksdale; that was a secret he would have to keep. Maybelle stepped over to Decker and she put her hand on his forehead and out came that loud voice again. "This is one fine looking boy, Lois, he is a keeper. So handsome, got his momma's pretty face and his daddy's charm, umm umm he is a keeper!" His momma giggled a little, she loved it when folks gushed over her kids. "What do you say to Mrs. Maybelle for helping you tonight, Deck?" His momma shortened his name when she was in a really good mood, which seemed to happen quite a bit lately. "Thank you for helping, Mrs. Maybelle." Decker was shy and just hated to talk to anyone, but he found it kinda easy to talk to Mrs. Maybelle. She was so easy to be around.

Her voice remained loud, and she remained big. She still had a pretty face, but she was so big that she had blocked Decker's view and didn't see his daddy leave the room. He had gone across the hall to say "hello" to Donnie Ray Richards, who was in the room next door. He had his arm in the exact same sling that Decker had except his sling was much bigger. Donnie was a big kid and he was only a junior in high school. He was an inch taller than Decker's daddy which he never noticed because he had never actually stood as close to Donnie as he did to his daddy. He was just a kid and besides, you can't just walk up to a football star just too see how tall they are. He noticed it more today because when his daddy walked back into the room he said, "Look who wants to see Decker and his broken collar bone." And then in walked Donnie Ray Richards. Decker was dumbfounded; he was shocked to see Donnie standing next to his daddy and even more shocked to find out that there was someone bigger than his daddy in the world.

His momma went right up to Donnie and hugged him ever so gently, because his arm was in a sling too, and Decker thought, *if his pain was a bad as what Decker felt he didn't want any hugs from anyone!* His momma actually kissed Donnie right on the cheek! He could not believe what he was seeing. She told him she was sorry about his collarbone and they would have won if he hadn't gotten hurt; Decker tried to listen, but he was still in awe. A real-life football star was standing in his room, wearing the same sling he was, and his momma gave him a kiss on the cheek! This was just about more than Decker could process and then Donnie walked right over to Decker's bed. "Hurts, doesn't it?" he said with a smile. Decker nodded his head up and down because he couldn't find the words; they were stuck in his throat somewhere.

He knew what to say when you met someone; his momma had gone over it a thousand times with him just like she had made him practice how to answer the phone. She was big on being polite and having good manners. She would tell him to judge people on their actions and deeds, not their appearances or wallets. She would say that everyone is God's creation and should be treated with respect. She said it so much that he could almost recite it himself without missing a word, although he had never thought to have someone show him his or her wallet. He wasn't sure how to judge that one, but he assumed he would figure it out eventually. "I heard you like to watch me play football?" At first Decker shook his head in the "no" direction and realized his mistake – then began to nod his head up and down that was supposed to clearly signal that he not only liked to watch him play, he loved to watch him play. "Now, Decker, has the cat got your tongue? Donnie came across here to say 'hello' to you and you need say something to him." His momma put her hand on his leg as she was saying it. Decker felt the pressure to speak welling up inside him, but he couldn't.

He knew what he wanted to say. He wanted to say that he thought Donnie was the best football player in the whole state of Mississippi, probably the whole world, but nothing would come up. Then the worst thing ever happened, the most embarrassing thing that he could ever imagine, a tear rolled down his eye; he couldn't stop it, he was about to cry! He was about to cry in front of the best football player in the world and instead of words coming up, tears were coming up! Donnie didn't miss a beat and bailed him out of the worst jam he could ever remember being in "I know man, mine still hurts like crazy too. I cried over there." He motioned over his shoulder as to indicate that he had been crying over in the privacy of his room. Decker doubted that Donnie was crying at any time but *Thank the Good Lord*, Decker thought. Donnie had just done something that Decker would learn that friends do for each other; they help you out in your worst times no matter what. Somehow, he knew that Donnie knew he wasn't crying because of the pain in his shoulder or the eye that was now turning black, he was crying because he couldn't get his mouth to form one single word.

Donnie patted him on the same leg his momma had patted him and told him that since the two of them were lame ducks for the rest of the football season that maybe they could grab a shake or something. Decker could not believe what he was hearing. The most popular and famous man in Webb was asking him if he wanted to have a shake with him! Of course he did and he hoped everyone in town saw it when he did! He nodded again but this time he managed to get out "yes", that was it, that was all he could say to Donnie Ray Richards, YES. Donnie Ray Richards smiled at him and looked at him with those sparkling green eyes. "I will come by your place next week and pick you up. How's that, Deck?" Holy cow! Donnie Ray had just shortened his name to Deck like his momma! This was by far the best day of Decker's life.

Donnie left the room and his daddy followed him out. The doctor came in as Donnie and his daddy were leaving. The doctor was a scary man to Decker. He was round like *Humpty Dumpty*, he had hair coming out the back of his shirt collar, and he was always smoking a big round cigar. He would take the cigar out of his mouth to examine a patient and that was about the only time he ever took a cigar out of his mouth. Some kids said they saw him go swimming at the community pool once and he smoked a cigar underwater. Decker wasn't stupid enough to believe that, but he did wonder if the pool drains might have gotten clogged with all his hair. When he was examining you, he kept the cigar in between his thumb and in index finger. His breath was terrible, and the smoke would drift in your eyes. Decker hated seeing him, but he was the only doctor in Webb and momma said he was a good man. When she told him to not judge people by their appearances but by their actions and deeds he should have asked if it was ok to judge them on their breath.

Chapter 6

⁂

AT FIRST IT WAS COOL HAVING HIS ARM IN A SLING
but then it just got in the way. His shoulder still hurt, and he
had to admit, every time he thought it didn't hurt anymore he
would try to take his arm out of the sling so he could be normal
again. But the pain would shoot out from his shoulder so badly
that he would nearly start crying all over again. He hadn't clearly
thought through all the problems of having your arm in a sling.
The attention was awesome, that was for sure, but simple stuff
like eating was a task. This was his good arm, the arm that he used
to write with and throw the ball with. He found he couldn't do a
lick with the other hand. He never knew how much he counted
on his good hand.

He couldn't even eat correctly. His sister laughed at him
when she watched him trying to scoop up some black-eyed
peas with his free hand. First, he tried a fork, then a spoon,

but nothing worked. The peas would just scoot away from the utensils like they were playing a game of tag with him. He was getting frustrated with it and his sister knew it. She reached over and dropped a little scoop of mayonnaise on the peas and mixed it all up. Now the peas were in sort of a little clump and he could scoop them right up with either his fork or his spoon, not to mention that this tasted so good to him. He had never thought of doing this until his sister thought it up for him.

She also helped him cut up his pork chop into little pieces so he could stab at them with his fork and shovel them into his mouth. His whole life he would remember that meant more than any other meal, Thanksgiving and Christmas included, which he admitted were such very fine memories, but this one was special. His sister had invented a new way to eat peas and he continued to eat his peas the same way for the rest of his life. There was one other obstacle that came to light shortly after dinner. During supper he drank about a gallon of sweat tea. For some reason momma's tea never tasted so good but then it hit him.

He needed to go. He didn't think much of it until he couldn't get his zipper down. He panicked; he tried to force his way through the pain and use his bad arm, but it hurt too much. Every time he pulled down on the zipper it would just pull a little ways and get stuck. He felt like he was in a real life and death struggle with this zipper. Then it happened, he tried his best to stop it but once he started whizzing he couldn't stop it. He just kept peeing. It seemed like he peed for an hour. His pants were covered, waist to cuff. He stood there in the bathroom trying to think of what to do. His underwear was stuck to him now, his pants were covered in pee and he was standing in a puddle.

To think just a few short hours ago he was carrying on a

manly conversation with a football legend and now here he was, a little red-headed kid standing in his own pee. He was amazed at how quickly a day could turn sour on a person. He wondered what Donnie Ray would do at a time like this and then realized that Donnie Ray probably never had to go to the bathroom. He did the only thing he knew to do, he yelled for his momma. Of course, because of the situation and the fact that everyone was on high alert, not only did his momma come into the bathroom, his daddy and sister did too. Yep, this has now become the worst day of his life. He would rather get beaten up at school than to have to stand here in front of his whole family covered in pee.

To his surprise, nobody laughed. In fact, his daddy made sense of it all by saying that we just didn't realize how much we take for granted and that it had never occurred to him that just going to the bathroom would be a chore. That made Decker feel much better, but it also made him think about what he would have to do at school Monday. He knew right then that he would have to practice not drinking anything all day Saturday so he could monitor his peeing cycle. He'd never paid any attention to how many times he peed a day but he better figure it out before Monday. POOP! Holy cow, what happened when he had to poop! He was in full four-alarm panic now. Well, he would just not eat or drink anything until this sling was off! He had no other choice; it was probably what Donnie Ray would do, that is, if Donnie Ray actually went to the bathroom.

Chapter 7

❧

HE SPENT ALL DAY SATURDAY FIGURING OUT WHAT he could and could not do with one hand. He even practiced unbuckling and unzipping his jeans. He went through all his clothes and tried on every pair of jeans he had. He had a brand-new pair of *Wranglers* that were so stiff that the pants seemed to stay in place while he tugged on the zipper both up and down. He had found the solution, a brand-new pair of *Wranglers*. Of course, the kids would make fun of brand-new jeans like they did every first day of school, but it was better than having the teacher or a classmate help him get his tally whacker out of his pants to pee. He would be so embarrassed if he peed his britches in front of her.

He went outside to just feel the outdoors and the fall air. He could smell the hogs in the next farm over and he didn't care much for that smell at all. They lived on 80 acres of land that his daddy said had been in his family since the Civil War. Their land sat in sort of a triangle with the Martin's land and the Buckles' land. The Buckles didn't have much but what they had they used it to run a junk and salvage yard.

The Martins had a lot of property, Decker wasn't sure how much but most of their property and the Martin's property butted up against each other. There was a mud bog separating the two, but Decker knew how to get through it without sinking in the quicksand. He loved to explore. When his daddy didn't take him to work or fishing he would spend all day exploring every square inch of their land and would snoop around the Martin's property just because he couldn't help it. He didn't go anywhere near the Buckles' junkyard because he didn't want to end up like that cat and he was sure that he would. Their place was a mess, and they didn't seem to care much. His daddy told him to make sure he stayed clear of there, not because the Buckles were dangerous, but he said that's where all the cottonmouths and copperheads were hiding. Snakes didn't scare Decker, but he wasn't going to take any chances of getting bitten by a snake or burned like a cat. Yep, he wasn't stupid; he knew how to be careful.

He had built a makeshift fort on a ridge that overlooked all three properties at once. He had worked on it all last summer and this summer he had camouflaged it with leaves and tree branches, so nobody could see it. He was in it one day and a deer walked right up to his fort and didn't even know he was in there. He was proud of it and it was all his, nobody knew it was there but him. Since his daddy owned the store and was the sheriff, they didn't do much with the land, but they still had cows and they even grew watermelons, a bunch of them. Daddy would plant a bunch of them in the spring and by July they had more watermelons than they could eat. Daddy would let him and his sister take the truck, fill the back of it up with watermelons, and drive down to the end of the driveway that connected to the road leading to Webb and sell them out of the truck. He said whatever money they made, he would get 20% and they could keep the rest. His sister was smart at math, so she kept track of what they owed their daddy. Some days they made a lot of money, so much money that his sister would have to roll it in a ball, wrap a rubber band around it, and stick it in the truck. Some days they wouldn't make but a few dollars. Either way, he remembered the good times because his sister would talk to him and help him figure stuff out.

He could ask her anything and she would explain so he could understand it. He wasn't stupid, he just took longer than others to figure stuff out. He tried to pick up a baseball he had in the shed with his bad hand and it hurt to even squeeze it. He picked it up with his good hand and tried to throw it left-handed. It was awful. He thought he looked like a girl throwing and hoped no one saw him, but as his luck would have it, someone did.

Chapter 8

SINCE IT WAS CAMPAIGN SEASON, HIS DADDY TOOK them to as many churches in Webb as he could. Their normal church was the Baptist church on Laurel Road but today they were going to the First Pentecostal Church on 2nd Street. Decker didn't mind going there because he might get a chance to see her. He knew she went to church there with her granddaddy and grandma. Her daddy didn't go to church at all, and her momma, well nobody talked about her. Decker didn't know why her momma didn't live with her but there had to be a good reason.

He couldn't imagine at the time living without his momma. So many things went through his head when he thought about it and it made him sad, so he tried not thinking about it. But still, his momma's biscuits in the morning were the best. He would smother them in the gravy she made out of some flour and bacon grease. On special weekends and holidays, she would make her biscuits and some chocolate gravy. He loved that stuff. That was like having dessert first thing in the morning. He could not imagine a holiday being worth much without his momma and as it would later turn out, they really weren't. His momma would make him wear a suit to church; he only had one and she kept it clean. It was a nice dark blue suit she had bought over in Clarksdale. When she first brought it home it was too big, but she said he would grow into it, but it he hadn't had it that long and it was already pretty tight. He noticed this morning that his pants were a little higher than they were last Sunday. He didn't have to wear the jacket this Sunday because of his broken collarbone but she did make him put on the tie. He hated the tie more than anything. He could feel it slowly choking him. He imagined that the minute it was around his neck it would begin to get tighter and tighter until he couldn't breathe anymore and then his eyes would pop right out if his head. They would have to stop church and pick his eyeballs up off the floor. It would be a huge distraction and he would probably get a whoopin' from his daddy for allowing his eyes to pop out in church. He wasn't allowed to do anything in church but sit arrow-straight and listen to the preacher.

It was so hard for him. He found that if he sat still too long he would nod off to sleep and then his head would bob up and down. That seemed to happen a lot because when it did, his momma would pinch him on the leg and that hurt. He walked into the church right behind his sister; he immediately began looking for her. He hoped that maybe they would sit in the same pew, but it didn't happen. Folks came up and shook hands with his daddy; he heard them say they would vote for him because they could count on him. Decker sat the furthest away from the aisle – that had just recently become the rule – his daddy sat at the end, then his momma, then his sister, then him. He liked the new rule because his momma couldn't reach to pinch him if he nodded off.

After he had taken his position on the seat, he continued his search for her. It would be the best Sunday ever for him if she sat by him. Maybe she would really like the way he looked all dressed up in a tie and she would want to marry him sooner than expected. After a few minutes of straining his neck to twist and turn all around the church, he found her. There she was! She was just two rows in front of him! His heart started beating fast and his palms got sweaty. He couldn't see her at first because there was a lady with a giant head blocking his view, but she had to move down a little because the church got filled up right before the service started. She was as beautiful today as she ever was. She had on a pink dress; at least he thought it was a dress, she was sitting so he couldn't tell. He just assumed since it was church she would be wearing a dress. She was sitting right between her granddaddy and grandma and the angle that he had to see her now was perfect. He was staring at the back of her head when he realized he wasn't staring at the back of her head anymore.

She had turned around and was looking directly at him! *Oh no!* he thought. She caught him looking at her. He tried quickly to think of something cool or tough to do but nothing came out. All he could muster up was a dorky goofy smile. She smiled at him and waved a very little wave and then turned around. *What just happened*, he thought? *Did she just wave at me?* He turned around to see if maybe she was waving at someone else. There was no mistaking; Jeannine Martin had just acknowledged him in church! He felt flush, his face must be getting red, and he couldn't tell but his mouth got really dry and he was breathing heavily.

His sister saw the entire thing happen. She looked down at Decker and smiled a type of smile that Decker knew very well. It was a smile that only brothers and sisters know. It was sort of a secret code smile so parents won't know you are up to something. She put her hand on his leg and patted him. She approved! Yep, today was a good day. Decker continued to daydream in church about Jeannine Martin, but the preacher got very loud at some point and brought him back to reality.

The preacher was a small man, but he was loud. He would come out from behind the preacher's podium and walk around and held his bible in one hand and a handkerchief in the other. When he got really excited he would stop dead in his tracks and point the bible at the ceiling and wipe his face with the handkerchief. He would hear someone in the congregation say, "Amen", or one lady liked to holler, "Preach it, brother" and he would start moving again. Decker thought that the music in this church was fantastic. It was fast and happy and noisy.

Today the preacher talked about that Viet Nam and how we need to pray for our boys over there and that we need more love, kindness, and forgiveness in the world. Decker had missed most of what the preacher was saying because he was thinking about Jeannine Martin but when he heard that forgiveness and kindness part, he wished the preacher would tell that to the boys in his school.

After the service was over his daddy and momma stood next to the preacher so daddy could shake hands with everybody. His daddy called it *being a good Christian* and his momma called it *getting votes*. Either way, he and his sister stood off to the side waiting. They weren't too far away so Decker could hear the comments everyone was making to the preacher and his daddy. It was the same old grown-up stuff. He wasn't overly interested in it, but he kept his eye on them because he knew she would be coming out soon. "So, you really like that girl in the second row in front, huh?" His sister looked down at him with that smile he had seen in church. "What's her name? tell me about her!" Although he could tell his sister anything and she was sure to keep it a secret, he felt himself turning red and his mouth got dry again.

He started to tell his sister about Jeannine but didn't get the chance. She showed up right in front of them. "Decker Davis!" She said it with such excitement like she hadn't seen him in years. He was confused because they had just seen each other Friday in class. He was caught off-guard and was not on his game at all. He froze. He had no idea what to say but like always, the women in his life bailed him out. His sister introduced herself and stuck out her hand, which Jeannine took and shook like a girl. His daddy had told him about handshakes and that a man needed to grip hands firm and tight when he shook another man's hand. He said that was a sign of strength and confidence and that you could tell an awful lot about a man by his handshake and his eyes. He said he had to be gentler with a girl because they had skinny fingers and soft hands and a strong handshake just might break their knuckles if a fella wasn't careful.

At that moment, he had this vision of squashing Jeannine's hand in his because he shook it too hard and crushed it. He could see her screaming bloody murder, pulling back her hand only to find this mangled stump with blood squirting out every-where. He could hear his daddy saying, "Son, how many times do I have to tell you to be gentle when you shake a girl's hand?

Now see what you've done!" He snapped back into reality and realized that Jeannine was asking him about his arm and she had heard that he broke his collarbone. He felt his sister's hand on his shoulder; his good shoulder and that helped him steady himself. He explained to her how it happened but again, he didn't tell her that bullies tripped him, only that he was in such a hurry to get back and watch the game that he tripped and fell. He even told her how much he was looking forward to eating the popcorn and having the hot chocolate, then he caught himself and wished he hadn't shared that part with her. For some reason, it just didn't sound manly enough. He wished he could tell her that he was out working with a bunch of lumberjacks and he had to keep a tree from falling on a guy or something a little better than: he tripped running to get some hot chocolate. *What a dope!* he thought. Jeannine didn't seem to mind that the story wasn't quite so manly.

While he was telling her the real story, she actually touched his sore shoulder. He felt a little pain but then he froze. He was not going to show her that anything hurt; he had to be strong at this moment. Just as he was about to tell her about talking to Donnie Ray, his parents and her grandparents walked up. His daddy looked down at Jeannine and said, "Honey, you have to be the prettiest girl in church today. I can't believe how big you have gotten, why, you are taller than Deck now." That was it – he was ruined. His daddy had just ruined everything for him. Decker knew she was a little taller than he, but was hoping she wouldn't notice it. Now his daddy had just shot it out there like a cannon for everyone to see. Suddenly to Decker, she looked like a giant. She was towering over him. She was reaching down and rubbing his head like grown-ups always did. Then his momma made matters worse by saying that girls grew faster than boys and they were lucky because Decker hadn't had to change shoe sizes yet this year. Now that was the final nail.

The one girl who actually spoke to him in school would now realize that Decker was just a peewee with small feet and red hair. It was the only time in his life that he wished the bullies would interrupt and beat him up again. Please get this over with. "Hey, Decker, the Martins are coming over to have Sunday lunch at our house. They want to try out your momma's friend chicken." Did his daddy just tell him that the Martins were coming to his house? Did that mean that Jeannine would be coming to his house too?

This was a full-alarm panic moment. He looked around for a place to hide but there was none. He felt the grip his sister had on his shoulder tightened just a little. He knew that was her signal to him that everything would be all right and he needed to breathe. "I will see you in a little bit, we are just going to change clothes and then be over. I can teach you how to throw with your left hand." *What?* And she ran off to catch up to two other girls that he recognized from school. His sister looked down at him again and said, "Let's talk a little when we get home."

Chapter 9

HIS DADDY TALKED ABOUT HOW GOOD THE SERVICE was on the way home and that they needed to go to that church more often. His momma agreed and asked him if he felt anything odd about it since he really only went there today because it was election season. Decker thought that sounded funny, that election season thing. It sounded like deer season or turkey season. He remembered that this fall was going to be his first deer hunt with his daddy. His daddy had promised to take him this year if he managed to do all his chores and stay out of trouble for the whole year. Decker was certain that he had done that. He hadn't fought back in school, he listened to what the teachers had to say, and he was finally making good grades. He couldn't understand why he had to study so hard. Reading was just hard for him. He struggled to make out his words and now that they had introduced cursive writing into the mix, he really struggled.

It just all seemed like gibberish. Because he so badly wanted to go deer hunting this year with his daddy and a bunch of his daddy's buddies from work, he had put lots of extra time into practicing reading and writing. It was helping, and his grades showed it.

He dashed off to his room in a hurry to change clothes and into his jeans and then realized with his arm the way it was, he was not going to be in a hurry to do anything. That's when his sister came into his room and shut the door. She only shut the door when she had a secret, or she knew that he had a secret that she needed to hear. "Let me help you get out of that shirt and tie and into your play clothes." He didn't mind his sister helping, she had seen him change clothes before, and she had even seen him in no clothes at all. She was more than a sister; she was like another momma actually. She started helping him with the tie and started talking about life and people and cultures. It was all very interesting, but he wasn't sure why she was talking about subjects like that. She usually liked to talk about music and especially about the *Beatles*. She was crazy about them and would sing their songs all the time. She had every 45 record they had put out and had just gotten a new stereo for her birthday that had an 8-track player in it. She didn't have any 8-tracks yet but said she was going to use some of her watermelon money she saved to buy a *Beatles* 8-track.

She just kept telling him that people were different and that some people had a hard time with differences and that not everyone saw the world like he did. He knew that was true or the other kids in school wouldn't pick on him like they did. If they only knew how much it hurt to get picked on all the time they wouldn't do it. She slowly pulled his shirt over his bad collarbone and threw the white dress shirt in the laundry basket. "What'd you do that for?" He made a frustrated face and told her that the shirt wasn't dirty; he had only worn it to church and he would just hang it back up and use it next Sunday. He grabbed it out of the laundry basket and handed it to her. She shook her head and put it on a hanger. She pulled the jeans out of the drawer and asked if the pair she held up were ok? They were. They were his favorite; *Levi's* with enough length at the bottom to get a nice roll going, perfect for all occasions! She continued to help him get out of his dress pants and into his jeans. "All I'm saying, buddy, is that I know you like this girl – and she is definitely pretty – but some folks in this town may not like the fact that you like her. You just need to be prepared for whatever they might say or think." It sounded like good advice to him, but he really couldn't imagine anyone not liking her. He could imagine them not liking him because it seemed that way in school already. He really thought that if he was seen with her and she really liked him then everyone might treat him a little better. Sort of in the same way they treated him differently when he was with his sister and his daddy. And the way they were sure to treat him differently whenever they saw him having a milkshake at Milholen's Drug Store with Donnie Ray Richards. He would sure be in high cotton then.

Their driveway was dirt and gravel and it was almost a half-mile long, so they knew when someone was coming. It was nearly impossible to sneak up on the Davis' home. The dust from the driveway kicked up the minute you left the main highway. He could see the Martin's station wagon coming down the driveway and felt himself tense up, she would actually be in his home. He had no idea what he would do. He only had one arm;

they couldn't play baseball or football. Maybe they could draw or something, but he nixed that idea because he couldn't draw or write with his left hand. He would look goofy. He couldn't figure out why he could not get his left hand to move the way he got his right hand to move. He knew how to make his letters, but when he tried with his left hand, nothing worked. Everything he tried to write down just turned into gibberish.

His momma had already started the chicken and after his sister helped him get changed out of his Sunday clothes, she started peeling potatoes. Momma always made mashed potatoes when she made fried chicken. Decker loved fried chicken and he was especially looking forward to eating a couple chicken legs, which were his favorite part. His daddy was sitting on the porch listening to the radio. He had put an old *Admiral* radio right on the front porch so he could listen to a station out of Memphis that played all kinds of music, but his daddy preferred Country. The sound was always so clear on the porch and sometimes when the mood struck them his momma and daddy would get up and slow dance right there on the front porch. His momma tried to show him how to dance one time, but he never got the hang of it and figured he would quit it for good.

That radio playing loudly and sitting on that front porch is where he would be on Saturdays so he could listen to the Ole Miss Rebel football games. They were rarely on the television. He was especially excited to listen to the games this year because they had a really good quarterback, Archie something, he couldn't remember his name, but he knew he was the talk of the town now that Donnie Ray Richards had broken his collarbone.

The Martins came in after greetings and hugs. He couldn't take his eyes off her. He really couldn't believe she was standing

right there in his living room! Mrs. Martin and his momma
darted off to the kitchen where they started talking about all
kinds of boring stuff. Decker thought that Mrs. Martin didn't
look like any grandma he knew. She seemed to sort of look like
his momma, but he really couldn't tell. She was still a grown up
and he tried not to get into their business. His daddy and Mr.
Martin sat and talked about that Archie guy and how Donnie
Ray would probably go to Ole Miss after he finished his senior
year and replace that other guy because he would go on and be
a pro. His sister took an immediate liking to Jeannine and took
her off to her room to show her some of the dolls and stuff she
used to play with.

Decker could hear them laughing down the hall. So, there
he stood, in the living room, all by himself. He thought about
going down to his sister's room but that was just too girly for
him. He didn't want to play with a doll, that was for sure. Deep
down he was kind relieved that he didn't have to talk to Jeannine
because he wasn't sure what to say. He had tried to think of some
subjects that were cool and fun to talk about but not many came
to mind. He liked whales and dinosaurs, but he didn't think
Jeannine would care much for either. He decided to go back out
onto the front porch and just sit on the swing. He was making
the swing go back and forth slowly and daydreaming.

He was thinking about how when he got to high school
he would be the star of the football team just like Donnie Ray
Richards. He even went all the way through the long bombs
he would throw with pin-point accuracy that float right into
the receivers' hands as they were in full-stride. He heard the
announcer say, "Another touchdown pass for superstar quarterback Decker Davis! Folks, that kid is something special. Better

get an eyeful because next year he will be playing at Ole Miss and then on to the Pro's!" He heard the screen door on the front porch squeak then slam and he snapped out of his imaginary football heroism. There she was, standing right in front of him. She had on a pair of jeans just like he did. He couldn't tell if hers were *Levi's* and he hadn't even noticed when she first came into his house what she was wearing. He had focused completely on her face. He would never tell anyone that he thought she was pretty. He would have to eventually get around to telling her if he ever planned to marry her but that could wait. "Your momma said for me to come out and tell you that it was time to eat." She smiled when she said it, but she did something that he never expected – she stuck out her hand – that must have indicated that she wanted him to take her hand? He wasn't sure; he panicked and sprung up off the porch swing nearly knocking her to the ground.

It was the first of a few embarrassing things he would do today. They both recovered quickly, and he bolted inside the house. He stopped about mid-way through the living room and realized that he had forgotten to hold the door for her. Not only had he not held the door for her, he went in first! If his daddy found out he didn't hold the door for a girl, he was sure to get a whoopin'. He turned to run back to the door to repair the damage of poor manners as quickly as he could, but she had already opened the door and came in on her own. He looked around to see if anyone had seen his poor behavior and luckily no one had. He didn't know what to say to her, so he froze. He wasn't about to walk into the dining room in front of her. He would stay in this spot all day if he had to. He managed to point out where the dining room was, and she walked to where he was pointing. He could hear the noise of the plates already, so he followed her. They took the last two seats available.

They didn't normally eat in this dining room, they normally ate at the little table in the kitchen. This was a real treat for him. They only ate here on holidays and today wasn't even a holiday and they were eating off momma's good plates! His momma scolded him for not washing his hands and he told her that he could only wash one hand, so it seemed like a waste of time. Mr. Martin got a good laugh out of that one for some reason but what was worse – Mrs. Martin gave Jeannine instructions to go help Decker wash his hands. She was going to have to touch him! She was going to have to wash his hands! She panicked as much as Decker but both kids knew this was something they had to do and something they had to do in a hurry because the food was hot and Mr. Martin was itchin' to say grace and dig into that chicken. Decker had heard him say it. They both stood in front of the sink for a second, not sure how to accomplish this mission, when she made the first move.

She reached up and unhooked the sling but held his arm in place. She slowly moved his bad arm up to the sink, turned on the water and actually checked to make sure the water was just the right before she slid his bad hand under the faucet. He rubbed some soap on his hand and slowly washed it until she was satisfied it was clean. She grabbed the towel and wrapped his hand in it. She asked for his good hand, which he gave to her without a fuss. She mesmerized him. She was as gentle as she could be with him. This was the same girl that moved like greased lightning jumping rope and could outrun everyone in school. And she was standing here in his bathroom washing his hands with as much softness in her actions as his momma and sister did. He felt it slip out. He knew it was coming and he did everything he could do to keep it from happening, but he couldn't stop it. He broke wind. Just like the fat guy at the concession stand...he farted. This was no dainty fart, either, this one came out roaring like a gorilla. His face immediately turned bright red. He tried to say, "Excuse me" but when nothing came out, she burst out laughing. He thought at first she was laughing at him but it was more than that. She was laughing so hard, she farted too! From then on, she was all right by him. Yep, he would definitely marry her someday. Even though she was only in fifth grade, he knew she was already the perfect woman.

Chapter 10

⚜

AFTER LUNCH WHEN HE HAD DEVOURED THREE chicken legs, a big heap of mashed potatoes, and two full glasses of sweet tea, he was told by his momma to show Jeannine the yard, shop, and barn, but don't wander off too far. Which really meant to get out of the grown-up's way. The two walked out to the barn where he showed her all the cool tools, especially the pitchfork. The pitchfork and its purpose fascinated him for many years. It kinda scared him a little because it looked like if you fell on it, it would poke a hole through you and then someone would have to come yank it out of you.

He imagined laying on the ground with the pitchfork stuck through him and pinning him to the ground like he had done with spiders before. He would poke a nail through the big spiders and leave them stuck in the ground; their legs would be moving up and down and trying to move but they couldn't go anywhere. He imagined having someone put their foot in the middle of his back like those spiders he would spear while they told him to hold still and they would yank it out of him. It would hurt for sure, but he still thought it was a cool tool. He had never actually used it; probably because they hadn't needed any hay to be moved from one place to the other lately and the cows seemed to pretty much find it wherever it was.

Jeannine listened to everything he was saying. She would ask a question every now and then but was completely fascinated, not with the tour of their stuff but fascinated with the fact that this was the same kid that stood off by himself at recess, the same kid who sat in the back of the class, the same kid that the other boys picked on and here he was, talking to her like any normal kid would. He thought he was cute with his red hair, but there was more to him than one could see, and there was way more to him than what he let people see. In his element, he moved with confidence, he didn't seem scared, he certainly didn't seem lost for words because after she had helped him wash his hands and they both farted in the bathroom, he talked to her like he had known her his whole life. Technically he had, both had gone to the same school since the first grade but had never had a class together until this year.

She knew his name and she knew his daddy was the sheriff but that was about it. She thought that being the sheriff's kid would have some advantages but it sure didn't with him. He got picked on anyway. She had paid attention to him this year because he was bigger than the other kids. When the bell would ring for recess to be over he would be the first back into the classroom because he was faster than everyone on the playground, except her, of course. She could outrun anyone, and she liked to prove it. She would race anyone, especially the boys because they would get so mad when she would beat them. She got along with everyone and she made straight A's in all her subjects.

Her favorite subject was math. She loved to figure things out and loved the thought of solving problems that no one else could. She was so good at it that the teacher had to develop her own lessons for her because the teacher said that the math the rest of the kids were learning didn't challenge her enough. She enjoyed school; she was a weird kid, her daddy would tell her, but she enjoyed being around other kids...except Lonnie Buckles. Lonnie was the last of the Buckles boys and he was just as mean as all the rest of them. They say he wasn't near as mean as Brett and he hadn't lit any cats on fire that she knew of, but he was definitely mean. He was always stealing stuff from the other kids. If you didn't have your name on whatever it was, it was sure to end up in Lonnie's desk somewhere. That would cause a problem sometimes because you just couldn't put your name on everything.

She understood the rules of dealing with Lonnie better than anyone because unfortunately she had been in every class with him since first grade. She prayed every year that she wouldn't be but every year, there he was, sitting there in his smelly shirt and worn-out jeans. He definitely had a hygiene problem, he smelled like chicken poop to her and she once asked the fourth-grade teacher if she could be moved further away. But the teacher scolded her for being judgmental and, based off her stature in life, she had no right to judge anyone. She had no idea what that meant but she endured the rest of her fourth-grade year sitting right next to smelly Lonnie.

Their fifth-grade year, she had managed to get this cool eraser out of a box of those small bags of chips that kids take to school. It was some sort of promotion and not every box had the eraser, so she thought she had hit the jackpot when her grandma bought one to use for her school lunch and it had the eraser in it. It was a Bandito guy that fit on the top of your pencil. He was really cool and fun to play with when she was bored in class. She normally took it home with her and kept it with her, even during recess – after all, this was the prize eraser! They had them on TV commercials and everyone wanted one, but she had it. She went out for recess and forgot it one day. When she came back from recess it was gone. She looked all through her desk but couldn't find it. It was a complete tragedy in her mind and then she looked up and saw it dancing on the end of Lonnie Buckles' pencil. She was furious.

She yelled in the middle of the teacher's lesson that he had stolen her Bandito eraser! Of course, he lied about it and said that he had it all year and just never showed it to anyone. She was so upset she said he was a damn liar and punched him in the shoulder. She had never before used a cuss word in public nor had she ever hit anyone, even though she had heard plenty of cuss words from her daddy, but she knew better than to use them herself. The hitting caught her off guard. She knew she had messed up for sure when she smacked him because he acted like she had broken his arm or something. He started hollering and fell off his desk onto the floor and rolling around.

It was a giant spectacle and all the other kids started laughing. Lonnie was enjoying the attention and enjoying the fact that someone else in school was going to get in trouble besides him. The teacher also didn't care for the language or the punching and because she had no proof that it was hers, SHE got in trouble and was sent down to the principal's office. Her grandma had to come pick her up from school. Luckily her grandparents believed her and supported her but not the language or the punching. They told her that there were better ways to settle a dispute than with language and hitting, and in life she wasn't always going to win every dispute.

She listened intently as Decker explained all about his barn and the cows and shed and the shop and whole bunch of other stuff that she didn't care about. What she really cared about at this very moment was that she was learning something. She was learning not to be too quick to pass judgment on people. Her grandma had always told her that you can't judge a book by its cover, that you have to open it up and read it, turn it from page to page, explore its ups and downs and then after you have closed the book on its last page, then and only then can you decide if it was a good book. She said that people were just like books; you had to turn way more than just a few pages to understand them. She had turned all the pages she wanted to turn on Lonnie Buckles and she knew he was a rotten book, but Decker was a different story. She listened to him and realized that he wasn't stupid like she thought, he was actually funny!

And he was smart. She wanted to turn a bunch more pages of Decker Davis and see what kind of book he was. She smiled every time he tried to pick something up and show her. He wasn't coordinated with his left hand at all. She started to interrupt him a few times to help him, but she decided he was the type that had to do things on his own. She liked that very much. Decker was not like all the other kids at school. He was comfortable with himself – he was not comfortable letting them world see him.

Chapter 11

⊕

DECKER FINISHED SHOWING HER THE WORKSHOP
and all the tools that were in the shop and a thought occurred to
him – he was going to show her the fort. No other person on the
planet knew about his fort, not even the deer. He was thinking
that she was so much fun to hang out with. She followed him
around; she actually cared about tools and all the stuff that he
cared about! She really was everything he thought she would be.
"Do you like to pretend stuff?" It just came out. He had run out
of stuff to say and didn't want to just blurt out that he had a fort
and he'd like to show her. He felt it was best to just guide her
that way. It was going to be a long walk and he was sure that she
wouldn't mind.

It was a nice October Sunday, so they wouldn't get too hot.
She took a minute to think about it and then explained to Decker

that pretending is what all kids do, some more than others and that sometimes, pretending was all a kid had. As she followed him along the path that led to the fence line which eventually led to the back of their property and the fort he had built, she told him about her momma and daddy and how she came to be with her grandparents. She said he struggled with stuff, but he was a good man. He never missed a birthday or anything important. He worked hard but he had a temper and had a hard time being told what to do. He didn't like bossy people. She said he really liked working as a guard at Parchman but he had a hard time with some of the inmates. He said they didn't have any respect for people but wanted everybody to respect them. He would tell her that life didn't work that way, that if you wanted respect you had to earn it and the quickest way to earn it was to show respect for others. Her and her daddy had moved in with her grandparents before she could even remember things. Her momma left them when she was just a baby and her daddy couldn't handle raising a baby all by himself, so her grandparents took over. She still listens to her daddy, but her grandparents were actually her parents now.

Decker was confused by all of it and would have to think about it for quite a while longer before he felt comfortable with it. She never said why her momma left her and her daddy. He wanted to ask but he decided it wasn't really important for now. He liked listening to her. She talked so fast that he had to pay attention more than he was used to. He didn't like to interrupt anyone who was talking to him because it was so rare that anyone other than his parents or sister talked to him and he usually just went with it. He guided her around bad spots in the trail; there were several of them that had tree branches and heavy brush and kinds of stuff. When he was alone, and he would hit the bad spots, he usually just crawled under or over or just figured a way to get through it.

But today he was with a girl, not just any girl, he was with Jeannine Martin. He wanted to keep her happy and clean. If they tried to go through the bad spots the way he normally did, she would make it back to the house covered in dirt and nobody would be happy. She talked to him about how she loved to run, how she could hear the wind in her ears when she was at top speed, and that her granddaddy said that was God's way of letting her know she was special. That was Him whispering in her ear. That He whispered in her ear all the time but when she ran, He whispered the loudest so she could hear Him. She told him how she loved math and that there was something really fun about solving a problem, especially a really hard problem that she had to think about for a long time. She said when she first started with algebra that she would get stuck and have to go out and play or read, or anything to get away from the problem, and when she would finally come back to the problem, it seemed clearer and easier to understand. She said she learned that from her grandma, helping her in the kitchen and watching her, especially when she would bake. She would ask all kinds of questions about how much sugar to put in and how much flour and how much salt and her grandma would always say something like, "Until it tastes good". Her grandma explained to her that sometimes you have to experiment, sometimes you have to throw the whole cake out because it just didn't taste good. She said when you practice and do things enough, you get good at it. When you practice it and then you love doing it, you get great at it.

Decker told her that he didn't like math that much, but he didn't mind it. He wasn't too bad at it, but he wasn't good either. He told her that he hated to read because the words just didn't make any sense to him and he got really upset when other people would get upset at him. He loved to hear stories and if he could have someone read books to him, he figured he would be a lot smarter. His momma and his sister would read to him when he was little, but they didn't do too much of it now. His sister once read a book to him that his momma told her she could not read to him, so she would sneak it into his room and read it when she didn't think they would get in trouble. He told Jeannine that it was fun because it was like he was doing something he wasn't supposed to be doing and he was learning something at the same time. She wanted to know what the book was, and he couldn't remember the name of it, but he explained it to her. It was about a bunch of boys that got stuck on this island and there weren't any grown-ups around and they had to figure stuff out on their own.

Then things got really bad and the boys got to be really mean to each other and actually started trying to kill each other. He said there were some parts in that book that were scary, but he REALLY enjoyed it. He sort of felt like the playground some days was a lot like that book. The boys in their school would be mean just because they could. She asked him why he didn't tell the teacher that they were mean to him. He thought about it for just a few minutes as they walked in silence.

The pause was so long she told him that he didn't have to answer if he didn't want to. He learned very quickly in this conversation that Jeannine Martin wasn't pushy or nosy, if you didn't want to answer something she quickly moved on to another subject. It seemed to Decker that she just wanted to keep the conversation going. She started to change the subject and he interrupted her, "Because if I tell, then they will NEVER be my friends." She stopped and looked at him, to Decker she was trying to look through him; she was almost scary at that moment. "Why do you want friends that would treat anyone that way?" This was a hard conversation for Decker because he didn't think anyone would understand his way of thinking. He didn't have any friends at all. He figured sometimes people could change their minds, sometimes people could change the way they thought about things. He had seen two boys get into a fight in fourth grade, one of those fights where actual fists come out and they wallop the other one before the teacher can get to them to break it up. And then the very next year in fifth grade the same two boys would be best friends. He figured he just hadn't had the right changes yet. He figured maybe sixth grade would be better. When he told her that he thought that sixth grade would be better she started laughing. "You just don't get it." She tried to explain it in so many words, but he never understood what she was talking about and he would seriously rather change the subject anyway. Just when he was trying to figure out a new subject to talk about, they reached the fort.

Chapter 12

HE MADE HER STOP SO SHE COULD SEE THE FORT. He was hoping that he had camouflaged it so well that she couldn't see it, but she could. She pointed out all the reasons why she could still see it and he had to agree. He was disappointed that he hadn't thought of some of the things she had said but then again, she was much smarter than he was. He opened the makeshift door which was one of the things she pointed out. He had nailed some wood across two tree branches then used an old hinge he found from his daddy's shop and it worked.

When he made the door, he was quite proud of it. It was the first time he had used his own creativity and through his imagination, he had made a door that worked. She said he should have painted the hinge black or brown or something that matched the trees if he really wanted it to be a secret. She said she could see the gold hinge from way back. He had to agree. He would have to swipe a can of spray paint from the shop and bring it out here and cover it. He made a mental note to do that after school one day this week. "Well, well, well, look what we have here, guys, dumbass Decker Davis and a colored girl." The voice was distinct, and he knew exactly who it was, Lonnie Buckles.

He couldn't remember the names of the other two boys with him, but he saw their faces in school sometimes. They weren't in the class with him, Jeannine and Lonnie, but they were in the same school. He thought they might even be in sixth grade already, maybe even middle school. He was sure that one of them had a mustache. Decker got that terrible feeling in his stomach, like when his sister was reading that book to him that he wasn't supposed to read, and they were about to kill that one fat kid they called *piggy*. He wanted to run right then and there, but he couldn't run off and leave Jeannine by herself. What if he took off running and she didn't follow? He really hoped she would take off running now and he would follow her. He couldn't figure out why she didn't because she was faster than everyone. "You're on Davis property, Lonnie, you need to leave!" Jeannine stepped right up to Lonnie as she was yelling at him. She said something about being in big trouble for trespassing, but she talked really fast. He could tell that Lonnie was having a hard time keeping up with her too. He seemed confused as to why she was even here. "What are you doing out here with the moron, coon, your kind don't belong out here. You two love birds come here to smooch is what it is probably! Hey, boys, Jeannine and Decker snuck into the woods for a look at his pecker!" They all laughed like it was the funniest thing they had ever heard. Decker didn't know what to say, he didn't understand what he meant by "her kind" and he sure didn't know what raccoons had to do with any of this.

However, he did understand the pecker comment and was a bit embarrassed to hear it in front of a girl. "Go home, Lonnie, you're the one that don't belong here. If my daddy catches you here he will arrest you." He was pretty proud of himself...he actually spoke but it didn't seem to do any good. Lonnie started laughing again and said, "Yeah – just let your daddy try, you idiot. My brother already popped your sorry ass daddy right in the eye and gave him a good shiner. He will damn sure do it again. As a matter a fact, you need one to match your daddy's!" and without any warning he punched Decker right in the eye. Decker sure didn't expect it and even if he had, Lonnie hit him on the side that had the arm in the sling and he couldn't even hold up a hand to block it. He fell back and hit his head on the side wall of the fort. He felt dizzy all the sudden and thought maybe he needed to throw up. Pain shot though his shoulder when he hit the ground and he screamed.

One of the other kids from sixth grade, he thought maybe it was the one with the mustache, started kicking him. He could hear Jeannine screaming for them to stop and to leave him alone but when he looked up he saw Lonnie wrestling with her. She was punching and kicking him with everything she had. Lonnie was much bigger than her and eventually got her pinned to the ground with her arm bent behind her back. He shoved her arm up towards her shoulder blades and she screamed. He released the pressure just a little and Decker could hear her crying. "Say you came here to see his pecker!" She didn't say anything and as he pushed her arm up higher, she screamed again. "Say you came here to see a Decker pecker!" She screamed again and this time she said it through her tears.

It was almost a whisper, "I came to see a pecker." That wasn't good enough for Lonnie; he intended to humiliate her and Decker before he was done. "That's not what I said! Say you came here to see a Decker pecker!" He pushed her arm way up her back and this time it was loud and clear, "I CAME HERE TO SEE A DECKER PECKER!" Lonnie started laughing hysterically. Decker had had enough, and he was MAD now. He jumped to his feet with the pain in his shoulder throbbing and punched the kid with the mustache right in the nose. He saw blood come out and the kid screamed his own little scream and dropped to his knees with his hands over his face. He could hear the kid crying and he found it quite satisfying. He was very pleased with the punch since he threw it with his bad arm, the same arm he had thrown a baseball like a girl yesterday. He got in a good kick on Lonnie's back before the third kid tackled him.

The kick to Lonnie's back knocked Lonnie off Jeannine and she sprung up like lightning. Decker managed to scream for her to run and get his daddy. He knew they would beat him up some more, but he also knew it wouldn't be forever. He thought they would be in a hurry to leave now if they thought his daddy might be coming and there was no way that any of these kids were going to catch Jeannine in a foot race back to the house. Jeannine must have understood the plan because she took off like nobody's business and he thought she left a dust trail she was gone so fast. The kid that tackled Decker was still on him when Lonnie came over. "You're gonna pay for that, you stupid little retard." He started kicking Decker, as did the other kid. He didn't know where the kid he had socked in the nose was, he really didn't care, he was just glad it was only two boys kicking him and Jeannine was getting away. All Decker could do was try and cover his head, but his arm was caught in that sling, so he could only use one arm to cover his face. They kicked him for what seemed like an hour to Decker and just like that, they were gone. He lay there in the dirt beside his now not-so-secret fort and thought to himself; he was glad he wasn't a cat.

Chapter 13

❦

DECKER HAD HEARD THAT IF A BEAR ATTACKED you, your best chance was to lay on the ground and play dead. He wasn't sure where he heard that, but he figured he had played dead long enough; it was time to get up. Besides, Lonnie wasn't a bear. He pushed himself into a sitting position with his good arm. He scooted backwards so that he could lean his back up against the fort wall. His stomach hurt, and his face hurt, but other than that, he seemed to feel ok. He had been in his first fight ever and he had given another man a good pop in the nose. He smiled to himself and realized that his lip hurt when he smiled. He touched his lip with his shirtsleeve and saw the blood on his shirt. He thought it was probably ok and there was no need to panic.

If his sister were here she would panic. She panicked when she saw blood. One night before bed, he had been wrestling on the bed with his sister, which they weren't supposed to do, but she would pick him up like he was one of those pro wrestlers he saw on Saturday morning TV at the Mid-South Coliseum in Memphis. She would pretend to body slam him on the bed and then pin him on the count of three. This time she swooped him up and went to slam him down on the bed but hadn't measured the distance to the middle correctly and his head hit the bedpost. It really didn't hurt but it knocked a hole in the back of his head and blood was everywhere. His sister started screaming and running all over the place, which caused his momma to come running into the bedroom. In her hurry, she slipped on the rug beside his bed and fell on top of her bleeding son. That hurt more than his head did because her elbow landed right between his legs. His own momma had popped him in the nads. It was embarrassing. His daddy came in and took over the situation like he always did when someone was bleeding. He only got one stitch out of it but it sure was a lot of blood.

He pulled himself to his feet and was surprised to feel as good as he did. He decided he didn't want to wait around for Lonnie to come back so he headed back toward the house. He had made it through two or three rough spots on the way back by crawling under most of the brush when he reached the dry creek bed. That was always his marker home. He knew that if he found the dry creek bed he would just follow it the rest of the way home because it ran right up to the side of his house. That's when he ran into Jeannine sitting in the middle of the dry creek bed with her head in her hands crying and making these awful sad sounds. She didn't hear him come up behind her and Decker realized after the fact that he probably should have warned her. He walked up behind her and touched her on the shoulder. He wanted her to know that he was there, and it was going to be ok. He couldn't figure out why she was sitting there and hadn't gone to get his daddy.

As soon as he touched her, she jumped up and socked him square in the chest. It knocked him back, but he didn't fall. Through her tears, she realized she had just hit Decker, then she took a step forward and grabbed him. She hugged him so tight that it hurt his shoulder, but he didn't say anything. He sort of liked it. "I'm so sorry, Decker, I thought you were Lonnie coming back to break my arm and beat me up some more! I'm so sorry! I didn't mean to hit you. Oh, look at you, your face, and your lip, and your eye! You are a mess!" She put her arms around him again and continued to cry. She kept her head on his shoulder with her arms around him. "I'm so sorry, I shouldn't have left you!" He wasn't very good at affection and he wasn't sure what to say or do. He patted her on the back; it was an awkward pat. His momma knew how to hug and console. She always made him feel better when he had a bad day. He wished he could hug and pat like his momma could, but he just didn't know how.

"How come you didn't go back to the house?" It was probably not the best thing you could say to someone when you were trying to console them, but his curiosity got the best of him. "Because I got lost, goofy! I didn't know which way to go so I just sat down and cried. I couldn't get back to you and I didn't know which way to get to your house. I was lost, and you were hurt, and I was helpless!" Decker thought that was kinda funny. She was the smartest person in school and she got lost? She let go of him and looked at his face. She still had tears running down her eyes. "We can't go back now, not right now.

We need to think this through." Decker didn't see the need to go back now anyway. He didn't feel like he needed to throw up anymore.

His shoulder still hurt like crazy, but it always hurt so he wasn't sure if Lonnie had anything to do with it or not. He wasn't sure what she wanted to think through. She told Decker that she had a bad feeling about what would happen if they told their parents the truth. She said it might cause some real problems and some people might get hurt if they weren't careful. He was confused by the thought process she was sharing. She would talk out loud, but he could tell she wasn't talking to him or anyone else, she was talking to herself. "Decker, those Buckles boys are mean. I don't need to tell you that but if we run and tell, your daddy and my granddaddy are both gonna get steaming mad. Your daddy is gonna wanna go out to the Buckles' junk yard and throw them all in jail. You and I both know that whole family is crazy. They might try to shoot him or something when he shows up at their place. Decker, I don't want to see anyone else get hurt because of us."

He knew he had to tell his parents; there was no way around that. He never lied to his parents and he would have to explain his fat lip. He didn't realize that his eye was swelling up and it would soon turn black. He tried to lie to his momma one time and he was terrible at it. He had swiped a pack of gum from the *Piggly Wiggly* checkout counter while they were standing in line. Nobody saw him do it and he wasn't really even sure why he did it, he just saw the pack of *Juicy Fruit* and decided he needed it.

More than likely, if he had just asked, his momma would have bought it for him, but for some stupid reason he just decided to save them the money and put it in his jeans pocket.

He probably would have gotten away with it had he chosen to chew in the privacy of his bedroom or somewhere else, but he decided that he would just chew it in the back seat of the *Ford Falcon* his momma drove. She saw him opening the pack in the rear-view mirror and immediately turned the car around. She asked him where he got it and that is when he discovered he was a terrible liar. First, he said he bought it. She asked where he got the money; he didn't have an answer. Then he changed his story to the "manager gave it to me." That didn't work so he said he traded it with another kid in the store. She asked him what kid he traded with and he couldn't think of any, so he finally he decided to spill the beans and he admitted he stole it. He was sweating by now and his stomach was all tied up in knots and he felt like he needed to poop.

They were already back in the parking lot of the *Piggly Wiggly* when he was in tears because he had told a lie and because he needed to poop really badly. His momma marched him in the store and asked for the manager. He danced around waiting on the manager to show up, tears in his eyes, praying he would hurry so he could find the bathroom. Just listening to Jeannine suggest that they not tell his parents something was causing the same problems he had with the stolen gum. He felt like he needed to poop. It sure wasn't as bad as it was in the *Piggly Wiggly*, but his stomach was definitely rumbling.

That was a bad day and he promised he would never repeat that mistake again. He was going to tell his parents everything, no matter what. Jeannine saw things differently than Decker did, but she relented to his way of thinking.

Chapter 14

❦

DECKER AND JEANNINE MADE THEIR WAY ALONG the fence line heading back to the house. It was the same way they had taken to get to the fort, but the view seemed different to both of them. Jeannine noticed some fall roses that were growing wild that she had not noticed before. She even asked Decker if they were walking home a different way. Each time she asked he said "no" but he was seeing things he'd never seen before.

Maybe it wasn't so much what he was seeing or that he couldn't remember seeing it, it probably had more to do with who he was seeing it with. Jeannine walked and talked more than anyone he had ever been with and he liked hearing her. She talked about all the books she liked to read and that a guy named *Charles Dickens* was her favorite writer. She liked him because he wrote all kinds of different stuff. He wrote Christmas stories and stories about orphan kids. She said he had a book for every mood.

Decker didn't think he was ever in the mood to read a book. It was just too hard. He would try, but the gibberish never cleared up for him. He had never heard someone get so excited about reading a book. He could get excited about football or baseball, but reading was not something he never got excited about, it made him feel stupid.

"What do you think will happen when your daddy finds out what happened today?" Decker had already thought about that but hadn't come to a conclusion yet. He definitely knew he wouldn't get in trouble because he hadn't done anything wrong and neither had Jeannine. His daddy didn't have a temper that he recalled. Around the house he was fun to be around because he liked to laugh and tell jokes. He played with Decker as much as he could. He taught him how to throw the football and baseball. Nobody at school knew that Decker could throw a spiral pass through a swinging tire that his daddy had hung from a tree. He had become really good at it. He wished he had a bunch more footballs though; he would get tired of throwing the ball through the tire and then having to go get it each time. If he had a few more footballs he wouldn't have to work so hard at it. He enjoyed it so much more when his daddy would stand on the other side of the tire and throw the balls back to him. Those were some of the best times. He could throw all day.

The kids at school would soon find out that he could be more than a tackling dummy for the playground bullies. He would be old enough for Pop Warner football next year and he intended to play. He knew what his daddy was like at home, but he really didn't know what he was like as sheriff. He expected he would be the same there as he was it home. He couldn't imagine someone having to be different at work than they were at home.

"My daddy will be just fine, it's my sister that will be mad. She ain't scared of nobody and she gets riled up about the Buckles." His sister was a pretty girl for sure but too many folks made the mistake of thinking she was just a girl.

His momma and sister had taken some karate lessons over in Sumner. His momma quit going but his sister loved it too much to quit. Momma said she loved it because the instructor was easy to look at and he was just a few years older than his sister. His sister stayed with it for a long time. As far as he knew, she was still driving over to Sumner every Wednesday and Friday nights for more lessons. He and his daddy had driven over one Friday night to watch her fight these three fellas…not all at once, but after she was through, everybody clapped, and they bowed at each other and the guy that momma said was easy to look at took her brown belt away from her and gave her a black one. They got pictures of it.

Daddy laughed and said her belt now matched her eye – she had a black eye in the picture. Yeah, his sister was scary when she got mad. She was bound to get mad. "Is my lip swollen?" Decker had no idea what he looked like. In spite of the way they all kicked him when he was down, he didn't feel bad at all. He could feel his lip swelling up and if he looked down with just his eyes, he could see a lump that wasn't normally there. Jeannine stopped and grabbed his arm to stop him. When they were stopped, she stood directly in front of him, placed both her hands on his cheeks as if she was examining a piece of fruit, looked from his forehead to his chin, and proclaimed that he wasn't too bad.

Yes, he had a bit of a swollen lip but that would be gone soon enough. His eye that Lonnie had tried to make black to match the one that Brett gave his daddy never happened. He just needed to wash up and he was probably as good as new. Maybe this wouldn't be as bad as Jeannine had first thought it would be. She licked her fingers and tried to press the cowlick down that had formed during the fight. Normally he didn't care for anyone other than his sister or momma messing with his hair, but Jeannine had just become his best friend, maybe his girlfriend. He wasn't sure how that worked but he knew when he socked that other kid in the nose, his whole life had somehow changed. He had no idea just how much.

Chapter 15

❧

JEANNINE AND DECKER CAME IN THROUGH THE
back kitchen door. The screen door had a horrible squeak when
it opened so there was no sneaking in, but nobody even paid
attention to them coming in. He could hear them talking and
laughing out on the front porch, so Jeannine figured they had
time to clean up a little. She got a towel from the counter and
wet it in the sink. She rubbed the dirt off his face and fixed his
hair the best she could. She didn't want to do too good of a job
on his hair, after all, he was a boy and it was supposed to be
messy. She looked him over one last time and decided he was
good to go.

He showed her where the hall bathroom was, and she went
in, shut the door, and cleaned her face and fixed her hair. She
had dirt on her clothes, but she figured a kid out on a farm was
bound to have dirty clothes. She thought maybe they wouldn't

even get asked about the events of the day and they could just go back to school on Monday and she would figure out a way to deal with dumb ole Lonnie Buckles.

Decker went into the living room but realized that everyone was out on the front porch. It was such a nice cool day and they were enjoying the weather. Daddy decided some homemade ice cream would hit the spot, so he was out churning the bucket. Decker usually did that churning, but since he wasn't there when his daddy decided to do it, he didn't get to. Decker liked doing it because his daddy said that whoever put the most work into making it should get the first bowl. Daddy's ice cream was so good. He suddenly got really hungry and forgot all about the fight at the fort. He waited in the living room for Jeannine to come out of the bathroom. When she came out, besides the dirt stains on her clothes, she looked the same to Decker. "How do I look?" Decker froze, it was now or never, and he knew he wouldn't get a better opportunity than this. His heart was beating very fast and his mouth got dry. He forgot all about the delicious ice cream that was soon to arrive on the front porch. He opened his mouth, but nothing came out. He tried to force the words up through his throat, but they were stuck. He swallowed hard thinking maybe that a new batch of words would come up more smoothly, but they did not.

"What's wrong with you? You look like you need to go to the bathroom." She continued to stare at him, waiting on him to answer her last round of questions. He couldn't. He was frozen in his own body, unable to speak, unable to tell her she was pretty, even though he knew it was exactly what he wanted to say and couldn't. All he could do was shake his head in no particular motion that indicated yes or no. He imagined that he looked like one of those stupid dogs that his Uncle Robert put on the dashboard of his pickup and when you popped it on the head it just shook around and gave you a continuous dumb look. Yep, she might even call him dumb ole Dashboard Dog Decker now. He could hear it in his ears and he would deserve it. "Oh, forget it, boys are just goofy. Stop shaking your head like that, you look like a dog on a dashboard." She walked towards the front door, turned to look back at him, smiled, and went out onto the porch.

He joined her on the porch and there was a lot of fuss over her dirty clothes and his. "What in the world did you kids do to get so dirty and, Decker, what did you do to your lip?" Mr. Martin was really fussing over Decker's lip; he was fussing over Decker's lip more than his own parents were. Jeannine was waiting on Decker to see what Decker would say; he looked at Jeannine and could see that she was begging with her eyes not to say anything about the fight.

He thought it over one more time. "We went way out towards the mud bog and just got dirty on the way there. The path along this fence is kinda rough." Jeannine wouldn't let him add anymore before she jumped into the conversation with excitement. "You all should see it! Decker built a fort all by himself and he got it covered so you can't even see it. It's really something! Why don't ya'll come out and see it for yourselves!" Decker thought she was perhaps the smartest girl he had ever met and ever will meet.

He hadn't lied. The path was rough, and they did go all the way out to the fence, but because she jumped in and suggested that the grown-ups go all the way out to see a kid's homemade fort changed the conversation from one of fact-finding to one of excuses. "Oh, honey I'd love to go out and see Decker's fort but you know my knees hurt all the time now. Why don't you babies just sit here and have some ice cream with us?" Mr. Martin sat back in his chair. He stopped examining Decker's fat lip and Decker took over the churning of the ice cream. Just like that, it was over. They couldn't see Decker's face as he was sitting on the floor of the front porch turning that handle on the ice cream maker with his one good arm, but if they could, they would see this huge grin on his face. Jeannine had just shown him how it's done. *What a woman,* he thought…*and I couldn't even tell her she was pretty.*

Chapter 16

LONNIE BUCKLES WAS SITTING ON THE WORN-OUT couch when Brett came in. The couch had a blanket thrown over it, so you couldn't see all the stains and holes in it. He was watching their only TV, a black and white *Zenith* that Brett had stolen out of an office building in downtown Webb. Lonnie remembered that Brett laughed when he told everyone that they didn't need a dang TV in the office and said the lazy SOB's needed to be workin' and not watchin' TV and he probably did them a favor by taking it off their hands. The TV wasn't much, and they had to put tinfoil on the antennas to get any stations to come in, and even when you got a station to come in, it was fuzzy.

Today was Sunday so Lonnie had managed to get the football game. "Where you been all day, you little fart?" Brett kicked Lonnie on the leg when he said it. Lonnie recoiled and hollered back for him to leave him alone. Brett never took to back-talk very much, especially from his little brothers, and he backhanded Lonnie right across the mouth. Lonnie felt the pain shoot through his face as the back of his brother's hand met him square on the jaw and lips. Brett laughed but leaned over and got right in Lonnie's face who was now covering his bleeding lip with both hands. Lonnie wanted to cry but he knew that if he cried, Brett would just beat him some more. "I already told you, boy, sassin' me ain't a good idea. Now get outta my seat and get me a beer while you are up!" Lonnie was just as stubborn as all the other Buckles boys. They all pushed things to the absolute limit, even when they knew they were beaten, they would continue to mouth off. "Get it your damn self!" Brett really smacked him this time. It was another backhand but this time he did it with real anger, the first one was just because he was mean and enjoyed it. "Boy, you better move your butt and I better have that beer in two seconds or this belt is coming off and you won't be able to sit on that lazy butt of yours for a month! I'm the only one around here that gets anything done! If it weren't for me, you'd starve, and look at you! You ain't starving, you are as fat as an Arkansas Hog. You don't do a thing around here but eat my food! Now move!" Lonnie slowly got up and he was a little dizzy from that last pop Brett had given him.

As he was walking towards the kitchen where the refrigerator was, Brett kicked him in the backside. It was swift and it hurt. Lonnie felt the lump come up in his throat but he choked it back. He was so mad and wanted to cry but he couldn't. He thought of his big brother, Donnie, who he was sort of named after – his daddy wanted them to rhyme so he got Donnie and Lonnie.

Folks around town said they made it rhyme because there were too many Buckles to remember all their names and it was easier on Lonnie if his big brother Donnie hadn't been shipped off to war. Brett would never hit him like that. Donnie would beat the crap out of Brett if he knew he was beating him that way. He wished that stupid war would get over so Donnie could come back and beat Brett to a pulp for being a drunken idiot. He grabbed the beer from the refrigerator and paused with the door open so Brett couldn't see that he was shaking the beer can with all he had. When he was satisfied that he had created a mini volcano just waiting to erupt, he took the can to Brett along with an opener and bolted out the front door. Brett poked a hole in the can with the opener and it spewed all over his face. He screamed a bunch of cuss words that Lonnie could hear as he was walking away from the house.

Lonnie smiled as he continued to walk away. *I reckon I got the best of him*, was the thought that went through his head until he heard the gunshots and he saw the dust fly up to the side of him. He turned in shock to see that Brett was standing on the stoop with a .22 rifle in his hands and was shooting at him! He took off running for the woods and heard another few gunshots. When he reached the woods, he checked himself over and couldn't find any holes, so Brett must have been too drunk to aim straight, or he would be dead. He really didn't think that Brett wanted to kill him; he just knew that was Brett being completely crazy and stupid. His brother didn't know when to quit. He would have to find a way to kill some time until either Brett left or he passed out. He couldn't go back to the house until either of those things happened.

Every day he wished that Donnie would come home. He didn't care about his daddy. He hadn't seen his daddy in nearly 5 years, and he could barely remember that man. He heard the talk around Webb, that his daddy wasn't just mean, but that he was evil. He didn't know enough about his daddy to agree or disagree, except that he remembered the night there was some kind of party at their house and all kinds of people were roaming around the house. He and his middle brother, Judd, had to stay outside because some grown-ups were using their bedroom. He and Judd shared a bed but didn't ever get to sleep in it when there was a party going on. Momma told him that they were renting his room out to help pay the rent for night. That night it was especially noisy; he was hungry, so he snuck back in the kitchen to get him something to eat. He saw his momma was huggin' some other man and when she saw him, she yelled at him to leave so he ran to his bedroom to grab a coat because it was cold outside, and he and Judd were cold. He saw some grown-ups wrestling in his bed, so he just grabbed his and Judd's coats and took off. The party broke up not long after that. He heard his daddy yelling at his momma and then he heard the gunshots.

The police came and then the ambulance came, and he later found out that his momma was dead and that his daddy had shot her and that other man that was in the kitchen with her when he snuck back in to get some food. As far as he was concerned, Donnie had been his daddy and that was all that mattered to him. He spent the rest of the evening roaming the streets of Webb. He would normally hang out with his two best friends but one of them got into big trouble with his parents and the other had a broken nose from getting punched by that little Davis retard. He didn't think the little moron had it in him to fight but I guess he did. He figured he would need to be more careful around him in school now, but it wouldn't stop him from picking on the retard. He still needed to kill some time and let Brett pass out and then he would go home and go to bed.

Chapter 17

＠

HE RODE THE BUS TO SCHOOL LIKE HE DID EVERY Monday morning, but this one was a special Monday, at least for him. Although he had gotten beaten up for about the umpteenth time, he realized that for the first time since kindergarten, he would have a friend at school. He thought he had a friend in first grade, but he moved away. He was a tall kid, taller than Decker in first grade, which wasn't saying a whole lot since Decker was smaller than everyone back then. It wasn't until he got to fifth grade that he caught up in height with most of the other boys and he had even passed some. But even back then, this kid was tall. He was taller than everybody. He remembered that the kid was kinda clumsy, even clumsier than Decker. He was always tripping on something or bumping into a wall.

Everyone would laugh at him and a lot of times he would cry because the kids would laugh at him. Decker learned back then just by watching him that crying only made things worse. He couldn't remember his name, but he sure remembered how he looked and how clumsy he was. He also remembered that they sat next to each other in the classroom and they also sat next to each other in the cafeteria. He remembered that he always had a banana in his lunch box and he never ate it. He said he hated bananas, so he would give it to Decker.

Sometimes Decker would get his momma to throw another half slice of his sandwich in his box so he could give it to that kid. He just felt like he needed to give him something for the banana because it just didn't seem fair to take something from him every day and not give anything. Decker asked him one day why he didn't tell his momma he didn't like bananas and maybe she could put an apple or an orange or something in his lunch instead. He remembered his answer to this day. He didn't understand it back then, but he did now. The kid said it wasn't his momma that packed his lunch, it was his daddy, and that his momma had gone to heaven. Decker didn't know what to say so said something about his daddy not being able to pack a lunch. He tried to change the subject because the boy looked like he was going to cry again and that meant that the other kids would start picking on them for sure. He never understood why it wasn't ok for a boy to cry but it was ok for girls to cry all the time. In fact, it seemed like when a girl cried, people would fall all over themselves trying to get them to stop and make them feel better. If a boy did it, good grief, every other boy would laugh, and the girls would blush and then the boys would start torture.

Anyway, he told the kid about his daddy and that he was a cop and owned a store. He told him about all the trips his daddy would have to take to help with tornadoes and floods and earthquakes and stuff. He was one of the people that knew best what to do when people were in bad shape. He tried to describe all the places that his daddy had been, but it was difficult because Decker had never been outside the state of Mississippi; he wasn't sure if he'd ever been outside of Tallahatchie County. He told the kid that a long time ago, before he was even born, his daddy got caught up in a hurricane somewhere trying to help people and nearly got killed. He didn't know much more than that since he was just trying to keep the kid from crying. He loved hearing all his daddy's stories about all his adventures but there were so many that he just couldn't remember all the details. In fact, when he tried to repeat some of the stories he would mix details of different stories up and make it just one big long adventure. To him, his daddy was like those two explorers his momma read about, *Clark* and some other guy. Those two guys had it made. They didn't have to take a bath, they floated every river, ate all the fish they wanted, shot all the bears and squirrels they could eat, and then they got to skin the animals and make clothes out of the skin. Yes, sir, that was the life for him, and his daddy was as close to one of those two men as he figured anyone could get. He wished he could read more about them, but he hated to read.

He was usually one of the first kids on the bus, so he always took a seat right behind the bus driver. Kids didn't pick on him so much if he stayed close to Mr. Johns. That was the bus driver's name, Mr. Johns. He was a kinda short fat man that smoked a pipe. Decker liked the pipe smell; it always smelled like cherries to him. He hoped one day he could smoke a pipe just to see if it was like eating cherries all day long. Mr. Johns was a nice man. He always called the kids by their names and on the last day of school he pretty much let the kids do whatever they wanted. It was usually a spitball fight or just a paper fight. Decker didn't care much for the last day of school and he usually found a way to get out of riding the bus the last day. He got picked on enough without grown-ups knowing about it, he sure didn't care to be picked on with them knowing about it.

Today he sat there in the seat behind Mr. Johns and looked out the window at all the grass that was in the middle of going from green to brown. It was by far his favorite time of the year. He thought that the trees were the most beautiful when they would change colors. He loved the orange colored ones, but his favorites were the trees that seemed to turn bright red. His momma told him that they turned that color to say goodbye to you and that they were letting you know they needed to rest for the winter and they would be back in the spring. She always had such a way of explaining things that made more sense to him than the teachers did. He saw them pass the Martin farm but the bus never stopped there. He couldn't figure out why she didn't ride the bus with them, but she was always at school when he got there. She was always the first person in the class. She sat right in the front row, which was a place that Decker avoided.

He liked to sit in the back. In fact, he would sit in the hall-way and just listen to the teacher if they would let him, but they never did. He remembered he got in trouble one day in class in fourth grade and the teacher made him sit out in the hall. She made him take his desk out there and everything! He really couldn't remember why he had gotten in trouble but when he realized how peaceful the hallway was when there weren't any kids running up and down and screaming and yelling, he figured that she could punish him every day if she wanted to. He liked it in the hall all by himself.

Aside from the looks that someone would give him if they happened to be in the hall during class, it was probably the most comfortable he ever was in school. He could hear the teacher through the door and he just understood what she was talking about way better when he didn't have to look at the blackboard or one of his books. He just remembered things better that way.

The bus was unusually quiet that day until they stopped at the Buckles' farm. Even though Decker knew it was his stop and he dreaded it, Brett had a distinct way of getting on the bus. When Mr. Johns would open the door, from the ground, he would hop on to the first step with both feet. Then he would pound the next two steps like he was stomping out a fire. Mr. Johns always shook his head and let out a little chuckle, but he always had the same warning for Lonnie. "Don't make today a good day for walking, you better behave yourself on my bus." Decker had never seen him kick any kid off the bus but that was the reputation he had. It must have happened before Decker started going to school because he had been Decker's bus driver for as long as he could remember, and he had never seen anyone get kicked off.

The bus was usually safer than school. The bus wasn't full today when Lonnie got on but instead of going all the way to the back of the bus like he normally did, he forced his way next to Decker. Decker wasn't pleased about this for a couple reasons: Lonnie usually liked to pick on Decker at school, but he thought because of this weekend's fight with his friends, he was in a hurry to get started and secondly, he stunk. No matter what time of the day it was you could count on Lonnie Buckles smelling like a cross between burned leaves and a pig's butt. Some days were more tolerable than others but today wasn't one of them.

"Scoot over, retard." He heard Mr. Johns say, "Lonnie..." in a very low tone. Decker was thankful for Mr. Johns because he ran a tight ship and didn't put up with any monkey business for sure. Lonnie smiled and waved at Mr. Johns as he could see Mr. Johns staring at him in his overhead mirror. "Just talking to my friend, Decker Davis, Mr. Johns." Mr. Johns gave him a nod in the mirror and then put his eyes back on the road. He looked at Decker and stopped smiling. "You know the game we played yesterday ain't over." Decker didn't say anything back to him and just turned his head and looked out the window. "You and your girlfriend are dead meat, retard." He said it with a whisper in Decker's ear then he was sure to smile and pretend like he said something funny, so Mr. Johns would be none the wiser. Decker didn't care what he said, he was going to school where a friend was probably waiting on him. That was something new and nothing that dumb ole Lonnie Buckles and his stinky breath could say that would change that.

Decker was feeling good about today, in fact, he felt so different today that he could hardly sit still. He turned to Lonnie and did something that he would have never considered doing before...he stood up for himself. "Oh, yeah, well how bout I just sock you in your nose like I did your buddy." It must have caught Lonnie by surprise because Decker didn't whisper it, he said it so that Mr. Johns and every other kid on the bus could hear it quite easily. "You boys settle down or you walk to school this morning." Decker continued to stare at Lonnie. Lonnie stared back at Decker, but he wasn't sure what to do.

Usually at this point, Decker had slunk away, and he would continue his assault, but this morning was different for Lonnie too. They both sat there in silence just staring at each other until they felt the bus stop. "Knock it off, boys, it's time for school. Go put that energy to some good use instead of this nonsense." Mr. Johns stood at the foot of the steps and watched all the kids get off the bus. He was good about wishing all the kids a good day.

Chapter 18

❦

SHE GOT READY FOR SCHOOL THE SAME WAY SHE always did. Her grandma would come in her room, flip on the light, put a hand on her, then lean over and whisper in her ear, "Wake up, baby, today you accomplish so many wonderful things but not from that bed." She would grumble like she always did. She wasn't really a morning person, but she didn't mind it either. She rolled out of bed and headed off to the bathroom. She shared the bathroom with her daddy who stayed in the room down the hall. She really didn't have to share it because he was never really there. Her granddaddy and daddy never seemed to get along.

They didn't fight but there was just always something cold between them. Her granddaddy would make a remark about her daddy needing to settle down and that he should have never lost that job out at Parchman and since he wasn't working he probably should do more around the house. Jeannine didn't think anything was wrong with that, but it would sure make her daddy mad. After all, she had tons of chores to do around the house. It was her job to wash the dishes and it was her job to clean the bathrooms, it was her job to rake the leaves when they fell – which it just hit her that in one month the yard would be covered in leaves.

She really loved the fall. She loved the different colors the trees would change into, but she hated raking the leaves when they were finished falling to the ground. This morning with all that stuff about chores and her daddy not being around so much, she thought about Decker too. That had never happened before. She never stopped thinking. She always had ideas popping into her head: how to solve a math problem that she was stumped on or how many steps she took to wash the dishes and how she could cut down the number of steps and still get the dishes clean and be done faster. That was just the way her mind worked, but above everything, she loved to dream. Her granddaddy called her his little dreamer. She wanted to be the first woman in space, she wanted to win an Oscar, and she wanted to win an Olympic medal in ladies 4x4 400 meters.

She had dreamed about being the anchor leg and crossing that finish line. She loved the idea of being on a team and winning. Oh, make no mistake, she would love to run the 100 meters all by herself and win a medal, but to her, there was something special about being on a team, and everybody on that team had to do their best to win. She read everything she could get her hands on about *Wilma Rudolph* and *Amelia Earhart*. She even dreamed about finding *Amelia Earhart*. It made her sad to think of her all by herself on some island somewhere. When she learned to fly and before she went into space, she was going to fly a plane over every island in the Pacific looking for her.

Oh, she loved to dream for sure, but today she had Decker on the brain. There was just something about him that she really liked. She had seen the kids pick on him and sometimes she even wanted to say something, but she never did. In fact, no one ever did. She had even ignored him sometimes because in her school, you get picked on for the least little reason. Especially her being a different color than most of the kids, she felt like she just needed stay away from trouble until she could get into a bigger school where stuff like that didn't matter so much. After this weekend, listening to Decker or at least hanging out with Decker, he didn't really say that much. She had done all the talking and realized that she had misjudged Decker and he wasn't at all like she thought. He wasn't stupid, he liked to laugh, he ate the same food she did, and he had a way about him that she had not seen; not only in him but in anybody she had ever met.

What she noticed most is that he looked at her differently, different in a good way. It was like he could see who she was. She spewed toothpaste all over the mirror when she remembered that she had farted in front of a boy! Her grandma would simply have a cow if she knew that her little granddaughter was in the kitchen with Decker and both of them were farting! She laughed and had to stop brushing her teeth and regain her composure. She was about to regain composure when one of her rhymes hit her and she had to get it out, *Jeannine and Decker washing in the sink, cleaning up the blood and letting out a stink...* She laughed so hard she let out her own fart just then. She needed to write that one down. She would never use it, but she thought it would be funny to use in *Double Dutch*. She had notebooks full of poems.

If she wasn't dreaming or solving math problems, she was writing poems. She loved to write poems. She didn't dare show anyone though. Some of them were just silly girl stuff but she thought she was good at it. There was this contest that was in the back of the TV guide that you could write a poem and send in a drawing and you could win $500. The drawing had to be of a horse and the poem had to be about the horse. She wrote the poem about the horse, but she couldn't draw very well so she never sent it in. She loved the *TV Guide* too. She would help her grandma solve the puzzle in the back and she couldn't wait to get the new *TV Guide* every week.

When she was satisfied that she could pass her grandma's tooth-brushing inspection she headed down stairs to get breakfast. She could already smell it coming upstairs. She knew it was bacon, biscuits and eggs. She knew it was bacon because not only could she smell it, she could hear it crackling. Besides the Thanksgiving and Christmas meals with all the family, she thought that breakfast was her favorite meal. It seemed like everyone in her house was in the best mood of the day.

On the weekends her grandma would wake her up and make her help make breakfast. Her grandma would talk to her the whole time they were making breakfast. She would show her how to make the biscuits which was the hardest part to her. She would get flour all over the place, but her grandma would just say that a god breakfast comes from making a mess. She enjoyed the time with her grandma, but this wasn't a weekend; this was a school day and she was in a hurry to get to school. She had something on her mind and she was determined to talk to the teacher about it before any other kid got to school. She skipped every other step on the way down the stairs and turned down the hall to the kitchen. She saw her granddaddy sitting there reading the paper like he always did. He would read some of the articles to her grandma while she was getting things ready. She heard him say something about *Bobby Kennedy* right before she entered the room. He heard her, and he put the paper down and gave her the once over just like he did every morning. "Honey, you are exactly what God intended a pretty little girl to look like." He would laugh when he said it, but she knew he meant it.

Her grandparents were the best. She and her granddaddy had the same routine every morning at breakfast before he would drive her to school. First, he told her how pretty she was and second, he would say, "Whatcha gonna do today?" and it was up to her to say, "I'm gonna change the world today." He would laugh and say, "Is that so, whatcha gonna change it to?" And she had to say, "A better place". She couldn't remember when that little game got started and some days she wished it hadn't but then some days she was glad it did. Today was a day she was glad it did because she meant to make some changes today, but she only wanted to help change one person, not the whole world. She wanted to help the kid that was willing to get beaten up to save her; she wanted to help change Decker Davis.

Chapter 19

❧

DECKER WALKED INTO THE CLASSROOM WITH about 15 other kids. They were shuffling their feet as though none of them seemed excited to be there. Monday was always tough for all the kids because they were still thinking about all the cool things they did over the weekend. For Decker, he had met Donnie Ray Richards, he had broken his collarbone just like Donnie Ray Richards, Donnie Ray Richards had come to visit him in his hospital room for the short time he was there – which practically made he and Decker best friends. At least that's the way Decker saw it, and he had punched a kid square in the nose. It was definitely a monumental weekend.

Decker also knew that Monday was the beginning of the torment as the kids would pick on him and he would probably do something stupid in class and the teacher would send him to the hall. He recalled that time in fourth grade when he was in the back row like he normally was, and he had this giant booger that was blocking his breathing. He didn't think anybody was looking and he was trying to wrestle it out with his finger when he heard Debbie Dalton say, "Ewww" really loudly and everyone turned to see what she was screeching about.

When he realized it was HIM they were all pointing at with his finger stuck in his nose. He tried to pull his finger out of his nose really quickly, but the booger was attached firmly and not only that, the biggest, longest snot trail come right out with it. There he was, dumb ole Decker sitting in the back of class, everyone staring at him with a giant booger on his finger and a snot trail as long as his arm would stretch that he had no idea what to do with. He couldn't remember for sure but that was probably a Monday. He wasn't in a hurry and didn't need to be because his desk was in the back and it was the closest to the door. After all the kids had filed in and the bell had rung he was the last one to step over the threshold and immediately knew something was wrong because his desk was gone. He stood there for a second. He didn't like change, and this was definitely wrong. "Uh, Mr. Davis – I've moved your desk up here. I think this will be more beneficial for you." All the kids that were now seated turned to look at him and some giggles went through the room.

Strangely he looked at both hands to make sure he didn't have a finger from either hand stuck in his nose, he didn't. That was quite a relief actually. He looked towards the front of the class where he saw the empty desk awaiting his arrival. From where he stood, it was so far away that it may as well have been in a different state. He forced his legs to move as he realized the quicker he got to his new seat, the quicker everyone would stop staring at him. At first it was just a shuffle, but the pace picked up considerably when he realized his desk was right next to hers. His daddy told him one time that there is a good and a bad in every situation and this seemed to be a perfect example. The bad was that he had to sit up front and the good was that he sat right next to Jeannine Martin. She began this morning's class like she did every morning. Each student had to stand and tell the class what they did with their time over the weekend.

Some kids could talk for an hour it seemed like, but others were like him, he tried to keep it short and simple and sit right back down. Besides, he never really did anything interesting. But today was different; today he had something to talk about except he wasn't sure if punching a kid in the snoz was appropriate. He usually talked about playing ball with his daddy, or if they happened to go fishing, he would talk about that for a minute. He knew he better think fast because now he was in the front row and that is where the teacher always started.

Jeannine went first, and she talked about reading the paper with her granddaddy and how she solved a math problem that had something to do with trajectory. Decker had never heard that word before, but he liked it. He would have to ask her later what that meant and would try to use it himself later. To him, trajectory just sounded cool. The kids always paid attention to Jeannine because she always had something interesting to talk about, or at least she made it sound interesting. He, on the other hand, did not like speaking in front of groups and always seemed to say or do something that made people laugh, but he wasn't trying to be funny, so he knew they were laughing at him.

When Jeannine was finished she smiled and took a little bow to the class and sat down in her seat. The teacher looked at Decker and helped him out just a little. "Mr. Davis, I see you have your arm in a sling and it looks like you have some very interesting tales from the weekend." She had done it, she had managed to help him think of something other than socking a kid in the head. He had almost forgotten that his arm was in a sling. He had really gotten used to it so much that he barely noticed it, plus he was getting pretty nifty with his left arm. He swung his legs out from the desk, planted his feet on the floor, and stood to face the class. So many things went through his head at that moment. His sister helped him remember the Gettysburg Address by reading it over and over until he could recite it all by himself. Not for homework or school but because he liked it. He liked Abraham Lincoln because he heard that some people thought that Lincoln was kinda stupid too, but he went on to be President. Plus, measuring time in scores seemed cool to him – you know – that "Four score and seven years ago".

His sister helped him figure that out too. One score was 20 years and since he had said, "Four score", that meant that it was 80 years plus seven, 87 years. He felt so smart every time he thought about that day he figured something out that most people didn't even know. He was about to tell them that he broke his collarbone and how he had met Donnie Ray Richards but as soon as he opened his mouth, all that came out was, "Four score and seven years ago." He had no idea why, he couldn't stop it, it was just like words that had to spew out of his mouth. All the kids laughed, and his face turned red. He started to sit back down when he felt the tug on the seat of his pants.

It was a tug that no one else could see but it was real enough. It was Jeannine. He turned his head to see her looking at him except it was more like a soft stare, the one his momma would give him in church to let him know to sit up straight. He turned his head back to class and while they were still laughing he said, "I had an accident and broke my collarbone. The collarbone runs from your shoulder to your neck. You can't fix it, you just have to let heal. It hurts really bad, but it hurt less when I met Donnie Ray Richards in the hospital because he broke his collarbone too." The class stopped laughing and there were lots of "OOH's" that came from the kids. He started to sit down but the teacher asked him another question, a question that he never expected in a million years…she asked him what "four score" meant! He couldn't believe it! He knew the answer and he was actually excited to be able to answer it!

He started to speak but before he could answer he felt that tug on the back of his pants again. He once again glanced down at Jeannine and this time she winked. He turned his head to the teacher instead of the class because she was the one who asked him the question, so he felt he should probably look at her. "It's a way of keeping track of time back in the old days. One score meant twenty years. So, it was 87 years." He sat back down quickly because he didn't want to give her time to ask any more questions. He had said more in the last five minutes than he had said since the beginning of fifth grade. He looked at Jeannine when he got situated back in his desk. He could feel that his face was still red, but the funny thing was, he couldn't hear anyone laughing like they usually were.

Jeannine smiled at him and just looked back at the teacher. The teacher turned to the blackboard and asked if anyone knew what speech Mr. Davis had just referred to. He was stunned when not one single kid could give her the answer. He waited for what seemed like forever, the wait was so long he thought the bell would ring for lunch soon. "Mr. Davis, what is the name of the speech?" No way! She was asking him another question that he knew the answer to! He felt the gas churning in his stomach now though. This was not normal behavior in class; he never got questions, and if he did, he didn't know the answer to them. He was sure to break wind if something didn't change soon and he would be back to being laughed at. Jeannine hit him on the arm, the bad one in the sling. That really hurt for sure. He turned to give her a dirty look, but she mouthed the word "Gettysburg" so no one could see her do it or be heard doing it. She knew the answer but wasn't answering? That didn't make any sense to him, but it took his mind off the big gas bubble that he was now fighting to keep contained in his backside. "It was the Gettysburg Address, ma'am." As soon as he said it he felt the pressure in this stomach slowly reduce to just sort of a hungry growl.

He was glad that was over, but the fear of a silencer filled his head. Sometimes gas would trick him that way. It would change from a giant bubble that wanted to force its way out to something sneakier that just kinda slowly seeped out. When that happened, it was awful. The smell was often unbearable and every kid in the classroom would start pinching their noses shut and fanning their faces. That's how you could tell where it came from, the nose pinch would start from the closest point of the gas leak and work its way outward from there. Today, he was lucky there were no noises and no silent deadly gas, just Jeannine smiling at him. He was ok with sitting in the front row now.

Chapter 20

❧

BRETT CONSENTED TO A SEARCH JUST LIKE HE always did when he went to go see his daddy. It was Monday and it was his scheduled time to go see him. He was pretty lucky to be able to go to Parchman this time. He didn't think he would make bail. Bail was only $50 for disturbing the peace. He thought it would be more since he managed to punch that idiot sheriff in the eye. That was the intention anyway. It was a little payback for the last time Sheriff Davis threw him in county lockup. That sheriff had it in for him; in fact, he had it in for him and his whole family. The Martins could do whatever they wanted to do. They could lie, cheat, steal anytime and anywhere and the sheriff wouldn't do a thing because he protected them. He protected them and didn't do a thing to help his kind.

None of it made sense to Brett but he was sure he'd get even with the sheriff and that Bobby Martin. Bobby Martin was a good-for-nothing punk and the world would be a better place if they just got rid of him, his family, and his kind. His daddy had already gotten a little payback on Bobby when he got him fired as a guard at Parchman. His daddy figured out a way to push ole Bobby's buttons, then he would get other inmates to push his buttons and boy ole Bobby would yank a night stick out and just wail away on some dumbass inmate. His daddy had been the recipient of the last little bit of punishment that Bobby had dealt out. His daddy told him it wasn't so much about the punishment as it was the timing. Bobby was on thin ice with the review board already because he couldn't control that temper of his. Bobby had a bad temper for sure. Everybody says it was because he thought he was gonna play professional football, but instead he went up to that hick state Arkansas to play football for that college instead of Ole Miss and blew out his knee. Served him right anyway for being a traitor and not playing for the Rebels. The whole state hated him for doing that. Brett didn't care one way or the other, he just figured it was one less of them in the state he had to worry about. His daddy said it was chow time and he saw Bobby walking towards him so he just kinda bumped into him on purpose.

Nothing happened really but his daddy pretended that Bobby hit him and went flying across the floor. His daddy laughed when he told him about it because he said he should go to Hollywood because his acting was something to see. He said he dropped his tray and made a racket, then slid across the floor so everybody would see him and then, he said this was the best part, he starts hollering and crying and saying, "Don't hit me no more, Boss Martin, please, Boss Martin, I can't take no more." The other guards came runnin' up and picked him up and took him out of the chow hall. He left Bobby Martin standing there just as confused and stupid looking as he ever was. His daddy had enough friends inside of Parchman that all claimed that they saw ole Bobby wail on him.

The warden did a full review, called a bunch of witnesses in, and decided that prison work wasn't for Bobby Martin and sent him packin'. His daddy loved to tell that story. The Martins and Buckles had never gotten along. The two families had property that backed up to each other; at least a small piece of it did. The Martins were always complaining about the junk spilling over onto their property. Every time the Martins would complain about something, he and his younger brothers would wait until the wind draft was blowing onto the Martin's farm and they would light a bunch of old tires on fire with some diesel fuel and let that black smoke just drift right up to their house. Sometimes them tires would burn for days. Brett hated the Martins and so did his daddy. Their older brother wouldn't let them do that kind of stuff like their daddy did, so he was kinda glad that his big brother got drafted and was off killing people in another county. He hoped it would make him meaner when he came back. He always thought Donnie needed to be meaner. He sure didn't try to make Donnie mad because Donnie could whoop the fire out of all of them and they all knew it. Donnie wasn't mean, but he was one tough boy. Everybody in town knew it too.

The guard was a little too frisky for Brett's liking when he was checked. He expressed his anger with the places the guard was touching, and the guard told him he could always leave if he didn't like the procedures. Brett didn't say anything back after that. He saw his daddy sitting there at the table in his black and white uniform. The pants were gray and had a nice long black stripe down the outside of each side and the shirt was as white as a sheet. They always looked uncomfortable to Brett; they had so much starch in them that they were as stiff as a board. His daddy told him he was lucky to wear these because the fellas that worked out on the farm were nasty and had nasty clothes. "You got it set up yet, boy?" His daddy wasn't much for small talk but then neither was Brett. "Not yet but I'm mighty close, daddy. That boy will be history come Saturday. That's if he goes to Sumner. I figure he'll go like he always does and that will be the end of him. I reckon then we will have settled up with him, huh?" His daddy looked around the room at all the other people that had sat down at the tables for visitation. They all were yacking about the dumbest stuff. They talked about kids and family and Christmas and a whole bunch of other stuff that didn't matter to him. He wasn't ever going to see a Christmas outside the walls of Parchman. He knew that, and he was good with it.

Life was easier in here. He didn't have to pay bills, he didn't have to send snotty kids off to school, and he dang sure didn't have to worry about his wife cheating on him in his own damn kitchen. "Yeah, that will do it. You heard from Donnie?" Brett knew when his daddy asked him about Donnie that it was time to leave. Donnie and his daddy didn't get along every well. Donnie didn't have the same momma as the rest of the boys. Donnie's momma died in a car crash when Donnie was still in her belly. They managed to save Donnie but not his momma. His daddy used to tell Donnie that they saved the wrong one.

Donnie and his daddy fought a lot mainly because Donnie wouldn't let him pick on the other boys. A lot of times when their daddy was drinking hard, he would beat Donnie black and blue and Donnie would just take it, but that was just the way Donnie was; he would step in and take the beating for all the boys. When his daddy would ask about Donnie it meant that he was getting angry inside and Brett didn't care if his daddy was in prison or not, he was still scared to death of him. "No, I ain't heard from him." His daddy looked around the room and let out a sigh, "Hell, maybe he's dead. You get done what I told you to get done. Don't bother coming back until you do." He rose up from the table, turned his back on Brett, hollered for the guard, and they led him through the door where the prisoners go back inside the prison. Brett sat there at the table for a few minutes with his head down. He let out his own sigh and said to himself, "I hope not."

Chapter 21

＊

DECKER SAT THERE AT THE DESK, AND FOR THE FIRST time he could remember, he tried to focus on what the teacher said. He would do pretty well at understanding what she was talking about but when she turned around and started writing on the blackboard he would lose focus. After all the other kids had stood up and talked about what they did for their weekends, the teacher started in on the first lesson and for the first time for as long as he could remember, he was actually trying to concentrate on what she was saying.

Every now and then he would glance over at Jeannine. He knew she had something to do with his desk being moved but he didn't really mind now. Something felt different and he liked it. She caught him looking at her a few times and she would give the head nod that was meant to tell him to focus in the teacher.

He did as he was told, and it seemed to make the day go by so much faster than he could remember. The teacher was in the middle of explaining neutrons and protons when the bell rang for lunch. Ms. Piper didn't handle chaos very well. She wouldn't allow you to just bolt up from your desk and spill out into the hallway. She was big on order in every way. When the bell rang in her class you had to put your stuff away neatly, slide it all back under your desk, stand at the side of your desk, and in order of desk rows, begin to line up at the door.

After the line was formed, she would open the door and all the kids would march single-file all the way down to the cafeteria. The rest of the kids in the hallway that weren't in Ms. Piper's class were going nuts, running and screaming and knocking each other over, but when they saw Ms. Piper's class come out single-file, they all seemed to step aside and let the line go through. Nobody got in the way of a Ms. Piper line. He was amazed that her class could maintain order when the rest of the school seemed to go bonkers when they heard that bell ring. He would tell his momma about it and she would tell him that it was an example of how the world worked, that when a group of people were organized with a destination and a purpose, the rest of the world stepped aside without even knowing they were stepping aside. Decker also realized that when he was in that line, nobody noticed him, and nobody picked on him for sure. That's one of the reasons he couldn't wait to play Pop Warner football next year. He would be a part of a team. He kinda felt like he was a part of a team in Ms. Piper's class, at least until recess.

Once Ms. Piper's line of kids made it to the cafeteria, they got in the food line. You could bring your own lunch if you wanted to and some kids did, Decker even did sometimes but today was cheeseburger day and he wouldn't miss that for anything. The school's cheeseburgers weren't nearly as good as his daddy's at the bait shop and they sure weren't as good as Donnie's Hamburger Shack, but they were still pretty good.

Because his arm was in a sling, he was struggling with handling the tray and grabbing the utensils at the same time. Jeannine took over the whole operation. She grabbed two forks and two knives and two spoons, and grabbed the chocolate milk for both of them. The ladies behind the counter put the burgers on the plates along with a big pile of crinkle fries, which turned out to be one of Jeannine's favorite parts of the meal. She didn't care much for the burgers, but she loved the fries. It turned out to be a super good deal for Decker because he would get half of Jeannine's burger and she would get half of his fries. They both enjoyed the exchange and laughed while they were eating at a little round table away from the rows of long tables. This was the first lunch of the year that Decker didn't eat alone, and he wondered how she knew he liked chocolate milk instead of the regular? That was amazing to him.

While they were eating, she asked him about his shoulder and how long would it take to heal his collarbone. He really didn't know. He told her that he hoped it would heal soon because he hated the sling, and without even thinking about it, he told her that he had trouble peeing. His face turned red the minute he said it, because he had totally forgotten for a minute that she was a girl, a pretty girl at that. Holy crap, he had just mentioned peeing in front of a girl! His momma was really gonna work him over if she found out he was so blunt around a lady. He could hear his momma's voice in his head, "Now, Decker, you apologize to the lady, you know that gentlemen never pick their noses, fart or burp in public, look at themselves in the mirror, and they certainly don't discuss peeing!" He could see her shaking her finger at him. His momma didn't know it, but he had now done all those things.

Well maybe not look at himself in the mirror. There was a mirror at *JC Penny's* that he walked by once and saw himself walking and he panicked, told his momma what he had done and that it was purely accidental, and she surprisingly let it go. She told him that mirrors in department stores didn't count but he thought it best if he not take any chances in the future, so he avoided mirrors. His momma was serious about her boy being a gentleman and treating ladies with respect. Well, technically Jeannine wasn't a lady yet; she didn't wear high heels, earrings or lipstick. To Decker, you couldn't be a lady until you did those things. "Well you are on your own with that, Decker Davis! I am not going to go into no old nasty boy's bathroom to help you go." His face got even redder if that was possible. She looked at him with this very angry look on her face and his heart started beating fast. He was sure he had just lost the one friend he had just made, and he had for sure blown any chance of marrying her all because he had trouble with peeing!

After she was satisfied that she had him right where she wanted, scared and confused, she started laughing. "I'm just messin' with you, Decker Davis! I am still not gonna help you pee though." She started laughing again and he relaxed. He wasn't laughing with her, but he relaxed. He promised himself he would be more careful from here on out. He didn't want to say boy stuff around her even though he found it was easy to say anything around her. He was as relaxed around her as he was with his family at home.

They sat there at the table together until it was time to go back to class, and right before the bell rang to go back, she said, "I asked Ms. Piper if she could move your desk next to mine. It's where you belong, Decker Davis." He was dunking the last big juicy crinkle fry into a pile of ketchup and had totally misjudged the crinkle fry to dipping ratio and squirted way too much out. Jeannine scolded him a little for wasting ketchup and for a minute she sounded just like his momma. He fully expected her to tell him that there were starving kids in China that needed that ketchup, but she didn't. His momma said that a lot at the dinner table, especially when she flopped out a big pile of steamed vegetables.

Inside of all those steamed vegetables were carrots, buried in the pile so he might not see them. But there was no hiding a carrot from Decker. He hated carrots, he hated the look, the smell, the taste, he hated everything about them. He would rather eat dirt than eat carrots. His sister tricked him into eating a worm one time when she told him it was a noodle. She got in trouble for it and to tell the truth, it really wasn't that bad. She felt horrible about it and never pulled a trick on him again. Well he would rather eat that worm again than eat a carrot, yuck.

His momma even told him it would help him see as far and sharp as a hawk. She quickly sent him to his room when he suggested they eat the hawk instead of eating a carrot. She never gave up trying though, but she never won the carrot battle with Decker. He never ate his carrots. "How come?" He wasn't avoiding the subject of his desk being moved but he had sort of moved past it. "You aren't stupid, Decker Davis. Sitting in the back of the classroom not learning anything is not helping you either. I am going to help you the rest of the year, but you have to try." Decker thought he had been trying and started to say so, but she kept going, "There is something we are missing about you that I will figure out soon enough. You knew the whole Gettysburg Address, how come you know that?" He started to answer, but again she wasn't finished. He would learn that Jeannine asked a thousand questions a minute and never really waited for the answer to come out. She just kept asking more. "I mean, no other boy in the class can recite the Gettysburg Address but you can, yet everyone thinks you are retarded. They think you are weak, but you beat a kid up for me this weekend and nobody has ever done that." Since she had no intention of letting him answer any of the questions, he jammed the entire french fry that was dripping ketchup into his mouth.

Some of the ketchup trail landed on his chin and his shirt. He was wearing a brown shirt, so you really couldn't see the ketchup, so he wasn't worried about it. "Decker Davis! You got ketchup all over your chin and your shirt. Good grief!" She grabbed a napkin, dipped it in her water glass, and began wiping Decker's chin and his shirt clean. The bell rang and they got up, grabbed their lunch trays, piled the milk cartons and utensils on the trays, and dropped them off at the little pass-through window that was to the right of the cafeteria before you left the window.

It was positioned in a way for the kids to dump out their trash and then slide the tray through the window and head back to class. Decker thought the pass-through window was creepy. He thought it was super scary mysterious because you couldn't really see anyone back there, you just saw the tray slide through and disappear. He pictured it in his mind being very hot and steamy back there with a big fat guy with a beard in a white t-shirt that was dirty and probably had food stains all over it. He pictured that guy with a gold tooth in the front and would flash it right before he snatched another tray in hopes that one of the kids would let their arm linger too long around that window and he would snatch that kid and the tray through the window. He could see a kid's legs disappearing through that hole in the wall, never to be heard from again! He made a point of quickly pulling his arm back away from the pass-through tray window for that very reason. No way was he gonna get yanked through that window.

"My granddaddy is going to pick me up after school and take me to the Webb Library, do you want to go? We usually stop at Milholen's first and have a strawberry milkshake. He tells me every single time to not tell grandma and I don't, but she knows anyway." The thought of going to Milholen's and getting a shake and looking at all the comic books they had there sounded good to Decker, but he had chores to do when he got home so he couldn't. He told her all about what he had to do from cleaning out BettyJean's stall and mucking out the coup. BettyJean was their horse. She had been with the family before Decker came around. He liked her, but she was a biter.

If you weren't paying attention when you cleaned out her stall she bit a hunk out of whatever she could sink her teeth into, which was usually his backside. His daddy told him she never meant no harm by it and to not get upset, and that to her, she was just playing. If she really wanted to hurt you, she could just stomp a hole in your chest. Of course, she never did – she was a good horse except for the biting. She told him that her and her granddaddy go to the library every day and that she wanted him to come with her as much as he could. She said she loved the library; there was so much to do in there. So many books about everything you could imagine especially about math and space. She said that since they lived pretty close together that she was sure her granddaddy would drop him off at his house. Decker never even considered going to the library until now, but he knew his chores came first. He had to ride the bus home and get those things done before he could do anything.

Chapter 22

꧁꧂

THE BUS RIDE HOME FOR DECKER WAS EASY. FOR some reason, Lonnie Buckles was not on the bus home. Decker figured the police had come and taken him off to prison just for being a jerk. He didn't care what the reason was, he was just happy for a peaceful ride home. He didn't get to sit in the seat right behind Mr. Johns like he liked to though because the Brantley girl had already taken the seat. He knew her; she was an older girl in the sixth grade already. She was nice enough, but he hadn't really talked to her. He just knew that she didn't pick on him which made her ok in his book. He was trying to remember her name and thought it was Liz or Carrie or something like that, but it wasn't coming to him.

He knew her daddy was off to Viet Nam just like a lot of kids' daddies' in his class because he was with his daddy one time in the Scout when he stopped by to check on her family.

His daddy did that a lot. He would check on all the families that have had their daddies off to Viet Nam. He would tell Decker that it was just the right thing to do. Decker was just glad that his daddy didn't go off to Viet Nam too. He asked him one time how come he didn't have to go and he told him he was almost too old and was also a 4F. He knew his daddy was old but didn't know what a 4F was. When he brought it up, he could tell that his daddy didn't like talking about it, so Decker didn't press it much more.

He sat in the seat across from the Brantley girl and she actually spoke to him as he slid into his seat. It wasn't much but she said, "Hi" and that was way more than Decker was used to. He looked out the window at the countryside waiting for his stop. They dropped most of the kids off before he was dropped off. Being the first one picked up in the morning meant he was the last to be dropped off in the afternoon. For some reason, being the last one on the bus in the afternoon seemed way lonelier than it did early in the morning. He really wished Jeannine would ride the bus and wouldn't figure out until much later why she didn't.

Mr. Johns told him to eat a good supper and to make sure he did his homework and then let him off at the end of the long drive way. He liked the long walk home because it gave him time to think about the day. He knew his momma would ask him all kinds of questions when he got home. He liked to be prepared, or at least as prepared as he could. He enjoyed his time talking with his momma. She always asked some really good questions...questions that made him think.

He found a rock that looked just right for kicking as he walked the winding driveway towards his house. The driveway, if you could call it that, was a mix of gravel and dirt. It was really hard to drive on when it rained because it would get pretty muddy and that's why they had the Scout, it could get through anything. They hadn't had much rain lately, so it was as dry as a bone. He made it past one of the last long curves that allowed him to see his house. He could see that his daddy was there because the Scout was there, but there were a few other cars there that he didn't recognize. It was pretty unusual to have company this early in the evening, but there was always something exciting to him about having company. He liked to watch his parents because they acted a little different when they had company. Daddy didn't take off his shoes and walk around in his socks, he would leave them on until the company was gone. His momma was pretty much the same either way. She was always dressed very pretty; to Decker she looked like she was always ready for church. His sister would just go to her room and listen to records and now her 8-track until it was clear for her to come out and "be normal", as she called it. Decker got to the back door and opened it. You could hear the squeak of the screen and that was fine with Decker; he didn't like to be sneaky. He really wanted everyone to know he was home.

Usually, he went right for the fridge and took a big ole drink of milk before anyone could catch him drinking straight from the bottle. Before he could even throw his satchel down and grab the milk, he heard his daddy call him. "Decker, is that you? Come on in here a minute, please." That didn't sound good to Decker. It was not ordinary for his daddy to be home at this time of the day and it was not ordinary for his daddy to want to talk to him at this time of the day. Usually, he could wait until after supper to get a whoopin' if he was in trouble and he definitely wouldn't get a whoopin' with strangers in the house. He put is book satchel down on the counter and slowly walked into the living room where he found his daddy, momma, and one of daddy's deputies that everyone called Bubba. He wasn't sure if that was his real name but that's what Decker called him. There was a freckle-faced man with one of those Bandito-looking mustaches that hung way down past his mouth.

It looked to Decker like he might accidently eat part of it if he wasn't careful. He was wearing a *John Deere* baseball cap and sitting there in the living room at the end of his couch drinking a glass of tea. "Decker, come here, buddy." Decker walked over to his daddy who was sitting on a kitchen table chair that had been brought into the living room so everyone would have a place to sit. When he got in front of his daddy, he was sure that he was in some kind of trouble, but he didn't know what kind of trouble. He racked his brain, everything had gone pretty smoothly today. In fact, it was a pretty good day all the way around.

This was something he was not prepared for. He usually had a good idea of why he was in trouble. His daddy put a hand on each of Decker's hips and pulled him close to him. Decker knew this daddy-son position very well. His daddy had talked to him this way before. Decker couldn't remember it ever being bad, but he did remember that it was always serious, and it always resulted in him having to remember something. "Decker, you know Bubba, this is Mr. Homer King." Decker waved a short wave at Deputy Bubba and just nodded at Mr. Homer King. He thought that he knew everyone in Webb, but he had never met Mr. Homer King, although he kinda had an idea who he was. "Decker, Mr. King says his son came home Sunday with a broken nose and two swollen eyes and that you might have had something to do with it."

Decker now for sure knew who he was. It was Luke King's daddy. He could see the resemblance. Luke King was the kid that looked like he already had a mustache in sixth grade. He wasn't in Decker's grade, but he like to hang out with Lonnie Buckles. He also happened to be the kid that Decker had socked square in the nose on Sunday. When all the pieces of the puzzle came together in Decker's head, he let out a little chirp. It was a cross between a laugh and a cough. The cough was conjured up at the last minute to keep the laugh from surfacing. Decker may be young, but he was smart enough to know that his daddy would take a piece of his hide later if he didn't take this seriously. Knowing his daddy the way he knew him, Decker knew he was safe and not in trouble. All he had to do was tell the truth and he would be fine and this wasn't going to be any different. "Decker, look at me son, do you know anything about it?" Decker didn't hesitate one bit. He plowed into the story with gusto and tried not to miss any details but sometimes had to go back and fill in some of the gaps.

The words that drew the story like an artist with a canvas came spewing out of him like a shaken-up soda can. He placed heavy emphasis on Lonnie Buckles holding Jeannine down and making her say the word "pecker". Sometime during Decker's recital of the story, Mr. Homer King had set his tea glass on momma's coffee table and he hadn't bothered to use one those coasters that momma made everybody use. She would pitch a fit if she saw one of those rings that a wet glass made on her coffee table. Decker noticed it right off and wondered if his momma would scold Mr. Homer King for possibly ruining her antique coffee table. She never did. His daddy never took his hands off Decker's hips, but he could feel the grip he originally had on him loosened considerably.

When Decker was satisfied that he hadn't left out any details he looked directly at his daddy. Decker saw two things in his daddy's eyes that he loved to see: the first was pride and the second was relief. He could tell that his daddy was relieved that his only son hadn't done anything wrong and was extremely proud that he had helped a friend that needed it. "Son, why didn't you tell us that when you got home?" Decker thought about this and this was an area he thought could be dangerous territory. It was dangerous because Jeannine didn't want anyone to know and she had helped him work his way around not telling the grown-ups. If he told the truth then he might risk Jeannine not liking him anymore and he didn't have a whole lot of friends to spare, so if he didn't tell the truth and his daddy found out he lied, then he would risk his daddy never trusting him again. He couldn't risk his daddy not trusting him, so he told him. "Jeannine didn't want anyone to get in trouble. She said that things like this got grown-ups stirred up and she just didn't want trouble." His daddy smiled at him, moved his hands from his hips and placed them in each side of Decker's head, pulled him close and kissed Decker on the forehead. "You have some chores to do, partner – why don't you go change clothes and get started."

Decker didn't waste any time high-tailing it to his room to change. He had figured out how to change with one arm pretty well, but he had trouble with his work overalls. He knew his sister was in her room and she would help him if he needed it. He had one strap over his shoulder, but he couldn't latch it, so he walked into his sister's room and nearly knocked her over because she was standing against the door. She grabbed him and pulled him in the room. She gave him the shush sign, which was one finger over her lips. She whispered, "I want to hear what they are talking about. Sounds like you have a story to tell me, you little monster!" She smiled and fixed his overalls while she continued to listen and peek through the crack in the door.

"Mr. King, I'm sorry about your son but it sounds like he had it coming." Mr. Homer King rose from the chair, crossed his arms over his chest, and what he said stunned Decker like nobody's business. "You actually believe that pile of crap, Sheriff? No way in a howling moon would my son pick on a one-armed kid and a good-for-nothing little black girl."

Decker looked up at his sister and she could tell that he didn't understand. "I will explain later", she gave him the shush sign again. Decker could see his momma stand up quickly which prompted Deputy Bubba to jump to his feet and take a step towards Mr. Homer King. "Bubba!" His daddy had a booming voice when he needed to and that one set a record for all-time booms as far as Decker was concerned. Bubba stopped in his tracks like a wizard or something had frozen him. Decker didn't blame Bubba for freezing in his tracks; his daddy had made him freeze plenty of times. "Mr. King, my son doesn't lie, it's not in him to do so. I want to remind you that I invited you into my house to try and settle this squarely, but when it comes to my son, this uniform doesn't apply. Insinuate that my son is a liar or show your ignorant societal views one more time and I will personally kick your ass from here to Jackson." He saw his daddy rise to his feet after he had said what he said, and Decker reminded himself to ask his sister what *ignorant societal views* meant. He knew what a liar was, and he knew what it meant and even better, his daddy wasn't going to let this man call his son a liar. Decker was smiling through the crack in the door. He looked up at his sister and she was smiling too.

When his daddy got to his feet, Decker thought that his daddy looked bigger than he had ever remembered. In fact, at that moment, to Decker, his daddy looked like the *Jolly Green Giant*, only he was wearing his all brown sheriff uniform. "Now, I will forgive your misguided statements and misplaced excitement as a man trying to protect his son, sort of a one daddy to another courtesy, but I wouldn't press me on it. I am gonna take the deputy here and drive out to the Martin farm and talk to that little girl. If she corroborates Decker's story here, I might come out to your place and arrest your son for assault and battery." Mr. Homer King turned and started walking towards the front door but stopped half-way and turned back to look at Decker's daddy. "I noticed you didn't say you'll go out the Buckles place to corroborate my son's story. You already made up your mind, Sheriff, you always have, and you always will. You take their side on everything in this city and I have to tell you that the good folks of Webb are just about sick of you and your colored friends. Election is coming up next, Sheriff. I'd plan on going into the bait business full-time." He turned back around and walked out the door.

He slammed it shut, which was something that Decker was never allowed to do. He always wanted to sometime but never had. His momma would holler not to slam the door and say something like "you'll break the hinge". Turns out she was right; Mr. Homer King had broken their front screen door. Decker saw his momma grab the glass that Mr. Homer King left behind off her antique coffee table, walk into the kitchen, and throw the glass in the trash. His daddy looked at Bubba and shook his head like he didn't understand. When his momma came back into their living room, she quietly said, "Nobody in this family will ever be forced to drink out of the same glass that worthless piece of trash drank from." Decker looked back up at his sister and both had wide eyes. His momma never said mean things. This was a first. "You kids get busy doing what you are supposed to be doing." His daddy knew they were peeking through the door the whole time. Both he and his sister scrambled to get busy.

Chapter 23

❦

ELMER DAVIS DIDN'T RATTLE EASILY AND WAS WELL-known around Webb and Tallahatchie County as being cool under pressure, level headed, and no matter who you asked, pretty much all of them would say he was fair in all his dealings both professionally and personally. He was born in Tupelo, but his daddy moved to Webb when he was just a baby. He was a local high school football and basketball star and because he was so tall he got a basketball scholarship at Wake Forest in North Carolina. That's where he got his degree in Criminal Justice and that's also where he met Bubba.

Bubba was on the same basketball team at Wake Forest. Bubba was a Winston-Salem local and had never been outside the state of North Carolina. Elmer Davis was known to be tough as nails, but he had a huge, soft heart. Over his time as sheriff, he helped so many people find a job or would hand them an extra few dollars to get through rough times. That's how Bubba became a deputy.

Elmer walked over to his wife and put his hand on her hips and pulled her close to him. She was still mad about what Mr. Homer King had said in their own living room. "Honey, you can't let a moron like that get to you. He can't help that he's stupid." She smiled and kissed him on the chin since she couldn't reach up high enough to get to his lips. "I know people like that have no place in the world today! I just wish you could throw him in jail and throw away the key! The world would be a better place I promise you that!" Decker's momma didn't rattle easily either but when she did, look out. Elmer laughed and gave her a big hug, lifting her feet off the ground when he did it. She giggled and blushed a little at the open affection her husband was showing her right in front of Bubba. "Honey, if I threw folks in jail for being stupid I would have to lock myself up." He lowered her feet back to the ground and kissed her on the lips. "I will be back before supper, we can practice the dance some more this evening. I am feeling like I might be able to pull off that spin tonight." Decker's momma loved to dance, and she was good at it. His daddy really only did it because it made his momma happy.

She had entered them in a dance contest at the dance hall in Sumner and this Saturday night was the big contest. She had circled it on the calendar that hung beside the refrigerator. She had just written "Tango" on the date. "You better practice, Elmer Davis, we are going to win this time." Elmer let go of Lois and started for the door. "Come on, Bubba, we need go visit with Dub at the barbershop." Bubba followed Elmer out the door.

Chapter 24

DUB MARTIN HADN'T MADE IT BACK FROM THE barbershop yet. HE was still with Jeannine at the library but was on his way home with her after having stopped for a strawberry shake. Her part of the deal was to never tell her grandma that she got a shake nearly every day and she had to sweep out the barbershop and refill the pop machine. Once she was done with that, she would sit in chair 3 and read her book until it was time for them to go home.

She liked hanging out at the barbershop; one because her granddaddy treated her like a little princess and two, because when she was refilling the pop machine she would get to sneak a *Mountain Dew* out for herself. It wasn't like she had to sneak anything; her granddaddy was the one who told her she could have one. It was just another secret she had to keep from her grandma. Her grandma always told her that too much sugar would keep her up at night but that couldn't be true because she would lay down in bed, open her book, and she would be out.

Most of the time, her grandma would have to come in, turn the lights out, and take the book off her chest where she had dropped it. Today she checked out a book on gravity and its effects on the body's equilibrium with a heavy emphasis on weightlessness. She was fascinated with floating around in space. Their teacher showed a movie in class about the astronauts and their space training and how they had to prepare for being as light as feather and what effects that had on their bodies so that when they landed on the moon they would know how to walk and stuff. She wanted to be prepared when it came her turn go into space, so she read everything she could on it. She was fascinated with the video and had sort of a secret crush on one astronaut in particular. The film the teacher showed it on a projector and had mesmerized her.

In order to see the film better, the teacher had to turn the lights down. Most of the other kids fell asleep because of the dark room and that smooth clicking sound the projector made when those reels were spinning. But not her, she wanted to watch it again, but one viewing was all she got. The teacher said the other classes had schedules to watch it too.

Dub saw the sheriff's Scout parked in front of his little barbershop as he turned into the small gravel parking area. The barber pole sign was working just fine. He had trouble with it since the day he bought the thing. He drove all the way to Memphis to get it when he found out a barbershop there was going out of business and they would give it to him if he would come get it. He hooked it up himself and at first it worked really well, he could even adjust the speed the colors turned inside the thing, but then it started acting up. Today it was working just fine, and he was quite proud. It was one of his first attempts at electrical wiring. He was very proud of that.

The sheriff and Bubba were sitting in the customer waiting chairs reading. Bubba had yesterday's Webb Tribune and the sheriff had last month's *LIFE Magazine*. "Sheriff, I just gave you a trim two days ago, can't be time for another. What brings you out here?" Dub never cared much for Bubba so he never really acknowledged him being there other than a nod. To Dub, there was just something weird about that boy. He didn't seem to fit in anywhere, but the sheriff renewed his contract every year. Bubba wasn't elected like the sheriff was, he was hired by the sheriff. "Hey, Dub, good to see you – I see you got your beautiful little helper with you." Elmer put the paper on the table, got up, and went to the soda machine. He slid the top open because it was one of those deep-well soda coolers. You just slid the top open and picked the flavor you wanted. He grabbed a *Dr. Pepper* and laid a dime on the counter.

After he opened the bottle on the side of cooler, he took his seat again. He was a very large man and didn't want to seem like he was towering over the little girl. "I'm sorry to bother ya'll, but you remember yesterday when the two kids came back to the house with dirty clothes?" Jeannine tried to sneak out the back door when she heard that, but Dub told her to hold on just a second. "I need to ask Jeannine about what happened out in the woods. Dub slid his barber smock on and asked Jeannine to come sit in the chair and talk to the sheriff for just a minute. He assured her that she could sweep and restock later. "Honey, I already talked to Decker, can you tell me what happened?" Jeannine squirmed in chair 2 for just a little bit. She looked around and looked at her granddaddy and remembered what Decker told her in the woods – he would never lie to his parents.

Elmer could tell she was scared and thought she might be in trouble, so he calmed her down as best he could. "Honey, I promise you that you aren't in trouble. I just need to hear you tell me what happened that got your clothes dirty like that." Her granddaddy walked over to her and kissed her on the top of the head. "Honey, granddaddy would never let anyone hurt you so go on and tell the sheriff what happened." She was about ready to speak when Bobby walked in. "What's going on here?" The sheriff and Bubba knew that Bobby had a short fuse and didn't need him scaring the girl or causing any trouble. "Hey, Bobby – we were just about to ask Jeannine some questions. You are more than welcome to join us. You doin' all right these days?" Bobby walked over to the soda cooler, slid the top open, and grabbed a *Mountain Dew*. "I'm fine, Sheriff; was at a job interview today over in Grenada. Gonna work construction – tired of cuttin' meat at Andy's."

Andy's was the butcher shop in town. Decker's momma got all their meat there. Bobby took the job after he got fired from Parchman and he hated it. "What you want ask my baby girl?" He popped the top off the bottle of his *Mountain Dew* with the opener attached to the machine and then went and sat in chair 1. "Honey, you want to tell me about yesterday?" Everybody in the room could tell that Jeannine had become even more nervous now that her daddy had arrived. Her granddaddy walked back over to Jeannine and stood behind her in the chair. He put his hands on her shoulders and leaned over and kissed the top of her head again. "It's ok, baby, the quicker you tell the sheriff what caused you to get your clothes dirty yesterday, the quicker we can get back to grandma and supper." Since she had already made up her mind earlier to tell the truth, it was easier to restart this time, although she didn't like the idea of telling her daddy what happened. She knew her daddy would get really mad. She didn't let that stop her though. She told the same story that Decker had told them. The sheriff could see Bobby getting angry when she was telling about having her arm pressed up behind her back and making her say what she said. She started to tear up at that part, because she remembered how helpless she felt and how embarrassed she was to be forced to say something so dirty. Dub stayed behind her with his hands on her shoulder as she spoke.

When she got to the part about her arm being twisted and forced to say she was there to see a Decker pecker, she started to tear up. She hadn't intended to cry but just remembering how much having her arm twisted behind her back had hurt and how little she could do to stop it caused the tears to stream down her cheek. She used her sleeve to wipe them away from her face; at that point is where Bobby shot up out of his chair and walked towards the door. His pace was slow, but it was deliberate and firm.

Bobby was going to get some payback and the Buckles were going to pay for hurting his little girl. Everybody in the room knew how he would react; Bubba jumped up from his chair and stood in front of the door. Bobby looked at Bubba; the sheriff could see that he had his fist clinched. "Bobby!" Elmer had used his booming voice twice that day and both times it had had its intended effect; it stopped Bobby in his tracks. "What?!" Bobby continued to stare at Bubba who was blocking the front door. Dub retrieved a tissue from the counter and was helping Jeannine clean up the tears that she didn't get with her sleeve.

The sheriff easily saw the tenderness and love that Dub had for his granddaughter and knew those emotions well, and although Decker had not cried as he told the exact same story that Jeannine had, Elmer felt a love for his son that could never be explained. He knew exactly what Dub was feeling. He knew that Dub's first instincts were probably like his were; he wanted to go find these kids, beat the hell out of their parents, and lock the kids up. But he knew that kids do what they see their parents do and in this case, restraint was the best and wisest choice. It was also the most difficult when it comes to seeing your child in tears.

The sheriff also was amazed by the incredible awareness and maturity Jeannine showed. Her reasons for not telling anyone were spot-on but coming to her conclusions was not something that a girl her age would come to. The sheriff knew right then and there that her grandparents were the reason for her wisdom, not her daddy. "Where you goin', Bobby?" Just like his encounter with Mr. Homer King, the sheriff never got up from his chair. He set his *Dr. Pepper* on the table beside him. "Sheriff, ain't nobody gonna hurt my baby like that." He looked down at the floor when he said it, but he looked up and directly at Bubba who was still blocking the door. "You gonna move or do I have to make you move?" Dub and the sheriff made eye contact.

In Dub's eyes he saw all the years of frustration of not being able to get through to his son, not being able to stop trying to solve everything with violence and anger. Bobby had been in more fights than anyone the sheriff knew. His memory of Bobby's temper went all the way back to elementary school. His sixth-grade teacher kicked him out of class and refused to let him back in her class. She said he was incorrigible and she would waste no more time on him. He had been a hand-full for Dub and the sheriff could see the stress appear on Dub's face. He knew he needed to get Bobby calmed down or there would be some real trouble. The history between Bobby Martin and the Buckles family was legendary. Bobby had been in a fight with one or all of them at the same time. The only one that Bobby couldn't whip for sure was off in Viet Nam now. "We will handle this, Bobby. We don't need your help." Bobby looked back down at the floor, shook his head in a sarcastic way, then turned towards the sheriff. "Sheriff, you ain't gonna handle nothin'. My baby got assaulted on your property and you sit there and tell me you gonna handle it? Everybody in this town knows you favor your kind and you ain't gonna do nothin'. Them Buckles been doing whatever they want for as long as they want all because they know you ain't gonna do squat. You showin' up in our church and in our barbershop pretendin' to be a man of the people is nothin' but a way to get a vote and everybody knows it. No, sir, Sheriff, you ain't foolin' nobody, Sheriff, especially me." Dub took a step out from behind Jeannine.

The sheriff could tell he was about to confront his son and he didn't need that. It would just make things worse and Jeannine was sitting there watching all of it. He stood up; he towered over everyone and he wanted that image in Bobby's head. Bobby only understood strength and power and he was hoping that his size would be a reminder of his own strength and power. "There ain't nobody in this room that understands what you are feeling and what you want to do right now. You must have missed that part in the story where Jeannine said they beat and kicked my son while he was on the ground AND he only had one arm to defend himself. I don't take to people pickin' on my son any more than you take to anyone pickin' on your daughter." The sheriff could see Bobby relax his hands and no longer had them in a fist.

The sheriff continued, "Oh, yeah, you also missed the part where your own daughter, who appears to wise beyond her years, didn't want to tell anyone because she knew somebody would get mad and then someone would get hurt, and then the hurt would never stop. You got a smart little girl in that chair over there and you'd be wise to turn around and tell her how damn proud you are of her right now instead of flyin' off the handle and endin' up in county lockup tonight." Bobby was now looking up at the sheriff. He didn't have his fists clinched but his eyes were still crazy. He looked like he could just explode at any minute.

The sheriff stuck his hands in his pockets and wanted no outward sign of aggression other than his imposing size. "I suggest you try being a daddy instead of a vigilante." Bobby walked over to Jeannine who was still in the chair with her granddaddy's hands on her shoulder. He put his hands on her cheeks and kissed her nose. "You ok, baby? Does your arm hurt?" Jeannine shook her head and said, "No". "I always knew you were smart, baby." He turned back around to the sheriff and took a step towards him. Bubba, who was still in front of the door, took a step towards the two men thinking that there still might be trouble. Elmer caught the motion and gave Bubba a look. Bubba stopped. "Sheriff, you better handle this or I will. I remind you that next year is an election year." The sheriff smiled at him and said, "So I've heard." The sheriff turned to Dub and Jeannine. "Honey, you are definitely the smartest person in this room. You are probably the smartest person in the whole state of Mississippi and you are confirmed as one of the prettiest. You come back over to the house any time you want to." He patted her on the knee and then patted Dub on the arm. "I will be back in a couple days for a trim, Dub." Dub smiled at him and he could see and feel the tension leave the room, maybe except for his son who was still very tense.

As the sheriff turned to leave, Jeannine stopped him. "Sheriff." Her voice was soft and as calm as ever now. The tears were gone and she was back to being her normal cute little self. He turned back to look at her. "Yes, baby?" she smiled at him, a smile that could melt statues. "Do you think Decker can come to the library with me tomorrow? I will help him with his chores if you let him come with me. My granddaddy takes me every day after school. You don't mind, do you, granddaddy?" She looked up at her granddaddy when she said it. He smiled back down at her and affirmed that it was perfectly fine and that he would drop Decker off at the sheriff's house when they were finished. The sheriff let out a huge laugh. "Honey, if you can get Decker to set foot inside a library you have even more charm than I thought you did. That boy hates to read; he'd rather muck out a chicken coup than read a book. Of course he can go but I doubt you'll get him to go with you." He patted her on the knee again and started towards the door. Bobby was still standing in-between the door and the sheriff. He made the move to step around Bobby, as Bobby didn't seem like he wanted to move. Bobby grabbed the sheriff by his arm when they were side-by-side.

The sheriff stopped and slowly looked down at Bobby's hand on his arm then slowly looked up at Bobby. "I mean it, Sheriff." The sheriff took his other hand and placed it on Bobby's hand, gripped it with the force of a bear trap which caused Bobby to wince and try to step back but couldn't because the sheriff's grip was like a vice. The sheriff knew he was causing Bobby considerable pain. He smiled at Bobby for a second and then his smile turned to a steely-eyed stare. "You can vote as many times as you can figure out how to vote next year but you only get to threaten me once. The next time I will deal with it Bobby Martin style." He let Bobby go and walked towards the front door where Bubba had already turned and opened the door so that they both could leave.

Bobby grabbed the wrist that the sheriff had just clamped down on. He could still see the sheriff's finger dents in his skin. When the door closed, Dub looked at his son, shook his head and said, "Maybe one of these days you will realize that when you mess with the bull, you gonna get the horns."

Chapter 25

BUBBA HELD THE DOOR FOR THE SHERIFF TO WALK through, more in awe than out of courtesy. He was amazed at his calmness in very hot situations. Bobby was a hot head, but he was also a very savvy hot head. He had probably been in a fight with every capable man in Tallahatchie County, at least the ones that were willing to square up with him and he had whipped them all, except Donnie Buckles. Those two had butted heads quite a few times and every single time, Donnie got the best of Bobby.

Bubba never could figure out why Bobby kept trying because every time he tried he would get a severe butt whoppin'. Donnie wasn't bigger than Bobby but there was something about him – he was gritty with lightning fast hands. It seemed like Donnie could land five or six punches to Bobby's one. Donnie never went looking for a fight. The sheriff told Bubba that Donnie had become like the fastest gunslinger in town and now every-body who thought they could fight measured themselves against Donnie. He also knew that Donnie would go out of his way to avoid a fight, folks had even seen him walking away, but fights always found him. The sheriff thought Donnie was a good kid who just seemed to find trouble wherever he went, or at least trouble found him.

The last fight between Bobby and Donnie was at a bar on the edge of town called Lollygags. It was a decent place well-known for their food and the music. They always had a live band and lots of atmosphere. It wasn't a bad place, but it wasn't really a place where you took a first date. Maybe a second date. Bubba was the first deputy to arrive after Bobby and Donnie had mixed it up. Donnie was already set to go off to basic training the next day. Something happened between Bobby and Donnie and the fight ended up out in the parking lot. By the time Bubba got there, there really wasn't much to do other than to take some statements. He didn't even really do that because neither man pressed any charges, but it was clear by the look on Bobby's face that he had come up short again. "What now?" Bubba was walk-ing behind Elmer as they left the barbershop. "We go out to see Brett." Bubba let out a sigh and slid into the passenger seat. "I hate going out there." The sheriff turned the key in the ignition and the Scout fired right up. "Me too."

Navigating the junk to get to the Buckles place was more of a challenge than Elmer Davis remembered. There didn't seem to be a bare spot on the entire property. There were old cars, washing machines, old refrigerators, and engine parts. The sheriff drove really slowly, thinking the whole way up the drive he would surely pop a tire on something jagged or sharp. He finally reached the house and he could sure tell that Donnie hadn't been there in a long time. Donnie made the other boys keep the house clean and the property organized...as organized as you could get for a junkyard. "Do not let Brett get under your skin, Bubba."

The sheriff knocked on the screen door; it didn't take but just a few minutes for Brett to show up. "What do you want, Sheriff?" Brett had a beer in his hand and looked like he had just woken up. "I want to talk to Lonnie, can we come in?" Brett stepped back from the door and made a signal to come in. Brett hollered for Lonnie to come into the living room, but he didn't show up. "Lonnie, you better get your butt out here now!" Brett took a drink of his beer and turned towards the back hallway. He walked down the hallway to Lonnie's room, but he wasn't there. "Lonnie, you little shit, you better get your butt out here now!" The sheriff stood in the living room waiting. He made eye contact with Bubba and both of them were having a hard time with the smell of the house.

The house smelled like dirty diapers or someone had left rotting fish in the trash a week ago. They weren't very excited about the way the place looked either. It needed more than a woman's touch, it needed to be burned. "He ain't here just now, Sheriff, you all will have to come back when he is here." The sheriff looked amused for a minute then he spoke, "It's a school night, it's almost dark and you don't know where he is?" Brett took another drink and said he didn't say he didn't know where he was, he just said he wasn't here. He explained that there is a big difference.

The sheriff struggled to understand the difference especially after Brett had just walked through the house looking for Lonnie.

It was clear he had no idea where Lonnie was. "Alright, Brett, as soon as Lonnie comes back I need you to call me." The sheriff motioned for Bubba to leave and Bubba walked out leaving the sheriff alone with Brett. As soon as Bubba walked out the sheriff looked at Brett. "Brett, your little brother beat up a little girl and has to answer for it. I suggest you find him soon and bring him to me." Brett took another drink from his beer and just smiled a very wicked smile. Elmer turned and walked out the door.

The sheriff and Bubba rode back to the office with the sheriff behind the wheel as always. He never let Bubba drive while he was in the car. "I want you to get with Webb PD and tell them we are looking for Lonnie Buckles. Nothing serious so they don't need to make a scene or arrest the kid if they see him, they just need to let us know where he is. I'm sure the King kid already figured a way to let Lonnie know that they're in a little trouble, so he might be hiding. Hell, he may have been hiding in the that house somewhere and with all the junk and trash he could have been hiding in the living room we were standing in! Geez, that place was a wreck." Bubba agreed that the place was a wreck but wondered out loud if maybe the kid ran away. The two talked about how quickly a family could spiral out of control when there was no authority figure in the house with Lonnie's daddy in prison and his older and most stable brother off fighting a war that the sheriff didn't fully understand yet. He figured he would get his mind around it soon enough but to him, it sure didn't seem like any business of theirs to be over there.

He dropped Bubba off at the office and made his way back home. He intentionally drove by Dub's just to see if Bobby's car was still there and it was. His car being there made him feel better for the night at least. He just had a feeling in his stomach that Bobby and Brett were destined to lock horns and he was afraid that this time somebody would get seriously hurt.

He walked in and threw his keys on the hall table like he always did. He headed straight into the kitchen where he knew Lois would be. Lois was standing over the stove stirring a pot of beans. Elmer hadn't eaten all day and wasn't hungry until he smelled the pinto beans. Lois was making one of his favorite meals, pinto beans and cornbread. He could eat a whole pot of beans all by himself if he wasn't careful, but he would sure pay for it the next day. In fact, everybody in the house would be passing gas the next day with giggles from his daughter and wife every time they let one loose. To Elmer, the gas was worth the trouble that a pot of pinto beans caused.

Because of the visit from Mr. Homer King and his trips out to the Martin and Buckles places, he was way overdue for supper. He was always amazed at Lois's ability to anticipate when he would be home and would always have dinner ready. He told Lois about the conversations of the night but he laughed when he talked about Jeannine asking if Decker could go to the library with her and that she even volunteered to help him with his chores just so he could go. He reinforced his belief that Decker would not go anywhere near the library. He thought that Lois would laugh but she only smiled and shook her head. "Is there something on your mind that I should know? That wasn't the reaction I was expecting from you." She got up, grabbed a bottle of *Red Label* from above the refrigerator, and poured two glasses. She set the glasses in front of them and Elmer. "This is a special day. It appears that our son has his first crush. I was thinking that called for a drink." She smiled and raised her glass, Elmer did the same thing, but he still had a confused look on his face. The two glasses clanked together, and each took a sip. "Good grief, he is just 11 years old, do 11-year-old boys even like girls? I have a hard time believing that." Lois got up and stirred the beans and then sat back down at the table. "Well guess who asked if he could go to the library over dinner tonight." She giggled and grabbed her glass and took another sip. "You're kidding! Decker hates to read. Holy cow, my boy doesn't have a crush, he is in LOVE. You see what you women do to us, make us do things we would never do on our own." The sheriff and Lois sat there at the table while he ate his beans and cornbread talking about Decker and Jeannine, and he didn't care whether Decker got his chores done or not as long as he could come home and explain what he read at the library.

It would be interesting to see if Jeannine would stick with her promise to help him with his chores, especially when it came to mucking out the chicken coup and BettyJean's stall. That would show really soon how deep Jeannine's love for their boy really was. "Is he still awake?" Lois confirmed that when she checked thirty minutes ago he was. The sheriff decided it was probably time for the man-to-man talk.

Chapter 26

❦

DECKER HAD JUST GOTTEN BACK TO HIS ROOM; he had been in his sister's room when he heard his daddy come home. Decker needed to work out all the day's events with his sister. She could explain things just as well as his momma could, sometimes even better because she still remembered what it was like to be 11. Decker was sure that his parents had forgotten what that was like a long time ago. After Mr. Homer King had been to their house, he had a lot of questions tonight that he had never thought of before.

Before they got into the deep subjects that were bothering him, he sat there in the middle of her bed Indian-style listening to her read. She was reading *Moby Dick* to him. She wasn't reading it for him but for her. She said she had to do a report on any novel she wanted to, and she picked *Moby Dick* because she knew that Decker would like the book if she made it sound exciting to read. She would read when he wasn't there but would always mark the place where she left off reading to him so she could keep track and still finish the book on time. She was happy with her choice, although because of the time it was written, some of the dialogue and words didn't make sense for modern day speak.

She found a good stopping point and as always said, "Ok, what's on your mind, Deck, what do you want to talk about tonight?" Decker was still thinking that Ahab was a cool name and he wished his folks would have named him Ahab because it just sounded so much better than Decker. It just sounded a lot tougher. He was fiddling with the quilt on her bed and looked up at her. "What is *ignorant societal views*?" Heather knew that would be his first question. Maybe not his first, but she knew that would be one of his questions that she had to explain very well. She knew her little brother didn't see color and she was proud of him for that. She wished that everyone saw the world the same way that Decker did and she didn't want anything she said tonight to change that. It was an important conversation and she wasn't sure she was completely prepared for it. "Well, how bout I try and answer that in a minute, but it would help me to explain it if you tell me why you punched that kid in the nose and how did it feel?" She smiled when she said it because she had heard him tell the story to their parents but what he never said was the what led him to do it. After all, Decker had sure been picked on and beaten up before.

It hurt every time she would see him come home with a new cut or bruise and there was nothing she could do about it. She also knew that he had grown quite a bit between the fourth and fifth grades and he had already gone through another shoe size just since school had started. Because of their daddy's size, she knew that Decker would do some serious growing, but she was worried that no matter how much he grew, he might already be trained mentally to be meek and she hoped he would grow out of that too. "Well, when Lonnie had Jeannine on the ground and he made her say that dirty word and then made her cry, I couldn't take it. I just knew I needed to do something more than just get beat up." He explained that getting beaten up was easy and he really didn't think much of it. Sometimes it hurt and sometimes it didn't. He told her that it had happened his whole life and he just figured he was supposed to get picked on and beaten up. She closed *Moby Dick* and set it on the nightstand, then she pulled her legs up and got into the Indian cross just like Decker so she could sit right in front of him.

Sometimes the things that he told her touched her deeply and she wanted so badly to hug him and take all his pain away, but she couldn't. "Listen, Deck man, I heard a story the other day that I wanted to tell you and if I don't tell you now while it's on my mind I might forget, so I will tell you that and then tell you what *ignorant societal views* are." He loved her stories, so he sat up a little straighter, but not too much because his shoulder had been hurting a little tonight. She told him the story about the baby elephant that stays chained to a stake in the ground all day every day. It wakes up and it is chained to that stake, so it realizes that it can't go any further than the chain tied to that stake.

It's so trained to obey the restraints of that stake and chain that even when it becomes a giant elephant, it doesn't realize that with its size and strength, it could rip the stake out of the ground and go anywhere it wants so it stays on the chain. He asked a few questions about how long the chain was and why it was chained, and she answered them all. She didn't know if he fully understood what she was trying to tell him because she sure didn't want to tell him that he could start breaking chains and beating people up, but she needed him to figure out for himself that getting beaten up was not something he had to put up with. "Now, the *Ignorant Societal Views* question." She started by saying that there were really stupid people in the world, Mr. Homer King and Lonnie Buckles to name a couple, and they saw the world differently than good people. She said that he was a good person, so he definitely saw things differently than Lonnie Buckles did. She said that people like Mr. Homer King think that they are better than other people because of their skin.

She started to continue, but Decker stopped her and asked her what was different about their skin than his. She explained that there was no difference in their skin than his, or hers for that matter, except that her skin was softer because she was a girl. She laughed when she said it, but she could tell that Decker didn't understand so she pressed on. "Decker, do you notice that Jeannine and her family are darker than we are?" She really didn't want to be that blunt, but she knew no other way. She wished she didn't have to be the one to point out color to him. That's when he heard his daddy come home and he knew he needed to be in his room at 9:00 p.m., those were the rules. Because of tonight's events, his daddy was home late, and it was past nine so Decker rolled out of his sister's bed and slipped back to his room. Before he got too far away from his sister she said, "Hey, little man – you forgot something!" He turned around quickly and kissed her on the cheek then snuck off to his room. Still confused on the *Ignorant Societal Views*.

His daddy walked into his room to find Decker flipping through a comic book. Decker knew he was coming and felt

like he needed to be doing something or it would look too obvious that he was waiting. He really had no idea why he felt that
way because he wasn't in trouble, so he could have been laying
there looking at the ceiling daydreaming like he normally did.
It was just something about his daddy that made him feel like
he needed to be doing something all the time. When the two of
them would be out fishing or working on the farm, he would talk
to Decker about never letting anyone think he was lazy. Decker
didn't think he was lazy, but it was always a good idea to be doing
something when his daddy was around. "Hey, buddy, how you
doin'? How's the shoulder, feeling better? Whatcha readin'
there?" His daddy asked a lot of questions when he wanted to
talk to Decker about something he thought was important.

Decker knew that for sure. The questions would come so fast
that he often never answered some of them because he couldn't
hold them all in his head that long. He held up the *Flash Gordon*
comic book and said he was just looking through it. He didn't
want a quiz on it because he hadn't really read it. "I left in such
a hurry after Mr. Homer King left that I didn't get a chance to
tell you how proud I was of you for sticking up for your friend
and sticking up for yourself. I also wanted to remind you that
you did everything right in this case but that you should use
violence as the very last resort. Understand, Decker?" Decker
understood for sure, he really didn't want to sock anyone in the
face ever again, but he was happy to know that he had it in him
to do so.

His daddy told him about his conversations with Brett
Buckles and wanted to know if maybe he knew where Lonnie
might be hiding. He knew it was a long shot that Decker would
even care where Lonnie was, but he was sort of doing a little

police work while he was talking to Decker. Decker watched his daddy pace around his room. He looked at the stuff that was on Decker's walls that he had seen a billion times and would make a comment about each one of them as if he was seeing it for the first time. He commented about the 1967 St. Louis Cardinal team picture he had on his wall. He said he really liked it and it was a great team with lots of speed and excellent pitching and they were once again in the pennant race this year.

Decker wanted to tell him that he was the one who gave it to him for Christmas, but he decided to just let that go. It really was one of his favorite Christmas gifts that year because he also got a brand-new *Lou Brock* fielders glove, which he spent all winter breaking in properly so that it would be ready for spring baseball. Decker sort of enjoyed watching his daddy pace around his room as he talked about all kinds of subjects. He even told Decker that this year he was going to take him quail hunting. He felt like it was probably time to try out that 4-10 shotgun that his daddy had swapped for the use of their bull. Decker didn't understand why anyone would want to use a bull, but it seemed like a pretty good deal and the guy went and got the bull and brought him back a week later with a *Mossberg 410* shotgun to boot. They didn't have to do a thing and Decker sure didn't mind the bull being gone for a week.

That bull was scary to Decker and he had to be careful when he would go exploring because the bull would charge at people he didn't like. Luckily for Decker, the bull seemed to like him because he never charged Decker, but he wasn't about to take any chances. Decker hadn't gotten to shoot the shotgun yet, but he was sure looking forward to it. "Say, champ, I was at Mr. Martin's barbershop. I had to visit with your friend to hear her tell the story that you told. Not that I didn't believe you, I most certainly did believe you, but it's just good police work to hear several different people tell the same story. It just makes things easier. She said the same thing that you did. She was sure grateful that you socked that kid in the nose although she didn't see it, but she did see you kick Lonnie off her. She sure is a pretty lady, huh?" His daddy finally stopped pacing and sat down on the bed beside Decker when he brought up the part about Jeannine being a pretty lady.

Decker had no idea why his daddy was saying this stuff and he felt his face get hot. That seemed to happen when he got nervous or he was embarrassed about something, like the time everyone in class was looking at him with a giant booger stuck to his finger. He wished at that moment he could have had a place to hide. Decker shrugged his shoulders like he wasn't sure, but the truth was that he did think she was pretty, but he didn't like talking about stuff like that. Decker started to say that Jeannine really wasn't a lady and that she didn't wear high heels and lip stick, but thought it better to say nothing at the moment.

He had no idea what his daddy wanted to talk about. "She asked me if you could go to the library with her. She even said she would help you with your chores if you got to go with her. What do you think? Do you want to go to the library after school?" Decker could feel a smile coming up on himself and he couldn't stop it. It was sort of embarrassing for him to want to go to the library. He wasn't sure why that was, but someone told him that only pansies went to the library. He knew now for certain that he wasn't a pansy, he had actually been in a fistfight! Pansies don't get into fistfights, but he sure wanted to go to the library with Jeannine. Decker nodded his head. He even told his daddy what had happened in class that day with Jeannine and how his desk got moved to the front and he actually answered a question about the Civil War that nobody in class knew but him, well except for Jeannine, and he had no idea why she didn't answer the question if she knew it. "Well its settled then, you get to go to the library with Jeannine and she gets to come back and do chores with you. You can take her back home when ya'll are done with the chores. You can cut across the south field and take her home or you can follow the road. It will be quicker if you two cut through the fields, but either way is fine by me. Your momma might even be able to give you a ride back to her house. I squared it up with Mr. Martin already, so you are good. Now, Decker, there is something else that I want to talk to you about since we are talking about pretty girls and boys."

Decker's daddy drew a deep breath; he thought he was ready to have this conversation but in truth he wasn't. It seemed so much easier when he was just thinking it was his duty as a daddy to talk to his son about the birds and the bees. Decker could tell that his daddy was really struggling with how to say whatever he was going to say so he decided to interrupt his thought and maybe that would help him get the words out. Decker was getting tired now and was ready to go to sleep. "Daddy, what does *Ignorant Societal Views* mean? I heard you say that to Mr. Homer King and I don't know what that means." The sheriff was so relieved that the subject shifted but also realized that the subject had shifted to an equally difficult topic, especially for a kid like Decker that had the correct societal views and never saw colors when dealing with people. His daddy took another deep breath, looked up at the ceiling of Decker's room, and allowed his eyes to roam the walls one more time. "Well it's hard to really explain,

Deck, but some people in this world, especially in this state and especially in this town, like to judge people by how they look instead of how they act. They think that everybody should stay separate and not be allowed to be friends. There are some people that won't like you being friends with Jeannine because you are different from her. You see, anyone who thinks that we should all be separated by the way we look has *Ignorant Societal Views*. Mr. Homer King is one of them and your classmate Lonnie Buckles is another. I doubt Lonnie really feels that way, but he is being taught by his brothers to behave that way. Right now, he is just doing what he thinks his big brothers want him to do, and eventually he will do those things because it is what HE wants to do. That's why I am so proud of you, you see a person's heart and brain, not their appearance." Decker's daddy really tried to avoid skin color in the conversation because he didn't want Decker to be forced to see something that right now he could not see.

Decker looked at the back of his hands and his palms as if he was examining his skin. "But don't I kinda do that with Jeannine? I see that she is pretty, that's why I like her. She is smart too. There is another girl in our class that is kinda ugly and I don't like her that much; she has a really big gap in her front teeth and every time she talks she whistles." He thought it was kinda cool at first because he hadn't learned how to whistle and here this girl could whistle without even thinking about it. But after a while you just wish she would talk normally and you couldn't see the back of her mouth through the gap in her front teeth. "Isn't that what I am doing? I like Jeannine because she is pretty, and I don't like Amanda because she is ugly?" The sheriff shook his head, and realized this was going to be tougher than he thought. Maybe he would put off the man-to-man talk for a later date.

His daddy told him that it was sort of that way and that he really should not judge Amanda and he should never openly say someone was ugly because it was just bad manners. The sheriff got a little frustrated because in a way, Decker was correct about pretty and ugly, but he still didn't see color. He decided that he would leave the conversation right where it was because Decker was as close to understanding it as he wanted him to be for now. "Just be nice to everybody, partner, and you will always come out on top." Decker was satisfied that he understood the subject better than before. His daddy kissed him on the forehead, told him he was proud of him again, and said goodnight. He flipped off Decker's lamp and said, "Go to sleep. Tomorrow you go to the library with a pretty girl, big man."

Chapter 27

⌖

AFTER HE CONVINCED HIMSELF THAT HE WAS
ready for school, Decker hurried to the kitchen for breakfast.
He was very excited this morning; nobody even had to wake
him. He couldn't ever remember being excited for school and
he wasn't sure how to deal with it. He didn't want everyone to
see he was excited to go to school because they would expect that
kind of behavior all the time. He was afraid that this might pass
after a while and didn't want to disappoint anyone. His momma
had made biscuits and gravy, not the chocolate kind that he liked
so much but the cream gravy; his momma's cream gravy came
in a pretty close second because she would put these tiny chunks
of sausage in it.

He had a process for this style of breakfast and it was very
important that he do it right or it just wouldn't taste the same.
He would open the biscuits so that he had a top and a bottom. He

would scoop the gravy out of the bowl with the ladle and pour the gravy all over his biscuits. Once the gravy had sufficiently covered the biscuits enough to satisfy him, he would then flip the biscuits over in his plate. This would expose the undersides of each. By doing it this way he could chop the biscuit into little pieces with his fork and he could savor each bite.

This particular morning, he was so excited to go to school that he skipped the biscuit flipping part and went right to cutting. He just couldn't afford to waste any more time. "Decker Davis! You have on two different pairs of sneakers!" His momma had one hand on her hip and another hand was flipping an egg over-easy for his daddy. Decker was amazed how she could talk, cook, and then be able to catch such details like mix-matched shoes, and he hadn't even noticed. He tried to shove more biscuits and gravy than he normally would into his mouth with each bite before going all the way back to his room to fix this shoe calamity. It was going to take precious time, time he didn't have this morning. Decker finished off his biscuits and gravy, mopping up the last little puddle of gravy with his finger then ran back to his room to find the right shoe.

Once he finally found the right shoe hiding under the bed he made the switch and headed back to the kitchen to grab his book satchel. "Decker, you be sure and stay with Mr. Martin today. He is going to bring you home. Got that?" Decker was already on the way out the back door. "YES MA'AM!" He ran the entire distance from the house to the end of the long winding gravel road that connected his house to the main road. He was out of breath when he reached the main road. He dropped his book satchel on the ground and leaned it against the mailbox. He had so much on his mind, all courtesy of a little girl that he couldn't wait to see in school.

The bus rolled to a stop with tires crunching the gravel as it swerved into the wide opening of Decker's driveway. The door swung open and as he started up the stairs, he caught his foot on the first step and fell forward. He caught himself before his head hit the top step, but he couldn't get his knees out of the way. They smacked into the side of the second step. He winced but it wasn't enough to dampen his enthusiasm. He looked up and saw Mr. Johns smiling and shaking his head. "You in a hurry this morning, Mr. Davis? Slow down a little. This bus won't leave without you, but aren't you forgetting something?" Decker looked down at his shoes out of instinct, but they were correct. He couldn't think what he had forgotten. "Your books, Deck, your books, kiddo." Decker realized he had left his book satchel by the mailbox. He backed up quickly and grabbed his books. This time he slowed down and took each step firmly and correctly. He was not about to fall again, his knee hurt enough already. He took the seat right behind Mr. Johns like he always did.

The bus rolled along heading towards Lonnie Buckles, but Decker could see that he wasn't at the stop like he normally was. He was dreading the encounter with Lonnie and he was relieved when he saw that he wasn't there. Mr. Johns made the slow swerve into the Buckles driveway and stopped the bus completely. Decker rose a little from his seat to see if he could see Lonnie running up his road towards the bus, but all Decker could see was piles of junk everywhere. The bus was quiet; Mr. Johns actually shut the bus off and walked down the steps. That wasn't abnormal for him to do, he liked to try to give the kids as much time as he thought he could afford.

Decker remembered that time that everybody in their houses overslept; his daddy was gone on one of those rescue missions down in Biloxi after a hurricane hit there and it was just him, his momma, and sister. His daddy was usually up early and got everybody else up. In fact, Decker used to think that his daddy never slept because he was always awake. His momma forgot to set an alarm clock and his sister was not an early riser at all. She was a bad morning person. Everybody in the house knew to give her some space in the morning and not to speak to her until she spoke to you. His daddy would tease him by telling him that he used to have a big brother, but he disappeared one morning after he accidently spoke to Heather in the morning before she was ready.

That morning, he ran to the bus like he did today but that day, he hadn't brushed his teeth or combed his hair. Mr. Johns kicked a few rocks and made a circle around the bus. When he felt like he had waited as long he could without making all the kids late for school, Mr. Johns climbed back on the bus, started it, shut the door, and resumed his route. Decker was relieved that Lonnie wasn't on the bus this morning but was also curious why. He felt like Lonnie was too mean to get sick and enjoyed terrorizing all the kids at school too much.

Chapter 28

BRETT WOKE UP MONDAY MORNING THE SAME way he always did, hungover. His head was pounding like someone was inside his skull trying to smash their way out with a hammer and the route they were taking this morning was directly through his eye sockets. He slowly rolled over and put his feet on the floor that was littered with dirty clothes and discarded hamburger wrappers from Lee's Place. It was a beer and burger joint on the edge of town where he and his friends liked to hang out. None of the respected citizens of Webb or Sumner ever went there. Brett and his friends had been there most of the day Sunday shooting pool and getting drunk.

Brett's best friend was a semi-loser named Charlie Scott. The only reason he wasn't a complete loser like Brett was because he was a mechanic in town and held down a steady job at Busters Garage. He was actually a pretty good mechanic from what all the folks in town said, they just didn't like to be around him because he always smelled like a combination of diesel fuel and B.O. He was kinda fat so he grew up with the nickname Chub so that's what everybody in town called him, Chub. He didn't seem to mind.

Decker always thought it was kinda mean to call people names since he had been called his share, but if Chub didn't mind then he guessed it was ok. Decker remembered a time when he was in Milholen's Drug Store one day with his momma when Chub walked in. He was picking up some medicine or something and had to walk by Decker and his momma. His momma was examining some lipstick colors and Decker was flipping through a rack of comic books when Chub walked by. Decker didn't notice anyone come in as he was deeply involved in *The Hulk* comic book he had in his hand, but he caught a whiff of something that he absolutely did not like. As Decker was prone to do, he hollered to his momma who was on the next aisle to let her know that, "Something STINKS! It smells like stinky feet and farts!" His momma slid the lipstick tube back into the spot she had found it, walked over to Decker in the next aisle, took the comic book from this hand, turned to smile at Mr. Milholen and said, "Thank you", and ushered Decker out of the drug store.

She had a nice firm grip on his arm as she nearly dragged him through the door. He knew from the grip she had on him that he had done something wrong, but he was at a loss. He also knew he was about to find out by way of a swift smack on the backside, or if it wasn't too bad of an offense, she would sort of smack him in the back of the head. He liked the head smacks way more than the butt smacks. If she took time to grab one of his arms to smack him on the backside with her other hand, he had seriously messed up.

As they got to the sidewalk in front of Milholen's, he felt the smack on the back of the head. She also realized that in her haste to dole out some punishment, Decker was unsure of the reason and he had walked out of the store with *The Hulk* comic book in his hand. She reached into her purse, fished out a dime, handed it to him, and told him to run back in and give Mr. Milholen the dime. He did as he was told but he was really confused now. She never let him buy anything when he was in trouble. He ran back into the store with the dime in his hand and when he got to counter where Mr. Milholen was always working on something, he put the dime on the counter and told Mr. Milholen that it was for the comic book and they were in a hurry because something in the store just smelled too bad to stay any longer. He turned and ran back out to the sidewalk where she was waiting. "Decker Davis! You never shout out loud in public that something stinks! What's the matter with you?! You know better than to behave like that!" She grabbed his arm and began the walk down the sidewalk to where she had parked the car. It was one of those quick hurried walks where Decker had to work pretty hard to keep up or risk getting dragged.

Brett stumbled to the bathroom and threw up in the bowl. He always felt a little better after throwing up. He walked down the hall, passed through the living room, and went into the kitchen. He opened the refrigerator, surveyed what was inside which was a tub of butter, some moldy cheese, and two bottles of *Pabst Blue Ribbon*. He grabbed a *Blue Ribbon*, opened it, and took a long drink. He headed out the front door to the chicken coup where he roused a few hens from nesting and stole 4 eggs from them.

He made it back inside where he cracked the eggs and threw them in a frying pan that he had to retrieve from the sink. "Get up, you worthless little fart! Eggs will be ready in a minute!" He scraped what remained from yesterday's eggs out of the pan and lit the stove. "Lonnie! Get your lazy ass up, I said! Your gonna miss the bus again and I ain't haulin' your lazy butt to school! You can walk!" Brett dumped the now cracked and scrambled eggs into the frying pan. He mumbled that his little brother was good for nothing but sleeping and eating. He headed down the hall to Lonnie's room, slammed the door open, and started to yell at him some more but he stopped when he saw that Lonnie wasn't there. His room wasn't in much better shape than Brett's, but he could tell he hadn't been there. He walked through the rest of the house and checked the back porch.

Sometimes when it was too hot in the house, Lonnie would sleep on the back porch because it was much cooler, unless there was a hole in the screen and the skeeters would eat you alive. Brett had put tape in several places around the back porch to cover the holes in the screen; he didn't care much for skeeters. He hated being the guardian of his little brother; it was just too much responsibility and he never missed an opportunity to tell Lonnie how much he hated being his guardian. One time when Decker was with his daddy at the bait store, Brett came in with Chub and Lonnie, they were all headed out to the lake to go fishing. Lonnie accidently knocked over a rack of fishing lures that were for sale.

Decker heard the crash and knew exactly what it was because a few other customers had knocked it over too. It was a wobbly display and Decker didn't like it because he was the one who had to pick it back up and put all the lures back on it. That was dangerous work to Decker because the little hooks on the lures would poke his fingers if he wasn't careful, so when he heard the crash it really made him mad that he would have to pick them all up, but even worse because he was sure without even looking that Lonnie Buckles had done it. When he came, he saw Brett hitting Lonnie in the face. He wasn't really hitting him but slapping him and it looked pretty hard to Decker. For a minute, Decker felt sorry for Lonnie. Decker had had his share of spankin's but nobody had ever slapped him in the face before. Lonnie was trying to block the slaps with his arms and hands but that just made Brett madder and he started hitting him harder. Decker felt like he needed to hide, he really felt uncomfortable watching Lonnie get smacked in the face and head like that.

Just when he was about to turn and go back into the storeroom he saw his daddy catch Brett's arm in mid-air, as he was about to hit Lonnie again. "That's enough, Brett." Decker could see Brett's eyes as he seemed like he was surprised that someone was stopping him from hitting Lonnie. Then he saw Brett just get really mean looking and he was really angry. "Get your hands off me, Sheriff! He's mine to discipline any way I feel like so mind your own damn business!" The sheriff tightened his grip on Brett's wrist, which was still frozen in the place that his daddy had stopped it. Decker could tell his daddy was tightening his grip because Brett's face started to change from mean and angry to more pain and scared.

Chub saw what was happening to his friend, Brett, and took a step toward Decker's daddy. "Chub, one more step and I will break his arm off and beat you to death with it." Decker's daddy towered over these two and even though Chub was fat, Decker's daddy made even him look small. Chub froze right where he heard the booming voice and Decker figured it would have been cool to see his daddy yank Brett's arm off and then start beating Chub with it. He saw the image in his head and actually felt kinda bad because he was enjoying it. The sheriff turned his stare from Chub back to Brett. "Not in my store you don't, Brett. Don't ever let me catch you hittin' this boy again or I won't be so nice next time." His voice was calm when he said it. Brett didn't respond. Decker knew that was a mistake for him not to respond.

When his daddy was serious, he expected you to acknowledge that you understood him. A simple "yes, sir" was all it took and everything would be fine but Brett didn't understand the rules like Decker did. The sheriff now pulled Brett really close to him to where the two men were nearly nose-to-nose. "I said do you understand me, Brett!" Decker had heard that voice too, this voice meant impending doom and required swift and decisive action, and this was where a simple "yes, sir" might not work anymore. This was very dangerous ground for Brett to be on. Decker was pleased to see that Brett wasn't as dumb as he thought he was when he heard Brett say, "I understand!" The sheriff let Brett's arm go as soon as he heard what he needed to hear.

Brett grabbed his wrist and rubbed it to help the pain. Brett gave Chub a mean look, and told both Lonnie and Chub that it was time to go and he didn't need any stinkin' bait from this trash heap – they could dig up some worms when they got to the lake. And with that, all three left the bait store. Decker was still frozen in place when he realized that Lonnie was looking directly at him. He saw a look on Lonnie's face that he never thought he would ever see. He saw the look that Decker gets when he hears his daddy coming up the driveway after his momma has given him one of those "wait till your daddy gets home". Lonnie looked scared.

Brett continued to talk to himself about how much he was gonna beat that kid as soon as he found him. They didn't have a phone at the Buckles' house, but even if they did, he wouldn't know who to call and sure wasn't going to call the police. He wasn't too concerned because Lonnie had run off before, but he always came back, or the police brought him back. He finished his eggs, found what he thought were some relatively clean jeans to put on along with a t-shirt, found the keys to the truck, and out the door he went.

Chapter 29

THE SHERIFF WAS DOWNSTAIRS HAVING COFFEE when Decker's momma came into the kitchen. There was never a time that anyone in the house woke up before his daddy. After their normal morning kiss, she started making the biscuits and gravy that Decker would later inhale in a hurry to catch the bus. He told her what was in the paper as she made breakfast. He always skipped over the clips that said anything about him or any subject he just wanted to avoid. He ran out of coffee so he made another pot and sat down at the kitchen table again. "What are your plans today?" She was cutting perfectly round biscuits out of the dough she had pounded together.

She used an old glass she had and she would just press it into sheet of dough and pull out a biscuit. Decker had only been away one time to see her do it. He had been sick, actually he had eaten a bunch of candy that he found in his toy box he had hidden there a few Halloweens back and had forgotten about it. When he discovered it, he thought he had discovered a gold mine. It all looked the same as the day he got it. After he ate most all of it, he started to feel sick.

His stomach started growling and rumbling and making noises that he could actually hear. He figured it had to have been the *Mounds* bars. They weren't his favorite because they had coconut in them but when he found the stash in the toy box, he felt like it was best if he at it all before he got caught. After his stomach started making noises he got a really bad case of the squirts. He ran into the bathroom but it all came out so fast he didn't make it. At the time, he couldn't remember ever having made such a mess in his pants. He stood there in the bathroom not knowing what to do. He threw the squirt-spotted underwear in the tub and figured he could clean them later, but later never came. He couldn't leave the comfort of the toilet. Every time he tried to get up and go back to his room, the squirts would hit him again. It was like they knew when he was trying to leave and made him dash back to the toilet. He thought he had the situation under control until he ran out of toilet paper. Then he really panicked.

He weighed his options as best he could and decided he would have to holler for his momma to bring some toilet paper. He did and she did, but she spotted the dirty underwear in the tub and that was the end of the secret. He had to tell her about the squirts, the dirty shorts, and the candy stash from last Halloween. The morning he saw her make biscuits was the morning she brought him into the kitchen to make sure she could watch him. There was a little breakfast nook that nobody ever used that she turned into a little bed he could lay down in while she made breakfast. He laid there in the nook and watched her make those perfectly round biscuits.

"Are you going to arrest that little Buckles boy today?" He put down his paper and took a sip of coffee. He set the coffee cup back in the saucer. "Honey, he's just a boy, I just need to talk some sense into him. Lord knows nobody will talk any sense into him in that house he lives in." Lois never stopped cutting the biscuits out of the dough and never turned around to look at him when she spoke. "He's a bully, he beat up a little girl…probably could have broken her arm from what Decker says AND he beat up our baby." The sheriff picked up the coffee cup again only to realize that it was empty, so he got up to pour another cup. "Yes, he did all that and he is still just a boy. You know, I think he may have done something for our boy that nobody else has been able to do so far." He waited to see if she would ask him what that was, and she waited to see if he would finish the thought. There was a pause with nothing but the soft noise of her cutting biscuits. "Ok, let's hear it. What did that bully do for our baby?"

The sheriff had the cup of coffee in his hand and he walked up and stood beside her so he could look at her face. "He made him stand up for himself…well maybe not for himself but he stood up for that little girl. Honey, I would never teach him to be violent and punch people, but a bully only knows one thing… force. Our son punched another kid in the nose so he could get to the bully that was tormenting his friend. He's never cared enough about anyone or anything to punch back. Don't you see? Didn't you see the light in our boy's eyes when she was around? I know he's only in fifth grade, but that girl flipped a switch in our baby that we couldn't." Lois stopped cutting biscuits for a minute, turned towards him, crossed her arms, and spoke. "I see all that too, Elmer Davis, but settling things with fists is no way to understand how to solve problems." He walked back over to the kitchen table and sat down and as always with Decker's daddy, he had the last word. "Neither is throwing an 11-year-old boy in the county jail." He didn't see it, but Lois actually smiled as she finished the biscuit cutting. She knew he was right, but she wasn't going to let him know it. It was good time for a break in the conversation anyway because Bubba showed up at the back door. He never knocked, and he never used the front door, he just came in. He had been with Decker's daddy for so long that nobody ever thought a thing about it. Bubba was as much a part of their family as anyone was. "Good morning, Sheriff". He turned and saw Lois at the oven about to shove a pan of biscuits in. "Good morning, Lois." Bubba got greetings from both Lois and the sheriff. "Sit down, Bubba, breakfast will be ready in about twenty minutes, pour yourself some coffee if you want some."

The sheriff could tell there was something wrong as Bubba was very jittery and sweating. Bubba was always sweating but he usually didn't start until after they had finished breakfast. "No, thank you, Lois, the sheriff and I need to get going this morning. There is some police work to do." The sheriff sat up in his chair. "Can't we have breakfast first, Bubba? What could be all fired important that it can't wait until after breakfast?" Bubba looked around like he was looking for someone else in the room to help him. "I think it's best you grab your hat and we just get going." The sheriff felt uneasy now, Bubba never wanted to skip breakfast. "Ok, Bubba." The sheriff got it, poured a thermos of coffee, grabbed his hat, and both men left through the back screen door. It screeched as it slammed shut.

Chapter 30

AFTER THEY WERE THROUGH THE BACK DOOR, Bubba took the lead to the car. He was walking so fast that the sheriff had a hard time keeping up with him. "Bubba, we aren't the volunteer fire department today are we? You wanna tell me what's goin' on?" Bubba reached the car before the sheriff and he immediately went to the driver's side, something that he never did. "Sheriff, I'd rather you just get in the car. I will tell you on the way there." The sheriff stopped and looked back at the house then turned back towards to car. "Ok, Bubba, I trust you, let's go."

Once they were in the car, Bubba put both his hands on the steering wheel and paused before he reached to start the car. "Old Man Barlow opened up the hardware store this morning. He needed to go through some boxes in the dumpster before he opened for business so when he went to the back alley where the dumpster is, he found Lonnie Buckles lying beside the bunker. At first, he thought he was asleep, the way he was curled up. He yelled at him to get the hell up and get out of his alley, but he didn't move. He swears he didn't kick the boy, but I know he did, he's mean that way, but he didn't move so when he put his hands on him to shake him awake, he said he knew something was wrong cause the boy was stiff and wouldn't budge. Turns out he had been stabbed in the stomach. The coroner is there now but I told them that they couldn't move the boy until you had a chance to look things over. You are good at figuring stuff out, so they are waiting for you. We need to get there in a hurry. I just hate seeing that boy laying there. I've never seen anything like it, actually made me sick to my stomach. I couldn't help it, but I heaved a clod right there when I saw him." The sheriff processed the information as best he could.

It was Monday and he certainly wasn't expecting this kind of information to smack him in the face this early. "He's dead?" Bubba kept driving but turned to look at the sheriff like he had just asked a silly question, which was something he never had the opportunity to do. To Bubba, Elmer Davis was one of the smartest guys he had ever met. "Uh, we wouldn't call the coroner if he was alive, Elmer." The sheriff shook his head in amazement of his own stupid question and let out a huge breath. Was Bubba talking about the kid that his son had just been in a fight with? The same kid that made his wife so mad that she wanted him to arrest him just 15 minutes ago. What just happened?

He was really struggling with the death of Lonnie Buckles but then the reality of the situation hit him, and he tried to tell himself that he was over thinking things; he needed to wait until he got to Barlow's Hardware Store and he would know more. "How do you know he was stabbed and did you at least step away from the scene before you chucked your supper?" The sheriff had always known that Bubba was really weak in the knees when it came to blood; Bubba fainted on the sheriff when they went to handle his first car accident fatality. It was a single car accident, but it was a messy one. Nobody knows for sure what happened to this day, but the car lost control on a gravel road that connected Tippo and Sharkey. The road wasn't used much other than by farmers and if you tried to use it as a short cut and happened to get behind a tractor, you were stuck for a while. When they got to the scene, the car had somehow lost control and flipped several times. The car ended up upside down in the middle of a cotton field. The car was easy enough to see but they had to search for quite a while to find the driver. The cotton was just about in full bloom; it was as high as it was going to get that year, so they had to go row by row until they found him. It looked to the sheriff like he had been catapulted out of the car through the back window because the front and side windows were smashed but still intact. Sliding through that back window sliced that poor fella in two pieces. The sheriff had to admit that it was a pretty gruesome sight, but he handled it just fine. Bubba did not. "Answer the question Bubba, how did you know he was stabbed?" Bubba kept his eyes straight ahead on the road, he may have even accelerated a little bit. "You'll see when we get there."

Chapter 31

❦

DECKER ENJOYED THE BUS RIDE TO SCHOOL THIS morning more than he could ever remember in his whole life. He wasn't being picked on by that dumb ole Lonnie; he had the front seat behind Mr. Johns all to himself. He kept his nose to the bus window as he looked at all the fields and farms on the way to school. He thought of what he would do in school. How would he react if he was asked another question? He even thought about Jeannine helping him clean out BettyJean's stall. The thoughts that flooded his head were overwhelming.

He didn't even know the bus had arrived at school and hadn't even noticed that every kid on the bus had already gotten off the bus. He felt the nudge on his shoulder and turned to see Mr. Johns standing over him, smiling. "Mr. Davis, daydreaming this early in the morning can be a good and bad thing but you better get your mind to work, see you this afternoon." Mr. Johns

turned and walked down the steps. Decker followed him down
the steps, and before he could get two steps away, Mr. Johns said,
"Forgetting something again, Deck?" This time Decker didn't
have to look at his shoes, he knew exactly what Mr. Johns was
talking about. He ran back up the steps of the bus and grabbed
his book satchel. He ran through the front doors of the school
and got called down by the assistant principal, Mr. Hardwick.
The kids all called him *Mr. Headthick* when he wasn't around.
Decker wasn't sure why they called him that, but he didn't like
him much. He was always in the halls and bathrooms, checking
on things and yelling at kids to get busy or get to class. He had a
beard and Decker always thought he smelled like peanut butter.
He would snap his fingers as he walked through the hall. Decker
got to the classroom and went straight to his desk. She wasn't
there yet which he was kind of excited about because he wanted
to have all his stuff put away in his desk before she arrived. He
was seeing the classroom differently than he had ever seen it. The
blackboard was bigger, the teacher's desk seemed to be pressed
against his, the only thing he didn't like was that he couldn't see
the other kids like he used to. It was always easy to spot trouble
when he could keep his eye on it and up until Monday, everyone
in class was trouble.

     She brushed against him as she put her stuff away. He had
somehow slipped back into daydream mode and she snuck up on
him. He turned to see her but didn't know what to say. He had
never greeted anyone in the morning besides his momma and
daddy so wasn't sure what the rules were or if there were any. He
thought about a handshake. He had seen the grown-ups do it
all the time and a few grown-ups that had met him while he was
with his daddy had actually shaken his hand. The only thing his

daddy told him about handshakes was to make sure you grip a man's hand tight, but he never told him if he should grip a girl's hand tight. He thought about it a little while longer and decided he wasn't comfortable with the handshake and settled on, "Hi".

She seemed rushed as she rummaged through her own book satchel, but she managed to say, "Hi" back to Decker, but she didn't look at him when she said it. Usually when his sister did that, she was mad at him about something, but he hadn't done anything yet, so she couldn't be mad at him. "Something wrong?" He was careful not say it too loud. Even though he was in the front of the classroom he was still careful about not drawing attention to himself. "Well I don't have a pencil that is one thing that is wrong, the second is that I knew I didn't have a pencil so granddaddy stopped by Milholen's and let me get a new one before school but they had the street blocked off cause something was going on at the hardware store and the police wouldn't let anyone through that street so then we had to take the old route which made me late and I don't like being late so if you tell me you are going to meet me at a time then you better meet me at that time Decker Davis." Decker usually didn't get dressed down like this unless it was his momma and he was at a loss for what to do or say. This was Jeannine Martin talking to him like she was his momma so all he could manage to say in return was, "Yes, ma'am".

The teacher walked in as Decker was reaching for his paper tablet. He had forgotten to take it out when watching Jeannine get organized as she was giving him the what-for about being late for meeting her. He laid his pencil on top of Jeannine's desk as the teacher was walking up to her desk. He never used it anyway, he just listened as best he could and tried to remember it all. Everything he wrote down looked like gibberish. She looked down at the pencil and he could see a smile come across her face. She looked over at him and started to say something, but the teacher already tapped her desk with her pointing stick, which meant it was time for class to start. From this spot in the classroom, the rustling of the desks and all the kids standing up to recite the Pledge of Allegiance sounded different. It seemed noisier from the front row. Once every kid was firmly in place beside their desks, the teacher would begin and then they would all follow along. Decker really enjoyed the Pledge of Allegiance because it was one of the only times in class that he felt a part of the class. As best as he could recall, his sister taught him the Pledge of Allegiance before he ever set foot in school and he was the only kid in first grade who knew the Pledge before all the other kids. It was the last time that he was ahead of the class on any subject. Jeannine Martin had done her research at the library on Monday and was about to change all that.

Chapter 32

⁕

THE SHERIFF ARRIVED AT THE ALLEY BEHIND THE hardware store where he saw the caution crime scene tape already strung up from the corner of the building to a fence post that was a part of the open field behind the hardware store and all the other stores along the main drag of town and the dumpster that Milholen's and Barlow's shared. The coroner's wagon was parked in the side alley just down from Milholen's, blocking any access to the back alley from that angle. The Webb PD was already on the scene.

The County Sheriff and City PD got along extremely well so the sheriff wasn't worried about anyone screwing around with the crime scene before he got there. He saw the chief of police standing in the back alley smoking a cigarette talking to the coroner. Bubba stopped the car and blocked the only other access there might be to the back alley. The sheriff exited the Scout and walked towards the two men standing there. "Morning, fellas. You already got a good grasp on what happened?" The chief of police was a young man who had lived in Webb almost all his life. His family moved to Webb when he was in elementary school so for all practical purposes, he was a Webbster. That's what they called anyone who grew up in Webb and never left. He was a nice enough guy, but Decker's daddy used to say that he was just a little too young for the job and hoped he would grow into it. His name was Aubrey Bigelow and he wanted more than anything to be mayor and then later go on to the capitol in Jackson. He was a smooth talker, but his daddy said he wasn't always to be trusted to do everything he said he would do and that any man who wanted to be a career politician had a screw loose. "Morning, Elmer. I guess you know it's the youngest Buckles boy. Makes me sick to my stomach to see this. Let me show you what we know and what we think." The chief started walking towards the dumpster and the coroner motioned with his head to follow him to where Lonnie was still lying on the other side of the dumpster, where the sheriff could not see him.

The coroner was also the town's funeral home director and mortician. That's pretty much how he got the job. He had gone to med school but just never liked dealing with patients, so he came back home from Starkville, bought Anderson's Funeral Home and went into business for himself. The mayor appointed him coroner long before Decker was born. Decker's daddy would say that Buster Halfacre was a good guy, but he was more comfortable with dead people than he was with living people. The sheriff always thought that was just a little strange. The sheriff followed Aubrey around the dumpster and saw the little boy curled up in the fetal position with his face pressed against the bottom side of the dumpster as if he was trying to hide his face from view.

There was a visibly small pool of blood around his torso area but not so much that the sheriff could see. "Sheriff, we haven't moved the boy yet. We've taken a ton of pictures, but we wanted you to be here to take it all in before we tried to turn him over. We've checked his pulse and he's gone for sure, but Buster here managed to get a temp on the body and says that the temp along with the rigor that has set in already, he's been gone for at least four hours." Buster nodded in agreement with the chiefs' statements then added, "Now that you are here, and we can move the body, we can get a better look at him and figure out some more stuff." The coroner put on a new set of gloves; they made that popping sound when he got them stretched into place on all five fingers of both hands. He bent down and gently put his hand on Lonnie's shoulder and he rolled him on his back so they could have a look at his front side. The chief let out a gasp but the sheriff held steady.

Lonnie had been beaten up pretty good. One of his eyes had swelling under it and he had a busted lip and quite a lot of blood around his lips. But as Buster rolled him over they saw both of Lonnie's hands wrapped around what looked to be a pretty large stainless-steel knife that was still firmly stuck between his chest bone and his stomach. "Good God, Amighty" came out of Aubrey's mouth before he realized that he said it out loud. The chief, with his eyes set firmly on life in politics, tried very hard to hide his southern accent, but when he got rattled, it came through loud and clear. He clearly meant to say *Good God, Almighty,* but the scene of a little boy laying on the ground in front of him holding the knife that was stuck in his chest caused him to revert back to Webbster.

Lonnie was already pretty stiff, so when they rolled him over, he remained in the fetal position. He now looked like a dog doing some tricks, but this was no trick. Lonnie was as dead as a doornail and he died painfully. "You think that boy had enough of Brett's backhands and killed himself? I read an article about teen suicide the other day. It's going around all over the East Coast, maybe that's what this is? Do you think that is what it was, Elmer?" The sheriff actually gave it a thought for a second as he didn't like to get stuck in one immediate train of thought. That was how mistakes were made. "I don't think so, Aubrey, but we are sure gonna need Buster to do a thorough exam on this one." The chief turned his back on the scene for just a minute and took in three long gulps of air. Before he turned back around, he squinted his eyes and looked at the sun. "That little boy won't see another sunrise. Damn. What do you see, Elmer? Talk out loud. I've known you my whole life and you process information better than anyone I know." Elmer bent down next to Lonnie and put his hand on the boy's face as he had done so many times with Decker.

It was a loving touch; a touch that he hoped Donnie could feel in heaven. He ran through his head that this boy didn't deserve to grow up the way he did. He had to fend for himself way too much and he only mimicked what he saw his idiot older brothers doing. "Well, from the looks of this knife and where it's stuck in his chest, it had to have punctured a lung and maybe punctured his heart, or at least nicked it. That would explain the blood around his upper and lower lips and around his nostrils. Every time he tried to breathe, his lungs would kick out some blood with the air. There sure isn't much blood around this body, just a little pool, which to me means that maybe someone brought him here and dumped him before he was dead. I don't like that he isn't wearing any shoes and I especially don't like that his pants are unzipped." The coroner took all the samples from the scene that he could and then started taking pictures of everything." The chief took a step back and let another *God Amighty* out before he knew it.

The sheriff asked Buster how long it would take him to do an autopsy and Buster told him he could have it for sure by midnight tonight. He said he would make it his only job for the day and sometimes things went fast and other times they went slow. He didn't want to miss a thing on this little boy, *God rest his soul,* as he put it. Buster took out two more sets of gloves and handed them to the sheriff and the chief. "I'm gonna need you two to help me get him in the wagon." The two men helped Buster get Lonnie into a body bag, zipped up, and into the coroner's wagon.

By now, people were trying to see what was going on, but thankfully they had Lonnie in the wagon and out of view before any of the merchants and townspeople saw what the sheriff now wishes he could un-see. Buster drove off with Lonnie in the back, clutching a knife that was jammed in his chest. The sheriff and the chief had a discussion about what to say if anyone from the paper asked because they needed to have the same story. Then the sheriff told Aubrey something that Aubrey was clearly not prepared for. "Aubrey, because of some stuff that happened this weekend between my boy and the Buckles kid, I could easily be considered a suspect. I expect that's what Brett is gonna holler when I tell him. Nothing could be further from the truth, but I know the Buckles, especially Brett, and he will take any excuse to blame me for this, or worse, Bobby Martin." The sheriff told him the story about what happened Sunday and that made it easier for the chief to understand where the sheriff was coming from. "That family is a mess for sure, but that boy sure didn't deserve to die with a knife stuck in his chest in a back alley slid up against that smelly dumpster."

The sheriff took one final long look at the entire scene from where he was standing to make sure he took it all in. He had never had a murder inside Webb city limits and he wanted to make sure he didn't screw up. "Aubrey, did ya'll pick anything up from the scene before I got here? What am I missing?" Without hesitation, Aubrey said they hadn't picked anything up except a couple of old valve stems and a valve stem puller. "Ok, did you bag 'em?" Aubrey looked a little embarrassed but tried to recover and say that they weren't near the crime scene. He said when he first saw the boy he chucked his breakfast in the field and when he had his hands on his knees all bent over he saw the stems and the puller laying there in the grass. He picked them up and threw them further out in the field to relieve some stress. He was embarrassed at first that he couldn't keep his breakfast down when he saw a dead boy, but now he was embarrassed that he forgot that everything around the crime scene was off-limits to touch.

The sheriff just smiled and shook his head. "It's probably nothing but I'd like you to find those stems and the puller. Be sure and wear gloves when you find them and bag them. Also, bag everything that is in the dumpster and if it's too big to bag then have your men secure a spot at the station to store it." Aubrey gave Elmer a look like he was crazy. "Elmer, that stuff in that dumpster stinks. I'm not storing it at the station and I have no idea where I threw those stems, geez. I have a pretty good arm and I was letting off some steam!" The sheriff, looked in the direction of the field where Aubrey had thrown the valve stems and then back to the dumpster, then directly at Aubrey, then he took a step toward Aubrey so they were nose-to-nose. "Then you better get busy finding them before it gets hot. The forecast says it's gonna be unseasonably warm today. And rent a warehouse for the contents of the dumpster, I don't care if you store it in your damn living room. I don't care either way but I gotta go talk to some folks." With that, the sheriff turned around and motioned for Bubba to leave and they both climbed into the Scout with Bubba still in the driver's seat. "Are we going to see Brett?" The sheriff didn't answer but he shook his head. He was deep in thought.

This could get ugly if he didn't handle this right. He was trying to figure out how to get word to Donnie, who was in a different country fighting a war and worse, he was afraid that Bobby Martin sure might be a prime suspect. He just didn't think that Bobby had it in him to kill someone, much less a kid, but the kid that was lying next to that dumpster had just this last weekend beaten up his little girl. He actually tried to make something good out of Lonnie's death; maybe they would get Donnie out of combat and let him come home. Then it hit him that that kid with a knife in his stomach had beaten up his kid too.

This sure was turning out to be a terrible mess. "No, I am not but you are. I need you to find Brett and tell him what's happened. You can drop me off at the Sheriff's Office before you head out to the Buckles place. I also want you to stop by the coroner's office and make sure that Buster got started on the autopsy. He will piddle fart around at first, but I can't afford to

have him wait to get started. I need that information way before
the midnight deadline he set for himself. I want to call the local
recruiting office and see if they can help me get word to Donnie.
Then I'm going to pick up Bobby. He is the first suspect." Bubba
was a little apprehensive about telling Brett his little brother was
dead. He knew Brett was a hot head and could do some really
stupid stuff when he was mad, so he wasn't thrilled about the
task, and it must have shown in his facial expression. "Good
Lord, Bubba. You're a deputy sheriff in Tallahatchie County…
now act like it." The sheriff would get frustrated with Bubba
because he sometimes lacked the confidence necessary to carry
out the duties of a deputy sheriff. Bubba was a good man with a
sensitive personality, he just needed to be told from time to time
that he was doing a good job, and that would provide him with
enough emotional fuel to give him the confidence to do his job.
"Look, Bubba, you saw the same thing I did. That little boy was
murdered. I have no doubt, but he wasn't wearing any shoes or
shirt and his damn fly was unzipped. I get a terrible feeling that
his last few hours on this Earth were terrible. I can't catch the
person who did this without you. I need you to act like a deputy
and be tough, can you do that?" Bubba immediately felt better
the minute that Elmer Davis told him that he needed him. That
was all he needed to hear, and he would bust down walls for the
sheriff if he had to.

Chapter 33

⁂

DECKER SPENT THE DAY SCRIBBLING WITH THE EXTRA pencil HE found in the bottom of his book satchel. He wasn't really writing anything down because he couldn't with his left hand but just felt like he needed to look like he was writing stuff down. He would try to write his name but when he was done it looked like how he wrote his name when he was first learning to write. He wondered why a person favored one hand over the other and how that happened. *It would be fun to be able to write with either hand*, he thought.

Jeannine would look at him from time to time, see that he was doodling on his paper tablet and would just shake her head and smile. They were learning about the 13 Colonies. This was right up Decker's alley! He loved everything about American History and loved to try to put himself in the story as it made the story more interesting. His sister read him the story about *Paul*

Revere one night and how he had to ride his horse really fast into town so he could tell everybody that the British were coming.

That weekend, he threw a saddle on BettyJean and tried to get her to run fast but she wouldn't cooperate. She got up to a slow trot, but he still rode around the farm yelling at the chickens that the British were coming. It didn't sound very good because when BettyJean just trotted, it bounced him up and down in the saddle so much that his words came out choppy. It reminded him of when he would try to talk into a fan and his voice sounded weird. It wasn't long before BettyJean got tired and wanted to stop, so when he wasn't concentrating on her head like he was supposed to, she reached back and bit him on the leg. She got him a good one that pinched a blue mark on the side of his calf. He tried to get even by yanking on her mane, but she didn't even notice. He thought for sure that she just peeled her lips back and smiled at him. He gave up on trying to be *Paul Revere* for the day and walked her back to the barn.

The bell for recess went off. That was the most anxious time of the day for Decker and all the students. The teacher was as adamant about order in preparation for recess as she was about being in order for lunch. All the students had to put things away in their desks, clean the tops of their desks, and then stand for inspection. Once she felt like the room was neat enough to go outside and play she would give the go-ahead sign to head out the back door onto the playground. The school was in a U-shape, so each class had a back door that led out to the playground. Even when she gave the ok to exit the classroom you had to line up in order of rows in the class.

This was another upside to being in the front row; Decker got to go out to the playground first. Jeannine helped him with putting his stuff away before they were allowed to line up by the back door. Once they were out on the playground, the noise of kids letting out the morning steam was crazy. Decker couldn't do much because his arm was still in a sling. He didn't think he really needed it anymore. He had learned how to hold his arm in just the right spot without the sling and found that if held it in that spot, his collarbone didn't hurt so much. He had to admit that while in the sling his arm didn't hurt at all, but he was tired of answering all the questions about what happened to him. He wanted to start making up stories about how he saved a bunch of orphans from a train wreck or he got caught in a stampede because somehow falling at the concession stand had become very boring and he was tired of telling the story. At least when he was with Jeannine he didn't have to say much as she still did all the talking.

The two were the first out the door of the classroom and onto the playground, so it felt a little strange to Decker. He was used to coming out last and then he would stay on the outer edges of all the activities that sprang to life in a matter of minutes. Luke King and his pals had already started a football game. Although the swelling had gone down, Luke still had two black eyes. Decker thought he looked like a raccoon and apparently the rest of the class thought so too because they started calling him Coon Luke. Decker felt odd hearing another kid get picked on, but he was glad nobody was picking on him that day. He saw the four-square court filled up, the monkey bars had kids hanging everywhere, the tether ball had a line and two boys were already arguing that one "roped" and should be out.

A kickball game had already formed and the jump rope section, where Jeannine like to be because she was the best in school, had already started to make its popping noise each time the rope hit the concrete. Decker thought that when Jeannine was in the rope and the other girls were trying to swing the rope as fast as they could, it sounded like firecrackers going off. "What do you want to do, Decker Davis?" He had no idea. He really couldn't do anything fun because his arm was still in a sling, so he had planned to just walk around and look at stuff like he always did. "I think I will just watch. I can't do much." Jeannine rolled her eyes; he noticed that the more time he spent with her the more he noticed her rolling her eyes. He started to notice that she was pretty dramatic in all her expressions. "Decker Davis! I swear! Stop being so helpless and shy! You still got one good arm so let's use it!" She grabbed his good arm and nearly dragged him to the jump rope court.

When she stepped onto the court, the other girls acted like a queen or somebody important had shown up because they all stopped what they were doing and waited for her. She still had a firm grip on his good arm so while they were all looking at her, she belted out, "This is my friend, Decker Davis. He has one good arm and he is going to work one side of the rope for us!" That was that. All the other girls seemed happy to have Decker on the court with them. One girl dropped her side of the rope and told Decker he could have her spot and she jumped in line. Jeannine lowered her voice and whispered in his ear, "It's not hard. Go on, take the rope and swing it around as fast as you can." From that moment on, she was in charge of the both of them and Decker knew it. He didn't mind at all because it wasn't like bossy in charge or parents in charge or being in charge like a bully, she just always seemed to know what she wanted, when she wanted it, and how she was going to get it, and she certainly wasn't afraid to tell people about it. Decker swung that rope for the entire recess. He had a little trouble at first but figured it out, and for the first time since first grade, the bell signaling recess was over rang and he wasn't relieved.

Chapter 34

꧁

BRETT WAS STILL CURSING HIS LITTLE BROTHER
under his breath as he was sliding into the seat of his truck. He put
the keys in the ignition and started it. It was an ugly truck, but it
was faithful, mainly because Chub helped him keep the engine
running like a top. The truck was a 1960 *Chevy* that Donnie had
picked up from a wreck where the owner of the truck got drunk
one night and tried to make it back to Charleston and hit another
car head-on.

Donnie had told them it was a bad wreck and some people
were killed but the drunk man walked away without a scratch.
Donne said it was because the truck was a beast and was tough
as a tank. The insurance company totaled the truck, so Donnie
repaired it with parts they had all over their property and it
turned out to be a pretty good truck. Brett pushed the clutch,
pushed the gear up into reverse, and was about to back away

from the house when the truck jerked a little then stalled. He depressed the clutch and turned the ignition again and it started. As soon as he pumped the clutch it stalled again.

He was getting mad, very mad; Brett did not like to have trouble with cars, especially this one. He got out, went to the front of the truck, and saw what the problem was. He had parked it a little too close to the house the night before because he was drunk and could actually see that he had rammed into the corner of the back side of the house and the bumper was hung up underneath one of the porch floor beams. He would have to figure a way to pry it loose because he figured if he tried to force it loose by using the accelerator more, he might yank the house down. He found a crowbar on the back porch and started to work the bumper loose from the house. He would try to free the bumper with the crowbar a little and then he would try to back up the truck. Little by little, he managed to loosen the grip the house had on his front bumper. He started the truck again, shoved it in reverse, and gave the truck just a little gas and felt the truck pop loose. He was proud of himself for not tearing down the house and for not ripping the bumper off the truck.

He was tired now and wasn't as concerned about his stupid little brother as he was stopping by the Jackpot. He loved to stop at the Jackpot in the mornings before he went what he called "treasure huntin'", which amounted to nothing more than junk hunting. He would scour the countryside for things in other peoples' barns and yards, if they would let him, for stuff that he thought he could buy from them cheap and resell for a profit. Sometimes he would get permission from the owners and sometimes he wouldn't. That was one of the many reasons Sheriff Davis had arrested Brett in the past.

The entire Buckles property was nothing but junk according to everyone in town, but Brett thought he was sitting on a fortune. He pulled into the Jackpot gravel parking lot. There were already a few other patrons in the bar, but he knew one of the cars was the owner's, a woman named Becky O'Neil. The Jackpot was a metal building with a big gaudy yellow and pink sign that flashed on and off 24 hours a day. It had a few tables and a stage area for a band or singers, but nobody ever performed at the Jackpot anymore. It was just strictly for drinking, poker, and some other stuff that went on in the back rooms. And even though she was quite a bit older than Brett, Becky and Brett had been sort of a couple for a while, but then again, there was gossip around town that everybody had been a couple with Becky. She used to say that she just needed someone to keep Billy's side of the bed warm until he got out. Billy was her husband who went off to Parchman around the same time Brett's daddy had gone off to Parchman. He was a part-time drug dealer and a full-time moonshiner. He ran stills all over the backwoods of Mississippi. Decker had overheard some people in town at Milholen's one day saying that the O'Neil's had the best maple shine in all of Mississippi. It sounded pretty good to Decker because he loved maple syrup. The sheriff got some dirty looks around town after he shut down the O'Neil's illegal operations.

Brett walked into the Jackpot and could see two men in the back playing cards and drinking shots. Becky was behind the bar with a towel over her shoulder like she always did and was smoking a cigar like she always did. Becky loved cigars more than any man ever did. She always had one burning in an ashtray on the bar or she had it stuck in the side of her mouth. "You're in early this morning, sweetie, you need more than drink, don't you?" She winked at Brett and he smiled. He knew his mood would change for the better if he started it off right. "I do need beer but not sure I will have time for the other this morning." She sighed like she was disappointed and reached under the bar and grabbed a *Schlitz* out of the slide-top cooler. She slid the bottle under the opener and pushed down on it which sent the cap falling directly into a can underneath the opener. She wiped the counter and set the bottle in front of Brett. He took a long drink and placed it back on the counter. She softly put her hand on Brett's and rubbed the back of his hand. "You sure? It's slow this morning and I could use some myself. It's half-price for you this morning." Brett smiled and looked at the two men in the back of the bar then looked back at Becky. "I wish I could, can I get a raincheck though? That's a bargain. I gotta go find my idiot brother. He wasn't in his room this mornin'. The little fart probably slept over at Luke Kings again and didn't tell me. He was sassin' me bad last night and I put a pop knot on him. I will make a man outta that boy yet." Becky turned around and put a few things away behind the bar and cleaned some more of the counter as she was talking. She was always cleaning. The bar may have looked like a dump from the outside but on the inside, it was always pretty clean, despite the disgusting patrons who frequented the place.

"Well if you change your mind, you know where to find me, sugar." Brett sat and sipped on his beer for just a little while longer then guzzled the rest of it. He stood and felt for his wallet in one fluid motion. He found it, opened it, and after realizing it had no money in it, he tried to remember the night before. The last he remembered he had almost a hundred dollars in it from selling a whole load of old washing machine motors the day before. He had no idea where the money had gone. He surely hadn't intended to blow a hundred bucks, that was a lot of money. The thought just made him angry, so he fumbled around in his pockets long enough to find a wadded-up dollar bill and threw it down on the counter. He looked at Becky who was already shaking her head in amusement. "You can give me a tip when you have more time, and not the money kind." She smiled and winked again when she said it. He forgot about the missing hundred bucks for a second. She had that effect on him. He thought that if she weren't already married, he would marry her.

He walked out the door of the Jackpot and was blinded by the sunlight for just a second. He fished his truck keys from his front pocket and decided he would shoot by the garage and see if Chub had seen Lonnie. If he hadn't, he had to worry about Lonnie later because he had a big salvage deal working with a construction company in Corinth he had to go meet with and he was going to be gone for the day. He pulled out onto the highway and headed towards Webb. He jammed a *Rolling Stones* 8-track into the dash radio, and *Mick Jagger* immediately started singing *Jumpin' Jack Flash*. He came to the stoplight right before the railroad tracks that led into town. He sat there at the light and saw the police cars blocking the back-alley entrance to stores on the West side of the street. He thought maybe someone had broken into Milholen's again; someone was always breaking into Milholen's and taking all the fun drugs.

That was his description; he didn't figure they were break-ing into the drug store to get drugs for a bad case of gout. He cruised right through the center of town until he reached the garage where Chub worked. He pulled under the awning which used to cover gas pumps. Chub's Garage was a filling station a few years back but the owner caught his wife in bed with a vacuum salesman from Marks. The previous owner nearly beat that vacuum salesman to death. After that, the owner and his wife moved to Charleston to try and work things out. He hadn't heard if they worked it out, but the gas station closed and a greasy fat man from Locke Station bought it and turned it into a garage. He liked to wear sunglasses all the time and his hair was always slicked back with some kind of grease. Even Brett Buckles didn't like being around him and would tell Chub that the man gave him the creeps. His wife wasn't much better; she was rail thin with ample bosoms but with leathery skin.

Brett couldn't remember a time that she didn't have a lit *Camel* hanging out of the side of her mouth, with as much of her bosoms on display as she could get away with, and she like to call everybody "sweetheart". The day they were supposed to move into the apartment behind the filling station, their car broke down on the way into Webb and Chub happened to be passing by and helped him get his car fixed. That's how Chub got the job as a mechanic. Up until that point, Chub took whatever job he could get, and he got fired from most of them. This job as the mechanic was the longest he had ever held down steady employment. The garage was still locked, and Brett looked inside and could see that Chub's *VW* was gone, so he figured he may have had to run over to Sumner that morning to pick up some parts. The owner was always sending him over there or making Chub go with him. Brett decided he couldn't wait around on Chub to show up. If the cops didn't find Lonnie skipping school somewhere in town, he would find him when he got back from Corinth.

Chapter 35

THE SHERIFF WALKED INTO THE OFFICE AND SAW Lavera, as he had every morning for nearly the last ten years. She was a classy looking woman who was always dressed to perfection and kept a full thick head of gray hair. She wore some pearl colored horn rim glasses that made her look a little older than she actually was. He guessed she was around 65 but when she put on her glasses she added a few years. Her husband ran the one and only bean hauling company in North-Central Mississippi and they were pretty well-off, but she liked to keep busy, so she got a job at the Sheriff's Office back in 1953 and had been a fixture around the place ever since then. She was never in a bad mood that the sheriff had ever seen but she was strict. No cussing allowed in earshot of her and you couldn't smoke in the same room with her. She would have none of either and would verbally dress down anyone who dared violate her code of ethics.

The sheriff never had any trouble with either one of those things since he didn't smoke and he rarely cussed. Lois had the same conduct code at home, so it was not as hard for him to conform to as it was for some of the others. Bubba had a little trouble at first because he liked to cuss a blue streak when he was mad and since Bubba got mad easily, he always caught all kinds of hell from Lavera. She said, "Hello" back to him but she added, "It's a shame about that little Buckles kid, Elmer." The sheriff stopped in his tracks then turned to look back at her. "How do you know about that already, Lavera? That's not information I want out to the public yet. I just sent Bubba to the Buckles place to find Brett and break the news to him." She pretended to look for something on her desk, but Elmer knew it was just for theatrics. She was the most organized woman in the office for sure and possibly the most organized woman he had ever met. He also knew that there were no secrets in Lavera's world. She knew everything about everybody. "Buster called just a minute ago and he wants you to call him. Would you like me to get him on the line, Elmer?" Besides Lois and occasionally Bubba, she was the only one in town who ever called him Elmer. "Yeah, please do, but I also want to talk to the marine recruiting sergeant in Sumner. I need him to help me get in contact with Donnie's C.O. in Viet Nam." He started to continue to walk down the hall when she replied. "I already called him…he was in a meeting but would either call you this morning or stop by. He had to be at a recruiting event at the high school." The sheriff shook his head in amazement. She really was the most organized, intuitive person he had ever met. "Thank you, Lavera."

He continued down the hall to his office. He was shaking his head as he entered his office, still amazed at how she anticipated what he would want and had already handled everything. He figured he might just start taking her to crime scenes; she just might be able to be of some help. The phone on his desk rang; he looked at it then looked in the direction of Lavera's desk, geez she was good. He hit the speaker button on the phone, "Sheriff Davis." That was always his phone greeting, good mood or bad, he never wanted the person on the other end of the line to be able to tell what kind of mood he was in or what kind of day he was having. He believed strongly that the sheriff had an obligation to remain sort of neutral in the way he carried himself. "He was molested, Sheriff." Buster had an uneasy elevation to his voice. Child molestation and murder were not occurrences that Webb was used to.

Although he was nervously excited, he was whispering like he was trying to keep a secret with the sheriff. "Are you done with the autopsy, Buster?" There was a long pause on the other end of the line as the sheriff waited patiently for an answer. "Not yet, I just thought you should know right away what we are dealing with here." The sheriff didn't think he could feel worse than he did than when he first saw that little boy laying there next to the dumpster. It sure appeared that he died a painful death and now to find out that he was humiliated as he was being murdered made the sheriff feel even worse. Why in the world would anyone want to hurt that boy? "Thank you, Buster, finish your work and don't miss a lick. I want to catch this son of a bitch who did this." He heard Lavera holler down the hall that there was no need for that type of language. He just shook his head. "Anything else, Buster?" He waited again for a reply, but he sensed that people around the office were listening to the call, so he pulled the phone from the cradle and took it off speaker.

"No, not much. His pants were covered in oil; makes the office here smell bad, that's about it."

The sheriff was about to say something again but Buster enthusiastically interrupted, "Oh, yeah, and the knife, it was stainless steel and it was from Andy's." The sheriff nearly dropped the phone as he had put the phone on his shoulder and was holding it by bending his neck. When he heard the knife was from Andy's, he straightened his head and the phone nearly fell on his desk. He caught it and put it back to his ear. He took a breath. "How the hell do you know that, Buster?" He heard Lavera down the hall again but ignored it. "A few years back, Andy had a guy working for him who was stealing his knives and selling them in Jackson. Andy's knives are the best in the business – sharp as razors and sturdy as a hammer.

Anyway, he started having the handles engraved with the name ANDY'S on it, but he would also engrave STOLEN on the handle so that if anyone tried to sell them at least the pawnshops would have to think twice about buying them. The knife in that little boy was from Andy's." The sheriff let out a sigh; he knew who worked at Andy's too. "Thank you, Buster, and not a word of this to anyone but me, you got that?" Buster didn't waste any time answering the sheriff on that one. "Copy that." He hung up the phone and was staring down at his desk when he heard the knock on his door. He looked up and saw the marine recruiting sergeant standing at his door. "Hi, Sheriff, I heard you wanted to see me, so I stopped by." The sheriff stood up and walked over to the marine and shook his hand.

He explained as much as he cold without revealing that Lonnie had been murdered. He asked if the sergeant could help get in touch with Donnie and bring him home. The sergeant was tactful and quite helpful. He used the sheriff's desk phone to make a few calls. When he was done talking to whoever he was talking to, he told the sheriff that he managed to reach his C.O, but he found out that Donnie's unit was out on a patrol and would not be checking in for at least 24 hours. As soon as they checked in, he would extract Donnie and have him routed back to the states ASAP. He did warn the sheriff that the C.O had mentioned that they had been encountering some pretty heavy resistance and Donnie's unit would probably see some serious combat in the next couple days. He believed the C.O. when he said he would get him pulled as soon as it was humanly possible. When he left the office, the sheriff felt a little better. He knew that the sergeant had also been in combat and understood the loss of a brother as he had lost his brother in some war. The sergeant had a calming demeanor about him and it was exactly the tone that the sheriff needed. Lavera yelling at him about his language this morning wasn't helping him either.

Chapter 36

⁓✦⁓

DECKER COULD HARDLY BELIEVE IT WHEN THE
bell rang for school to let out. He had not realized that the time
had gone by so fast. The teacher yelled some final instructions
as each kid was deciding what to take home with them and what
to leave in their desks. Decker decided he needed to take his
math book home with him and get his sister to help him with
fractions. He really struggled with fractions and couldn't figure
out what function that a fraction played in real life.

He had been to the store with his momma before and he had
actually helped his daddy at the bait shop and never once had he
heard anyone use a fraction. He tried to imagine hearing it one
time, *that will be one dollar and one-fourth, Mr. Davis.* At which point
he would reach in his pocket and pull out one-fourth of a penny
or quarter or whatever. He just didn't get it and truth be known,
he didn't really want to get it. "Decker Davis, stop daydreaming

and let's go, you are going to the library with me. I have something to show you when we get there." Decker snapped out of his daydreaming and finished collecting his books. He shoved them in his book satchel. They didn't seem to fit very well, and he realized that something was keeping the books from resting nicely on the bottom.

He pulled the books back out only to realize that they were now covered in banana goo. He had forgotten to eat his banana at lunch, which was something that never happened. He would toss the carrots in the trash, but he never forgot to eat his banana. Today was a blur for Decker. He seemed like he had something going on at every minute of the day and he had become so busy listening to Jeannine that he had actually forgotten to eat his banana. "That's gross, Decker!" He ran to the back of the class, grabbed some paper napkins that were on the shelf, and cleaned his books the best he could. He had to admit that even though he loved bananas, having squished bananas all over his books was kinda gross. Once he had it cleaned up, the two headed for the hallway and out the front door.

Jeannine immediately spotted her granddaddy's car as it was in the same spot it was every day of school for as long as she could remember. She took off running to the car leaving Decker standing there. Decker wasn't in the mood for running because if he ran, it reminded him that his shoulder still hurt, so he followed Jeannine but at a much slower pace. She waited on Decker to get to the car and opened the back door for him since his arm was still in a sling. They both slid into the back seat. "Hi, granddaddy!" She normally sat in the front seat with her granddaddy, but it just felt strange to leave Decker in the back seat alone. "Hello, little dreamer, what did you do today?" She smiled, and responded like she always did, "I tried to change the world today!" He laughed his normal belly laugh that Decker had heard so many times at the barbershop. "And what are you trying to change it to?" Decker was enjoying this back and forth. He didn't realize it was a routine until it happened every time they got into her granddaddy's car. "To a better place, granddaddy!" He laughed again, started the car and then looked in the rearview mirror. "Hello, Mr. Davis." Decker waved at him with his good arm but didn't say anything, as was the case when he was in a new situation or environment. "A man of few words, I like it." Mr. Martin laughed and pulled out of the school parking lot.

Mr. Martin pulled into the library loop. It had a really long horse-shoe drive where you could almost pull up to the front door of the library, and it had parking off to both sides and in the back. It was the first building off the town square just kitty-corner to the courthouse. If you walked out of the library's front and made a quick right, the sidewalk would take you all the way down past the hardware store, the Ben Franklins, and then on to Milholen's.

If you kept going you would go on across the railroad tracks. Mr. Martin stopped the car and turned around so he could look at both Decker and Jeannine. "Now, little dreamer, you know the rules, you don't go anywhere but the library and I will be back here at 5:15 sharp to pick you and Mr. Davis up. Got it?" Jeannine was shaking her head the whole time as if she knew the routine. She had her hand on the door handle the entire time that her granddaddy was giving her the basic instructions, ready to explode out of the car door and burst into the library. Decker was staring at Jeannine and he believed that if he could somehow see himself, she had the same excited look on her face that he had to have had when he was headed to the football stadium and knew that he was going to get that box of popcorn and some hot chocolate. He couldn't believe anyone could get that excited about going to the library. "Yes, granddaddy!"

With that, she popped the handle on the door and shot out of the car like a cannon ball. Decker tried to follow but she was already through the front door before he even got out of the car. "Mr. Davis, same rules apply to you too. Don't go anywhere but here and I will be here to pick you up and take you home at 5:15 sharp. Tell the librarian what time you are getting picked up and she will make sure you are in place when I get here. Got it?" There was no hesitation in his answer at all, "Yes, sir." With Decker armed with his own set of instructions, he exited the car and walked up the steps to the library. He had never been in the library and wasn't sure what to expect, but the minute he opened the door he was shocked by how big it was and how many books were in the place.

It also smelled funny to him. It smelled like furniture polish and brand-new Manila paper. All the tables were dark-colored wood and the other thing that struck him was that it was quiet. He didn't think he was going to like being here at all. He looked around for a minute and wasn't quite sure what to do; he couldn't even see Jeannine. This place was so big and dark. He wondered how they were expected to read in such dimly-lit conditions. As he was taking in more of the surroundings, he heard his name. It was a soft faint call of his name, but he didn't recognize the voice. He turned around and behind him was a tall lady with gray hair standing behind him. "I can't believe we have the pleasure of having Mr. Decker Davis today. I was excited to hear from Jeannine that you were coming today." Decker knew who she was. She had been the librarian since his daddy was coming to the library when he was in school. Decker couldn't believe anyone could be that old. He didn't know what to say so he fell back on the best grown-up response he had, "Thank you." He looked down at his shoes and realized he had two different sneakers on again and nobody even noticed! Just when he felt like he had gotten away with a fashion screw-up, he heard Jeannine's voice, "Pssst...Decker, come over here, I have to show you something." She was sitting at a large table with a green lamp turned on so she could see in this dark building and already had a stack of books in front of her. He nodded at the librarian and walked towards the table where Jeannine was sitting.

With every step, he could hear the thud of the wood floor beneath his feet. The boards were very solid and because it was so quiet, even his mismatched sneakers made a lot of noise. He tried to soften his steps, but it didn't work. No matter how light he tried to make himself, he could hear every step echoing off the walls of the library. When he reached the table, he stood next to her as if he was awaiting further instructions. Jeannine had that effect on him. He noticed he followed her orders without question. She looked up at him where he was standing and tugged on his good arm. "Sit down, Decker Davis, I want to show you this!" She was so excited that her eyes were dancing all over the place and she could hardly sit still. Once Decker sat down next to her, she put her finger on the word at the top of the page. "I bet you have never seen this word and I bet you can't read it either."

At first Decker thought she was going to make fun of him like the other kids did and she must have realized what she said because she changed her tone and began to explain what she was talking about. "Look, this is YOU! This says that some people have what is called Dyslexia." Decker had never heard that word and he really had no idea what it meant. He pretended to lean over and read some of the book, but Jeannine saw right through it. "Look, it all looks like gibberish, right? The reason it looks like gibberish is because your brain doesn't process words the way mine does. In fact, your brain is much more complicated than mine which makes you pretty smart." She made that part up, but she knew she needed a hook to help him understand better. She figured he needed confidence because when she saw him talk about the Gettysburg Address, she could see confidence grow inside him somewhere. She knew he wasn't stupid although she had thought that very thing like all the other kids in school.

It bothered her enough that she started coming to the library and looking for books that gave reasons as to why certain kids didn't like to read. She had actually talked to the librarian about it and it was the librarian who started stacking every book she had on reading disorders in front of her. Jeannine read the entire book on Dyslexia and was confident that if she helped him focus on his letters and focus his mind, he would turn into not only a good reader, but also gain some confidence in the process. "Look, we just have to train your mind to read the letters differently. If we sort of trick your brain into seeing things the correct way, you can read anything you want, and you won't need anyone's help. This is it, Decker!" She was so excited her voice echoed off the walls like his footsteps did except her voice was even louder.

The librarian came over and put her hand on Jeannine's shoulder, but she didn't say anything to her other than wink and smile. Jeannine knew that meant that she needed to lower her voice. She put her arm around Decker's neck. She was careful not to hurt his shoulder, but she pulled him close to her; so close that they were cheek-to-cheek with both of them staring at the book below them. "If you come to the library with me every day, I can help you learn to read all over again. I promise I will!" She was whispering but as she spoke he could feel her cheek move against his. He was never much on affection with anyone other than his family, but he liked her closeness. She felt normal, but even better was that she made him feel normal. He didn't understand exactly what the book said or how she even figured out that he was Dyslexic. He wasn't sure he could pronounce it. He had only heard it so far. "Dis-what?" She laughed and turned him loose from the grip she had around his neck.

Their heads immediately separated but they stayed close together at the table. "Say it like this: DIS-LEX-E-UH." She sounded it out very slowly so that he could repeat it. She made him repeat it several times until she was comfortable that he could say the word. The two spent the rest of the time they had practicing the definition of Dyslexia and making him explain to her how he understood the definition. The librarian came over and interrupted them to let them know that it was time to pack up and meet Mr. Martin. They both scrambled to clean up the desk and put the books away. Decker couldn't wait to get home and tell his sister about Jeannine's tutoring session.

Mr. Martin was right where he said he would be and was right on time. Both Decker and Jeannine climbed in the back seat. Jeannine had the normal exchange with her granddaddy; Decker came to love this little exchange between the two. He noticed that she changed a little. Her demeanor changed; she was more of a little girl when she was around her granddaddy than when she was around just Decker. He liked both versions but when it was just her and him, she was definitely closer to being an actual grown-up.

Mr. Martin turned down the long driveway that led to the Davis farm. The gravel kicked up a cloud as he took each curve slowly. Decker could see BettyJean in the field and pretty soon, he and Jeannine would call her up to the barn, give her some oats, and brush her down. He was pretty sure that Jeannine would like that part because it was actually his favorite part. BettyJean loved the oats and she knew what time of the day it was before Decker did. If he wasn't at the barn at 6:00 p.m. sharp, she would make noises with her nose and would kick her head back and holler. His daddy would call it a *whinnie* but to Decker it didn't sound like a *whinnie*, it sounded like a cross between a cow and coyote.

Either way, she would kick up a fuss if she didn't get her oats and rub at 6:00 p.m. sharp. He didn't think that Jeannine would like cleaning out her stall; BettyJean would make a huge mess in there. She had the biggest poop Decker had ever seen and she dropped a lot of it when she did. She didn't seem to care where she was when she did it – she would just lift her tail and it would start dropping out. The stuff she dropped would have to be scooped out of her stall along with whatever hay she didn't eat, and then he would have to put some new hay in there. He really didn't mind much but you had to be careful around BettyJean. Not only did she like to bite, she was clumsy with her feet and would step on your foot if you weren't paying attention, and that hurt something terrible too. She had done it to Decker once but luckily his sister was with him and she sort of pushed BettyJean off his foot because she didn't seem to notice or care about his screams of pain. It made the top of his foot swell up and his toes turned black a few days later. He actually thought it looked kind of cool, but it sure hurt like the dickens to walk on it. His momma took him to see the doctor and they took a picture of his foot that showed the bones inside. Decker thought it was the coolest picture ever and asked if he could keep it and was disappointed when they wouldn't let him. They did say that all his bones were just fine and nothing was broken.

He saw the same kind of picture when he broke his collarbone. He thought that was just as cool...maybe even more because the doctor pointed at the part that was broken and he could actually see where it broke. He would need to watch Jeannine closely and make sure she didn't get bit or stepped on. Mr. Martin stopped the car in front of the house where Decker's momma came out of the front door to greet them. Decker didn't hear any of the conversation between Mr. Martin and his momma because he had already exited the car with Jeannine and they both were practically running to the barn. Mr. Martin yelled something at Jeannine as they were running for the barn and she threw her hand up to acknowledge that she heard him and kept running.

"This is BettyJean." She had already entered the barn now because it was straight up 6:00 p.m. "She's a Quarter Horse. She is mainly friendly, but she likes to be sneaky and bite you when you aren't looking. Her favorite target is your booty when you are trying to climb on her." He laughed when he said *booty*. He couldn't remember saying *booty* in front of a girl other than his sister and momma. She laughed when she heard him say it too.

The thought of getting bitten by BettyJean, the Quarter Horse, must not have scared her because she walked right up to BettyJean and started petting her neck. "She is beautiful.

She smells funny, but she is beautiful." Decker laughed. He never thought she smelled funny, she just smelled like a horse. He scooped some oats out of the bag and dumped them in her bucket. He showed her the stall and what had to be cleaned out. He laughed when she said GROSS. BettyJean had left plenty to clean up. She tried to hold her nose as they were scooping out the stall, but it was nearly impossible to work with one hand, although Decker had learned to do just that. He was becoming very good at using one hand.

When they finished cleaning out BettyJean's stall he showed her how to throw out some scratch for the chickens. They laughed and joked with each other throughout the process of completing Decker's chores and he had forgotten all he had learned about Dyslexia earlier in the afternoon. They both stopped what they were doing when they heard his momma holler for them to come in. This had turned out to be one of the best days Decker had had in a very long time. He wasn't in a hurry for it to end. He was so comfortable around Jeannine. He never thought it was possible that he would actually have fun cleaning out a stall and feeding chickens, and she was a GIRL!

Chapter 37

BUBBA DROPPED THE SHERIFF OFF AT THE OFFICE. After the conversation with the sheriff and hearing that he was needed, he felt better about having to deliver the news about Lonnie Buckles to Brett Buckles. He hoped the sheriff could manage to get Donnie out of Viet Nam because he knew that Donnie, although sort of rough around the edges, was a pretty decent guy and could get control of Brett and Judd. Bubba hadn't seen Judd in quite a while, but he was the third brother in-between Brett and Lonnie.

Everyone in town said that Judd had a different daddy, but it was never proven. He wasn't a swift thinker and didn't enjoy getting into fights like his older brothers. He never finished high school and by all rights should be off to Viet Nam too but because Donnie had volunteered for the Marines before he was drafted. The military wouldn't take any more brothers from the same family. Everyone in town wished Brett would have gone off to Viet Nam instead of Donnie but it didn't work out that way. He took the back roads to the Buckles home. He didn't want anyone in town to see him drive through the main drag on the way to the Buckles place and then start putting two and two together and realize that there might be a problem with the Buckles.

He turned up the radio a little louder to hear the *Johnny Cash* singing about being stuck in Folsom Prison. He loved that song because the bad guy got what was coming to him and *Johnny* sang it so well. Bubba could sing right along with him and it took his mind off having to deliver the terrible news to Brett. He may not have liked Brett or any of the Buckles for that matter, but he had sympathy for anyone who lost someone. He had never lost anyone. In fact, he was an orphan and bounced around from home to home until he graduated high school. Somewhere in all that moving he discovered he had a talent for basketball. The local high school coach also discovered he had a talent for basketball and ended up taking legal guardianship of him. He felt pretty fortunate when that happened because unlike some of the foster families he was forced to live with, the coach and his wife were very good people and pushed him not only to excel in basketball, but also to do well in school. He still had some scars from cigarette burns he received on his 13th birthday. He tried to block those days out of his mind because there were some pretty rough ones.

When he met Elmer Davis at Duke, Elmer was a junior and Bubba was a freshman. He liked Elmer from the minute he met him. He knew Elmer was a leader and inherently he was a follower. He liked the way Elmer took charge of everything and tried to use the same mannerisms that he observed from Elmer, but he just couldn't. Bubba was very protective of those who he admired and loved and he not only admired Elmer, he knew he loved him in a brotherly way. He was told a long time ago that he had a brother, but because he was an orphan, he wasn't sure if that was true.

Even if it was true, he had no idea where his brother would be. He always thought of Elmer as his big brother, which is why he turned down several job offers to become Elmer's deputy. He knew that if in the unlikely event that Elmer ever lost the election, he would probably be out of work, but he didn't care. Not only was he a three-sport star athlete, he was the valedictorian of his high school and had a Criminal Justice degree from Duke University. He hated that people thought he was weird. He didn't think he was weird, he just struggled with social situations. He liked living in rural Mississippi and was slowly figuring out his social issues and found himself more and more comfortable when Elmer Davis wasn't around. He still needed to hear from time to time that not only was he doing a good job, but also that he was needed.

Bubba made the turn down the gravel road that led to the entrance to the Buckles place. Once he made the turn he navigated all the junk that had been strewn all over the property. He was afraid he would run over something and puncture the tires. Luckily, he had been with the sheriff recently and remembered the path to the house pretty well. When he reached the house, he could see that the truck was gone so he didn't think anyone was home at the moment but needed to check anyway. He knocked on the screen door and could see inside the house through the screen. He pushed on the screen and it was unlocked. He pushed it open and hollered for Brett, and not hearing a reply, entered the house.

He wasn't there to arrest anyone, so he didn't need a warrant and just thought of it as being neighborly. *People should not leave home and leave their doors unlocked*, he thought. He walked through the house and from room to room and didn't find anyone, which he knew he wouldn't. He opened the refrigerator just to see what was in it. There were a few tubs of food that he didn't recognize and three *Pabst Blue Ribbon* beers. There sure wasn't much to feed anyone, much less a boy of Lonnie's age. He felt bad for the boy; it had to have been a tough life, one that may have reflected his own. He reached in and grabbed a bottle of beer, found an opener in one of drawers and downed it, every last drop. Elmer probably wouldn't appreciate him having a drink at the Buckles expense, but he didn't care. He just felt uneasy after seeing that little boy in the condition he was in. He started to throw the empty bottle in the trash can but couldn't find one. Then he realized that if he set the bottle on the kitchen counter, no one would notice as there were already several there. He thought about where to go next.

Brett wasn't a complicated creature and was either home or at the Jackpot, so he decided that the Jackpot would be his first stop. He made his way through the house, carefully navigating what looked like years of neglected laundry. Bubba was a neat freak by nature and just being in the Buckles home was giving him trouble. He liked order and being in a messy environment made him even more jumpy. He sat in the car for a minute just to make sure he was taking the correct steps. He really didn't want to make a mistake and make the department look bad or worse, make Elmer look bad. He had so much respect for the sheriff, but to him it ran deeper than just respect, he loved the sheriff like a brother.

Besides his last legal guardians that were good and decent people, the sheriff and his family was the only family he had. He grabbed the radio and called Lavera. She answered in her usual friendly voice. He told her that he struck out finding Brett at his home but was pretty confident that he would find him at the Jackpot. She gave him a "10/4, copy that" that never sounded correct coming from her. The way she said it was just too nice and too soft that it just didn't sound right.

He made his way out of the Buckles place, careful not to run over anything that might pop a tire. He actually let out a sigh of relief when he reached the gravel road that led towards town. He pulled into the gravel parking lot of the Jackpot and parked. The Jackpot was another place that made his heart rate go up. To him, it was a shady place and it was always dark in there. Anytime he had to go in there to break up a fight or haul out a rowdy drunk, he had to be careful if it was daytime. Walking out into the sun after being in the dungeon for even a few minutes, he had a hard time adjusting to the light. Bubba took a breath before he went into the Jackpot, not because he was nervous, but because he would need the air. The place was not only dark, it was stale with old smoke and God knows what else.

Chapter 38

AFTER THE MARINE RECRUITING SERGEANT LEFT his office, THE sheriff sat at his desk for a minute to figure out the best way to approach Bobby Martin. He didn't think for one second that Bobby was a murderer and he definitely wasn't a child molester. However, at the moment, all the evidence pointed right at Bobby Martin. He knew Bobby was hot-tempered and he knew that Lonnie Buckles had roughed up his little girl, but the sheriff saw it as child's play that might have gotten a little rough, and it sure wasn't worth someone getting killed over. He knew that Decker got bullied in school and it took everything he had in him not to interfere. Decker was growing so fast that he was certain that eventually Decker would be bigger than the bully. He also knew that size didn't matter because it was more of a confidence thing when it came to Decker. Decker lacked confidence in almost all public situations and that alone made him an easy target for boys. The sheriff hated bullies, but he also knew that if he tried to fix everything for Decker, he would never be able to stand alone, much less stand up to a bully. He was confident that the time would come when Decker would figure it out for himself. He already saw a flicker of something in Decker's eye that he hadn't seen before, and he was sure that little flicker had a name: Jeannine Martin. He pictured Decker and then he would see Bubba. Bubba had been bullied his whole life, not by kids but by grown-ups. It didn't matter that he now had a degree from Duke University, Bubba still lacked confidence because as far as the sheriff knew, he had never been allowed to find his own confidence through the help of friends and family. If that high school coach and his wife hadn't basically adopted Bubba for his high school years, there was no telling what dark path Bubba might have chosen. Bubba was a good person who still hadn't found his way. He was getting better, but he still badly needed the sheriff's help to keep him pointed in the right direction.

He decided the best action was to go to where Bobby worked. Just before he got up to grab his hat that was hanging on the tall hat rack beside his desk that had been given to him for Christmas by the office staff, Lavera walked in. She didn't knock as usual. "Elmer, I can't work in a place where bad language is tossed around like so many nouns, verbs and adjectives. I know it's a stressful time with that little boy being murdered right here in our peaceful town of Webb but that is no reason for you to allow yourself and others to descend into a nasty world of profanity. There is always a better choice." The sheriff felt his pulse rise in him. Was she seriously picking today, now, at this time to preach to him about language? He wanted so badly to lash out at her, and in his mind, he was telling her to just pack her stuff up and march right on out the door if she didn't like what was going on in the office, but he also knew she meant well. He liked the fact that no matter what the situation was she never compromised her position. She may not have had the muscle and brawn that Bubba had but she certainly had the confidence that he lacked. He wished he could balance it out. "Lavera, I can't force you stay and you know I love you, but I also can't promise that on days like today that I don't let loose some profanity that would embarrass a sailor. This isn't church, this is the Sheriff's Office, but because I love you with all my heart and truly thank the Lord every day for allowing me the opportunity to work with you and count you as my dearest friend, I will promise you that I will do my best." He could see the grin on her face, especially when he admitted that he thanked the Lord for her every day. To her that meant that he was a God-fearing man, even though he only went to church because Lois made him go to church, and if it weren't for Lois he would probably not go. He just had a knack for calming Lavera down when others would be arguing with her all day. "It's a terrible thing what happened to that little boy, Elmer. I want you to catch him and I am sorry that I let my temper get the best of me. It's what profanity does to me every time I hear it. I see good people who are highly intelligent chose to use words that any old silly adolescent uses to make themselves sound tough." Having said what she needed to say to help herself feel better, she turned to walk out but stopped before she reached the door. "I called Andy's and Bobby is working today." Then she turned and walked out. How the hell did she know where he was going? The lady obviously had a telepathic skill that he wished he had. Even though she knew everything going on in the investigation now without asking one single question, he knew she was not a gossiper. She was very serious about police work and she would never pass on information that wasn't meant to be. He placed his hat squarely on his head – another Christmas present from the staff. He never used to wear hats, but it seemed his staff lacked creativity or perhaps they felt HE lacked creativity and bought him a hat for nearly every occasion: birthdays, anniversaries, and Christmas. This hat was his favorite, mainly because it fit well. It wasn't a full-fledged cowboy hat as it did not have a full brim. He thought it was closer to a fedora than anything else, but Bubba said it made him look like Lyndon Johnson. He didn't take that as a compliment, but he really liked how the hat felt good on his head. It didn't match his brown uniform but being a cream color, it didn't stand out either. He walked by Lavera's desk and told her he would be back and made some joke about not waiting up. She didn't get it because she replied that she got off at 5:00 sharp. She was perhaps the smartest woman he had ever met but she was not given a funny bone.

Since Bubba had the Scout, he took the only car available, a pathetic puke green color 1963 *Dodge Dart*. It was all the department could afford at the time and it was purchased at an auction in Jackson. The town garage chipped in, cleaned up the engine, added some horsepower, painted it, and put *County Sheriff* on each front side door and handed it back to the department. It was ugly, but it ran like a top. They never changed the original green paint because they ran out of donation money. At least that's what they said. The sheriff actually thought it came in handy because it was difficult to spot amongst the trees in the summer, which was peak season for stills and illegal moonshine. Using that same car, he later busted Leroy B, the previous owner of the garage and a very good moonshiner in his prime. When he snuck up on Leroy's still, Leroy just laughed and said he should have painted that car bright pink and the sheriff wouldn't have been able to sneak up on him the way he had done that day. The sheriff wasn't too interested in stills, but Leroy had flaunted his stuff a little too much and the church folks like Lavera got organized and demanded the sheriff do something about it. Truth be known, the sheriff enjoyed Leroy's moonshine better than any store-bought stuff he ever had. Of course, he would never let Lavera see it, so he kept it in the barn and would take a sip every now and then. Ole Leroy spent the night in Jail. The church ladies were happy because the sheriff had done his sworn duty, so it was a win-win for everybody.

He pulled in to Dub's barbershop before he went to Andy's butcher shop. He and Dub had been very close friends for many years and he felt like he needed to tell Dub what he was about to do. It definitely wasn't standard police procedure, but he believed in the loyalty to friends as much as he believed in the badge. He thought he would certainly want to know beforehand if someone was going to arrest Decker or Heather. He wished sometimes the town wasn't so small and he could just be a cop. He decided it was best if he told Dub Martin the entire story and ask him to keep the details to himself. What he really wanted to do was to keep Bobby locked up and away from the Buckles family while he sorted this whole thing out. If Brett believed that Bobby killed his little brother, Brett would turn even more stupid than he already was, and he would exact revenge for sure. He didn't need a family feud in his town and he sure didn't need a race war breaking out. They had enough of that crap going on all over the state; he'd like to keep Webb out of it.

"Well hello. This is a mighty nice surprise, Sheriff, I know you ain't here for a trim. I just gave you one less than a week ago and I already told you that you got my vote so what brings you to the edge of town?" Dub was always cleaning when he spoke and couldn't sit still while he was in his shop. The sheriff freely admitted that Dub's shop was always cleaner than Mac Hibdon's but Mac's was pretty sharp too. Both guys were fidgety and liked to be fixing or cleaning something while they didn't have customers. Dub didn't have any customers and the sheriff was thankful for that. He would have to run anyone off while he told Bobby the story about the day's events. The sheriff pulled his hat off and fidgeted with it for just a minute. He thought he had rehearsed how he was going to tell Dub he was about to arrest his son for murder, but his brain got stuck on the sight of the little boy again and that always threw him off. "Out with it, Sheriff. I've known you for most of our lives, and I know you fidget with that ugly Johnson hat every time you don't know what to say, so now just go on and get it out. That's the best way to get something stuck in your crawl out to the surface." The sheriff tilted his head back and looked at the ceiling; even the ceiling was cobweb free, spotless from what he could see. He lowered his eyes to meet Dub's and told him the story outright. He left out the fact that the boy had been molested though, which to him was a subliminal sign that he really didn't think that Bobby had anything to do with this terrible crime. He knew it would cause Dub some unnecessary internal pain if he shared that detail. When he finished with all the details that he thought he should share with Dub, he could see that Dub had a tear running down his cheek. Dub was fighting off the emotions that only a daddy could understand, the eternal loss of a son as the

Buckles family had now suffered and the potential loss of a son he now faced. "Good Lord, that poor little boy died right there by that dumpster you say?" Dub stopped cleaning and sat down in his own barber chair. When he sat it was like all the life came out of him and he started to cry. He grabbed a towel from the counter and rubbed his face. After he regained a little composure he said, "Sheriff, you have a job to do so go on and do it, but I gotta tell you that Bobby may be a hot head but he ain't no killer. He didn't have nothin' to do with that little boy's murder, God rest his soul. I know you'll figure that out soon enough." The sheriff stood there fidgeting with his hat even more than before. He knew at that moment that he was perhaps looking at one of the finest men he would ever meet in his lifetime with his heart breaking right in front of him. It was emotional for him too. "Dub, I'm sorry it's me who has to go do this, but I promise I will treat him fairly and I promise I will find out the truth." Dub didn't say anything back and just stared straight ahead. The sheriff turned and walked out the door.

He walked out of Dub's barbershop feeling as low and bad as he could ever remember feeling. He had seen some terrible things while as the Sheriff of Tallahatchie County, but mainly when he was doing search and rescue for a couple of the hurricane-stricken areas down around the Gulf, especially in Pascagoula. He had terrible memories from that hurricane. He was sent down there by the governor to head up recovery along with a team of two doctors, two nurses, and a deputy from Jackson that was a rising star in the Mississippi political world. It was a good team. Very sharp doctors from different parts of the state and two tough, sharp nurses, one being Maybelle Richards. They extracted bodies from all kinds of places, but the worst one was the little girl. Maybelle just so happened to look up and see her lifeless body in a palm tree. She had been up there for quite some time after the hurricane made its mark and nobody spotted her until Maybelle just so happened to look up to enjoy the beautiful blue sky that day. Seeing Lonnie beside that dumpster reminded him of that time so many years ago. At the time, Maybelle understandably broke down in tears and was nearly inconsolable for days after that. Seeing that little girl in that tree and that little boy beside that dumpster 18 years apart reminded him that there are some things that can't be unseen and some wounds that simply won't heal. He hoped that Dub would heal from having to hear that his son was being arrested for murder.

Chapter 39

DECKER WATCHED AS JEANNINE FINISHED THROW-
ing down some new hay in BettyJean's stall. All of his chores
were now complete. When they heard his momma call them,
Jeannine started to leave the stall, even though they weren't
done. He let her know that the general routine was that his
momma would call once just to let him know that it was time to
start finishing the chores. The second call was for him to make
sure that everything was put away and the third call meant he
was in trouble for lollygagging around. He had only made it to
the third call once and that was when he was chasing a barn
snake though the hay. He actually caught it once, but it slipped
out of this hand and when it did, it took off like lightning. He
had no idea a snake could move that fast. He was disappointed
that he never caught it because he was planning on taking it to
school for show and tell. He told Jeannine that story and she told

him that if he had brought that gross snake to school with him she would have smacked him a good one. He showed her how to latch the stalls and secure all the buckets so that they were easy to find the next day. He told her that his daddy had told him that the more organized he was about putting things away the easier and faster it would be for him to complete his chores. He had done this so many times that he now understood it. He hated it when his sister did the chores for him sometimes because he was sick or visiting a relative because she never put things back where they belonged. It would nearly take him to his momma's third call before he got everything done because he spent too much time trying to find where she put everything. He never griped at her though because he didn't want her to get mad at him and then maybe not read to him that night. He was good at adapting anyway.

After he was confident that they had put everything away, the two started to walk towards the house. He tried to walk next to her, but she would walk faster each time he got next to her and pretty soon they were both running for the back door. He was a little embarrassed that she beat him to the door and he quickly let her know how hard it was to run in a sling. He couldn't move his arms fast and after all, it was his arms that generated some extra speed. She rolled her eyes and pulled on the screen door where they saw Decker's momma standing over a skillet of fried chicken, which was one of Decker's favorites. "Check your shoes kids, make sure BettyJean hasn't snuck into the house with you!" Jeannine looked confused but caught the implication when she saw Decker looking at the bottom of his shoes. Neither had managed to step in BettyJean's poop. "Jeannine, it is so sweet of you to help Decker today and to take him to the library with you. Do you wish you hadn't now? That barn is a nasty place and BettyJean has no manners." She giggled like a girl when she said it, which made Jeannine feel right at home. "Oh, no, ma'am, I love horses. They smell funny, but I do think they are pretty and BettyJean didn't bite me like Decker said she would!" Decker watched the exchange between Jeannine and his momma and he was kind of impressed with his momma. She was acting differently than she normally did; it was like she was trying to be a little girl again. The two girls jabbered on about everything under the sun until they heard her granddaddy's car pull up to house. "Oh, Good Lord, I have completely lost track of time, Jeannine – I didn't put a thing in your belly and your granddaddy is already here to pick you up! I promise not to make the same mistake tomorrow. You are coming back tomorrow, aren't you?" Jeannine was gathering up her schoolbooks as Decker's momma was fussing over not feeding her. Decker thought that she took too much stuff home with her every day. He didn't take home half the stuff she did, and he thought his book satchel was too heavy already. "Oh, yes, ma'am, I will be back every day until Decker can use his arm again." His momma walked over to where Jeannine was but to Decker, she glided. He never actually saw her feet move, she just sort of slid from place to place. He never could understand how she never seemed to make any noise when she walked. She stood right in front of Jeannine and then put both her hands on Jeannine's cheeks. She was very soft in her motions and the way she touched her. "My, you are such a beautiful young lady. Thank you for helping Decker with his chores. I will make sure I feed you next time." Having said that, she bent over and planted a kiss on Jeannine's forehead. Jeannine smiled this giant smile like Decker had never seen. His momma was so gifted at making kids and other people feel good. The same kiss she had just given Jeannine, she had given him a thousand times. On his bad days she'd plant a kiss on his forehead that nearly made him forget all about getting picked on. Maybe one of these days he would give Jeannine a kiss right on the forehead just like that. Jeannine ran out the door and jumped into the car. Decker's momma talked to Mr. Martin for just a few minutes and apologized for not feeding her. She told him that she could stay later the rest if the week if she wanted to and she could stay and eat with them. He couldn't hear what Mr. Martin said back because he was in the car, but he could see him smile and nod and then he drove off. Decker was inside already nibbling at some of the chicken that his momma had pulled from the frying pan already. "Decker Davis! You go wash those nasty hands before you pick at my chicken!" He took off for the bathroom without another word.

As Mr. Martin neared the road at the end of the driveway, he interrupted Jeannine, who was talking as fast as he had ever heard. She was clearly excited about the day, the library, the discovery, the horse, the chickens, and even the horse poop. "Baby, I have a piece of bad news that I need to talk to you about. I sure don't want to upset you but it's important that you hear it from me."

Dub Martin told her that her daddy had been arrested and was in jail. Of course, he couldn't tell her just one piece of the story without telling her why. It's a little easier to hear some bad news when you are distant from it, but he worried how she would react to finding out that the boy who had twisted her arm and roughed her up just a few days earlier was now dead and even worse, that some folks would think her daddy did it. He felt like that was just too much for a child to handle. In typical Jeannine fashion, she asked him a thousand questions as he continued to drive them home. *Why do they think her daddy did it? How come Decker didn't know? Where did they take her daddy?* The questions just kept coming out of her like a machine gun, but Dub Martin was the perfect person to handle it. He was the calmest and most patient man. He loved his granddaughter more than anything and he always tried to protect her but treat her as much like an adult as he could. Things were still shaky in this part of the country and the more she could think like a grown up, the safer she would be.

Chapter 40

BUBBA PULLED ON THE METAL HANDLE OF THE Jackpot door that was very hot and he pulled his hand back quickly. It should not have been a surprise, but it was. The door faced West and got baked by the sun most of the day. He used his sleeve to grab it the second time and pulled the door open. Immediately, he felt like he was in the dark and had entered a cave; the only thing he was missing was a lamp on top of his head to light the way. He heard her greeting before his eyes adjusted and he heard the rustling of chairs, but he couldn't tell who was doing the rustling. Most likely it was someone that was skittish about seeing a cop walk into the bar, so they more than likely headed out the back door. "Don't get the pleasure of having you here, Deputy, what are ya drinkin'? It's on the house. Nothin' but top-shelf service for the county's law is what I always say." Bubba detected the sarcasm in her voice but ignored it. "Thank

you, Ms. Becky, I will take a raincheck on that free drink, but I
am on duty at the moment. "Well since you can't drink on duty
are you in the mood for somethin' else? I can give you a discount
on that. I promise it will be the best money you will spend this
month, maybe even this year." He heard a few laughs from the
back but ignored them too. He knew what she was selling, and
he wouldn't have anything to do with her if she was the last
woman in Earth. One of the laughers from the back yelled, "I
will take two then, Becky!" She threw a towel in their direction.
Bubba's eyes had adjusted to the dimly-lit bar now and he could
see the guys in the back. He thought he knew one of them but
the other he didn't recognize. "Thank you, ma'am, I know I'm
a fool for passing up such a bargain but I'm here looking for
Brett Buckles." She picked up another towel from somewhere
under the bar and threw it over her shoulder, then pretended
to clean. Bubba thought the place was a dump and couldn't tell
if it had ever been cleaned. He noticed as he walked across the
rough concrete floor that his boot would stick in certain places.
He hated to think of what his boots were walking through, but
to each his own. She had to make a living too. "What's that idiot
done now, Deputy? Did he rob a candy store, shoot someone's
dog, or did he light another cat on fire?" The laughs were pretty
loud with that last cat comment and Bubba had to stop himself from laughing too. She was witty, and he knew he couldn't
match her wit, so he decided the best course of action was to
stay on the job and not get cute. "No, ma'am, we just need to
visit with him. He isn't in any trouble, just need to have few
words with him." She lifted the bar top that allowed access to
floor and walked through it towards Bubba. Bubba was always
a little jumpy and he was trying to figure out why she needed to

come out from behind the bar. After she was standing right in front of him he realized she was just trying to keep the prying ears in the back from hearing what she said. He knew that deep down Becky was a good one who was dealt a really crappy hand in the poker game of life and she was doing the best she could at it. He didn't like her business much, but he respected her for making a living without hurting anyone. He also knew it was illegal what she was doing but everybody kinda looked the other way. The sheriff himself even said once that she was a great stress reliever for the very mischievous in town. He said if it weren't for her, there would be a lot more crime in the county. "Deputy, he came by here this morning. He was lookin' for his brother, but he said he had some business in Corinth and didn't know if he would make it back today or even tomorrow, but he did say he was going to stop by Chub's before he left. Those two are just weird, especially that Chub. That's all I know." She kept her voice to a high whisper. He heard every word and was certain that the gallery in the back had not heard a single word. He admired her in a tender-hearted way, a trait that he had that the sheriff told him he should never lose, but would have to hide in this business. "Thank you, Ms. Becky. If he happens to stop by, just let him know we'd really like to talk to him." He tipped his hat, because he was certain that was what southern gentlemen did, plus he was proud of his hat and wanted people to notice it. It was a genuine cowboy hat that he bought down in Jackson when he and Elmer were at a military auction for used equipment. Elmer was always finding a bargain and he sure did that trip. They hit the jackpot on some tactical gear that they bought for pennies on the dollar, so Elmer was in a good mood and they snuck off from the auction, bought the hat and had it custom-fit to his head. He as very proud of it and loved the feel of it. He started to turn around and walk out but she grabbed his hand. He turned back to look at her. He was surprised to see a tear running down her face. He was more surprised that he spotted it in this dim lighting. It caught him off-guard and was not sure what to do. "Deputy, find that little brother of his first. When Brett comes back I just know he will beat that boy black and blue and he don't deserve that. He's just a little boy that is in a bad spot, but even worse, find him before that smelly gross mechanic finds him. He's a creep for sure. He is one of the only ones in town who I won't do for any price." Bubba felt a lump raise up in his throat and had to quickly gather himself. He now admired her quite a bit more than he did before. She really cared about that boy's well-being. He had just learned something else that Elmer Davis had already told him before, he told him not to judge too quickly, people would surprise you in good ways and to be careful because they will surprise you in bad ways too... just be able to recognize the difference. He knew he had sort of misjudged Ms. Becky O'Neil. He reached out and put his hand on her shoulder. It was an awkward moment for him, but she didn't seem to mind the small effort of his sympathy. "Thank you, Ms. Becky. I will do that." He felt guilty for knowing that the little boy she was referring to had already been found and Brett was not going to beat him black and blue ever again.

Leaving the Jackpot, Bubba felt a sad feeling, a feeling like he should have been able to do something for that boy. He had been sort of in the same situation except the people who liked to beat on him weren't family, most were total strangers who put on a good show for the people who ran the foster family organization. He remembered one man and woman that had kids of their own already but for the extra money they would take in foster kids. The daddy would beat him on the butt and back so that the agent who came to check on them couldn't see the marks. He would be told to be polite and make sure that he said he was having the time of his life. He should have been able to see all the signs, but he didn't. Maybe he didn't want to. It didn't matter now, but he should have done something.

He decided he would drop by the garage and see if by chance Brett had stopped by like Ms. Becky had mentioned. If he wasn't there, he would get the oil changed in the Scout. It was long overdue.

He stopped by Chub's garage and parked the Scout inside one of the big garage openings. He saw Chub talking to a customer at the front counter, it was Mrs. Schoenthal. She was the matriarch of the only Jewish family in Webb. She was a sweet lady but feisty as hell when she had to be. Bubba got to see her feisty side one day when he tried to give her a parking ticket for parking in a loading zone downtown. She told him in no uncertain terms that she should not be given a ticket because she was dropping off blankets and toys at Sterlings where the Baptist minister worked part-time at Christmas just to make a little extra cash for the holidays. She told him that it was very insensitive and unchristian like to give her a ticket for doing good work for the pastor, and the fact that she was Jewish and trying to help poor kids all over the county have a better Christmas was a sign that he was totally in the wrong. He relented and just told her to have a good day. He wasn't much for arguing with anyone much less a lady who not only had dressed him down right there on the sidewalk of downtown Webb but had also dressed him down for improperly pronouncing her name. He said it like it was spelled and thought he was correct, but that day during his lesson in Christianity and Judaism, she told him that it was pronounced SHANE-TALL not SHOW-IN-THAL. He had been pronouncing it wrong for as long as he could remember, but after that day when she said she was fed up with his ignorance of culture, he never mispronounced it again.

He walked through the shop to the front of office where Mrs. Schoenthal was telling Chub that he had not fixed her brakes properly and she expected him to correct the issue. She said they still made a squeaking noise when she stopped. She admitted that it was much less of a noise than before he had worked on it but nevertheless, it was still there. Chub seemed irritated because he kept running his hands through his greasy hair, a motion that seemed to irritate Mrs. Schoenthal even more. As he walked into the room, both Chub and Mrs. Schoenthal looked at him but didn't say anything. "Stop running your hands through your hair when I am talking to you. That is improper manners if ever I have seen them and if you expect me to shake your hand after such a disgusting display of poor hygiene you have another think coming." From where Bubba was standing, he could see both of their faces. Mrs. Schoenthal didn't even blink, even though she was about a foot shorter than Chub and Chub was no giant. She was clearly intimidating when she got like this. Chub started to run his hands through his hair again but caught himself before he did and rubbed the back of his neck instead. Since Chub was always kinda on the dirty side, Bubba didn't think that was much more sanitary than running his hands though his hair, but it must have been permissible to Mrs. Schoenthal because she didn't say a word. She started to say something else and Chub slammed his hand down on the counter. It was loud and aggressive. It surprised Mrs. Schoenthal and it surprised Bubba too. Chub was usually as thick as a tree stump upstairs and never got riled up about anything. Bubba felt the need to step in now, so he interrupted to help break the tension that was rising in the air. "Uh, hello, Mrs. SHANE-TALL, it's nice to see you today. I'm sorry to interrupt but I am on some serious police business that I need to visit with Chub about in private. Time is certainly of the essence. If Chub here promises to fix your brakes so they are smooth as silk would you mind giving us a few minutes?" He took his hat off when he was talking to her. He knew better than to show her that kind of disrespect and he dang sure made a conscious effort not to run his hands through his hair. Just like someone had flipped a switch inside her, she turned to Bubba and became the woman she was about 99% of the time, the most charming and graceful woman you could possibly meet. She was right there with Lois Davis in the class department. "Deputy, it is so nice to see you today, you know I would never interfere with a police matter. I have some shopping to do and I will be happy to come back when Chub has the brakes fixed as they should have been already." She smiled a smile that could melt an iceberg. She stuck out her hand to Bubba and like a southern gentleman he was trying to become, he clasped her tiny hand ever so gently, brought it up as high as he dared, leaned over and kissed the top of her hand. He wasn't sure if he had done that right or if there was a target that he was supposed to hit when kissing a woman's hand. He would have to ask Elmer about that, but he must have done it correctly because Mrs. Schoenthal seemed delighted to be treated with such southern manners. He let go of her hand as softly as he could so she could turn and leave. Before she left, she nodded very sweetly at both Chub and Bubba and he could have sworn that she did one of those royal looking bows. He couldn't remember what it was called, *curt* something.

When she exited the garage office, Chub turned to look at Bubba. "I was gonna fix her brakes anyway, all I said was that it would be difficult today and she got mad at me. I will get even with her someday." Bubba saw a look on Chub that he had never seen. It was cold, and he didn't like it. "Oh, now, she is a good woman, she just wants her brakes to quit squeaking. Say, have you seen Brett?" Chub seemed to get agitated at the question and turned and walked out to the garage. "Why does everyone think I know where Brett is? I don't care where Brett is, we aren't joined at the hip you know!" He raised his voice and grabbed a shop towel on the way to the car that was on the rack. "No need to get upset, I just asked. I need to visit with him so let him know if he stops by. Say, can I get an oil change while I am here?" Chub stopped fiddling with the undercarriage of the car and turned to look at Bubba as if he had two heads. "Since you just told Mrs. SHANE-TALL that I would fix her brakes today, I don't have time." For some reason, Bubba felt silly for asking now, Chub had a point. "Ok, that's fine, I can get it done tomorrow. Say, can I use the toilet? I gotta go." Chub told him that the head was behind the tire rack; first door on the left and to turn out the light when he was done and make sure the toilet didn't stay running after he flushed. "Sometimes you have to jiggle the handle." Bubba made his way behind the tire rack and found the bathroom with ease. He flipped the light on. The switch was very old and very heavy. It made a huge clicking-popping sound when he hit the switch. He thought it was a lot of noise for one single small bulb in the middle of the tiny bathroom that had obviously been painted to match the green tire rack. It was pretty disgusting too, he doubted anyone had cleaned the bathroom in years. There was crap all over the floor, the toilet was a mix of old white porcelain and rust and Lord knows what else. In the corner behind the toilet was a small pair of sneakers. He chuckled and wondered how many times those sneakers had been peed on being as they were in the corner right beside the toilet. He only thought that because he had let his stream wander right off onto the shoes. At first, he felt bad, but seeing as the conditions of the bathroom were deplorable, he thought, *no wonder Chub smelled so bad all the time*; he couldn't imagine Chub actually putting those sneakers on later, that was too much to stomach. Then he thought, *Chub has some really small feet.* He was careful not to touch anything. The sink was so disgusting that he figured his private parts were probably cleaner than that sink. He would skip the hand washing in this bathroom. When he walked out of the bathroom, Chub was standing in the hall behind the rack, leaning against the wall with his arms crossed. The hallway was still a little dark, so it made Bubba jump just a little. "Dang, man, you ought not hang around outside in a dark hallway like that!" Chub pushed himself off the wall; didn't say anything to Bubba and went into the bathroom and closed the door. Bubba just shook his head and thought to himself, "That Chub is one weird cat".

Chapter 41

THE SHERIFF PARKED THE UGLY GREEN CAR IN THE first spot in front of Andy's butcher shop. There weren't any other customers around so that was a small blessing. He was about to step out of the car when Lavera's voice came crackling over the radio. "Elmer, are you there? Hello? Elmer?" Lavera was never up to speed nor did she care about proper police radio dialogue and protocol. He picked up the mike on the CB and responded, "I'm here Lavera, something wrong?" He waited a long time for her to respond and was getting frustrated because he knew she liked to multi-task. She thought she was good at it, but she really wasn't. She was the smartest woman he knew but she only did one smart thing at a time. If someone called or walked up to her desk she would forget that she had just tried to reach him on the police radio. "Oh, good! Elmer, Aubrey called and said that he had found the valve stems and the puller, he had them bagged and was sending them over. He also said that the contents of the dumpster were at A-1 refrigerated storage and that everything had been marked and tagged." The sheriff raised his eyebrows. He was a little surprised. Aubrey was a good man, but he wasn't a very thorough cop. He didn't like details and he didn't like a lot of hard work. It sounded like he had done both. "Thank you, Lavera." He hung the mike back on the hook, stepped out of the car, and adjusted his belt buckle. He thought about opening the trunk to retrieve his gun and holster but that just wasn't his style. He was going to arrest Bobby Martin, a man he had known his whole life, and he was certain Bobby wouldn't cause any trouble.

He stepped through the door of the butcher shop and was hit with the cold air and the smell of fresh meat. He was struck by how white everything was in there. This is where Lois got the meat for their family. He had been in there a few times, but it had been a long time. The last time he was in the shop was over three years ago. He brought in a 12-point buck to have Andy process. Andy was the best at getting every ounce of meat possible from a buck and everybody in town used him during hunting season. He would get so busy with the deer processing that he would have to hire extra help to handle the regular customers. That's how Bobby got his job after he was fired out at Parchman. As it turned out, Bobby was nearly as good a meat cutter as Andy. Bobby didn't have the same way with customers that Andy did though, so Andy kept Bobby in the back of the shop as much as he could.

"Hello, Andy." Andy was cutting meat at the front counter and was obviously deeply engrossed in what he was doing because he didn't hear the sheriff come in. When he heard the sheriff say "hello" he looked up with his usual cigarette hanging out of his mouth. When he looked up, part of the ash hanging off the end of the cigarette dropped to the counter. The sheriff didn't see where it dropped but he hoped that Andy wasn't completing an order for Lois. "Hello, Sheriff, what brings you here? I am working on Lois's order right now; give me just a few more minutes and I will have Bobby bring it out." He stubbed out his cigarette somewhere behind the counter and rubbed his hands on his white apron leaving some blood marks on it. "She said she would send you by to pick it up, but she said it would be much later than this. Good thing I got Bobby started on it right away." The sheriff took a few more steps toward the counter but wasn't sure he wanted to. No telling where Andy stubbed that cigarette out but since he couldn't ever remember anyone getting sick from Andy's beef he figured Andy was pretty safe. He was also glad to hear that the man he was about to arrest for murder was working on his family's meat supply for the next week. It all seemed a bit off to him. "Oh, thanks Andy, but I wasn't here to pick up the meat. Actually, Lois hadn't managed to send today's honey-do list to me yet." The sheriff took off his hat and held it in his right hand. "I was actually hoping to speak to Bobby, is he here?" Andy wiped his hands again and came out from behind the counter. He stuck out his hand for Andy to shake, and Andy reluctantly did but he tried not to show it. "Is there something wrong, Sheriff?" Elmer shook his head and held Andy's hand in the shake mode for just a little longer than normal, long enough for Andy to get uncomfortable with the handshake, which was what the sheriff intended to happen. Sometimes people in this town could be too nosy for their own good so by making Andy feel uncomfortable with the really tight grip and the very long handshake, he was sending Andy a subliminal message. "Not as far as you're concerned, Andy. I just need to visit with Bobby and for privacy sake, I need him to come to the office with me. You say he is in the back working on my wife's order, right?" The sheriff let go of Andy's hand and pointed and nodded towards the back so that Andy knew he didn't need any help finding his way around. "I will just go back and visit with him. Say, Andy, why don't you go have a smoke outside while I visit with Bobby and if we aren't here when you are done with your smoke, feel free to complete Lois's order and I will come back and pick it up later. How's that?" Andy wasn't stupid, he understood just by the handshake alone that the sheriff didn't want him around at the moment. He took off his apron, went behind the counter to retrieve his cigarettes, looked for something else but didn't find it, then came back around to the customer side of the shop. "Sheriff, I will make sure Mrs. Davis's order is complete by five today. If you can't make it by then, don't worry. I will be at the house, just ring the bell and I will come get it out of the cooler for you." Andy lived right behind the butcher shop and customers often went straight to his house to get him to cut some meat. The poor man never really took a day off, but he didn't seem to mind. When the *Piggly Wiggly* came to town, everybody said that Andy would probably close up shop because they had a big nice brand-new butcher shop at the back of the store, but from what everybody could see, Andy didn't miss a beat. You could never wake the manager of the *Piggly Wiggly* up at 10:00 at night and expect him to cut some meat for you, but you could with Andy. Most folks never bothered him after hours, but occasionally there was an emergency, or someone underestimated the amount needed for a party on Saturday night, but other than that, Andy was pretty much an 8:00 to 5:00 shop. "Thank you, Andy, that's mighty kind of you. I will try not to be after 5:00." Andy walked out the front door leaving the sheriff standing there in the front of the shop by himself. He drew in a deep breath and walked behind the meat cases and then through the door leading back to the stock room area where Bobby would be. He walked down a hallway that had cooler doors on both sides until he reached an open area where the work counter, bone saw, and meat grinder were. Bobby was cutting through a huge slab of what used to be half a cow. Bobby looked up and smiled, said, "Hello" to the sheriff, put his knife down, wiped his hands on his apron, then washed them in the sink. "Hang on, Sheriff, I wouldn't shake your hand like this." When he was finished drying he walked up to the sheriff and the two shook hands. Elmer could tell right away that Bobby Martin, just by his actions alone, was not the killer. He didn't seem nervous. He took the time wash his hands and by the smile on his face he was genuinely happy to see the sheriff. He wished he didn't have to arrest him. "What can I help you with, Sheriff? I would have come out to see you; no need to come back to this mess." The sheriff took off his hat, which he now recognized was a nervous habit. Every time he was about to say something he didn't want to say he tended to reach for his hat and pull it off his head. "Bobby, I wish I was here just to see you work your magic on that carcass, but I am actually here on official business." Bobby looked confused and that was no surprise to the sheriff. "Bobby, I am here to arrest you for the murder of Lonnie Buckles." He went into the Miranda Rights segment of the arrest and after he was finished, Bobby was more dumbfounded than he was when the sheriff said he was there on official business. The sheriff didn't make any moves to handcuff

Bobby. He wanted to give him time to process what he had just told him. Bobby shuffled his feet, spun all the way around, and paced the room. "Sheriff! I didn't kill that little boy, I ain't even seen that boy or his idiot brothers! I swear I didn't have anything to do with this." His voice was very shaky and for a second the sheriff thought he would have to catch him and keep him from falling on the floor. "What happened to him, Sheriff? I am a lot of things but I ain't no killer." The sheriff started to reach for the cuffs that were in a holster on the side of his belt, but he decided not to. "Bobby, I need to take you down to the office and that way we can sit and try and figure this out. By rule, I am supposed to handcuff you before I put you in the squad car, but rules were meant to be broken. I'd like for the towns folks, especially Andy, to see you get in the front seat with me and just drive off. There will be a lot less gossiping that way." The sheriff stood there for a few more minutes and let the silence get drowned out by the fans in coolers making their noises. One of them obviously needed adjusting because it was making a terrible metal-on-metal sound that the sheriff hadn't noticed as much a few minutes ago. Bobby pulled his apron over his head, threw it in a barrel that was full of other dirty aprons and said, "Let's go, Sheriff, let's get this mess cleaned up now."

Bobby sat down in the front seat just like the sheriff had suggested. Even though they both nodded at Andy, who was on the sidewalk smoking a cigarette, nobody thought it was weird for Bobby to get in the front seat with the sheriff. They especially didn't think he was being arrested. That was certainly not the way you arrested someone.

He and Bobby later walked into the Sheriff's Office to the stares of everyone who was there. Lavera expected Bobby to be in handcuffs like everyone else. They made their way back to the interrogation room, which doubled as a place where the sheriff had private conversations with employees that weren't doing a good job or needed to be straightened out in some way. Either way, the room had negative connotations. Bobby sat down in one of the chairs and the sheriff sat down in the other chair. They were now face-to-face. "I need you to tell me everything you did starting from the minute you walked out of your daddy's barbershop when you were upset and reminding me that it was an election year." The sheriff took his hat off and sat it on the table that separated the two men. Bobby put his head down on the table, so the sheriff couldn't see his face and started to talk but he stopped. The seriousness of a murder charge was now sinking in. He raised his head up, the sheriff could see the streams of tears running down his face, definitely not the face of a cold-blooded child killer. "Do I need a lawyer, Sheriff?" The sheriff was sitting up straight in his chair with his hands clasped in his lap when he heard the question. He put his elbows on the desk and leaned forward so that he was closer to Bobby. "Bobby, I don't think for one minute that you killed that Buckles boy, but..." He paused and looked around the room like he was trying to keep a secret. "The evidence all points to you right now. I'm doing my job and I need you to do what you think is best for you. So, in short, I can't answer that for you. Only you can." Bobby leaned back in his chair. He was wearing a short sleeve t-shirt so he pulled the sleeve out as far as he could and wiped his eyes. "I don't need a lawyer. I didn't lay a hand on that boy even after I knew he beat up my little girl, and your boy, Sheriff. How come you ain't on the other side of this table?" The sheriff knew that Bobby would ask him that question. "Because my whereabouts from the barbershop to now have already been accounted for. I need you to do the same thing." Bobby shook his head as if he understood and drew in a deep breath. He began to tell the sheriff all about his weekend, even that he admitted he was "running hot" after he left the barbershop. The sheriff didn't need to have him explain "running hot", he knew exactly what Bobby meant. He detailed every move he made all weekend, but when he got to around midnight Monday night, he started to struggle. All he could say was that he went to bed around midnight and was back at Andy's at 8:00 a.m. the next morning. The sheriff asked him if there was any way that he could corroborate that he was at home and in bed by midnight Sunday night. The only thing he would say was that he lived alone and that it was impossible to get someone to corroborate that. The sheriff knew that was true but was frustrated because that was the most important time frame. He needed Bobby to fill in that blank somehow and he could let him free, but until he could do that, he would have to lock him up. "Bobby, I have to lock you up until we can get some more information and hopefully figure a way to place you at home Sunday night or dig up some more evidence. I'm sorry I have to do this." He asked Bobby to stand up and turn around. Bobby didn't say a word. His time in Parchman told him what to do next so he turned around, put his hands behind his back, and allowed the sheriff to put cuffs on him. A few minutes later, the sheriff closed and locked the cell door on Bobby Martin.

He walked down the hall towards his house. He was so focused on what he needed to do as he was walking down the hallway that he literally bumped into Lisa Bradshaw, who worked for the Sumner Gazette. He knocked the papers she was carrying out of her hand. He bent down to help her pick them up. He knew she would want to talk about the events of the day, but he was in no mood. "Hello, Ms. Bradshaw, sorry about that." He tried to keep from saying anything else but as they were both kneeling in the hallway she said, "Sheriff, I know it's been a tough day. I am not here to badger you, but I have to put something in the paper tomorrow. The town is already talking about the murder." The sheriff knew something like this couldn't stay quiet for long. He hated gossip in every form, but he guessed that finding a boy in the back alley of downtown Webb was a subject folks were bound to talk about. This was a small town, and this was a big deal. He couldn't blame them. "Lisa, I would rather not comment on anything now. It is too soon, and we don't know much." She grabbed the last piece of paper off the floor and stood up. He followed her. She was a very tall lady and it surprised him for just a second that they were nearly eye-to-eye. He figured she had to be at least 6-foot 3 and she was not wearing high heels. "You know enough to arrest a man for the murder of a little boy. One is white, and one is black. I'd say that is quite a bit." The sheriff knew what she was getting at and wasn't surprised. "What do you want, Lisa? I am tired, and I need to make some phone calls." Lisa took the papers from his hand that he had helped pick up. "Get out in front of this, Sheriff. The best way to stifle the gossip is to control it. I just need a statement from you on what you know so far." The sheriff thought about it for a minute and realized that she was right. If he didn't try to control the misinformation he would have a miserable time finishing this investigation. She wasn't a bad lady at all. He met her a long time ago when she first got the job at Sumner and thought she was honest and always kept her word. He liked her, but he simply didn't like her profession.

He gave her what he knew, but since he had not been able to contact anyone in the Buckles clan yet, to please leave the name of the boy out of the paper. She agreed but she also said that she had to print Bobby Martin's name because it was now a matter of public record. The minute he arrested him and read him his rights it became public information. He understood that but didn't like it. He knew that Bobby didn't kill that boy and hoped that he could prove it before anyone did anything stupid, especially Brett.

When he was finished with Lisa Bradshaw, he continued down the hall until he got to Lavera's desk and was surprised to see that she was still there. She never stayed past her 5:00 p.m. shift. "Elmer, I got Andy on the phone for you." He stood over her desk looking at her with a puzzled look; he was making her feel uncomfortable which was not easy to do to Lavera. "What did you do that for and why are you still here?" She fidgeted with her desk to deflect the attention; she really didn't like the attention she was getting from the sheriff at the moment. "Elmer, I figured you would want to ask him if anything had been stolen recently from his shop, and this is not a normal week. If you aren't already under a lot of pressure, you soon will be when that tall lady prints whatever she is going to print tomorrow. I am just trying to help, Sheriff." He had thought earlier that he needed to talk to Andy about the missing knife but had forgotten. He was actually a little embarrassed that he had to be reminded about good police work from his secretary, but then again, she was not an ordinary secretary, and did she just call him Sheriff? "Thank you, Lavera, I appreciate you calling Andy for me, and did you just call me Sheriff?" Lavera put her head down, started writing something and said, "Of course not."

After he had finished talking to Andy – who had no idea if one of his knives was stolen or not – he hung up the phone, flipped off the desk lamp, and headed for home. He had leftover chicken on his mind. He would call Bubba from his house to see if he had any luck finding Brett or Judd.

Chapter 42

❧

DECKER FINISHED WASHING HIS HANDS AND WENT
back into the kitchen where his momma was now busy making
some mashed potatoes, and from his experience, that meant that
supper was just about ready. He could hardly stand it anymore.
The chicken smelled so good and the sound of her blender
working over the potatoes in that bowl was overwhelming. She
stopped the blending when she saw him come back into the
kitchen. She set the blender down on the counter. Decker could
see the mashed-up potatoes hanging off the blender blades and
wanted so badly to go over and lick those blades like he had done
so many times before. "Decker, run and get your sister, tell her
that she needs to help set the table and pour the tea. Your daddy
will be here shortly, and we can eat." Before she could get the
last words out of her mouth, he bolted for his sister's room. He
slammed into the door and turned the handle at the same time.

She was sitting on the bed with her legs crossed. "You know, little man, you need to start knocking on the door." She put the book down that she was reading. "Is the house on fire?" She was smiling. She had been through this routine many times before… he was hungry and in a hurry to eat. Decker was the most impatient kid in town when he was hungry. "I'm hungry and ready to eat. Momma wants you to set the table." He bolted out the door and back down to the kitchen. His momma had restarted the blender after he left and now he could see that the potatoes were very creamy. His momma looked at him and knew what he was thinking. She turned the blender off and set the blender on the counter where he could see the blades were covered in wonderful creamy mashed potatoes. She hit a button on the back of the blender and popped the blades out of the machine. "Decker, come put these in the sink please." His momma would never openly tell him to lick the blades of the blender, so by telling him to put them in the sink, she knew that he would lick them clean before he ever even got there. Decker grabbed the blades and had them licked clean, but he had to stop at the sink for just a little bit to finish the job. Once he was finished licking the blades, his momma asked him how school was today. He normally answered with a typical, "It was fine", but today he felt like he needed to say more. He told her again about being moved up to the front of the class, he told her about recess and how he helped with the jump rope and that nobody picked on him. His sister had arrived in the kitchen and was pulling glasses out of the cabinet to first fill with ice then with tea. She was listening to him talk; neither momma nor Decker could see her smiling. She had suffered with her brother more than anyone. She held him close when he cried after being picked on all day.

She had allowed him to fall asleep in her bed while she read to him and would pick him up and carry him to his room. He never remembered her carrying him to bed, he would just wake up the next morning in the place he thought he should be. She had told him over and over that he was special and one day everyone else would know it too. She hoped that this little girl who had suddenly stolen his thoughts and probably his heart would be the gateway to so many more good things for her little brother. As she listened to him tell his momma about his day, she realized that she had never heard him talk so much. She was setting the table when he got to the part about Dexia. Somehow Decker had shortened the word, either because he couldn't remember how to pronounce it, or he believed that was how it was pronounced. His momma stopped and asked him to say the word again and he again repeated Dexia. Heather walked back into the kitchen and said, "Hey, buddy, do you mean Dyslexia?" Without missing a beat, Decker said, "That's what I said, didn't you hear me?" Heather smiled, he was on a tear right now and there was no correcting Decker when he was on a tear. She knew she could go back and fix the pronunciation later, but it was best to let him go. "Dyslexia, huh?" His momma pulled the salt and pepper shakers out of the cabinet and placed them on the counter for Heather to take to the table. "I have heard of that before, I believe that is where you read things backwards?" Decker took a hunk of skin from a chicken leg that was hanging off the platter and shoved it into his mouth. While he was chewing, he laughed a little when she said it and had to stop and chew a little faster so he could answer it. "No, momma, not really, it just means that my brain sees letters in weird ways. My brain won't let me put them together to make words!" His momma grabbed some napkins from the tray and handed them to Heather. She didn't say anything nor did Heather. Neither had ever thought that Decker might have a reading problem but it kind of made sense. Decker wasn't stupid at all, they both knew that he was smart, but he didn't like to read. Looking at it now, he didn't like to read but he loved to be read to. Both Heather and Lois were in deep thought as they watched their little man picking at a chicken leg on the platter until it was nothing but the bone. His momma was about to say something when the phone rang. Without asking permission, Decker reached up to the big yellow phone hanging at the end of the counter he was sitting on and said, "Davis residence, Decker speaking." Both Heather and Lois looked at each other; both were smiling on the inside and the outside. Their little guy was figuring some stuff out. The sheriff wasn't expecting Decker to answer the phone and was pretty surprised too. He chuckled a little because there was something weird about talking to his son on the phone. He hadn't expected to do that but as it turned out, it helped put him in a better mood. "Well hello, Mr. Decker Davis." Decker started to pick at another piece of chicken and his momma smacked his hand; she said there was no eating while you are talking on the phone. Decker had never been this far in proper phone manners, so he pulled his hand back from the platter. "Hey, daddy! Dinner's ready. Are you coming because that hollow leg you say I have is empty!" Decker's momma could hear Elmer laugh through the phone and shook her head. "I'm gonna be late, big man, so you go ahead and fill up that hollow leg. Put your momma on the phone, ok?" Decker handed the phone to his momma as soon as he heard that, but she wouldn't take it back just yet. "You must tell the caller good bye and then you hand the phone to the person they are asking for." Decker shook his head as if he understood it. He put the phone back up to his ear and said, "Good bye." He then handed the phone back to his momma and he could hear his sister Heather laughing in the background. Elmer told Lois he would be late and to eat without him. He would eat some leftovers when he got home. She told him she wasn't sure that there would be anything left after Decker got through with it.

Jeannine had a terrible time sleeping that night. She had so many things spinning around in her head that she just couldn't sleep. She spent the evening talking to her grandparents about everything under the sun. They were good at explaining things to help her see the broader picture. As much as they would like to avoid it, they wanted her to see the implications of a crime that involved different races. Her granddaddy told her that sometimes things like this awoke demons in people that they didn't even know they had, and that they had to do their best to trust that God would help everyone stay rational and help them keep those demons from waking up. She had a lot of questions, like *how demons can live in someone and them not know it* and *if a kid who was the same color as she were killed, would he still be worried about those demons?* He explained that of course he would be worried, but it would be in a different way, but he always worried about the demons that are inside of some of the best people. Her grandparents wanted to go over what happened when she and Decker got into a fight with the Buckles kid. She went over the story again and didn't leave out a single detail. In a way, she wished it would just be over because she was tired of telling the story. After her granddaddy told her that the Buckles kid was no longer with us, that was how he put it, he didn't want to use any more strong language with her than he had too. He thought this was entirely too much for a child to handle. She should not have to deal with her daddy being locked up and she should not have to deal with skin color.

Jeannine was not sure what to think. Her grandparents had given her so much information to think about. It was kind of their way of attacking every situation. They liked to give her all the information they could give her and let her decide what her next questions were, if any, or what actions she should take. They knew she was a super smart girl and wanted her to behave that way. She lay there in bed thinking about tomorrow until she fell asleep.

When Elmer Davis came home he ate what was left of the chicken and potatoes. As he sat there at the table with just Lois, he told her about the day's events. He didn't care that it was confidential information. It would be out in the paper tomorrow and besides, he always told her what he did that day. He had no secrets from Lois. She was his sounding board for a bad day and she helped him work through things in a way that nobody else could. She would offer advice when he wanted it and when he didn't want it and she would tell him when he was wrong. She told him that he had to go in and talk to Decker before he fell asleep. He put up a little fuss about having to tell Decker about a crime, but she explained that if Decker didn't have a full grasp of the situation, he would not understand how to react to any comments or mean teasing that might be directed at Jeannine. Lois told him to think of any other time that he could remember when Decker was so excited about school, about going to the library. He was doing things that she wasn't sure she thought he would ever do; he was having fun at school. Elmer conceded and headed off to Decker's room, but he stopped by to talk to Heather first. He wanted her to be in on the conversation with Decker. She was good with Decker and often helped him understand some pretty complex stuff and this was certainly complex. Elmer explained much of what happened to Heather first. When she had a good grip on what her daddy's concerns were and how he wanted to explain it to Decker, she told him that he will have a hard time with the racial issues because she believed that he truly did not see color. She told her daddy that she thought Decker would have a harder time with the murder. Even though that kid picked on Decker relentlessly, Decker didn't have a mean bone in his body. He would never wish bad things to happen to anyone. She confided in her daddy that in her conversations with Decker, she realized that he may not have a mean bone in his body and he may not see color, and he was over-the-top protective of those who meant something to him. That's why he punched the kid in the nose, he felt like they were making Jeannine say bad words and were hurting her. She suggested that maybe if they sort of hint that Jeannine might get picked on tomorrow and they were counting on Decker to help look after her, then he would rise to the challenge because he would think that they expected something grown-up from him and it would help him block out the other stuff. If he was in protective mode, he wouldn't care about anything else. After listening to his nearly grown-up daughter, Elmer felt a lump raise up in his throat. He realized that he needed to pay more attention to her and Decker because she knew more about his son's emotions than he did. He didn't see that as knock against himself, it was actually a source of pride. Not only was he raising a son to become a man, his little girl had become a woman and he somehow missed some of it. She was beautiful, mature, and rational. He gave her a huge hug that lifted her feet off the ground. When he set her down, he kissed her on the forehead. Feeling like they were ready for the conversation with Decker, they both walked into Decker's room, only to find him sitting up with a book on his lap and sound asleep. The conversation with Decker would have to wait until tomorrow morning.

Chapter 43

THE NEXT MORNING THE BREAKFAST TABLES AT both the Martin and Davis homes were lively with conversations. Jeannine was still asking questions about demons. Mr. Martin sat listening to her very quietly and wished maybe he could have used a different term than demons in people. She seemed to be very hung up on the concept and maybe wasn't seeing the broader picture because of it. She told her granddaddy that she had a terrible time sleeping because she wondered what demon might be inside her and was scared that maybe while she slept the demon inside her would slip out and do bad things. She didn't like the idea of something inside of her that she couldn't control. Her granddaddy assured her that there was no way that there was a demon inside such a beautiful little girl. He said that demons were developed over time and that they were sometimes taught. He said that if she kept her heart pure and avoided hate, she would never have a problem with a demon. He said that hate and ignorance were the two main things a demon needed to eat daily to in order to thrive. She assured him that she didn't hate anyone; she admitted that she once said that she hated a kid in fourth grade because he would intentionally knock her down while she was jumping rope, plus he farted in class all the time even though the teacher would tell him not to do it. She said that kid had to have had a demon inside of him to fart like that all the time. Her granddaddy laughed while she was telling him the story about the farting demon. Her grandma didn't care much for the open discussion about farting at the breakfast table, but she let it go because she wanted her baby girl to get everything out. She was liable to have a pretty rough day with kids making fun of her daddy getting arrested, especially since the story was already in the Sumner Gazette that was sitting on the table with them. Mr. Davis saw it on the front page and he didn't read any more of the paper. It was the first time in nearly 40 years that he hadn't read the paper to her while she cooked in the kitchen. It was just too much for him to handle. Once the conversation was coming to an end, Mr. Martin went over the rules for the day and reminded her that he would pick her and Decker up from school and take them to the library.

At the Davis breakfast table, Heather and the sheriff were repeating everything they had discussed the night before. Decker listened but it was always difficult to tell if Decker was actually paying attention because he had to be doing something at all times. This morning as they were talking to him about the difference in skin color and the tragic death of Lonnie Buckles, he was breaking his bacon into one-inch pieces that he would then drag through the syrup, leftover from his pancakes, one at a time. He was very methodical about the size of the pieces. Every now and then Heather would get frustrated, stop the conversation and say, "Hey, little man, what did I just say?" Each time she asked, Decker would stop, and repeat verbatim what either she had said or what his daddy had said. Both Heather and Mr. Davis were amazed at how well he repeated back what they said when he didn't appear to be paying any attention at all. When they felt like they had covered everything, the table got quiet. Mrs. Davis decided it was her turn to see what Decker was thinking. She sat down next to Decker and ran her hand through his hair, she loved to do that and to be honest; Decker liked it too. Every time she ran her fingers through his hair, he just felt better. He didn't know why but he could feel how much his momma loved him just from her touch. It would be one of the many things that he would badly miss after she was gone. She didn't have to say anything to him, all she had to do was touch him and he just knew what she was trying to say. This morning she asked him if he wanted some more bacon and he smiled and shook his head yes. She got up, went to the counter, and brought back a platter of bacon. It seemed like everyone was staring at Decker and he knew it. He was kind of used to that at school but not at home. He dunked some more one-inch broken pieces into the maple syrup but before he was about to dunk the last piece he said, "I will make sure nobody picks on Jeannine, I always do that." But then he asked a question, "How come I feel bad that Lonnie died? He was always mean to me and everyone else in class. There's sure gonna be a lot of kids that won't mind him not being in class, but I still feel bad. How come?" Mrs. Davis wasn't about to let Heather or Elmer answer that one. "Because you're special, Decker Davis, you have a good heart." She ran her hand though his hair as she said it. "Now you know, Mr. Martin will pick you and Jeannine up from school so be ready, be good, and be safe. Ok, Deck?" He slammed the last piece of maple syrup-covered bacon in his mouth, jumped up and mumbled something about being late for the bus, and off he went. He took the time to grab his book satchel and he crashed through the back screen door. It squeaked as it slammed shut. He sprinted right past Bubba who was coming up the stone walking path that led from the side yard to the back door. Bubba tried to say something to Decker, but he got no response.

Bubba knocked on the back screen door then entered. The knock was more for social graces than anything. He had been told a million times that he need not knock, that he was family. Bubba sat down at the table with the sheriff. Mrs. Davis almost instantly sat a full plate in front of him and he wasted no time digging into it. This time he spent, nearly every morning, with the Davis family was probably some of his happiest times. He loved the smells and the sounds and especially the food. "Have you seen the paper?" The sheriff slid the paper over to Bubba for him to see. Bubba shoved a huge fork of syrup-covered pancakes into his mouth at almost the same time the paper slid into his view. Since he didn't want to talk with his mouth full, he nodded up and down to let the sheriff know that he had seen the paper. "We need to find Brett lickidy split this morning. No wasting time. Brett doesn't need to find out his little brother is dead from the newspaper." Bubba chewed what was left of his pancakes. "I'm gonna go back out to his place first thing and if he ain't there, I will drive to Corinth if I have to. I went by the Jackpot and the garage, his two favorite hangouts, and just missed him at the Jackpot but he hadn't been by the garage."

The sheriff laughed a little which caused some confusion for
Bubba because he was being serious, and the sheriff was laughing, about what, he had no idea. "What's so funny?" The sheriff
got up and poured another cup coffee but while he was pouring
the coffee with his back to Bubba he smiled and said, "Did you
squeeze in any time for Ms. Becky?" It was a mischievous comment and he knew it would get Bubba's blood pumping. He
always thought Bubba worked faster and much sharper when he
was a little edgy, that was for sure, the way he played basketball.
When they were on the same team at Duke, Elmer would prod
Bubba in practices and games. He would do things to intentionally get Bubba angry and all the sudden, Bubba would turn into
one of the best point guards he'd ever played the game with.
He wished he didn't have to push Bubba that way, but Bubba
didn't seem to have a switch of his own that he could flip on and
off. "Now that's not funny, Elmer Davis, you know darn well I
would never have anything to do with Ms. Becky and the goods
she sells out of that place! I don't know why we don't just shut
down her joint, nearly everything that woman does is illegal,
and we just sit here and let it go on. I should just go over there
and arrest them all then set fire to the place!" Bubba was very
upset that the sheriff would even joke about him spending any
time with Ms. Becky. He was so upset that he called the sheriff
Elmer, which is what he called him until he got the job of deputy
sheriff in Tallahatchie County, Mississippi. The sheriff was still
not looking at Bubba, but his smile had become increasingly
large. He was trying to suppress it, so he could turn around and
resume the conversation in a more rational tone. When he was
confident that he could carry on without a smile, he turned and
sat back down at the table. "If you went and did that I would

have to arrest you for arson and potentially homicide because most of the people in that building would be too drunk to know it was on fire. Not to mention some of Becky's backdoor customers are some of Webb's finest and most respected citizens, known to thump the Bible on Sunday and bump the headboard on Monday. Me and Lois have a nickname for them, we call them the T&B's, short for thump and bump." The sheriff had a devious little smile on his face. Bubba was still riled up about the prospect of spending time with Ms. Becky, but he was regaining his composure. "That's terrible, Sheriff. That place is nothing to joke about." The sheriff was still smiling as he leaned back in his chair. He was about to say something when Bubba added something about Ms. Becky that the sheriff wasn't expecting. "She's not a bad woman you know. She just got dealt a bad hand in life and is doing the best she can." The sheriff was surprised by that and actually thought for a moment that Bubba had in fact sampled the goods at the Jackpot, and now the sheriff lost his smile. "She said something to me yesterday that bothered me all night. She asked me to find that boy before Brett did because he would beat that boy black and blue, but then she said to find him before that smelly creepy mechanic did. I am pretty sure she was referring to Chub. That boy smells like a walking diesel engine that's been dipped in rotten farts. Good Lord." Bubba shook his head as he was telling the sheriff about what Ms. Becky said when the two were together. "Sounds like Ms. Becky might have changed your impression of her a little? I know you are dead on about Chub though, but he is harmless. He might smell bad, but he only hangs out with Brett because Brett makes him feel tough. Take Brett away and he is just a pushover." It was Bubba's turn to get some coffee from the pot now; it was actually the coffee pot he had given them for Christmas a year earlier. It was a brand-new *Mr. Coffee* with a clock on it and everything. He found it at *Sears* in Clarksdale and was quite proud of the fact that he was drinking coffee out of a pot he had gifted. It sort of affirmed his strong skill at gift selection. "Yeah, I caught Mrs. SHANE-TALL giving him the what-for yesterday because he didn't fix her brakes. He acted weird. I swear I thought he was gonna pop her one right in the snoz if I hadn't stepped in. He was as mad as I've ever seen him; usually he's pretty docile. She didn't seem to be put off by his unique aroma at all, but I sure was." He sat back down at the table and there was a slight pause in the conversation. Bubba took the time to finish his last few bites of eggs and bacon. "Since we have two cars, you go back out to the Buckles place and see if he made it back from Corinth. After that, you can check out the Jackpot again if you like." The sheriff was simply trying to stir Bubba's emotions again, but he didn't get any response, so he let it go. Bubba acted like he had just thought of something he forgot which turned out to be true. "Dang, I forgot to check on a report of still operating again. I really don't think its operating because it's too late in the shine season, all the leaves are falling off the trees, so they wouldn't start one now. Somebody in town told me that they thought there was one out on Old Wire Road." The sheriff nodded his head in agreement of his deputy's assessment of the moonshine season coming to a close for the winter. "Yeah, it's more than likely kids and a bonfire. The high school kids like to go out there to build a fire and make out. I imagine that's what you will find, a burned-out bonfire site." Bubba agreed, got up from the table, grabbed his plate, and cleaned it off in the sink. He never left dirty dishes anywhere; even in his own place he was very meticulous about being neat. While he was rinsing off the plate the sheriff poured the rest of the coffee pot contents into a thermos and screwed the top down tight. "Well meet me back at the station at 5:00 today. I don't want to drive this green bomb home any more than I have to. The cows complain that it makes them nauseous." Bubba laughed, finished drying his plate, and put it back in the cabinet. "Well you're the one that picked that ugly piece of crap out of the auction." The sheriff laughed and said, "Yeah, but the price was right, and she purrs like a kitten...wait are we talking about the car or you and Ms. Becky?" The sheriff howled with laughter. Bubba didn't appreciate the humor at all.

Chapter 44

﹏

Decker stood next to the mailbox just like he had every day of school. He could usually hear the bus coming before he actually saw it. There was a curve in the road that prevented him from seeing it until it was almost right at the entrance of his driveway. To Decker, the bus didn't make the same sound that other cars or even trucks did. He heard it coming and this time he made sure to pick up his book satchel that he had dropped by the mailbox out of habit. He didn't realize it when he set his book satchel next to the mailbox, but he had set it on a somewhat newly-formed ant hill. He was busy kicking an old beer can he found like a football. He was getting pretty good at lifting it off the ground pretty high, high enough to clear the mailbox. That was impressive as far as he was concerned. He was so good that he started aiming his kicks right at the mailbox. He wanted to hear the can hit the side of the mailbox and after a small adjustment in his follow through he was smacking the mailbox with every kick of the can. He heard the bus coming up the road with its distinctive sound. He kicked the can one last time and missed the mailbox but that was ok, he had hit it enough. He thought that after he and Jeannine were through with chores this afternoon, he would take a real football and impress her with how well he could kick it. He grabbed the book satchel from the ground and stood there diligently where he had been told to stand oh so many years ago. The standing place was a safe distance from the road and it allowed the bus to swerve into the entrance to the Davis driveway without going into the ditch. As he was standing there waiting for the bus to stop he felt something burning on his hand, and when he looked down at his hand, he was horrified to see what looked like a million ants on his hand – and to him it looked as if they were trying to gnaw the flesh right off the bone! He dropped the book satchel and started beating his hand on his thigh and swinging his hand in the air in hopes to hurl the ants into the air and off his arm. He still couldn't use his other hand very well, but he tried. The movement of this hand in the sling brought so much pain in his shoulder that he stopped trying to use that hand and simply smacked his good hand and arm against his pant leg. Mr. Johns could see Decker in the distance as he rounded the curve and it looked to him like he was dancing a weird dance where he would spin three times, smack his thigh, and spin three more. He couldn't wait to hear this story. Decker Davis was always good for a laugh in the morning in some weird way. As he got closer to Decker, he realized that Decker wasn't dancing, he looked to be fighting off bees. Mr. Johns slammed on the brakes, set the emergency brake, and yanked open the door of the bus. He nearly jumped down all three steps and started yelling at Decker to tell him what was wrong because he couldn't see any bees. Decker managed to yell that he was getting bitten by ants! Mr. Johns grabbed Decker around the waist in order not to hurt his broken collarbone; at least he stopped him from spinning long enough to see the ants on his arm. Decker had already managed to whip most of them off, he guessed, because he only saw a couple. He swatted them away and then inspected the rest of Decker's clothing but couldn't find any more. Decker kept squirming, which was testing Mr. Johns patience, but he finally managed to let Decker know that they were all off him as far as he could tell. Decker stood there and looked at his arm then looked up at Mr. Johns. Mr. Johns gave him the option to get on the bus with the ant bites burning a little and check in with the school nurse for some cream that would keep the burn and itch down, or he could turn around and walk back to the house and let his momma put something on it and then drive him to school. No way was Decker going back home; his momma might make him stay home from school and then he would have to stay indoors the whole day and that just couldn't happen. Once when Decker got a stomachache and stayed home from school, he threw up all morning but felt fine in the afternoon, but she still wouldn't let him go outside. He reckoned it was one of the worst afternoons he had ever had in his life. All he could do was sit and look outside. Mr. Johns started to pick up his book satchel for him but saw that it was covered in ants; he asked Decker what he wanted to do about that. Decker quickly decided that he didn't need a thing in that book satchel except for his lunch and he didn't even need that really, he could eat the cafeteria food. It wasn't so bad, but he hoped it wasn't a carrot day. "Just leave it

by the mailbox, I can pick it up when I get back home tonight."
Mr. Johns used his foot to scoot the book satchel as close to the
mailbox as he could. As he was walking away, he thought that it
might look a little strange to his parents if they saw a Decker bag
with no Decker at the end of the road, so he climbed back up
in the bus, grabbed a pencil and paper, and wrote a quick note
explaining the malaise that had just occurred this morning, but
emphasized in the note that Decker was just fine; he just had a
couple ant bites. By now Decker had already climbed up in the
bus and was once again thankful that he was the first to get on
the bus and at least nobody saw him getting attacked by killer
ants. Mr. Johns sat down in the driver's seat, closed the door, and
looked in the mirror at Decker sitting there rubbing his ant bites
on his corduroy pants. Not only could he see him doing it, he
could hear the sound of his skin rubbing against the corduroys.
"Well Mr. Davis, good morning. You sure make driving the bus
interesting. Now stop scratching the ant bites, you'll just make
them itch worse."

When he arrived at school, Mr. Johns went into the school
with Decker and took him right to the school nurses office. He
couldn't count on Decker to handle the task alone because he
would more than likely have gone straight to class and continued to rub his bites on his pant leg the rest of the day. If that
were to happen and he left that note at the mailbox saying that
Decker was fine, he would probably get an earful from the
sheriff, or worse, Mrs. Davis. Once he had Decker firmly in
the school nurse's control, he left the building and returned to
his bus. When Mr. Johns took him to the nurse's office, he was
surprised to see none other than Ms. Maybelle Richardson. He
was confused because she wasn't the school nurse. "Well Decker

Davis!" She came over and gave him a hug; it was a gentle hug, one like a momma gives. She bent down to look at him, touched his cheeks with her hands like she did at the football game last week and said, "What in the world are you doing here already this morning, is your shoulder hurting?" He raised his arm to show her the ant bites. When he raised it, he was surprised to see that there were only a few ant bites around his wrist area. At the time, he was certain that there were at least a million ants on his hand. He figured his spinning around and waving his arm and smacking his hand against his thigh strategy must have worked better than expected because the damage wasn't nearly as bad as he expected. He told Ms. Maybelle Richardson about the ants and the pain and the strategy and all the while he was telling her, she was rubbing some white cream on his arm. He immediately felt better. He didn't know what it was she was putting on his wrist, but it was sure taking the itch away. She told him that she was the new school nurse and that she was so happy not to drive to Clarksdale every day and that she would see him every day of school now. When she was finished with his arm, she told him to come back after the lunch break and she would rub some more cream on the bites. He really liked her; she looked at him like his momma looked at him.

He sat in his seat next to Jeannine. After the conversation with his sister and daddy that morning, he wasn't sure what to expect, but she looked normal to him. She looked pretty in the clothes she wore and the way she had combed her hair. He fully expected kids to be surrounding her desk and poking their fingers at her and calling her names, along with calling her daddy names, but none of that happened. He was prepared for that scenario; he was simply going to crash into all the kids surrounding her desk. He would use his one good shoulder to really lay into them, then he would drag her out of the pile with the one good arm and take her to the front office where they would give him some medals for being so brave and tough. He had worked it all out in his head on the bus. Now, it was just a normal day, and nobody was saying anything to her. The bell rang, and the door closed. He tried to say "good morning" to her, but the rustle of all the kids standing up to begin reciting the Pledge of Allegiance drowned him out.

He heard a few things that the teacher said that morning, but not much because he was so focused on protecting Jeannine that it was nearly impossible to concentrate on what she was saying. He wasn't sure when the attacks would come or where they would come from, but he was prepared for as many as he could think of. He promised his daddy that he would look after Jeannine and he intended to keep that promise. The bell rang for lunch and as was the rule, each kid had to put their stuff away, stand beside their desks, and exit the classroom row by row. There was a strict no talking policy in place and the consequences were dire. If you were caught talking in line or waiting beside your desk, you were forced to miss recess. It was the ultimate punishment for Decker. Even if the kids picked on him during that time, he still liked to get out and walk around the school playground and take in the sounds and let his imagination run free. It was hard to let your imagination run free when you were sitting by yourself at your desk in an empty classroom watching the clock over the teacher's desk tick.

He and Jeanine made it to the cafeteria where he told her about the ants and having to go through the food line today. She decided that she would go through the food line too even though she was carrying her lunch. As they scooted their trays along the rail that was in front of the cooks, Decker could see that it was Salisbury steak day. Not the best of days to eat the cafeteria food but it was tolerable. He also knew what came with the Salisbury steak...carrots. He would make sure that the lady didn't shovel any of that crap on his plate for sure. He'd rather starve. Jeannine was in front of him and grabbed two milks out of the deep well cooler for both her and Decker and made sure that she got the chocolate milk. She grabbed the utensils for her and Decker and began the journey down the food line. The first stop was the main course, but the lady behind the counter didn't give Jeannine anything, she just put the steak on Decker's plate and said, "Next". Decker thought maybe she didn't see Jeannine, so he said, "Hey, lady, you forgot hers." The lady didn't say anything, but Decker wasn't going to move. Jeannine had a feeling she knew what was happening but sure didn't expect it from grown-ups in the school. She had prepared for kids but not this. She told Decker just to keep moving but he hadn't caught on to what was happening. This time he yelled, "HEY, MISS, YOU FORGOT HERS!" This stopped the chatter in the whole cafeteria, which wasn't Decker's intention as he didn't like to draw attention to himself, but he had promised to look after Jeannine and he was keeping his word. "Young man, she has a lunch. We don't serve kids who brought their lunch, especially kids of murdering parents. Now move." He now understood everything his sister and his daddy had told him that morning. This was what they were talking about, he just didn't expect it in the lunchroom from a grown-up. The lunchroom was quiet now and he could see a teacher coming up to the line, so Decker took his tray that already had the Salisbury steak and a heap of gross

carrots on it, slid it to Jeannine, and pulled Jeannine's empty tray
to him. Jeannine looked frightened like she had just witnessed a
theft, but she didn't say anything. Her granddaddy had told her
that sometimes it was best just to keep quiet and move on and
that most of the times the demons wouldn't follow. The teacher
who came up to the line asked what was going on and the lady
behind the counter started to speak, but Decker interrupted her
and said, "She forgot to put some stuff on my tray is all." The
teacher looked at the lady behind the counter and then looked
back down at Decker, who had managed to put a very sad look
on his face, and he did look pitiful with one arm in a sling and
the other arm covered in white cream. "Oh, goodness, you poor
dear." She looked at the lady behind the counter and told her to
just put his food on the tray and she would help him take it to
the table. She smiled at Decker and rubbed his head. The lady
behind the counter must not have felt like arguing with another
grown-up so she put a little of everything on Decker's plate and
slid it down the line to where the teacher was waiting to grab it
and help Decker sit down. The teacher carried Decker's tray to
any empty table, sat it down, and told him if he needed anything
more just to holler and she would help him. She said, "Poor
dear" as she was walking away. Jeannine had this very angry look
on her face, even though she was already cutting into her steak.
She kept her eyes straight ahead and didn't look at him, but she
said, "You are gonna get me in trouble. There was no need for
you to kick up a fuss like that." She shoved a piece of steak into
her mouth and chewed it like she was mad. Decker sure didn't
understand. In his mind, they both had food in front of them
which was the objective, so why was she so mad? "Why are you
mad? I didn't do anything wrong." He was trying to cut his steak

with one hand, but it kept slipping around the plate. She saw this and took the knife from his hand, grabbed his fork, and cut it in little pieces. While she was cutting she said, "Because grand-daddy told me not to draw attention and to walk away from the demons and most of the time they wouldn't follow you if you stayed quiet!" She was trying to keep her voice down, but it was coming out like a growl and it kinda scared Decker a little. She realized that her voice and actions were scaring Decker a little and then she looked at him, she really looked at him. She saw the face and the tinge of red hair and the green eyes and all the ant bites and the arm in a sling and it hit her that the kid that she thought was a little stupid less than a week ago had just out-smarted two grown-ups, something she had never expected. She let out a breath as if all the tension she was feeling from being the center of attention when she was told not to be from her granddaddy last night and then again this morning was gone. "Decker Davis." That was all she said. They talked through the entire lunch. She even tried to talk him into eating a carrot but that was a deal breaker for Decker. She could get him to do just about anything, but she would never get him to eat a carrot.

The rest of the day went on like any other day except that Decker was still in protective mode. He would scan the class-room for any potential threats, but other than the little dust-up with the lady in the cafeteria, nothing happened. They both met her granddaddy outside the school and he took them to the library. Decker noticed that he wasn't as chipper as he was the previous day, but he did manage to ask her what she did today, and she answered with the usual, "I changed the world!" When he dropped them off at the library loop, he turned to look at them and gave them the normal instructions. He would be there to pick them up in an hour and to check with the librarian if they lost track of time.

Chapter 45

BRETT MET WITH THE CONSTRUCTION SUPERVISOR from Corinth and the two discussed the possibility of Brett helping with the remodel of three apartment buildings. The construction guy was going to tear out all the old fixtures and was hoping Brett's company would handle the tear-out of all the bathroom and kitchen fixtures. He told him that whatever he could salvage he could have and he would pay him a percentage of the contract with the builder. Brett wasn't really clear on the percentages part of the contract because all he could hear was that he could have what he could salvage. To him, free stuff was the best deal he could make. Brett wasn't the sharpest knife in the drawer when it came to handling contracts and the construction supervisor could tell. The construction supervisor was quite happy when Brett agreed to have all the stuff removed in a week. He knew that was nearly a twenty-four hour a day job and almost impossible to complete in a week. He also didn't tell Brett that the contract clearly stated that if Brett didn't have the old fixtures removed at the agreed time then there was no percentage of the contract allotted. It was a great deal for the construction supervisor because he and his crew could now concentrate on other more complicated demolition. Brett signed the sub-contractor agreement without even looking at it, believing that the construction supervisor was a straight-up dealer. The construction supervisor laughed as he walked away from Brett. He couldn't remember meeting anyone so dumb yet so anxious to prove it.

Brett finished his business in Corinth, but it was late when he finished so he stayed the night. He said he wanted to look over the scope of the project and formulate a strategy, but truth be known, he and the guy on the construction crew got into a drinking contest where they took turns drinking whiskey shots that the guys would light on fire and they would have to shoot them with the flame burning hot. It was something he had never done before but the construction guys goaded him into doing it. Their boss had already told them that "this guy" from Webb was as dumb as a bag of bent hammers. He never saw the guys doing the shots with the flame. They had perfected a way to blow out and shoot them all in one motion, a secret they did not share with Brett because it was fun watching him get burned at his own expense. When he woke the next morning, he swore from now on it would be best if he just stuck to regular shots. He swore his upper lip and the bottom of his nose were burned. He woke up the next morning with a hangover, not a really bad one, just a burned lip.

After he figured out where the truck keys were, he took care of his morning whiz before he headed back to Webb. He was anxious to get back to Webb so he could tell Judd what a deal he had made and that they were fixin' to make some serious money. He figured if he got Judd in gear, maybe ask Chub to help if he wasn't busy at the garage, and then take Lonnie out of school for a week, they could complete the job and walk away in great shape. He hadn't figured out that percentage thing yet, but he thought he would get Becky to help him read through that part over a few beers this evening, and maybe a little extra activity. He was feeling, rich, smart, and wealthy.

He pulled into the driveway of their property, and seeing how much merchandise was strewn everywhere, he started thinking about all the improvements he wanted to make before Donnie got home. He knew he would probably not see his daddy any time soon, but he really did look forward to Donnie being back and taking over the business again. Making big deals like he had just completed was not his thing, but he figured after today's success, he could learn to like it. As he got closer to the house, he could see Judd pacing back and forth in front of the house. Judd always paced back and forth when he was nervous, mad, upset, and amorist. Becky managed to help him out with the last one most of the time because not many girls were beating down the door to get at Judd. He was the least attractive of the brothers and Brett thought he was the dumbest. He conceded that Donnie was the smartest and maybe the best looking, but he fancied himself pretty good looking, so he figured it was a toss-up between he and Donnie. Lonnie hadn't filled out yet and he couldn't tell if he was going to be good looking like he and Donnie or not, but from what he could see, Lonnie was going to be dumber and lazier than Judd. He would try his best to make a man out of Lonnie, but he wasn't sure he could do it. Lonnie was just a fat stubborn kid who needed his butt kicked about once a week just to keep him straight.

Brett rolled the truck to a stop but nearly hit Judd because Judd was pacing with his eyes closed and that was usually a bad sign. He thought if he closed his eyes it would help make things go away quicker. He set the brake on the truck, jumped out, and slammed the door. He was upset that Judd nearly let himself get run over. "Judd! Stop your damn pacing back and forth! I nearly run over you. What the hell is the matter with you, boy?!" He grabbed him by the shoulders and made Judd look at him. He remembered the time Judd found out that their momma was dead, he went nuts like this; Donnie had more patience with him than Brett did but not much. "Look at me!" He slapped Judd in the face pretty hard and Judd opened his eyes. He started crying now that his eyes were open. "Brett, they found Lonnie dead this morning! They found him dead!" Brett let go of Judd's shoulders because he wasn't sure how that could be possible. Maybe Judd got things wrong. He wasn't very smart. "How do you know it was Lonnie and where did they find him and what happened?" Judd wiped his face with his sleeve and tried to gather himself so he could explain better. "It was in the Sumner Gazette this morning! He was murdered, Brett! They arrested Bobby Martin for killin' our brother! The sheriff got him locked up at county!" Judd ran into the house, and before Brett could even ask him where he was going, he came flying back out of the house with a paper in his hand. He handed it to Brett. "Our little brother is dead! Killed by that damn Bobby Martin!" Judd was nearly spinning in circles again. "If Donnie was here he would go bust that jail cell to pieces and drag Bobby Martin through the streets! I want Donnie home!" Judd was hysterical, but Brett thought he did have a point; Donnie would get even for this. Brett could handle this situation, but he was still in shock. He still didn't know how Lonnie was killed. The paper didn't say much other than he was found behind the hardware store and that they had arrested Bobby Martin. The sheriff had no other comment than that. He went through all the details in his head then he remembered that Lonnie beat up Bobby's little girl last Sunday along with that sheriff's retarded kid. He knew that for a fact, but he didn't think twistin' that little skanks arm behind her back was really beatin' her up. Lonnie was just playin' around anyway and what he did sure wasn't worth Bobby killin' him over it, but then that Bobby Martin was a hot head. He was as crazy as a barn rat and probably figured it was just payback for what Lonnie did to his little girl. When he finally got his arms around the fact that his little brother was dead, he wasn't sad at all, but he was mad...raging mad. He would have to step in for Donnie and exact revenge for this. He knew just where to start.

Chapter 46

AFTER HE PICKED UP JEANNINE AND DECKER FROM school and dropped them off at the library, he had to go back to the shop. He had two trims he knew were coming in and both were regular customer crews-cuts that missed their normal Saturday trim for various reasons and let him know they would be in that day after 3:00 p.m. They were easy cuts and he called them easy money because they were essentially a number one on the side and a number two on the top; a few quick and steady glides over the noggin and he was done. One and two were the two easiest settings on the trimmer. He would easily have both customers done in under an hour, plenty of time to get back and pick up Jeannine and Decker and take them out to the Davis place.

He unlocked the door to the barbershop, flipped the light switch and realized that in his rush to go pick up the kids at school, he didn't have time to sweep the floor from the day's last few customers. He hated a messy shop, even when he was working he usually swept up between customers, but today he was busier than usual, and couldn't afford to be late to pick up the kids. He never made appointments. To his customers who asked to make appointments, he would laugh and tell them that appointments were for the ladies and they needed to go see Ms. LuLu for that stuff, and that he only cut men's and if he couldn't give a man a hair cut in less than 15 minutes, he probably wasn't a man. He would laugh every time he said it. Some of his regular customers would goad him into the proclamation when they were paying at the counter and ask for an appointment for the following week. He would sometimes tell them he was too busy raking up a bouffant to see them next week. Everybody in the shop would get a huge laugh out of the back and forth and often the challenge of wits between customers and its owner. He was a man of routine and every time his customers joked about it, they got the same response.

He finished sweeping up the hair, cleaned the counters, and took the trash out the back door to the dumpster. He heard the front door open, so he tapped the trash can on the edge of the dumpster to make sure that any sticky contents didn't remain at that the bottom of the trash can. He walked in with the trash can in his hand, "Hello, Charlie! You here for your perm? Give me just a minute and I will heat up the rollers so they are nice and warm and won't hurt your ugly head!" He walked over and shook Charlie's hand. Both men laughed at the joke and Dub motioned for Charlie to sit down in the number 1 chair. Charlie Watts was a cotton farmer who was trying to get a field prepped for winter last Saturday and just couldn't leave work to get a haircut.

He actually didn't need much of a haircut because he was shiny bald on the top and just need the sides trimmed. Dub chatted with Charlie about the price of cotton and what the outlook was for next year's crops. When he finished trimming Charlie's hair, he did as he always did, he swooped the apron off so that the hair would fly away from the customer. While he was giving Charlie the dusting talc on the back of his neck, Elliot Jenkins came in as he said he would. This was going along perfectly for Dub. He would finish with Charlie, get Elliot done, and he would go back and pick the kids up from the library. Elliot Jenkins would take a little longer than Charlie as he had a full thick head of hair and he was very particular. Dub would joke with Elliot that he would have to start charging him more for all that hair or he may have to start going to see Ms. LuLu. Even though both Charlie and Elliot had seen the Sumner Gazette that morning and knew that Dub's son had been arrested, neither mentioned it. Even though Charlie appreciated that very much, he never said so. He didn't want anyone to know that it was eating him up inside. He prayed every day since the sheriff stopped by to tell him what he was about to do. He appreciated the sheriff very much for that. He knew that it wasn't police procedure to let a parent know their kid was about to be arrested for any reason, especially murder, but the sheriff did it for Dub Martin out of respect for him and his family. He thought the sheriff had done everything he could at the moment, but he prayed that someone would step in and find the real killer of the little boy. His son wasn't a killer. He had been hot-headed with a short fuse his whole life, but he didn't have it in him to kill anything. After all, it was Bobby Martin who caught that cat that Brett set on fire and put it out of its misery. He remembered his son coming home to tell him what

Brett did to that cat and how he saw the tears well up in his son's eyes when he was telling the story. That wasn't the action of anyone who would kill much less kill a small child. It had only been a day, but he trusted the sheriff and if anyone would figure out what happened, he would.

Even though Charlie was through with his haircut, he sat in the waiting chair listening to the conversation between Elliot and Dub. He figured it was close enough to 5 o'clock so he went over to the soda box, dug down to the bottom and came up with an ice-cold bottle of *Pabst Blue Ribbon*, snapped the lid off on the opener attached to the cooler, and sat back down. "Don't mind if I do, Dub Martin. I need something to steady my nerves after letting you work on my hair-do!" They all laughed. Dub asked Elliot if he wanted a beer but Elliot declined and said he had a date with his old lady and she didn't like him drinkin' before it. Dub was working very gently with the trimmers. "You need to go on and marry that woman, boy, you been tappin' that till how long now?" They all laughed and knew exactly what Dub meant. "Hells bells, I asked her a thousand times and she tells me she wouldn't marry a broke down old horse trader like me, she's is holding out for something better!" All three men howled with laughter. Dub actually had to step away from Elliot to gather himself again. Charlie took a huge gulp of his cold beer, swallowed it and said, "She is a smart woman, I knew that for sure!"

After Dub was finished with Elliot, they all settled up the bill and agreed to see each other in a week. Dub made another joke about Elliot's date with a smart woman. Once the front door was closed, he latched the screen and locked the front door. He would exit out the back like he always did. He grabbed a broom and swept up the hair the men left behind, scooped it up in a pan, and dumped it in the trash can. He shook out the aprons and hung them on the hooks by the mirror so they would be ready for tomorrow's customers. He noticed on the floor there was a big hunk of hair that obviously came from Elliot. He had either missed it or it came loose when he shook out the apron. He went back to get the broom and pan and bent down to sweep it up when he heard the back door open. The only person who ever used the back door besides him was Jeannine. Sometimes she would run home from school and come sit with him in the shop. He turned to see and realized quickly that it wasn't Jeannine.

"Well look what we have here, a murderer's daddy sweeping up his nasty old barbershop." Brett had entered the back door and was now standing in the middle of his shop just a few feet away from Dub. Dub glanced at the front door thinking that maybe he could just turn and walk out, but he wasn't going to run from this punk. Dub had fought bravely in the South Pacific during World War II and running wasn't his thing. He didn't care how old he was, he still felt like he could beat the hell out of this kid if he tried anything. "Brett, go on and turn around and walk out the same door you just came in before you do something silly." Brett took a few more steps inside and sat down in the number 2 chair. "The front door was locked old man, I'd just came in to get a haircut. I saw them other two fellas leave, and I thought to myself them boys look sharp as tacks, man that old fart Dub Martin sure knows how to cut some hair. I think I want to look sharp as a tack too but then I see that you've gone and locked me out. I gotta tell you old man, I think them fancy Kennedy boys would call that discrimination." He laughed when he said Kennedy boys, then he said, "If there are any left." Obviously making reference to the recent murder of *Bobby Kennedy*. Brett looked at himself in the mirror as if he was deciding what kind of haircut he wanted. "Say, it just occurred to me that you might not know how to cut white folks hair. But then I know you cut your boyfriend's hair." Brett had this evil look come over his face when he said *boyfriend*. He was obviously referring to the sheriff who was really the only white customer that Dub had. "How is that idiot sheriff? Did he come over and hold your hand and get your permission to arrest that murderin' SOB you raised?" Dub was getting pretty tired of this and he didn't like his beautiful wife being referred to in such a way. Dub started to take a step toward Brett, but he heard another voice. Judd had entered the barbershop. "Dub, you want to just stand where you are." Judd was holding a gun and worse, he was pointing it at Dub." Brett swung the chair around while Dub was looking down the barrel of Judd's gun and punched Dub right in the jaw. It happened so fast that Dub didn't see it coming and he staggered. Dub was tough, he could take a punch and had actually tried some boxing back in his younger days, but Brett had popped him when he wasn't watching and that made him dizzy. Before he could regain his balance, Brett was on him again, punching him all over the head and wherever else he could land punches. He tried to protect his head, but Brett had sort of pinned him against the counter where he kept the combs and clippers and cleaning solution. Brett had him so well pinned against the counter that he could neither fall nor stand; he felt like he was suspended against the counter. Brett was yelling things at him, but he didn't hear much of them because he was dizzy and felt like he was about to pass out. "I'm gonna teach all you damn Martins a lesson. You gotta know your place old man! You got one boy behind bars that I can't get to, but I am gonna get to every one of you before I am dead. I promise you that!" Brett continued to hit Dub in the head until Dub finally slid down to the shop floor. Dub was bleeding out of his nose, ears, and mouth. His eyes were almost swollen shut. Brett kneeled down next to Dub and said, "If you tell anyone it was me that done this, that little African princess granddaughter of yours is gonna feel me too, only I will turn her into a woman for you. You got that old man?" Brett looked at his knuckles and they were covered in Dub's blood. He saw one of Dub's teeth lying on the floor; he picked up the tooth and put it in Dub's shirt pocket then wiped his hands on Dub's shirt. "You might have old Doc Barnes fix that tooth for you." He laughed, stood up, picked up an old iron doorstop that was sitting beside the front door, and threw it into Dub's mirror behind the two chairs. It smashed the glass and rained down shards on Dub. Dub blacked out thinking the doorstop that Brett picked up was meant for him. He didn't see Brett and Judd leave through the back door, but not before Brett smashed his clippers into small little pieces and then urinated on both chairs.

Chapter 47

AFTER LEAVING THE SHERIFF'S HOUSE WITH HIS
stomach full of hot breakfast, Bubba drove out to the Buckles
place and once again found it empty. He took another tour of the
home and nothing looked different. It was still a pigpen. He
grabbed another beer from the refrigerator and chugged it. He
started thinking of Ms. Becky and thought he better stop by and
check the Jackpot to see if maybe Brett had shown up there
today. If he weren't there, he would stop by Chub's garage to
make sure that Mrs. Schoenthal wasn't there first and maybe get
his oil changed. When he pulled into Chub's garage he could see
there were a couple of cars parked there but there were no customers. He recognized one of the cars from the VFW. He
thought it belonged to the commander of the VFW, but he
couldn't be sure. He walked into the office area which used to be
the store part of the gas station. Now it was a place where you

talked to Chub or the owner and either waited for them to fix your car or handed them your keys and left it with them. Because they tended to keep cars there for several days in a row, they had changed the two big roll-up garage doors to where you couldn't see into them anymore. There wasn't anyone around, but the coffee pot was there, and it looked and smelled like it was fresh, so he helped himself to a cup. He flipped through some *Field & Stream* magazines while he sipped his coffee. He got bored really fast and was a little upset that nobody came out to greet him and at least find out what he needed. He thought he heard someone in the back area, so he put his magazine down and walked through the back shop entrance door. He still had his coffee in his hand because for some reason it tasted extremely good, best he had in a long time. He found it amusing that he thought the best cup of coffee in Webb could be found at Chub's garage. Everybody knew it wasn't Chub's garage, but somehow even though Chub didn't own the garage, everybody just called it Chub's garage. Bubba saw a *Chevy Camaro* on the rack; he thought it was pretty impressive. It had a nice new set of rims on it and it looked like it had a new paint job. Since it was still high on the rack, Bubba wanted to peek underneath it. He had never had the time to just see what a car looks like underneath before, so he walked over to it and stood there admiring the muffler system. He had no idea how long and detailed the muffler was underneath a car. He looked around and still didn't see anything or anyone and that just seemed weird to him. It was the middle of the day; the place was wide open with fresh coffee brewing and nobody around. Maybe they went on a parts run again and forgot to lock up. He opened a few of the tool drawers, not for any reason other than being nosy. He had a pretty good set of tools that Elmer and Lois had given him for Christmas last year, but he wasn't very handy with tools and hadn't figured out a way to use them. He was struck by how organized everything was in this garage. There was nothing out of place and he wished his tool shed was as organized. There was that green rack of tires in the back of the garage that went from the floor to the ceiling; at the bottom of the rack there were a few big baby blue oil drums. Behind the rack was that disgusting bathroom he had the privilege of using already. The hallway further down from the bathroom seemed even more dimly-lit than the last time he was there but that didn't dampen the need to snoop. The need to snoop was overpowering to Bubba. He had always had a passion for snooping, that's kind of why he liked police work so much, plus he wanted to get the oil changed on the Scout. He didn't have much to do until Brett came back to town, so he felt like now was as good a time as ever. As he walked down the hallway taking in large whiffs the new rubber tire smell, he really liked that smell. On the outer wall he found two doors; he remembered the first one, it was the small bathroom. He opened the door to have another look as if he needed another reminder of what disgusting looks like. He stuck his head in the bathroom. It was the same as the day before but the day before he hadn't noticed that there was a small showerhead in the open corner part of the disgusting bathroom. He had never seen a bathroom that had a sink, toilet, and shower all in the same place. The urge to pee hit him, which always happened any time he got near water or bathrooms, so he decided to take advantage of the facility. When he finished, he flushed the toilet and zipped up securely, careful not to rush through that because just last week he had rushed though the zipping stage a little too quickly and regretted it. He quickly washed his hands, out of habit this time, and after seeing the sink he regretted it, so he was careful not to touch anything but the faucet, and he even thought about just leaving the water running so he wouldn't have to touch the handle again. There were no towels anywhere, so he patted his hands on his hips and thighs to help his hands dry a little quicker. Once he was out of the bathroom, he took a few steps down the hall where he opened the second door. He was surprised to see that it had a single bed, a little closet, a desk, and a TV. Unlike the bathroom, this room was a little neater, but not much. There was a huge dark stain on the concrete floor and he could see the square outline of what he figured used to be a rug. He knew it because he had that same square outline on his porch at home. It was a smaller square than this one but after the rug had been there for so long, it kinda left a nice clean square on the porch after it was removed. And then it hit him. He stopped what he was doing and remembered the shoes beside the toilet; they were sneakers, small sneakers, sneakers that might belong to a little boy who was found barefoot with a knife in his stomach? He had a lump come up in his throat. He walked over to the dark spot in the concrete beside the bed and bent down to see if he could tell what it was. He first mashed his thumb on the spot to see if anything came up with his thumb. He expected his thumb to come back from the concrete with blood on it, but it didn't. Then he wiped all five fingers across the dark spot to see if he could rake up something, but he got nothing. Maybe he was letting the day's events make him jumpy and he was annoyed that he was letting his emotions get the best of him. He was still kneeling next to the dark stain thinking about how silly he was being now when he heard a voice behind him. "You always

snoop around peoples' homes when they ain't there, Deputy?"
He jumped up really quickly and was both a little scared and
embarrassed that he was a lawman and had let someone sneak up
on him. He stood up, turned to see who was behind him, and
tried to look official. It was difficult to look official because he
knew he really shouldn't be back in this part without permission,
but he was allowed to take some liberties because no one was in
the garage when he showed up. "Well I came in a while ago and
waited in the front for quite a while. I reckon I've been here for
twenty minutes or so now. Helped myself to some coffee."
Bubba held up the cup of coffee for a visual, but Chub didn't
change his expression at all. Bubba actually thought his expression got a little weirder when he held up the coffee cup. "Say,
what's this spot on the floor?" Bubba pointed to the spot by the
bed then turned back to look at Chub. Chub's expression had
changed considerably, and he seemed nervous as he kept shifting
his weight from one foot to the other. It looked to Bubba like he
needed to go to the bathroom. Something was not right about
Chub's behavior and Bubba wanted to press him a little more.
He flashed back to the shoes beside the toilet, the spot on the
floor, and now Chub is acting like a kid who has been caught
with his hand in the cookie jar. "I spilled some oil on my rug,
Deputy, it was ruined. Is that what you are here for, to inspect
my living quarters? Don't you need a warrant for that?" Bubba
took a step towards Chub, but Chub took a step back...a large
enough step back that he was now outside the room in the hallway. "So, you're a lawyer now are you, Chub?" Bubba was
regaining his composure after being startled by Chub. When
Bubba felt confident he could become very quick-witted, almost
closer to a smart ass, however, the nervous tension was in the

room. "Make yourself at home, Deputy. Take a nap for all I care, I have work to do." With that said, Chub disappeared from the hallway, leaving Bubba standing in his little living area alone. Bubba started feeling very uneasy about the whole situation. Something was simply not right. He hadn't figured it out just yet, but he would very soon, he was sure of it. He bent down one more time to check the spot on the floor, but nothing had changed, and he still couldn't get anything to stick to his fingers. He walked out of the little bedroom. He didn't see Chub and just figured Chub had gone to the shop area. The thought of the shoes flashed in his head again along with the vision of Lonnie lying next to the dumpster barefoot. He stuck his head in the little bathroom, flipped on the light, and heard that loud click-ing-popping sound from the ancient light switch. He could see the shoes were still there but this time, despite being peed on, he needed to check the size. If they were boy's shoes he may have stumbled onto something. Approaching the toilet, he could see that they were canvas sneakers. He thought he knew the brand name but could only come up with *Chuck* something. He bent over to pick up the sneakers to check the size, unaware that Chub had returned. He picked up the sneakers, stood back up, and realized he wasn't in the bathroom alone. The hair stood on up on his arms and he spun around. He was face-to-face with Chub; they were so close he was slightly nauseated by the diesel and body odor that Chub was famous for. He was so distracted by the smell that he didn't see the knife in Chub's hand until it entered his stomach. Bubba knew who killed that little boy now and he had definitely just screwed up. He forgot to pay attention to his surroundings. He was alone and forgot to watch his own back. Elmer had told him a million times to scan the room, find your weak spots, and don't get boxed in. He told him that being a small-town deputy meant that you often had to handle situations alone. The sheriff told him that when you were alone, you had to turn up what he called your personal radar. He had just failed at every one of those training lessons. The shock he felt was quickly followed by adrenalin. He pulled his revolver from his holster faster than he ever imagined he could. Chub saw him go for his gun and tried to stop him, but he was just a little too slow. Bubba pulled the trigger on his .357. At first, he thought he had missed because Chub recoiled the hand that was still attached to the knife that was presently jammed in his stomach. The knife came out with his hand. Bubba heard the splatter on the floor and knew that it was his blood making that noise, but what surprised Bubba even more was that Chub reinserted the knife. Bubba felt this second stab way more than the first. He felt a tinge of embarrassment for now being suckered a second time, and out of anger more than anything, fired every round he had left in the gun until all he could hear was the clicking of the hammer hitting empty chambers. Chub, slumped down in the little bathroom, tried to say something but could only gurgle. Bubba could still hear the blood spilling in the floor and didn't want to look down. He knew he was in trouble because he was already dizzy, and his legs were about to buckle beneath him. His mind was racing now. He saw everything that he should have done but it was much too late to cry over spilled milk, or spilled blood in this case. He needed to get out of this back room and to a phone quickly. He stumbled out of the bathroom; the knife was still in his stomach, he tried to move carefully but quickly. He had heard that a persons' guts could easily slide out of the sliced hole made by a knife, and when they started to find their way out of your stomach, it was like trying to stop some gory avalanche of intestines. He was already nauseated by the smell of his own insides. He leaned against the hallway with his shoulder and shuffled his feet until he was directly behind the big tire rack. In some way, he gained a little extra pep by reaching this point, for it meant that he was almost back to the shop. He reached out to grab the tire rack with the hand that wasn't holding his bleeding stomach so he could switch sides of the hallway, and he lost his balance. He fell behind the rack but had the directional grit to not fall on the knife that was sticking out of his stomach. He landed on his left shoulder causing his head to hit pretty hard on the concrete. He felt uncomfortable where he was and the urge to get comfortable was practically overpowering, so he rolled over onto his back. Staring up at the ceiling, he could see every cobweb, every spider, and every crack as if it were only inches from his face. He felt all his senses in his body come alive like they had never come alive before. Every fond memory he had which seemed to all center around Elmer Davis and the entire Davis family blew through his head with absolute clarity. He felt the warm blood sliding down his sides and hips and then he smiled and closed his eyes.

Chapter 48

FOR THE FIRST TIME IN A VERY LONG TIME, MAYBE
as far back as he could remember, the sheriff spent the entire
day in the office. He met with Buster Halfacre for almost two
hours. Buster covered everything that he found out during
Lonnie Buckles autopsy. The details were tough for the sheriff
to sit through. Buster pointed out again that there was no way
the Buckles kid got behind the hardware store on his own. He
was stabbed somewhere else and dumped there. He said that
he was still alive when he was dumped there but not for long.
He estimated, based off the rigor, that the time of death was
between midnight and 2:00 a.m. He needed more information
back from the lab in Jackson to help him pin-point it better; he
simply didn't have the equipment to determine some things very
accurately and this was one of them. The sheriff was listening
intently and decided he made a mistake by not bringing Aubrey

into the meeting. The Webb PD and the Sheriff's Department were going to have to work together to find the killer. They took a break while he asked Lavera to call Aubrey, but no surprise to him, she had already called him, and Aubrey was on his way but had to stop off at the school and talk to a sixth-grade class about the dangers of using drugs. He gave the speech every year and when he was done, he gave them a little quiz. It was a big deal in town and when the kids were done with his speech and class, they all got green ribbons. Buster tried to wiggle out of waiting around for Aubrey, but the sheriff wouldn't have it. Buster sat in the waiting room with Lavera while the sheriff went down to talk to Bobby one more time to see if maybe Bobby had thought of an alibi beside being home asleep.

Bobby walked into the conference room led by the jailer. He was wearing the black and white striped standard jumpsuit that they used. The jumpsuits were another bargain that the sheriff got from Parchman. Parchman updated the cloth to a little more breathable fabric and much cheaper, so they ditched the jumpsuits that they had been using which had the softness and appeal of a burlap sack. Bobby had his hands and ankles handcuffed when he was led into the room. The sheriff looked up as he heard Bobby come in and saw that Bobby had a fat lip and nose that looked to be swelling under his right eye. The jailer sat Bobby down and started to leave but the sheriff interrupted his departure. "Unlock his chains." The jailer stopped at the door and turned around with a frustrated look on his face. "Not operating procedure for a murderer, sir." The jailer turned back towards the door as if he was leaving again, obviously trying to use procedural rules from his boss as his reason for not following orders. "Son, I am not in the mood to have a junior jailer lecture me or quote procedures that he obviously hasn't read completely yet, because if he had, he would have read the part about the sheriff having full discretion to execute his job how he sees fit. Now turn your ass around and take those chains off him!" This got the young man's attention and he immediately unlocked Bobby's ankles and wrists, but he was making it clear through his facial expressions that he was not happy about it. When he was finished, he took the chains that he had collected from Bobby's ankles and wrists, plus the chain that looped around his waist, and threw them on the table. This was his last attempt at showing the sheriff his displeasure with the sheriff's actions and words. After he threw them on the table, he turned to leave, but when he had his back turned to the sheriff he said in sarcastic tone, "I ain't responsible if that boy tries anything with you. Holler when you're done." He once again started to reach for the door, but he was once again interrupted. "Say, do me a favor when you get out in the hall, head down to Lavera's desk, she will have some survey papers for you to fill out." Bobby was watching the back and forth with a great deal of enthusiasm. Just like the sheriff, he was anxious to hear the junior jailer's comeback now. "What kind of survey is it? Can I do it this afternoon? I've got two more prisoners that I need to process through holding." The sheriff rose from the table and immediately filled the room with his presence. He stood over the kid like a dark cloud. He smiled and stuck out his hand. The kid stuck his hand out, more out of reflex and courtesy than anything else, because he had no idea why the sheriff wanted to shake his hand. "No, it can't wait, it's a survey on the workplace environment. It's real important to know what people think of how the Sheriff's Office is run, how the sheriff handles himself professionally, etc. Standard survey we give to everyone when they leave the department." The kid was smiling but when he heard that it went away. He tried to pull his hand back from the sheriff, but anyone who had ever shaken the sheriff's hand knows that if he doesn't want you to let go, you aren't going anywhere unless you want to leave your hand behind. "I'm not leaving, sir." His voice was a little shaky and Bobby could tell that the sheriff was really squeezing this kid's hand hard. Bobby had felt that same handshake before. "Oh, now it's sir, huh? Just a minute ago you slung those chains on that desk and tried to show your feathers in front of my friend here. Well I got news for you Private Peacock, my feathers trump yours and I have decided that this sherrifin' business ain't your cup of tea. Read the policy manual while you're looking for a new job, it will tell you that I have full discretion on who does and who does not work in my jail!" He was poking the jailer's chest with his middle finger as if to send a subliminal message. He let go of the kid's hand and relaxed his expressions. Bobby saw him go from the most intimidating person he believed he had ever seen to the most sincere and nicest in just a matter of seconds. He patted the kid's shoulder and actually rubbed his hair like he was rubbing a red-headed kid's head for luck. "Lavera will have your pay ready for you." The kid couldn't get out of that room fast enough. Bobby looked down at the table so the sheriff couldn't see him smiling and shook his head. He thought, *the sheriff really is a good man.* He sat back down and changed from a smile to a very serious look. "What happened to your face?" Bobby shook his head as if to say he wasn't going to say anything. "Sheriff, I been on both sides of it now. I know what the rules are and ain't no way I am tellin' you a thing. A handshake and your feathers speech can't change that, ever." The sheriff sat back in his chair and crossed his right leg over his left and then clasped his fingers together over his knee. "I won't say a word but I gotta know if I got some folks outta line in here. I can't fix it if I don't know it's broke." Bobby laughed. "Let's just say that that some of your colleagues AND some of my colleagues in here don't take kindly to child murderers." The sheriff tried to get Bobby to tell him, but he never did. He tried to help him remember anything about where he was the night Lonnie Buckles was murdered but they came up with nothing. The sheriff left the room more frustrated than when he came in and by now Aubrey had shown up.

Buster continued his report on the autopsy and Aubrey sat through it but not easily. He would pull his handkerchief out of his back pocket and pat his forehead to wipe the beads of sweat that continued to form. The beads got heavier when Buster was describing the sexual abuse and the issues that had caused. He told them all that it was probably as much pain as that little boy ever had in his life and he probably didn't even feel the knife go into his stomach. When the knife entered the boy's abdomen it nearly sliced his liver in two pieces and it had punctured the stomach. The acid in his stomach contaminated most of his insides, which meant to him that if someone had gotten the boy to the hospital right after he was stabbed, they might have been able to save him, but as it was, he bled out. For theatrics he said, "It wouldn't be his first choice of how to go, for sure." He also told him that his feet were covered in oil, some kind of motor oil, like *Valvoline* or *Pennzoil* because it was fresh motor oil, not the kind you see after it has been used. The sheriff let Buster go after he was finished but he and Aubrey stayed together after Buster left to talk about what the plan was going to be. Aubrey seemed confused. "Sheriff, the boy was sodomized violently then stabbed, it was obviously a message to the Buckles family. You HAVE the killer in your jail right now, so I don't understand what the need for a plan would be?" The sheriff once again told Aubrey that he no more thought that Bobby Martin killed that boy than *Lee Harvey Oswald*. He stressed his belief that Bobby Martin was a hot head but not a killer and it was all just too convenient that the knife came from Andy's and the boy was killed right after he had a little dust-up with his son and Bobby's daughter. As he was talking he remembered the valve stems and the valve puller. He stopped in mid-sentence and was about to say something when Lavera bust into the office. "Elmer, I just got off the phone with Mrs. Shoenthal and she says you need to get to Chub's right now!" Lavera was panting and the sheriff could tell that she was scared. "What the hell, Lavera? What's wrong?" Lavera sat down in the empty seat in his house. Aubrey reached over and touched her shoulder. "She was there to get her brakes fixed and nobody was there, so she went back into the shop area and she saw an arm on the floor behind the tire rack. She won't go any further. She was scared to death." The sheriff jumped up from behind his desk and grabbed his hat. Aubrey told him he was coming and the two took off for Chub's.

Chapter 49

⁂

OK, YOU TWO, YOUR RIDE SHOULD BE WAITING for you Any minute. Time to put your stuff away neatly and absorb what you learned today." The librarian whispered as she talked to Decker and Jeannine. Jeannine looked around and there was no one else in the library but he and Jeannine so he couldn't figure out why she was whispering. He said, "Thank you" at the normal Decker tone and both Jeannine and the librarian gave him the "SHHHSH" with their fingers over their lips. This learning stuff was a lot of new territory for him and he was pretty sure that Jeannine helping him learn to read by using the focus techniques they had found through the library was actually helping, at least he thought it was. He could tell that she enjoyed teaching him as much as she enjoyed reading books and man could she read. He watched her with fascination, as she would use her finger to guide her across the lines of the page, and it seemed to him that her finger was moving so fast that she might get a blister on her finger if she did it too long. He laughed once when he saw her using her middle finger to guide her eyes instead of her pointing finger. He saw a guy show that middle finger to his daddy once and he had to ask what that meant. His daddy just told him that it was bad and meant bad words and that decent people never used that middle finger for anything which included picking their nose. He remembers laughing when his daddy got to the part about the nose picking. His daddy was always cracking a joke that made him laugh. Decker knew from experience that picking your nose with that middle finger was close to impossible. He had tried it a couple times and his finger was just too big to fit in one of those tiny holes in his nose.

That afternoon, Jeannine spent quite a bit of their library time explaining the Dewey Decimal System the library used for keeping track of all those books. She said that all you had to do was know what subject you wanted to read about, and the rest was easy. She always got so excited when she talked about books and reading. She even told him that the system was named after a librarian named Melvil Dewey, or maybe it was Melvil Decimal, he couldn't remember. He just thought that Melvil was a cool name and if they ever got another horse he was going to talk his daddy into naming it Melvil. He also found out that day that she had what she called a photographic memory; she said that was how she could read so fast. She explained that she basically took pictures of stuff in her mind and it was there forever; all she had to do was figure out a way to recall it when it she needed it. She said she had her own private Dewey Decimal System locked away in her head and she was the only one who understood how to use it.

After they put away the books they pulled from the shelf, Decker decided that he wanted to check out a book on the history of the Civil War. He was fascinated by the Civil War and now that he was slowly figuring out how to read a different way, he found he didn't have to go back and re-read the same page ten times before he understood what he was reading. He took the book to where the librarian was standing and told her that he wanted to take this one home with him. The librarian then told him that he needed a library card and she would help him fill one out quickly so that he could take the book home. When they were finished, and the librarian handed him the library card with his name on it as clear as day, he thought he would bust inside if he didn't get home soon to show his momma. The first thing that he would have to get was a wallet now because he needed something to put this new card in! He was so excited he showed it to Jeannine because he had never before had anything official with his name on it! Jeannine laughed and was very amused by his excitement over something so simple as a library card. After all, she had had one for as long as she could remember. "You are one silly boy, Decker Davis!" Then she did something that was completely unexpected and totally caught Decker off-guard, she kissed him right on the cheek! It shocked Decker so badly that he dropped the book, and it was a big book too. The Civil War was a big subject and obviously required many pages to cover it all. The noise of the book hitting floor echoed off the walls and that made Jeannine giggle. She acted like it was no big deal and she simply grabbed her book satchel and off to the front door she went. Decker stood there in shock, he placed his hand on his cheek where she had just kissed him as if he might be able to feel the mark she had left. He had no idea what to do or who to tell but he sure needed to tell someone. He knew standing there in that library, feeling the kiss of a girl his own age kissing him right on the face in public was a subject that he would have to discuss with his sister. He saw her kiss a boy one time when they had company over and she kissed him right smack on the lips. Decker was glad that Jeannine had not kissed him on the lips because that was just gross.

He caught up to her on the steps of the library. She was looking for her granddaddy, but he wasn't there yet. "Why did you do that?" Jeannine was not looking at Decker and she asked him what he was talking about. "Why did you kiss me?" She laughed and turned to look at him. "You don't have to have a reason to kiss somebody, Decker Davis, but you generally kiss people that you like a lot." He knew he liked her a lot too, but he didn't know that was how you told people you liked them a lot. This was all so confusing at the moment, so Decker decided it was best if he waited and sorted it all out with his sister. He was in a hurry to get home to talk to her about it, watch Jeannine shovel more horse poop, and put this book down. He was regretting having checked out such a big book. Now he would have to carry it all the way home.

They waited until 15 minutes after 5:00 which was the time her granddaddy told her that if for any reason he wasn't there to pick her up, she was to walk the few blocks down the main street across town and meet him at the barbershop. He told her that sometimes he would get a rush of unexpected customers and not only was it worth the money, he just simply couldn't refuse business. The barbershop and the library weren't that far apart so her and Decker took off for the barbershop. They crossed the street that separated the library from downtown and then made their way along the sidewalks. Decker stopped at the display window at Sterlings and saw they had put a brand-new genuine leather football in the window with a bunch of other stuff. Jeannine had no interest in the football and wouldn't let him linger long. Once they reached the end of that part of main street they had to cross the square to get to the side of downtown that her granddaddy's barbershop was on. Jeannine knew a short cut that ran behind the courthouse, so she told Decker to race her to see who could get to the end of the courthouse first. They both took off, but Decker knew he would lose, one because she was faster than he was and two, this book was as heavy as a rock. Jeannine reached the end of the courthouse before Decker. He could see her slowing down, so he tried to go a bit faster to close the distance so it wouldn't look like he gotten beaten so badly. That is when he spotted a man stepping out from behind one of the partitions that line the backside of the courthouse. He immediately didn't like the way he felt. His daddy had told him lots of times that your body knew long before your brain would admit that there was trouble. He said that some folks would keep going because they convinced themselves that those goose bumps they felt on their arms were just silly. He wanted to run in the other direction, but it was too late because Jeannine was already standing in front of the man and no way was he leaving her. When he got a few feet from where they were standing he could see that it was Brett Buckles. He knew this was nothing but trouble. He was Brett and they were potential cats.

"Well if it ain't the sheriff's retard kid." Decker eased up beside Jeannine, grabbed her arm and pulled her, and began walking again to walk around Brett. Every time the two tried to step around Brett he would take a step and stand in their way.

"What's a nice retarded kid doing with this little African princess, huh? You two sneaking around here behind the courthouse so that you give her kiss, maybe even more?" Brett had this grin on his face like he was really enjoying what he was doing. Jeannine took a step back away from Brett, which forced Decker to do the same thing since Decker still had a grip on her arm. "Leave us alone, Brett! My granddaddy is looking for us and when he finds us he is going mash you into little pieces!" Jeannine yelled as she continued to try and walk around Brett. He once again stepped in front of them but only this time he got really close to them. Brett swung and hit her in the side of the face with the backside of his hand. Her head turned with the force of the hit and she stumbled back just a little, but Decker had her arm and didn't let her fall. "Your granddaddy ain't nothin' to me kid, I can squash him and light him on fire if I want to and there ain't nothin' you or your murderin' daddy can do about it!" Brett raised his arm back to hit her again, only this time, Decker jumped in front of Jeannine and took Brett's fist in the back of the head. The force sent both Decker and Jeannine falling to the ground. Decker had been punched before but that one that he just took from Brett made him dizzy. He knew they were in trouble because if a grown-up was ready to raise a fist against two kids, there was not much he could do to stop it. He looked up and saw that Brett had moved over them and was raising his had to hit either him or Jeannine. He wasn't sure, so he grabbed his book satchel that had fallen beside them when he and Jeannine fell and quickly raised it to shield himself and Jeannine. It turned out to be an effective shield because Brett's fist collided with the history of the Civil War instead of their heads. Brett let out a curse word that Decker had heard before and it was a bad one, the worst of them all. He saw Brett spin around holding his hand and cursing more at the same time. That's when they heard another voice. "Leave them kids alone." The voice was calm but forceful; Decker still had his book satchel over their heads, so he couldn't see who it was. "Get your kicks out of picking on little kids, do you, Brett?" Decker lowered the book satchel so he could see and his heart jumped and his mouth opened with awe. There he was, Donnie Ray Richardson. Webb's superstar quarterback was standing right in front of them. There was no mistaking that to Decker, especially since he still had his arm in a sling, just like Decker. Even though he was shocked to see the greatest football player perhaps in world, Decker saw this as an opportunity to stand up, so he and Jeannine scrambled to their feet. "I get my kicks any way I want, and I don't need no afro-sportin', broke-down high school punk football player askin' me dumbass questions." Brett let go of his hand. Decker saw him change his expression from what looked like amused to evil. Decker was mixed about his feelings at the moment. He was happy that someone had stepped in to help him and Jeannine, but he also didn't want his hero hurt because he was already in a bad spot with his shoulder. He wanted to run but now he felt like he needed to help another friend of his. He liked the idea of saying that the famous Donnie Ray Richardson was a friend of his. Brett took a step toward Donnie, but Donnie took a quicker step than Brett did and managed to land a left hook that Brett clearly was not expecting. Decker was amazed now, not only was Donnie Ray the most famous person he'd ever met, he was clearly the toughest because Brett stumbled backwards, and it looked to Decker that if the back of the courthouse wall hadn't caught him, Brett would have surely fallen to the ground.

Donnie Ray didn't allow any time for Brett to recover before he was on him again. He was pounding Brett with his one good left hand when Decker saw a shadow out of the corner of his eye and then he saw something hit Donnie Ray in the back. It made a thud and Donnie Ray immediately stopped pounding on Brett and dropped to his knees. Donnie Ray managed to turn his head in time to see the next attempted blow from the baseball bat Judd was swinging and he rolled away from it. The bat hit the ground instead of Donnie Ray. Donnie Ray was still grimacing in pain when he yelled for Decker to run. Decker wanted to run but his feet were stuck, and he wanted so badly to help but he knew he couldn't do anything. Decker grabbed Jeannine's arm and took off as fast as he could run but never let go of Jeannine's arm until they were at the end of town and nearly to the barbershop. He figured from there, he would find Jeannine's granddaddy and he would help call his daddy. Decker and Jeannine were so scared that it never occurred to them to stop at one of the downtown stores and get someone to help and that maybe Donnie Ray Richardson would not have been beaten by Judd and Brett so severely with that baseball bat.

Chapter 50

THE SHERIFF HAD THAT FEELING THAT SOMETHING was wrong by the tone in Lavera's voice and this gut instinct that he was known for. With Aubrey in the passenger seat, he pressed the accelerator on the ugly green squad car in route to Chub's garage. It didn't take long. There was not a shoulder on the main drag or on the highway, which was usually case, but the sheriff also knew that every time he was in a hurry to go somewhere, he ended up behind a grain hauler or a hay tractor, but luckily today he had a clear path. He and Aubrey arrived at Chub's. He saw the sheriff's Scout parked in front of the garage and thought that he was glad that Lavera got in touch with Bubba. He didn't really trust Aubrey with any real police activity, especially any that required quick thinking. Aubrey was a good man and honest as there ever was one, but his ability to process information and quickly activate his critical thinking skills simply weren't that good. He was afraid that if he ever had to pull his gun that he might shoot his own foot off. He pulled under the awning of the garage right behind where Chub had parked earlier. He still wasn't carrying a gun of his own and it never occurred to him that he might even need it. He looked for Mrs. Schoenthal but she could not be found. Whatever it was that made her call must have scared her off. The sheriff saw that there was no one in the front area; he looked around while Aubrey circled the building outside. Aubrey had already drawn his side arm even though the sheriff had told him not to. Aubrey was not about to be caught off-guard and was prepared. The sheriff walked through the garage area and didn't see anyone. The only thing he saw was the *Camaro* on the rack. Other than that, the shop looked as neat and orderly as it always was. He let his eyes follow the outer wall, beginning with the front roll-up doors all the way around to the back wall, hoping to see what it was that scared Mrs. Schoenthal enough to call the office. When he got to the tire rack on the back wall, he spotted the hand with the wristwatch sticking out just enough to be seen from where he was standing. "Bubba! He yelled for Aubrey to come in since he wasn't wearing a gun, but it didn't stop him from running to where Bubba was laying. He knew it was Bubba's hand by the watch he had on his wrist. He and Lois had given it to him for his birthday. Lois had driven all the way to Memphis to buy it for him because it was the only place they could find the watch. It was a divers watch, tested up to 200 feet. Bubba liked to go diving in his off time; he had the gear and had even joined a dive club located outside of Biloxi. When he turned the corner behind the tire rack, he could see Bubba lying in a pool of blood around his abdomen area. Aubrey came running up behind the sheriff with his gun drawn. The sheriff was already kneeling over Bubba checking for a pulse. He couldn't be sure, but he thought he found a faint pulse in his neck. It wasn't as easy to find a pulse when his own heart rate was elevated and all his senses were exploding around him. He looked back at Aubrey who had a complete look of shock on his face. "Aubrey! Check those two rooms and call an ambulance! Now, damn it!" Aubrey stepped over Bubba and entered the bathroom where he saw Chub with his back against the wall, sitting on the ground with his head slumped over like he was taking a nap. "Chub is in here! He's down; Jesus H there is blood all over the place in here! What the hell happened?" The sheriff was holding Bubba's stomach trying to stop any more bleeding, but as far as he could tell, the bleeding had already stopped. He hoped it hadn't stopped because he was wrong about finding that faint pulse. "Aubrey, call a damn ambulance now!" Aubrey came running out of the bathroom and checked the second room as he was instructed to do and then ran to the desk to use the phone. The sheriff could hear him on the phone asking for an ambulance and could also hear him on the phone asking for assistance from both the Sheriff's Office and the PD. "Yes, I said get everybody here, damn it! There is an officer down! I want the ambulance here now and I want this scene secured. Now move your ass!" The sheriff was pleased with the urgency in Aubrey's voice. Aubrey was a good man and cared about the people of Webb much more than anyone and even though he and Aubrey often butted heads about how to do police work, he knew that they were both on the same team. Aubrey came running back to the sheriff then stepped over Bubba again and headed back into the bathroom where Chub was still slumped on the floor. Aubrey had forgotten to check to see if Chub was alive or dead, but then he wasn't sure if he could find a pulse with his excitement level raised to where it was. He thought for a minute that he would pass out from the dizziness and the queasiness he felt in his stomach. "I can't find a pulse, Sheriff, I think he is gone. Jesus there is so much blood all over the place! Someone either attacked these two or these two got into a fight with each other. I can't tell right now."

The ambulance arrived after what seemed like an eternity to Elmer. While he waited for the ambulance, he spoke to Bubba softly and calmly in his ear the whole time he was applying pressure to his abdomen. Bubba was not only his deputy, he was his best friend. He had never been this shaken up before and the thought of Bubba dying here on this garage floor with a knife stuck in his stomach was just about more than he could handle, but he would never let Bubba or anyone else know that he was rattled on the inside.

The ambulance guys arrived at almost the same time as the entire Webb PD and the Tallahatchie County Sheriff's Department did. They quickly put Bubba on a gurney and carried him to the ambulance. Once the sheriff saw Bubba was gone, he went into the bathroom where Chub was slumped over. Bubba's .357 was lying at the base of the toilet where he had dropped it after he realized it was empty. The sheriff didn't pick it up. He instead bent down and tried to find a pulse on Chub's neck and then his wrist and could find nothing. He was pretty sure that Chub had expired. He saw about mid-way up the bathroom wall above Chub's head there were several cracked porcelain tiles. "Is he bleeding from his stomach or chest area?" Aubrey replied, "Was." The sheriff looked the room up and down and saw the *Chuck Taylors* in the corner hidden behind the toilet almost next to where Bubba's gun was laying. He knelt and picked up one shoe by just barely pinching the tongue of the shoe, careful to touch as little of it as possible. He put the bottom of the shoe flat on his forearm sleeve so he wasn't touching any part of it. He pushed the tongue of the shoe back and could see just off to the left of where the size 6 was printed on the inside of the tongue were the initials LB. The initials were written with a blue pen and were a little faded, but there was no mistaking the LB and to the sheriff, that could mean nothing but Lonnie Buckles. It was pretty common practice for boys to write their names on the inside of their sneakers since nearly every kid in school had the exact same pair, either in black or white. You just weren't cool if you didn't wear *Chuck Taylor*; Decker had a pair just like these. "They weren't attacked. Chub molested and murdered that Buckles kid just as sure as I am standing here, and Bubba figured it out." Aubrey was still kneeling beside Chub and quickly stood up. "What? How in the hell do you know that?" The sheriff leaned over with the shoe on his arm and showed Aubrey the LB initials inside the shoe. He then set the shoe back where he found it beside the toilet and then picked up Bubba's .357, held it at angle, pushed the cylinder release, and then let the shells fall in his hand. "He used them all on Chub." He held his hand out with the empty shells piled in his palm so that Aubrey could see that every one had been fired. He then added, "Chub must have snuck up on him or surprised him or something and stuck Bubba with that knife right here in the bathroom. They were close together, but Bubba must have managed to pull his revolver and unload it right up against Chub's stomach because that is all the distance he could get for himself. The tiles on the wall will either have slugs in them or we will see the slugs on the floor behind Chub when we move him." Aubrey looked at the shoes in the corner, the blood on the floor, the shell casings that the sheriff was holding, then to the wall and said, "I'll be damned." He drew in a deep breath, rubbed his forehead and said, "So you were right, Bobby Martin didn't kill that little boy." The sheriff stepped out of the bathroom and said, "Aubrey, please make sure they get pictures of everything in this place, make sure they don't miss a thing. I want everything recorded." He kept walking but stopped and turned back towards the entrance to the second room. "Oh, and call Buster and ask him to get some fingerprints off that Buckles kid." As he walked into the little bedroom that Chub was using as a home, he saw the same outline on the floor of where a rug used to be. He did almost the exact same thing that Bubba had done before, pressing his thumb to the concrete then swiping his fingers, and he came up with the same result that Bubba came up with, nothing. Aubrey came into the room with him. "Sheriff, the unit radios are full of chatter. Some of the folks in town have those scanner things and they listen to all the juicy gossip around town when its reported, not going to be easy to keep this quiet. That lady from the Sumner paper is already calling for a statement. The whole town already knows that Bubba is on his way to the hospital in Clarksdale and that someone is dead in the garage; they are speculating but they don't know for sure. I'd like to be on the same page when I have to talk to that reporter." The sheriff was about to answer when another deputy interrupted him. "Sheriff, Lavera says there is trouble at Dub's barbershop and you need to get there fast." "Tell her I will get there ASAP, I need to finish what I am doing and tell her..." The deputy interrupted him, "Sheriff, she says that your son made the call from the barbershop." The sheriff bolted out the door without another thought other than getting to his son. He knew there had to be some real trouble for Decker to use the phone. He wasn't very good at it, but he and Lois had made him memorize the number to the Sheriff's Office and his home. He started to jump in the Scout, but realized that it might still be a part of a crime scene, so he jumped into the ugly green car and he was at the barbershop in less than 5 minutes.

Chapter 51

⁂

DECKER AND JEANNINE RAN THE REST OF THE WAY
to the barbershop. She could see that her granddaddy's car was
parked there but she didn't see any other cars, so she figured
he must have had a few walk-in customers. She had walked
from the library to the barbershop a million times before but
today was different, she was running and was scared that those
Buckles boys were running after her. She was still crying as she
hit the front door, but it was locked. She told Decker that they
would have to go around to the back door. She thought it was
strange to have the door locked; if he had customers inside why
would he lock them in? She sprinted around to the back door so
fast that Decker couldn't keep up. She yanked the screen door
open and ran through the back storeroom into the floor of the
barbershop. When she saw the glass broken she stopped crying.
She was scared. Something was wrong for sure, and that's when

she saw her granddaddy lying against the front wall beneath so many shards of broken glass. Decker could hear her scream as he was just now pulling the screen to the back door open. He had never been in the back storeroom before, but since it wasn't very big, he found his way to the door that led to the actual barbershop. Even though he was following Jeannine, he couldn't help but feel like he was in a place that he wasn't supposed to be. He actually felt relieved to get to the barbershop floor until he saw why Jeannine was screaming. He saw her kneeling on the floor next to her granddaddy, shaking him trying to get him to wake up. She was crying as much as Decker had ever seen someone cry. He ran over to where she was kneeling, not knowing what to do, but when he saw her granddaddy's face he immediately wished he hadn't. Decker had his share of bumps and bruises in his time, but he had never seen anything like this. If he didn't know where they were and who owned this barbershop, he wouldn't be able to recognize the man lying on the floor. *His face was swollen as much as a face could be swollen*, he thought. His eyes were completely shut, so much so that Decker thought he looked like a Halloween pumpkin except someone had forgotten to carve the eyes out like they were supposed to. "Help him, Decker! Don't let my granddaddy die!" She would shake him and yell, "Wake up, granddaddy!" and then lean over and hug him. Decker was at a complete loss; he had no idea what to do. Jeannine was going crazy right now, so he knew he had to do something. He tried to remember every injury he had ever had or seen that anyone else had. He remembered his big sister twisted her ankle playing volleyball against Tutwiler and his daddy kept ice packs on it all weekend while she kept her leg propped up on the sofa. He remembered his daddy telling his sister that she had to keep the swelling part up in the air, so he shoved a bunch of pillows under her leg which made her look like she was frozen in place while kicking a field goal. He jumped up from the floor to go find some ice if he could; even if it didn't work or it was the wrong thing to do, he wanted to show Jeannine that they were doing something, anything to help her feel better. He put his good hand on the ground to help himself stand up and felt a sharp pain. He looked down and saw that he had a piece of the mirror stuck on the bottom part of his palm. It was already bleeding but other than the initial pain of contact, he was surprised to realize that he didn't feel any pain at all and it was bleeding a lot. Normally when he saw his own blood he would panic a little and feel a strong urge to find his momma. He reached over with the semi-bad hand and pulled the glass shard out and threw it in the corner, a place where it couldn't get him again. He ran to the soda cooler and found lots of ice, so he grabbed a barber towel and filled it with ice. He couldn't help it, but he was getting blood all over the barber towel as he was filling it with ice. He figured it wouldn't matter much. Once he had the towel filled with ice, he made a nice ball out of it by twisting the top closed. He saw a pile of barber aprons in the corner and grabbed those too. He made it back to Jeannine where she was still yelling for her granddaddy not to die. "Here, slide these under his head like a pillow, you need to keep the swelling elevated." Jeannine continued to yell the same things and go through the same motions as if she wasn't hearing what Decker was saying to her. This time there could be no mistake, he got her attention, "JEANNINE!!!" She stopped crying for a minute, looked at Decker, and he repeated what he had said earlier. "Slide this under his head! You have to keep his head up!" He didn't know why they had to keep his head up, he was just repeating the remedy for swelling he had already heard. "Put this in his face! It's ice, it will help him feel better." He had been yelling but by the time he got to the last part he lowered his voice again. Jeannine wasn't screaming the way she was before at least. She elevated his head by shoving the barber aprons under him and then gently moved the ice pack all around his face. "I'm calling my daddy." Decker knew where the phone was as he had seen Mr. Martin use it before. It was pretty high up on the wall across the room so Decker slid a chair up to it so he could see the rotary dial right in front him. He slowly began to dial the number as he had been instructed to do by his momma; insert his finger in the chosen number and then rotate the dial with his finger remaining in that number hole all the way down to where it stopped. Since he still couldn't lift his regular dialing hand up very high, he had to use the bloody hand to dial. He didn't mind but he hoped he wouldn't get in trouble for getting blood all over Mr. Martin's pretty yellow phone. He heard the voice on the other end say, "Sheriff's Office". When he heard that, he followed the instructions he had been given once again. "Hello, this is Decker Davis, how are you today?" The voice on the other end became noticeable as she said, "Well hello, Decker Davis, I'm fine thank you, how are you and what can I do for you?" He looked over and saw that Jeannine was still crying but she wasn't yelling anymore, she was gently holding the ice pack on Mr. Martin's face. "I'm fine thank you for asking. I would like to speak to Elmer Davis, please." Lavera was getting a kick out of the professionalism in which Decker was handling this conversation but she knew she needed to hurry in case other call came in, after all, this was not a normal day. "Well Decker, he is out of the office at the moment, shall I have him call you when he gets back or is there something I can help you with?" Decker thought long and hard about this. He wasn't sure what he could tell a perfect stranger but the need for a grown-up's help was greater than the need for manners, so he fired away. "I am at Mr. Martin's barbershop with Jeannine Martin and Mr. Martin is hurt really bad. He is lying on the ground, his face is pretty ugly, and there is lots of glass everywhere. I lifted his head to stop the swelling and put some ice on his face, but he isn't talking so I don't know if he feels better now or not. Oh, and I need a *Band-Aid* because I cut my hand on some glass. Can you have my daddy come here?" Lavera panicked and told Decker to hang up, stay right where he was, and she would get in touch with his daddy and someone would be at Mr. Martin's barbershop right away. After he was finished, he hung the phone back in the cradle as instructed, and he fixed the cord so it wouldn't get all tangled up. As instructed.

Chapter 52

THE SHERIFF'S CAR CAME ROARING INTO THE parking lot of Dub's barbershop. He slammed it in park and bolted out of the car and nearly tripped on a beer bottle as he was making his way to the door. He pulled on the screen, but it was locked. He didn't like the idea of being told that his son was at this barbershop and the door was locked. He took two hands and ripped the screen off the hinges then tried the door handle, but it too was locked. He took one step back and with all his energy he kicked the door open to the shop. Decker and Jeannine jumped up as if they had been caught doing something wrong but when Decker saw that it was his daddy he immediately ran to his daddy and practically jumped into his arms. He had never in his life been so happy to see his daddy; one, because he was scared and two, he was tired of being a grown-up and didn't want to make any more grown-up decisions. He tried to stop but he started crying. He could feel his daddy's hand firmly press against his back and then gently rub as it patted him. "I'm sorry daddy, I didn't know what else to do! They hurt Jeannine, then they hurt Donnie and now I don't know who hurt Mr. Martin, but he is hurt bad." He continued to whimper with his head buried in his daddy's neck. "It's ok son, I'm gonna need your help now though. Let me check on Jeannine and Mr. Martin and while I do that I want you to call Lavera back just like you did before. Ok?" Decker lifted his head off his daddy's shoulder and rubbed his eyes with the hand that was bleeding. The sheriff saw that and set him down quickly to look at his hand. "What happened, Decker?!' Decker explained the glass part but while he was explaining, his daddy had already retrieved another towel from the counter and wrapped it around Decker's hand while leaving his fingers exposed so he could still dial with the finger. "Ok, son, go call Lavera." The sheriff went to Jeannine and Dub, knelt beside them, and lifted Jeannine's face with this right hand ever so gently. He could see she had a little cut on her bottom lip and it was a little swollen but not bad. He asked he if she was all right and she shook her head yes. He then asked her if she could go help Decker make the call and she again shook her head, got up, and went over to where Decker had already climbed on top of the chair again. As she was walking away the sheriff could see that she had cut her leg on the glass she sat on trying to help her granddaddy. "Jeannine, get a towel and wrap it around your leg, baby, ok?' Jeannine looked down and saw that she was bleeding, grabbed a towel on the counter sitting next to the jar of combs and wrapped her leg all without breaking stride. The sheriff thought to himself that these were some tough kids.

He was proud of both of them. He looked down at Dub and removed the blood-covered ice towel. Decker wasn't kidding, his face was mess. He once again felt for a pulse. He was really tired of doing that today and hoped he would never have to feel for another pulse for as long as he lived. To his relief, Mr. Martin had a strong pulse but was unconscious. He put the ice pack on the part of his face that he thought was the most swollen, but it was sure a toss-up. If he actually covered the swollen parts, Mr. Martin would die from suffocation. He decided he needed to secure the room, which meant he had to check the stock room. Someone had snuck up on Bubba today and it cost him dearly, he wasn't about to make that mistake too. He checked the stock-room only to find nothing but a mouse that scared him a little when it shot across the floor. As he was walking back into the barbershop, he heard Decker say, "Hello, this is Decker Davis." He took the phone from Decker. "I got it son, thank you, very good job. Can you take Jeannine over to the soda machine; grab a pop for the three of us then wait for me outside?" Decker did as instructed. The sheriff told Lavera what he found, but as he was talking to Lavera he remembered what Decker had said when he was holding him, "They hurt Donnie…" what did he mean *they hurt Donnie*? There wasn't anyone else here. "Hang on, Lavera, don't hang up but get an ambulance over here for Dub, I need to ask Decker something." He laid the phone down on the chair that Decker had been using as a stool to stand on. He walked outside where Decker and Jeannine were sitting on the bench out front that vigilantly stood watch over the main street morning, noon, and night. The bench had been there for as long as the sheriff could remember. "Say, buddy, you said they hurt Donnie, who are you talking about?" Decker handed his bottle of *Mountain Dew* to Jeannine for her to hold so he could stand up. He didn't feel right talking to his daddy while he was sitting. He didn't know why, he just knew he should be standing. "Donnie Ray Richardson, daddy. Brett Buckles tried to hurt Jeannine and me, but he wouldn't let them. He was beatin' up Brett pretty good for us but Judd snuck up and hit him with a baseball bat. Donnie Ray is the one that told us to run." The sheriff started to run back into the shop to tell Lavera where to send another ambulance, but he realized he didn't know where. Decker must have read his mind because he followed up with, "We were behind the courthouse when Donnie Ray started whippin' Brett." The sheriff immediately headed for the phone that was still lying on the chair. "Yeah, Lavera, send Aubrey and another ambulance, if there is one, to the courthouse. Decker says that the Buckles boys beat up Donnie Ray Richardson with a baseball bat. Yes, Lavera, this is the worst day in Webb history, now send Aubrey to the courthouse and tell him to call me here. I am going to stay with Dub until the ambulance gets here. Oh, and Lavera, call Lois and tell her to get to the barbershop now to pick up Decker and Jeannine, she will know how to make them feel better." He put the phone back in the cradle and went to sit with Dub until the ambulance came and took him away. While they were carrying Dub to the ambulance, the shop phone rang, it was Aubrey. "Jesus Sheriff, this kid is a mess, he's barley alive, somebody worked him over bad. Even left the baseball bat they did it with." The sheriff took off his hat. He knew who did it and he was about to go hunt them down. "It was the Buckles boys, Aubrey, the damn morons think they are getting some payback for their little brother. Donnie Ray just happened to be in the

wrong place at the wrong time but I'm selfishly glad he was."
He told Aubrey that he needed to go get Maybelle at her home
because he didn't want her to hear about her baby boy through
gossip. He hung up with Aubrey and figured he knew where to
go now. The Jackpot was the most logical place, he would go
there to celebrate and since Bobby Martin was still behind bars,
as far as Brett would be concerned, he had no more targets to
settle his moronic score. He would want to brag and drink. He
waited outside on the bench with Jeannine and Decker; the day
had taken its toll on both of them. Decker had leaned over and
laid his head on the sheriff's right leg and Jeannine had done the
same on the other side. He rested his hands on their backs. As he
rubbed their backs he could actually feel the stress leave their
little bodies. He thought to himself that he would get some
payback of his own, damn the badge and the rules, it was time
someone taught Brett Buckles some life lessons, and then Lois
arrived. She jumped out of the car and ran directly to them and
her beauty struck the sheriff as it always did. Among all this mess
today, just the sight of her made him smile and reflect on how
lucky he was. She fussed over both kids like she was so good at
doing. She kissed every square inch of both of their faces, both
kids reverted back to being kids after just a few seconds of Lois's
fussing. After she had both the kids secured in the back seat, she
closed the back door to the car and came around to where the
sheriff was standing. She placed her hands on his hips and pulled
him close to her. He put his arms around her and squeezed as
tightly as he could. "I will take them by the hospital to get those
cuts looked at and while I am there I will check on Bubba. I am
worried about you, Elmer Davis; you have that look in your

eye." He let up on his squeeze just a little, but he wasn't prepared to let her go just yet. She was good for his stress too. "And what look is that?" She pulled away a little so she could stare into his eyes. "It is the look you get when you're hyper-angry." Hyper-angry was her soft term for when he was mean. It took a lot for Elmer Davis to become mean and he had reached that point the minute he saw those two little kids trying to help Dub Martin on that barbershop floor.

Chapter 53

❦

BRETT TOLD JUDD TO HAND HIM THE BAT AND HE did as he was instructed. Brett was bleeding from a cut above his left eye. The left side of Brett's face took the brunt of Donnie Ray's punches. Even though Donnie Ray still had an arm in a sling, he was big enough and strong enough to nearly get the best of Brett with his good arm, and he would have if Judd hadn't snuck up behind him and sucker smacked him with that Louisville Slugger. Judd was a little late when he turned the corner of the courthouse. Originally, he was supposed to just come up behind the kids and keep them from running away. Brett cooked up the plan because he knew that Dub dropped them off at the library every day and he knew for sure that Dub wasn't going to be able to pick them up today. Judd and Brett were supposed to scare the kids. Brett said he was gonna just talk dirty to the little girl so that whenever Dub woke up, the little girl would tell him what Brett said to her and that would keep Dub from saying anything to the cops. Judd remembered how excited Brett got when he talked about the things he was gonna say to that little girl. Brett even said that he might actually touch her between the legs just to put a good scare into her. Judd wasn't sure about that part, he really felt like Brett was just talking tough like he always did, but he also knew how crazy and mean Brett could be. Judd had taken some of Brett's wrath over the years and he kinda felt bad that he was glad that Brett had turned his meanness towards Lonnie. Brett used to be mean to him all the time but when Lonnie grew nearly as tall as Judd, Brett started smacking him around. Instead of seeing the kids when he turned the corner, he saw a big black man wailing away on Brett and the two little kids laying on the ground hugging each other. He ran to help his brother and didn't realize it was Donnie Ray Richardson until he had already hit him in the small part of the back and sent him crumbling to his knees. Judd was pretty proud of that whack, he wasn't very good in sports, but he could swing a bat when he played little league and he put his experience to use on Donnie Ray Richardson. He felt bad when he realized it was the star quarterback, someone everybody knew. There wouldn't be any way to keep all this a secret for sure now. "Give me the bat, I'm gonna kill this son of a bitch." Judd handed him the bat and before Brett could hit him, Donnie Ray yelled for the kids to run. Brett was leaning against the courthouse with his head down when Judd knocked Donnie Ray to his knees, so he had seen his face. When Brett looked up and asked for the baseball bat, Judd could see that Brett's face looked almost as bad Dub's did when they left the barbershop. Brett hadn't beaten Dub as badly as Judd had ever seen any man get beaten. Now he was looking at his big brother with a pretty mangled-up face of his own and he was bleeding like a stuck pig. Yes, sir, Brett was a mess and Judd actually felt happy. Brett took the bat and started hitting Donnie Ray anywhere he could hit him. He was using both hands and was swinging down on Donnie Ray as if he was chopping wood. Judd knew by the way that Brett was swinging the bat that Brett intended to kill this kid. Brett was mad, someone had whooped him good and Brett could never let a fight end this way. He had seen Brett get whooped pretty good before. It wasn't too often that anyone got the best of Brett, mainly because Brett always struck first. He used to say that the first punch was usually the best punch and if you couldn't disorient a man quickly he might be able to whoop you because now he would be mad. That's why Brett always struck first. But even with him striking first, he had seen a man take the punch and then beat the crap out Brett only to have Brett wait for the man somewhere in the parking lot, surprise him with a tire iron, and then pummel the man nearly to death. Brett hated to lose a fight. In this case, Donnie Ray had obviously gotten the jump on Brett and now Brett was blood mad. Even though Judd didn't want to, he figured if he didn't do something his brother would beat this kid to death and up until now, they hadn't really hurt anybody – just put the fear of Buckles into them.

The two kids took off running and Brett didn't even notice. He was so mad that all he could think about was beating some respect into this kid. Brett was about to swing down on the kid's head when Judd grabbed the bat in mid-swing. The slap of the bat against the palm of Judd's hand could have been heard down at Milholen's. Judd felt the pain, but he knew he couldn't let go. Brett looked up at Judd with this wild-eyed crazy man look but

Judd didn't flinch. "You kill this kid and neither one of us will see the light of day, Brett. They will bury us under Parchman." Judd could just barely see the pupil in Brett's left eye as it was nearly swollen shut now, but he could clearly see the blind rage in the right eye and he just knew that Brett was about to turn that bat on him, maybe even set him on fire, but he did neither. The beating that Richardson kid had given him coupled with the energy he spent swinging that bat had taken quite a bit of the starch out of Brett. He let Judd take the bat from him. Judd took the bat and threw it on the ground next to Donnie Ray. Judd wiped Brett's bleeding face with his shirtsleeve as he helped him get to the truck. The truck was parked just off the corner of the main street and couldn't easily be seen. When they got into the truck, he asked Brett if he wanted him to take him home, but Brett was adamant that he wanted to go see Becky. Brett talked the whole time about how fun it was to beat those two men, well one was a man and the other was still a boy. At least in age he was a boy, but in size he was definitely a man. Judd figured if the Choctaws planned on getting their star quarterback back for at least the last couple of games, it wasn't gonna happen now. The collarbone would probably heal in time for Donnie Ray to play a game or two before the season ended but definitely not now. Brett laughed when he said he could actually hear that kid's skull crack.

They pulled into the Jackpot and parked in their usual spot right by the front door, but Brett made Judd pull around back so Judd did as he was told and parked under a Magnolia tree in the back. They tried to go in the back door, but it was locked. Becky liked to keep it locked so no one would try to slip out on a bill, either for liquor or the other stuff. They walked, well

Judd walked, Brett limped and moaned with every step. "I think that little bastard might have broken a rib. I hope I killed him, it will teach him to stick his damn nose in places he shouldn't ought to." Judd held the front door open for Brett and as Brett was walking by Judd holding the door he said, "What if you did kill him, Brett? You could go to jail like pop." Brett tilted his head back and let out a howl like a wolf or something. It made Judd jump back from the door and nearly lose his balance. He definitely did not expect him to howl like that. He didn't even know that Brett knew how to howl like that. When Brett was finished howling and scaring everyone that was inside the bar, which wasn't many, he looked at Judd. "You mean what if *we* killed him, huh, little brother? I believe you had a hand in it so don't you forget that." Brett was standing perfectly straight staring directly at Judd. He took a step closer to Judd so that he was nearly nose-to-nose with him. "In fact, I just might say something like; Sheriff, my little brother was so consumed with revenge and hate that when that football hero stepped in and tried to stop you from raping that little African princess, you beat him to death with that baseball bat. I will just say I tried to take the bat away from you to stop it and this is what you did to me!" He had this crazy look on his face, his eyes, or at least the one he could see out of, was as dark and cold as any eye he had ever seen. "You know the truth, Brett, I tried to help you! That kid was beatin' you to death!" Brett grabbed Judd by the collar with both of his hands then pulled him even closer. "You listen to me! There has never been one of their kind born that could whip me and there never will be! Everyone in town knows that and that's why they will believe me over a droolin' pea brain like you, so you keep your damn mouth shut and leave the thinking to us smart people! You got that?!" Brett was gritting his teeth now and keeping his voice low as he said it and it caused spit to come out of his mouth and spray all over Judd's face. He let go of Judd, turned around, and walked deeper into the bar. Judd heard him holler for Becky and a little later, Brett and Becky were gone to a back room. Judd was glad he was gone, and he was glad he was gone with Becky. He always came back from seeing Becky in a much better mood. Judd sat at the bar and started to order a beer but realized he didn't have any money, so he just sat there waiting, but not really sure what he was waiting for.

Chapter 54

THE SHERIFF WATCHED AS LOIS DROVE AWAY FROM Dub's barbeRshop with the kids safely in the back seat. Lois was right; he had an ember of hate smoldering inside him and seeing Dub on the floor, his kids crying, bleeding and scared, it had been ignited into a full-blown inferno. For all he knew, Dub Martin might not make it. He was getting up in years and it was very difficult to rebound from a beating like that. His deputy and best friend might not make it because a child molester had stuck a knife in his stomach and caused God knows what kind of damage and now this innocent kid who was trying to help his own son might have been beaten to death. He looked up at the sky as if looking for some divine guidance on what he should do. He knew he had to let Bobby Martin go, but he didn't want to let Bobby go until he had Brett behind bars, otherwise Bobby would really do something stupid. For now, he figured the best thing to do would be to keep them separated. He walked to his ugly green car and as he was walking to the car he thought about his side arm. He opened the trunk and saw it lying there, right where he put it. He stood there staring at the gun tucked neatly into its holster. It was a simple snub nose .38 that the department issued him when he was first elected. He never used it. Bubba always kept it clean for him, but he just didn't like how it felt when it was on his hip. He wanted to be approachable and to him it just seemed like a gun was a deterrent for that. He decided that in his current state of mind, it was best not to have a gun handy. He felt like he just might use it and then maybe regret it later. He could handle the Buckles clan just as easily without one. He slammed the trunk shut and made his way to the driver's side when he heard the radio crackle. It was Lavera. Her voice was very quiet, almost as if she was whispering, and he had a very hard time hearing her. In very low and measured tones she said, "Elmer, Aubrey asked that you go by PD please." At first, he couldn't understand her, so he asked her to speak up, but this time he rolled up the car window so the only thing he could hear would be her voice. "Aubrey asked you to go by PD." He listened intently enough to understand her this time. "What for? I am kinda busy right now. In fact, ask Aubrey to meet me at the Jackpot, that's where I am headed now. I suspect Brett will be there." She didn't respond. It was dead silent for a few minutes, but he didn't think anything of it as Lavera was notorious for multi-tasking then forgetting that she either had someone on hold or had left someone hanging on the radio. "Lavera?" It was still silent but just a few seconds later she replied, "Damn it, Elmer, just go by PD." He nearly dropped the mike. Lavera had used the word *damn*. He had never heard her use that or any other cuss words and was definitely shocked. All he could manage to say was, "copy".

He cut through Main Street trying to keep his ugly green car from going too fast. Something was definitely wrong with Lavera, but he wasn't sure what it was. He had a suspicion that Aubrey knew and that's why he was to stop by PD.

He pulled into PD. It was a small building but a nice building. It had been built in the summer of 1963 when the town experienced a little economic boom when the price of cotton skyrocketed. The town got a little cocky and decided to spend some of those new-found tax dollars; some of the spending was wise and some not. Elmer was not sure if this building was needed but at least they didn't overreach and build a huge three-store monster that would end up half empty when the price of cotton came back to normal. He saw Aubrey on the steps actually waiting for him. Now he became nervous. Aubrey liked to show off his new office. Any chance he could get to make sure the sheriff saw his nice posh office, he took it. The Sheriff's Office was actually bigger, but it was about 30 years older. It wasn't until a year ago that the Sheriff's Office actually put a phone line directly into his office. Most of the time he had to go out to the main desk and take a call. He grabbed his hat and got out of the car and started walking towards the front door, but Aubrey started walking towards him so he could close the distance quicker. "Aubrey, I was about to go arrest two morons by the name of Buckles, but I got diverted here for some reason that Lavera wouldn't tell me. She even used a cuss word to get me here. What the hell is going on?" Aubrey rubbed his chin as he looked around as if to check to see if anyone was listening, but since they were in the parking lot, the chances of that were slim to none. The sheriff noticed that Aubrey hadn't shaved in while and as he nervously rubbed his chin and jaw line, the sheriff could hear the bristle of his stubble. "We just heard from Coahoma County Hospital, we lost Bubba a few minutes ago. I'm sorry, Sheriff." The sheriff felt a huge lump raise up in his throat and he did his best to choke it back down. He started to say something, but the words came out shaky, so he cut himself off before his emotions came out with the words. Aubrey understood the relationship that the sheriff and Bubba had, as did everyone in town. He sensed he needed to try to fill some dead air to give the sheriff time to gather himself. "Lavera got the news and couldn't bring herself to tell you. She is mighty shook up and called me. It was the only thing she could think to do. I really am sorry it's me that has to tell you this, but I would rather you hear it from me as opposed to try and get Lavera to stop crying long enough to tell you." Aubrey put his hand on the sheriff's shoulder for just a minute, but he felt uncomfortable and removed it. The sheriff was still looking down at the ground and hadn't said anything yet. "Why don't you go home, Sheriff, let us go arrest Brett and Judd." The sheriff finally looked up, cleared his throat, and said with perfectly clarity, "No, sir, ain't nobody arresting that piece of shit but me." Aubrey shook his head then threw his hands up as a gesture that he wouldn't stop him, he knew better. "Sheriff, those boys beat Donnie Ray pretty good, but we think he is gonna be alright. I got Maybelle and she is at the hospital with him." The sheriff could tell that there was more that Aubrey wanted to say. "Something else, Aubrey?" Aubrey did that little look over his shoulder again to see if anyone was watching or listening. "We ain't sure if Dub is gonna make it though. He had a stroke while he was on the way to the hospital. I guess that beatin' he took was more than his body could handle." The sheriff felt his pain of losing his best friend and the sorrow that accompanied that pain turn into rage. Those idiots may have beaten a man to death for no reason at all. He spun around and headed to the ugly green car. "Sheriff, I'm coming with you!" The sheriff didn't respond but got into the car and was pulling out of the parking lot before Aubrey could catch up to him. Aubrey was caught in an open space and almost started to run after him, but he quickly nixed that idea, ran back into the building, grabbed his keys, and ran back to the parking lot to go after the sheriff. When he reached the car, he cursed a blue streak when he saw that the car had a flat tire.

The sheriff ignored all the rules, punched the accelerator, and was hell-bent for the Jackpot. He didn't know how he knew Brett would be there, but his instincts told him that he would be there. He rolled sideways into the parking lot as he slammed on the brakes. He was out of the car in seconds. In fact, he was out of the car so fast that he forgot to turn it off and he forgot to set the brake, so as soon as he was clear, the car rolled into the field beside the Jackpot. He hit the door so hard it slammed off the top hinge and hung there in the open position. The patrons who were in the bar all jumped and scrambled for cover as they were all certain that the sheriff would start shooting. "Where the hell is Brett?!" He looked around and a few patrons quickly looked away as if they didn't want to get involved. He looked behind the bar and could see the bartender peering over the top edge of the bar at him. The bartender shifted his eyes to a position behind the sheriff; the sheriff caught the look and quickly turned to see Judd pointing a gun at him. The sheriff took two steps towards Judd and with his left hand, grabbed the gun and raised his arm up so that the gun was pointing at the ceiling. It happened so fast that Judd tried to squeeze the trigger, but it discharged into the ceiling. Before Judd knew what happened, the sheriff punched him right in face and that was the end of Judd for today. Judd crumpled like a bath towel that fell off the hook. The sheriff took the gun, opened the cylinder, and let the bullets drop to the floor. They made a clanking sound when they hit the concrete floor of the Jackpot. When all the bullets were out, he threw the gun out the door of the Jackpot that was still stuck open. Since he didn't see Brett by now, he had an idea where he would be. He made his way towards the back and as he did he yelled for everyone to get the hell out of the place. Not a single person refused, they all scrambled for the front door. One patron hit the front door by accident on the way out and that was all it took to finish the door off, it fell to the side. Now there was just a doorframe. The sheriff continued to the back room where he kicked the door in. There he found Becky in one corner with the bed sheets wrapped around her and Brett in another corner with nothing wrapped around him. Without any more hesitation, the sheriff covered the distance between he and Brett in seconds, when he used his left hand to grab Brett by his throat and nearly lifted him off the ground. "Must be cold in here, you little weasel!", an obvious reference to Brett's private parts. The sheriff looked at Becky, who was now trying to make her way out of the room, but he didn't say anything. He turned to look at Brett and he saw Brett trying to crack a smile. It was more than he could stand. With his free right hand, he began to rain down blows anywhere he could hit Brett. Right then and there he made up his mind that he needed to be Brett's judge, jury, and executioner. Brett never uttered a word, never whimpered, it was almost as if he wanted the sheriff to beat him to death. The sheriff was about to smash another blow down on Brett's head, which he was sure would finish him off, but his arm was caught in mid-air. The sheriff still had his left hand on Brett's throat when he turned his head to see Donnie Buckles standing there, holding his arm, in his full Marine dress blues. It seemed very strange for the sheriff to see the beauty of that uniform here in this place, so close to him and preventing him from dealing Brett the death blow. He let go of Brett's throat and he could hear Brett's naked body slide down the wall to the floor. Donnie Buckles still had a solid grip on the sheriff's arm. The sheriff turned to square-up with the man who was holding his arm and the room became very quiet. Other than hearing Brett labor for breath, you could hear a pin drop. Donnie still had the sheriff's arm suspended in mid-air when he said, "Killing my brother ain't gonna change what's happened, Sheriff." Donnie looked down at Brett then looked back up at the sheriff. The sheriff was clearly taller and bigger than Donnie but for some reason, Donnie showed absolutely no fear. His voice was calm and rational; it was almost the same voice that the sheriff used when he was trying to bring calm to a situation. "A dead Brett Buckles won't bring Lonnie back, won't bring your deputy back, it won't do anything but cause more pain." Donnie let go of the sheriff's arm and the two men stood squared-up with each other. The sheriff looked down at his fist and it was covered in Brett's blood, then he looked at the white glove that Donnie had used to stop the sheriff from hitting Brett again and it now had blood spots on it. The reality of the situation came to him when he saw that. For the first time since he had been sheriff, he felt embarrassed. He wasn't embarrassed that he was pounding Brett; he was embarrassed because he couldn't stop himself from pounding Brett. For all he cared, Brett needed to get his ass kicked but he should have been able to stop. Maybe embarrassed wasn't the right emotion, the correct emotion was fear. He was scared of what he was capable of doing. He took a deep breath, looked around the room, then looked directly at Donnie. "You're right." He stepped to the side of Donnie and went around him. When he was almost to the door, Aubrey came running in. "What the hell happened?" The sheriff started to speak but Donnie interrupted. "The sheriff was arresting my brother for the assault of Dub Martin and Donnie Ray Richardson. My brother was resisting arrest." The sheriff turned to look back at Donnie, but he didn't know what to say. He simply nodded at Donnie, stepped around Aubrey, and walked out of the Jackpot.

Chapter 55

THE SHERIFF WENT TO THE HOSPITAL TO SEE DUB and Donnie Ray. He didn't realize his hands were still covered in blood when he walked in, so he stopped in the bathroom and tried to clean up. He looked in the mirror and saw the person that he wanted to be, not the person that had just nearly killed a man with his bare hands. The lump in his throat that he choked down when he heard the news of his best friends passing finally made its way to the surface; he couldn't stop the tears from running down his face. After he washed his face several times and was confident that he had *rung out the sponge*, as Lois used to say, he made his way to Donnie Ray's room. Maybelle was inside holding Donnie Ray's hand looking as sad but as pretty as she ever was. He could barely recognize the kid laying in that bed. Brett and Judd had really worked him over. He felt that little lump raise up in his throat again but this time he fought back.

Maybelle looked up and he could see that she was still crying. "Look what they did, Elmer, look what they did to our boy." She started bawling again then laid her head on the side of Donnie Ray's bed. He could see her body go up and down as she sobbed and tried to breathe at the same time. The sheriff walked over and put his hand on her back. It was really all he knew to do. "The doc outside said that he is tough and will be just fine. He will heal up and be starting quarterback next year. The Good Lord wouldn't take such a fine young man from us like that." She continued to sob, and he wasn't sure that she was listening. "Your son stepped in and may have kept bad things from happening to a little girl and my son, for that he is a hero." He patted her back again but got no response. "I will come back and check on him after I've gone to see Dub." The sheriff walked out of the room leaving her sobbing next to her son. Donnie Ray would go undefeated the next year, win the state title, and shock everyone by accepting a scholarship to play football at USC. The Ole Miss Rebels were not happy.

He walked down the hall and into Dub's room. Mrs. Martin, Jeannine, and a few of Dub's patrons were sitting with him. Dub was in the same shape as Donnie Ray was in, barely recognizable. He walked over to Mrs. Martin where she stood up and gave him a hug. "The doctor said he is a tough old codger, Sheriff. He says he just needs time to heal." She was still hugging him when she said it. "We don't need the doctor to tell us that he is a tough old codger, we already knew that." The patrons got a chuckle out of that and Mrs. Martin let go of the sheriff and he could then see that she had a smile on her face. "I got the boys that did this to him and now I need to go let your son out of jail." She smiled even bigger, stood on her

tiptoes, and kissed him on the cheek. "Thank you, Sheriff."
He turned to see Jeannine sitting in the chair, looking at him.
"Decker still needs your help reading and BettyJean is still
making messes." Jeannine smiled, stood up, walked over to the
sheriff, and hugged his leg. He felt that lump rising again and
shook his head. He patted the top of her head and she let him
go. He waved at the two patrons and walked out of the room.
Jeannine would later graduate at the top of her class and accept
a full-ride academic scholarship to MIT.

The sheriff needed Lois now more than ever; she was good
at helping him with the lump in his throat, but he had one
more thing to do.

He walked into the Sheriff's Office where he was met with a
huge hug from Lavera. He wished she hadn't, but she immediately
started crying. He held her for a long time while she continued
to cry. He had been hugged today more than he had ever been
hugged in his life. He wasn't good at this and he knew it. She
stopped crying but while her face was still buried in his chest, he
said, "I want you to know I won't tolerate bad language in this
office." He could feel her body shake a little, but she pulled away
and he could also see a smile on her face. Maybe he wasn't as bad
at this consoling thing as he thought he was. He let her go and
headed straight back to the jail.

He walked with the jailer right down to where they were
holding Bobby. The swelling under his eye he had incurred
from someone inside the jail had gone down a little and he
was sitting on his bunk. He waited for the jailer to unlock the
cell then stepped inside. He told Bobby everything, the good
stuff and the bad. Bobby got very upset when he learned
his daddy was in a coma but calmed down as the sheriff

unfolded the rest of the story. The sheriff made a swooping motion as to usher Bobby out of the cell and said, "Your family needs you." Bobby didn't waste any time leaving the cell and heading to the hospital to be with his family. Dub eventually recovered but the stroke took away his ability to use his left hand, so he gave up barbering, but Bobby took over the barbershop.

When he walked into the house, Decker met him at the door. Decker practically jumped into his daddy's arms. He held his son for a long time. Decker had seen more this week than any little boy should ever have to see, and he had met every obstacle like a man. He was proud of his son and he didn't mind telling him. Decker had a firm grip around his daddy's neck when Lois came in from the back bedroom. He could see her, and the tears started to well up. She came right to him, put her hands on his cheeks, and raised herself high enough on her toes to kiss him on the lips. He grabbed her around the waist and held her as he gathered himself. She didn't have to say anything, just her presence made him feel better. This time he wasn't the consoler, she was. She whispered in his ear, "We can skip the dance contest this Saturday night and just stay home. You need the rest." He tightened his grip and lifted her off her feet, which caused her to giggle a little. "No way, baby, I need to show off my beautiful bride on that dance floor." She laughed out loud, kissed him on the ear and said, "Are you sure? I really don't mind, it's not a big deal." He set her down gently but still had a firm grip on her. "I'm sure, I need for things to get back to normal."

Made in the USA
San Bernardino, CA
03 April 2018